EVILWAY

"Three hundred nine feet," John said quietly as he pointed toward the top. "Largest natural span of stone on earth." Norman grunted his acknowledgment.

"I'm going to climb to the top," John announced. "When I get to the top, take a picture of me waving. You want to come, Norm?"

Norman never paused during the ascent. He didn't look down until he stood at the highest point of the span. Far below, the women and children looked up, tiny bright specks of color against the desert landscape.

"Wow," John said. He stopped beside Norman and grinned. "What a view!"

"Sure is," Norman agreed. He glanced at his brother from the corners of his eyes, eyes that glittered as he smiled a thin smile. He moved several steps away from his brother and watched John waving at the others on the canyon floor.

John never saw the bird as it came out of the sun at his back. It was a big raven, a male, well over two pounds and diving with wings folded as it whistled through the air, a black feathered missile, its target the back of his head. John lowered his hands and was turning toward his brother when it struck.

With a look of surprise he pitched forward, twisting as he fell, screaming, screaming, falling a long time before he hit the rocks below.

EVILWAY

RYAN O. MOSES

ZEBRA BOOKS
KENSINGTON PUBLISHING CORP.

ZEBRA BOOKS

are published by

Kensington Publishing Corp.
475 Park Avenue South
New York, NY 10016

First printing: June, 1990

Printed in the United States of America

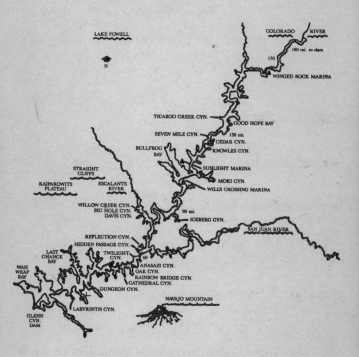

LAKE POWELL

N

COLORADO RIVER

180 mi. to dam
170

WINGED ROCK MARINA

TICABOO CREEK CYN.

GOOD HOPE BAY

SEVEN MILE CYN.

130 mi.

CEDAR CYN.

BULLFROG BAY

KNOWLES CYN.

SUNLIGHT MARINA

STRAIGHT CLIFFS

KAIPAROWITS PLATEAU

ESCALANTE RIVER

MOKI CYN.

WILES CROSSING MARINA

WILLOW CREEK CYN.
BIG HOLE CYN.
DAVIS CYN.

90 mi.

ICEBERG CYN.

SAN JUAN RIVER

REFLECTION CYN.

HIDDEN PASSAGE CYN.

LAST CHANCE BAY

TWILIGHT CYN.

60

WAH WEAP BAY

ANASAZI CYN.
OAK CYN.
RAINBOW BRIDGE CYN.
CATHEDRAL CYN.

DUNGEON CYN.

NAVAJO MOUNTAIN

GLENN CYN. DAM

LABYRINTH CYN.

One

When the boat entered the shadow of the cliff, Lance Redhill removed his sunglasses and polished them on his shirt. He looked back the way they had come and squinted against the brightness. Beyond the shade the lake glistened like molten metal, and blue in the distance, the rugged bluffs shimmered on the horizon. He hooked the earpieces carefully behind his ears and wiped his forehead with his sleeve.

"How many canyons have we searched, Dad?" He swayed as his knees absorbed the boat's gentle motion. "Seems like hundreds."

Joe Redhill shrugged. "I lose count. Fifteen or twenty on the Escalante River today. Many more yesterday on the main lake, and many more the day before that." He stood at the helm with one hand on the throttles and the other on the wheel. His weathered face was the color of the desert and his thin lips turned down at the corners. Stocky, broad-shouldered, he wore a denim work shirt, blue jeans, hand-sewn moccasins. A strip of red cloth bound his head just below the short-cropped silver hair.

"Well, I'm glad we're out of the sun," Lance said. He was taller than his father, slender and sinewy. He had high cheekbones and his skin was smooth and his raven black hair was combed straight back from his forehead. He wore blue jeans, a Grateful Dead T-shirt, and imported athletic shoes.

Joe nodded his agreement. The rumble of the outboards grew louder as they entered the confinement of a canyon. The water was calm, the cliffs high, and the division between the two uncertain. His dark eyes narrowed as he watched for hidden hazards. The canyon seemed to end a

7

short distance ahead but he maintained a steady seven-knot speed.

Lance glanced at his father as they approached the end, then reached a hand to brace himself on the steel rail encircling the steering console of the Boston Whaler. It seemed they would run into the wall of stone, but the illusion was revealed as Joe turned the boat through a sweeping curve that appeared to their right and the smooth sandstone, merging almost invisibly with its inverted reflection, shattered into a chaos of small wavelets as the boat disturbed the surface of the water.

Joe smiled faintly. "Things are often not as they seem in these canyons," he said.

"I'm glad you know them so well," Lance answered, "because I sure don't."

Now the channel gradually narrowed until only a few yards separated the boat from the enclosing walls. Joe eased the throttles back and they slowed, slowed, began to retreat as he pulled the throttles into reverse. Suddenly he shifted to neutral and peered at the canyon wall.

"Someone has been through here." He pointed at the sandstone, gouged and smeared with white. As they drifted closer, Lance removed his sunglasses and thrust them into a pocket, then leaned over the side and touched the scarred stone with his fingertips. He glanced up at his father and nodded.

"Pretty recent," he said. Joe idled the boat forward and the cliffs continued to close overhead until the sky was a slender, clear blue line. More scrapes appeared in the cliff face, along with smears of white paint and flakes of chrome. The boat was moving forward at a crawl now. Thirty feet into the tight passage, forty, and a submerged stone ledge to starboard showed a series of deep gouges in its surface.

The shadows grew deeper. Fifty feet, sixty, seventy. Eighty feet and they glided between two soaring columns of stone embedded in the cliffs, columns ten feet in diameter, symmetrical and polished by the endless winds except for their bases, which were shattered.

"Explosives," Joe said, raising his voice over the noise of

8

the engines. "Somebody blasted their way through."

"Why would they want to do that?" Lance asked. Joe shook his head.

The canyon widened beyond the columns, but not much. A hundred feet more and it curved gradually to the left, and as they rounded the turn their progress was blocked by the broad, white stern of a houseboat filling the canyon from wall to wall. They looked at each other with amazement. Then Lance grinned and said, "We found the sucker."

The houseboat's outboard motors were raised and the props, clear of the water, were battered and bent from contact with rocks. A folding chair was on deck, a beer can and some papers beside it. Propped against the railing was a fishing rod with its line in the water.

Joe switched off the ignition and they drifted forward until their bow bumped the stern of the houseboat. Lance tied a line to a cleat and the silence enfolded them, hot and oppressive. For a moment they both paused and listened; small waves slapping the hulls, the drone of a fly, a croak that could have been a frog nearby, or a raven far off. Joe shrugged. He cupped his hands around his mouth.

"Hello!" His yell echoed down the canyon and died away. They waited for a response, and when none came they climbed aboard, footsteps booming hollowly on the aluminum deck.

"Something stinks," Lance said.

Joe nodded. The air was perfectly still, not the faintest breeze stirring in the deep box canyon. He stepped to the door and peered through the glass. Slowly, almost reluctantly, he touched the door with his hand. It swung quietly inward and the shadows exhaled a stench of decay. His face wrinkled with distaste.

"Hello?" His voice rang down the hallway, but again there was no reply. A fly buzzed past him from the darkness, then another, circling his head and landing on his face. He waved it away and took a step inside. The floor creaked beneath his weight.

"Hey?" he waited, breathing shallowly, then backed out and turned to his son. The young man's face was somber.

9

"Guess I better have a look around," he said. "You can come or wait here."

"I'll come."

Joe nodded. He removed the cloth from his head and wrung the moisture out; a minute ago he hadn't even been sweating. He tied it across his face before entering the hall-way, and Lance cupped his hands over mouth and nose and followed.

The private cabins were aft, and Joe opened the door of the first one he came to. The room was dark, the blinds drawn, and he slid his hand along the wall until his fingers found a switch. He flipped it on and the halogen table lamps bathed the room in cold white light. A suitcase lay on a folding stand at the foot of the bed. The closet doors were open and he could see clothes hanging neatly inside. Several boots and a pair of thongs were arranged beside the dresser, a zippered shaving kit atop it. The queen-size bed was neatly made and directly in its center was a bowl.

They entered, gazing at the bowl. It was about twelve inches in diameter, light tan in color, and decorated with gray geometric designs.

"Anasazi," Joe muttered. He circled the room, careful not to touch anything, noting every detail. He nudged the door to the head open with his foot and peered inside. A tooth-brush and tube of toothpaste on the sink, a towel hanging over the open shower door. Nothing more. He motioned to Lance and went out into the hall. They checked the other three cabins and each was orderly; but when they came to the main salon it was a different story.

Papers and boxes were strewn across the beige carpet, piled on both couches, and crammed on the shelves. Some of the boxes were taped shut, numbers and letters printed on them in heavy black ink. Others were open, exposing pots, baskets, and items wrapped in brown kraft paper or bubble plastic. The stench was nauseating and Lance pulled his shirttail up to hold it over his face.

Flies buzzed in circles beneath the ceiling, crept over the boxes and furniture. On the coffee table was a plastic bag filled with arrowheads, and beside the bag an open notebook. Joe stopped to turn the pages; handwritten lists, pages of dates, initials, code numbers like those on the boxes. With a thoughtful expression he closed it and stood.

He spun around as a faint sound came from the galley, gentle as a sigh, and flies rose up in a cloud and buzzed about in agitation before settling down again, settling on something that lay just out of sight behind the breakfast bar separating the salon from the galley. With slow, cautious steps, Joe skirted the stools beside the counter and found the body.

It was sprawled on its back, dressed in a pair of khaki slacks and a blue short-sleeved shirt. The swollen flesh, distended with the gas of putrefaction, bulged against the clothing. The feet were bare and pale, puffed up like ghastly pastries. The arms and neck, where they exited the T-shirt, looked ready to explode.

It was the head, however, that the hungry desert flies were concerned with. The head was craned back, mouth open, and lay in a pool of dried blood on the white linoleum. The flies were crawling in and out of the nose, the ears, squeezing past the protruding purple globe of the tongue, creeping delicately across the glazed and sightless eyes.

The back was arched clear of the floor. The hands were clenched into fists atop the chest and gripped a straightened coat hanger in their fat, horribly comic fingers. The wire curved upward from the fists, arched above the chest and throat, plunged back down toward the face and into the right nostril.

Joe saw a fly emerge from that dark orifice, crawl several inches up the wire, and launch itself into the foul warm air. It flew straight at his face and he swatted wildly. He stumbled back into his son, who spun and headed for the forward exit, threw open the sliding glass door and burst out onto the foredeck with his father at his heels.

Joe tore aside the cloth and gulped fresh air while Lance hung his head over the railing and vomited. Joe turned his back on his son, giving him what privacy he could, avoiding with his eyes what his ears could not ignore.

He tipped his head back to scan the soaring vertical walls,

11

several hundred feet high, that formed a great bowl enclosing the houseboat. The patch of sky high above was blinding in contrast to the shadows and he blinked as he dropped his gaze. When the bright spot faded from his vision he stepped ashore to the narrow crescent of red sand below the bow. Recorded in the soft soil were the marks of heavy boots, the passage of many feet, a path that led to the cliffs.

He followed the path up the gentle rise of the beach and found a chasm directly before him. It was concealed within a natural fold of the cliff, only a few feet wide at the bottom, tapering to disappear in a slender crack ten feet above his head. As his eyes adjusted to the darkness, he could see that it continued into the cliff's interior.

"Dad?"

Joe turned at the sound of Lance's voice. His son was crouched beside the bow of the houseboat, hair dripping water as he splashed his face and head.

"Never seen anything like that before," he said, attempting a smile that looked more like a grimace. "Sorry I got sick. But . . . well, the way he died . . . and the smell. Do you . . . do you think he did that to himself?"

Joe shook his head. "Maybe. Maybe not. A very ugly death, however it happened. I do not recall seeing any worse, even in the service." He pinched his nose between his fingers and blew the stench clear as Lance walked up the slope and joined him.

"It is obvious why they chose this place," Joe said. "Well hidden, almost inaccessible, a perfect home base for pot-hunting expeditions. Some of those artifacts are probably worth more than I will make in ten years."

Lance's eyes widened. "Worth killing for?" he asked.

Joe grunted. "Maybe. Three men rented this boat, and I am wondering what happened to the other two."

"If they killed the guy on the boat, why didn't they take the bowls and stuff?"

Joe grunted again, shook his head slowly as he turned to peer into the shadowy chasm.

"I do not know what happened here," he said, "but I do know we better get back and report it. First, though, I want

12

to take a look up this gulley."

"I'll be right behind you."

Joe entered the chasm moving sideways in its confinement until, a short distance in, it began to widen. It ascended in a series of precipices that would be waterfalls during the rainy season but were now smoothly polished sandstone, cliffs within the cliff, varying between a few feet to ten or more in height. Where the climb was too high to scale easily, they found sturdy wooden ladders made from two-by-fours.

Joe climbed like a bear, relying on the great strength in his arms and legs as he moved steadily in and up, ladders creaking beneath his weight. His son climbed like a cat and made no sound, swarming up the rungs with sinewy grace. Several times they stopped to rest before at last emerging from the dark, narrow cleft to stand atop a plateau where a warm wind was blowing. They wiped the sweat from their faces, stretched, and tipped back their heads to breath the clean smell of sage and mesquite.

"That feels good!" Lance said. He shook his head and turned to face the wind, combing his hair out of his face with his fingers.

"I like it up top," Joe said, "to be able to see a long way off. Those close, dark places make me uneasy."

"Really?" Lance looked at his father with surprise. "I didn't think you were afraid of anything."

"Uneasy, not afraid." Joe grinned. "Look, see there?" He waved his hand toward the south, where a solitary mountain loomed in the vast expanse of Rainbow Plateau, its summit lost in a halo of clouds. "Navajo Mountain, Sleeping Woman's head. She is wrapping her head in darkness. Perhaps she is hiding from the ugly thing we have found."

"You sound like Grandfather when you talk like that," Lance said with a chuckle, "like an old Indian."

"I am an Indian," he replied with a smile, "but not that old. And Grandfather was a wise man. And you, my son, going to the white man's school, sound more like those *belli-canos* every day." He pulled a box of Callard & Bowser licorice from his pocket, shook the last piece of imported English candy into his hand, and held it out toward Lance.

"No thanks," Lance said. "Every so often I forget and think it's edible, but not right now. I don't know how you can eat that stuff."

Joe shrugged and popped it in his mouth, wadded the box and thrust it in his pocket as he sucked the rich toffee. He shaded his eyes with his hand and made a complete circle. In every direction the land was hunched up and folded down, riddled with canyons and fissures, studded with mesas and stone spires. To the east the Escalante River glistened between cliffs five hundred, a thousand feet high, cliffs painted in broad, sweeping bands of red, yellow, white, brown.

West, only a mile or so away, rose the Straight Cliffs, a towering wall of stone running northwest to southeast for over thirty miles, atop which was the Kaiparowits Plateau. To the north he could see the tormented stone formations of Waterpocket Fold where, since the creation of the continent, the Colorado River had cut deeply into the flesh of the earth. And beyond, hazy in the distance, there arose the forested peaks of the Henry Mountains. East he thought he could make out Nokai Dome, and farther yet, Red House Cliffs. All this and more, as far as the eye could see, was *Dine' Bikeyah,* the Navajo Land.

"What are you looking for?" Lance asked. Joe dropped his hand and blinked.

"Something," he said. "Not sure what. Come on." He started across the mesa, and now his gaze was fixed, not on distant horizons, but the ground directly before him. He indicated to his son the things he saw, signs of the passage of many men, with quick gestures of his hands. Here a rock had been kicked aside, there the black smear of a hiking boot, scuffs scrapes in the soft stone from hard-soled shoes. When they crossed pockets of soil where plants had established themselves, the vegetation was trampled and branches were broken.

"They were pretty sure of themselves up here," Joe said over his shoulder, "no worry at all to conceal their presence."

The main trail followed a direct route to the base of Straight Cliffs. Other less-traveled trails intersected it, but

14

Joe stayed with the most obvious path and soon they were climbing the rise to the foot of the cliffs. As they clambered up a ledge of broken sandstone, a raven arose with a rustle of wings from something dark lying almost in the shadow of the cliffs. It was crumpled and torn like a bit of wind-borne debris caught on the branches of a bush, and only when they drew near did they realize they had found a second body. Lance blew his breath out between pursed lips.

Joe nodded his agreement. "Takes a few weeks before the heat and the scavengers make a body look like this," he said. All that remained was a partially clothed skeleton with patches of desiccated flesh and skin clinging to it. The blue jeans and brown, long-sleeved shirt were in shreds. Several yards away, beside a stunted piñon tree, lay a hiking boot. The leather was chewed and the laces were missing.

They squatted several feet from the body. Joe picked up a small twig and twirled it in his fingers as he gazed at the wreckage and saw what pathetic scraps a man became when the vital spark was gone. The shattered skull stared sightlessly from empty sockets, jaw agape. Many bones were obviously broken. Badly broken. The coyotes had scattered the fingers and toes, had gnawed many of the larger bones, but it looked like the skeleton had been beaten with a huge hammer. Joe tipped back his head and looked up, up, to where red stone pierced blue sky. He nodded.

"Yes," he said in a thoughtful voice, "it must have been that way."

He stood and looked about but Lance continued to stare at the remains until his father touched him on the shoulder. When he arose his face was pinched, his forehead furrowed.

"He fell a long way Dad," he said, "and the animals have eaten him."

"Yes."

"Do you think he was murdered?"

Joe looked up again at the cliffs, as if they might hold an answer. He shrugged. "Who can say?"

His son shook his head, glancing again at the broken body. There were claw marks in the soil where the coyotes had fought over the carcass.

"You said there were three men," Lance said quietly.

"Yes." Joe squinted at the bright place on the horizon where the sun was just setting. "But we can look no further today. You lead." He motioned with his hand and his son started back along the path. Joe turned to follow and a bright flash of light caught his eye, something beside the body, and he paused to see what it was. The pocket of the jeans had been pulled inside-out, and lying beside the dirty white inner fabric, half-buried in the soil, was a single quartz crystal.

Joe's eyes narrowed and he hissed through his teeth. He cleared the dirt away from the stone with the twig, then stretched his fingers toward it. But his hand stopped short, and he suddenly arose and strode to the ledge where his son had already disappeared over the edge. As he let himself down a raven cawed somewhere high on the cliffs, the sound harsh and mocking. It echoed, and echoed, and seemed to follow him all the way back to the boat.

It was late at night when they reached Winged Rock Marina and idled between the lighted buoys marking the entrance. They had not even attempted to move the houseboat, but raced back up Lake Powell's glass-smooth waters with the throttles wide open. The lights were still on in the rental office as they tied the boat at the fuel dock.

"Someone has waited for you," Joe said as he glanced at his watch, "and I hope she is not charging me overtime." Lance hunched his shoulders and grinned. Joe said, "Well, she will have to wait a little longer while you fuel the boat and put it in the slip. I must go report what we found."

A shadow of disappointment crossed Lance's face, but he didn't protest and moved quickly to comply as his father walked off along the dock.

Joe paused outside the rental office. Fishermen were unloading gear beneath the lights, out toward the end of the docks, and their voices carried to him on the warm night air; sounds of laughter, of someone coughing.

A hundred feet beyond where he stood, the main walkway

met the shore, and a concrete path led to the parking lot and administration building. The transient slips lining this portion of the dock were completely filled with boats.

In the opposite direction the walkway extended another several hundred feet beyond the fuel dock, far out into the bay, and attached to it were twenty fingers, each with fifteen to thirty slips, depending on their size. Only two houseboats were in tonight, their cabins softly lit by the glow from the walkway lights. Painted on each cabin was a circle with black wings, and inside the circle were the red letters NTC, standing for Navajo Tribal Corporation.

Joe stepped to the office and opened the door. "Hey, good evening."

The young woman at the desk looked up with a startled expression, then smiled, all bright teeth, tan face, blond hair.

"I thought you might show up sooner or later," she said, tossing her head so the long hair flew back over her shoulder, "but I didn't think it would be later." Then she saw his expression and asked, "What's wrong?"

"We found the boat," he said, "and two of the men who rented it. I think."

"You think? Where are they? Didn't they come back with you?"

"Both dead."

"Oh my God!" Her smile faded, the color draining from her face beneath the tan.

"Keep it to yourself until we find out what has happened. And the police will be thick as flies here tomorrow, just to give you some advance warning." She nodded slightly and he started to close the door, then added, "By the way, Lance will probably be in after he puts the boat away."

"Okay." Her lips twitched in an uncertain smile. He nodded and shut the door, continued along the dock.

"Evening!" A fisherman passed carrying a tackle box.

"Good evening." He lifted a hand in greeting. Off to his left loomed a brightly lit building on floats which housed the marina dry dock, the houseboat maintenance facility, and his office. Where it connected to the main walkway was a

17

locked gate and out of habit he tugged the padlock in passing. It was secure.

He stepped ashore and followed the path to the crowded parking lot, threading his way among the trucks, cars, and boat trailers to the administration building. It took a moment before he found the correct key, let himself in, and switched on the lights. He turned right, past the information desk, and followed the hall to the door at its end. Beside the door was a small, tasteful brass sign that read, "Harold Lowtah—Resort Manager."

Inside, he crossed to the desk, lifted the phone from its cradle, and searched the telephone index to find "Sheriff—Mexican Hat." Electronic chirps filled his ear when he pushed the button and the phone rang five times before someone answered.

"San Juan County Sheriff's Department."

"Shirley? This is Joe Redhill over at Winged Rock Marina." He pressed the receiver hard against his ear, a look of concentration on his face as he stared at a photograph of Harold and the governor of Utah shaking hands.

"Oh, hi Joe! How are you?" The voice lost its official chill. "How are you?"

"I am good Shirley, how about you?"

"Just fine Joe, just fine, And Anna?"

"She is good, Shirley, thank you. Listen, I have a problem over here. Is the sheriff in?"

"As a matter of fact, by some miracle he is. Can you hold for a minute?"

"Sure." He propped the phone on his shoulder and plucked a pen from its holder. As he waited for the sheriff, his hand drew an egg-shaped circle on the note pad beside the phone. The scratching of the pen was audible in the silence of the office as two dark scribbles appeared for eyes, another for the nose, square pegs for teeth. Joe's face was impassive as he watched his hand draw. The movements were quick and sure, as if the hand had a life of its own controlled from within the blunt, powerful fingers.

"Joe?" The sheriff's deep voice boomed in his ear and the pen made a jagged line up the center of the picture.

18

"Hello Nathan, I am glad you were in. Afraid we have a bad situation here."

"What's up Joe?"

"It is about the houseboat we have been looking for; we found it this afternoon. There is a dead man aboard, and another up in the rocks. A third man is missing." Silence greeted his statement. He pressed the receiver harder against his ear.

"Nathan?"

"Yeah, I'm here Joe. Thinking. Where'd all this take place?"

"The boat is at the end of a canyon, up the Escalante River. We call it Big Hole Canyon, but it is not on many maps. The second body is below Straight Cliffs."

"What happened, could you tell?"

"We found the man on the boat with a wire run up into his brain. The other one fell a long way."

"Jesus Christ!" There was a pause, then, "We, who's we?"

"Myself and my son Lance. One more thing; the boat is filled with Anasazi artifacts."

"Well I'll be damned!" Again, silence followed as the sheriff digested the information, then, excited, "Right! All right. Where are you now Joe?"

"I am at the administration building."

"Okay. I'll be out there in about two hours."

Joe sighed. "It is late, Sheriff, I have not had supper yet, and I am tired. That boat is not going anywhere, and neither are the men."

"Yeah, guess you're right. Okay Joe, we'll be there first thing in the morning. Bright and early. Better cancel all your appointments."

"I will arrange it. Good night Sheriff."

He set the receiver in its cradle and his gaze fell on the note pad. Across the top of the sheet was printed Winged Rock Marina, and the NTC logo. Below this, the picture Joe had drawn, a grinning skull with dark, gaping eye sockets. A jagged line split the skull from the top to bottom. Joe tore the sheet from the tablet, wadded it into a ball, and tossed it into the trash can as he stood.

The night was quiet and still as he stepped outside and walked to the side of the building where his and Lance's Honda trail bikes were parked in the dirt. They gleamed yellow in the lights, bright pollen yellow, a cheerful, optimistic color. Joe straddled his bike and turned on the ignition, kicked the starter with his foot.

The engine sputtered to life and he chased the bright circle of its headlight along the paved two-lane road, past the campground and its pleasing smell of campfires. He turned left at the gas station, up the drive to the RV park, and into his own driveway. In front of the Ford pickup, he propped the bike on its stand and turned off the engine.

A few late parties were going on in the motor homes and trailers, muted sounds of laughter and music in the night, a baby crying. The windows of his own house trailer glowed dimly yellow. Alone amongst the orderly, straight rows of metal dwellings, his sat diagonally across its asphalt strip so the front door faced the east, as the homes of the *Diné*, the Navajo people, ever have. His trailer alone, amidst the barren RV park, was surrounded by trees and cactus, by pepperweed and tamarisk, yucca and indigo bush, redbud, primrose, herbs and vegetables.

He entered quietly, trying not to disturb his wife, Anna, who always retired early. But as he crept into the kitchen he heard movement and she appeared from their bedroom, the last door at the end of the hall. She crossed the living room and he met her halfway to put his arms around her.

"Go back to bed, Anna," he said. He kissed her on the forehead.

"But your supper—"

"I will fix it tonight. Get your rest, and wake me early, okay?"

She yawned. "Okay. I left some stew for you." She smiled sleepily and turned, and padded toward the bedroom. "You found the boat, didn't you?" she asked, pausing in the door.

"Yes."

"I thought you must have, to be out so late. Where?"

"Escalante River."

She waited for him to continue, watching him sleepily, her

20

curiosity competing with her drowsiness. When he didn't say anything more, she yawned again, fist over her mouth, gave a vague wave, and disappeared into the darkened bedroom.

He warmed a plate of mutton stew in the microwave and poured a cup of coffee from the insulated thermos on the counter, added a heavily buttered slab of bread, and carried it to the table. After he had eaten he carried the cup and dish to the sink and rinsed them clean. He washed his face and undressed, then joined his wife in bed. Some time later, just before sleep overtook him, he heard Lance come in.

He awoke before sunrise to the sound of Anna busy in the kitchen. He smelled breakfast cooking and slid swiftly out of bed and into the bathroom to shower and shave. As he seated himself at the kitchen table, she poured a cup of coffee and set it before him.

"Good morning," she said. "You had a late night."

He took a sip of the strong, black coffee and nodded. "A long day and a long night, and now an early morning." In a few sentences he told her about what they had found, sparing the gruesome details.

Spatula in hand, she stood before the stove and stared at him. "What could have happened?" she asked. "These grave robbers, are they getting as wealthy as the drug dealers?"

He shook his head. "I do not know, Anna. Maybe today we will learn something more."

She crossed her arms beneath her breasts and hugged herself as her dark eyes widened. "What of the *chindi?*" she asked quietly in Navajo. "The man's *chindi* would have been trapped inside the boat. All the evil of his life, all his bad thoughts and wrong deeds were released as a ghost when he died. It would've remained inside, waiting for someone to come along. Waiting for a victim."

"I do not know," Joe repeated uneasily in English. He gazed into his cup and frowned. "I do not feel worried, if that is what you mean. It was a white man's *chindi;* perhaps it will not affect a Navajo. And who believes in that sort of things these days anyway?"

"I do," she hissed in English, "and if you're *Dine'*, you do too."

"Do I?" He shook his head slowly. "I am not sure anymore. Besides, it was daytime, everyone knows *chindis* do their mischief at night."

She stared at him for a minute, then turned her back. The bacon was sizzling and she deftly flipped the strips to cook on the other side. Her hands were strong and tanned, and her black hair hung in a glistening braid almost to her waist. She was tall and slender like her son. Her father had been a Zuni of the ancient, powerful Macaw clan, and had died many years ago from drink. Her mother, still living, was a Navajo of the Mud clan, and when Joe and Anna first married they lived among her mother's people near Kayenta, Arizona.

"What about our son?" Anna said without turning, her voice short and tense. "Eighteen years old and he's been at the *bellicano*'s schools since he could walk, do you think the white man's *chindi* won't affect him? I probably sound foolish to you, but I've seen what happens.

"My uncle, old Raymond Lonepine, was in the hogan of a woman who died during childbirth. A month later he killed a man in a bar fight and ended up in jail. And that's where he died, too, in solitary confinement."

She turned to him and her voice softened. "The *bellicano* doctors said he was insane, Joe, but we knew better. That's a label they use to explain lots of things they don't understand. If Uncle Raymond had a Sing to chase out the *chindi*, none of it would've happened. I'll have a Listener stop by, and determine which ceremonial to use. Then we'll have a Sing for you and Lance."

She set three plates on the table, and Joe saw from her determined look that it would do no good to argue. She heaped his plate with scrambled eggs, added six strips of bacon, returned to the oven for a pan of corn bread. She refilled his cup, and as Lance came down the hall and dropped into a chair, she poured two more. Lance gulped at the coffee and hissed through his teeth.

"Wow!" he said, "that'll wake you up. Good morning."

"Good morning," Joe said. "Get enough sleep?"

"Four hours, that's plenty. Me and Chris had a lot to talk

22

about. What are we doing today, are we going to bring the boat in?"

Joe shrugged. "Depends on how the sheriff and his people want to handle it. We will take them to the boat and after that it is up to them."

Lance nodded, mouth filled with corn bread, eyes filled with excitement. They ate quickly and finished their breakfast in silence. Joe mopped his plate with corn bread and arose from the table.

"About time we were going," he said to Lance. And to Anna, "I would not expect us for lunch."

"I won't. It's my shopping day, remember?"

"I always forget." Joe bent to tie his moccasin as Anna smiled and shook her head. The moccasins were an object of amusement to everyone except Joe and the old man who made them for him, using double-thickness bullhide for the soles and oil-tanned elk for the uppers. They were the most comfortable shoes he had ever worn.

"They say your memory's the first thing to go, Dad," Lance said. He drained the last of his coffee and jumped from his chair, vanishing into his room before Joe could reply. Anna tipped back her head as Joe arose and he kissed her on the lips, touched her cheek lightly with his fingers. When he opened the front door he smelled the fragrance of the carnations Anna had persuaded to grow and the scent was spicy, like cinnamon, in the morning air.

"Drive carefully," he said.

"Yes. You will have the Sing, won't you?"

He shrugged. "If it makes you happy."

"It will. Is there anything special you want me to buy today?"

He nodded, gazing toward the lake. "Could you find some of that licorice I like? The fancy kind?"

"I might could arrange it." She smiled fondly at him.

"Thank you." He could tell from her smile that their argument was settled. Sometimes it was best to give in.

The sun was burning above the horizon as they rode their trail bikes to the administration building. A dozen or more police cars and emergency vehicles were clustered near the front steps where a group of men waited, clutching clipboards, cups of coffee, radios, talking in low tones and moving slowly if at all. Their attire varied from uniforms and suits to blue jeans and work shirts, and they all turned to watch as Joe and his son parked their bikes beside the building.

Harold Lowtah, tall, gangly, with a great beak of a nose dominating his mournful face, started toward them, but a man in uniform reached them first.

"Morning, Joe, Lance."

"Sheriff," Joe said. They shook hands, and as the sheriff gripped Lance's hand he said, "My boy tells me you'll be with him at Utah State University this fall."

"Yes sir, I got my letter of acceptance a couple of weeks ago."

"Well good for you, good for you, nice to have another local boy make it." He clapped Lance on the shoulder. Sheriff Nathan Andrews was a big man, four inches over six feet and heavily built. Sun-bleached hair hung over his collar from beneath a crisp, grey Stetson, and his weathered face had the flattened look of a professional boxer. He gestured toward a man in a plain suit as men crowded around them.

"This is Brian Thornton of the FBI. He was called in because we're on national park land. You know Bruce Lamar, Federal Bureau of Land Management, and this is David Evans, Utah State Archaeologist. The Navajo tribal police won't take a hand unless it should happen that the, ah, crime, occurred on reservation land. Gentlemen, this is Joe Redhill and his son Lance, and Harold Lowtah, the resort manager."

They exchanged greetings and shook hands. The BLM man was short and round with a ruddy face. He smiled constantly. David Evans was thin and dark and spoke so quietly his listeners had to strain to hear. The FBI man had the fair complexion of an office worker and wore his blond hair in a crewcut. His eyes were hidden behind sunglasses and his hands, shoved deep in his trouser pockets, jingled his keys nervously.

Joe answered their questions about when and how he and

24

Lance found the boat. The sheriff waited for a pause in the conversation, then interrupted in a respectful tone. "Excuse me gentlemen. I suggest we get moving while the day's still cool; anybody familiar with Lake Powell in August will know it could be a hot son-of-a-bitch this afternoon."

They nodded their agreement. The lawmen and technicians filed in orderly fashion to the boats, fifteen men, three women, and assorted equipment. They crowded aboard the NTC's Whaler and Harold Lowtah's personal boat, a thirty-foot Bertram cabin cruiser. The lake was calm and they made good time. Curious fishermen watched them pass from boats prowling below the shadowed cliff faces where they trolled the deep, dark water.

The houseboat was as they had left it, and the passengers, who had been talking and laughing during the ride, became all business as their training took over. Joe and Lance waited aboard the Whaler. People came and went, returning for this or that piece of equipment. The FBI man tried unsuccessfully to place a call to the regional office over the marine radio, and David Evans, the archaeologist, tried several times to contact the university, speaking excitedly into the microphone clutched in his fist, but for him, too, the only reply was the crackle of static from the speaker. After about an hour the sheriff appeared on the stern with a handkerchief held to his face. When he lowered it to speak he looked tired.

"We'd like you to take us to the other body," he said.

"Sure." Joe opened a storage locker and removed two canteens. He slung one over his shoulder and handed the other to Lance. Harold Lowtah waved languidly from the bridge of his boat, a scowl on his face and a cup in his hands.

"If you can get them to speed things along, I'd appreciate it Joe," he said.

Joe paused, one foot on the Whaler and one on the houseboat. "I will do what I can," he said. Harold smiled gloomily.

Five men waited for them on the shore: the FBI man Thornton, the BLM man Lamar, Sheriff Andrews and a deputy, and a technician wearing a backpack. They were silent and grim except for the BLM man and his perpetual

25

smile. With Joe in the lead, they started up the crevasse. Over an hour later they reached their destination.

"There."

Joe and Lance stopped some distance away as the others passed, eyes fixed on the grisly remains. The technician shrugged off his pack and withdrew a camera. He photographed the body from all angles while the sheriff and the FBI man made entries in their pocket notebooks.

"The coroner won't have any big job finding cause of death," the photographer said with a chuckle. Nobody replied or seemed to share his humor, and he quickly finished and put the camera away, shouldered his pack, and wandered a short distance across the plateau. The FBI man squatted beside the body as Lamar looked on.

"Mr. Redhill," the FBI man called, "what do you make of this."

Joe approached and shrugged. "A quartz crystal."

"Just something he picked up off the ground, huh?"

"Probably."

The BLM man looked sharply at Joe, then thrust his hands in his pockets and craned his neck to peer up at the cliffs. When he spoke his voice was thoughtful and addressed to no one in particular.

"Quartz crystal plays a part in lots of Indian rituals and ceremonies, doesn't it Mr. Redhill?" Without awaiting an answer he continued, "Sometimes it symbolizes fire, and one of the creation myths says that in the beginning of the world a crystal was put in each person's mouth so everything they said would come true. I understand that some Indians carry them in their medicine bundles to ensure personal safety. The Navajos carry the Four Mountains Bundle though, don't they?" He tugged his upper lip, thinking.

"Yeah, that's it; plants and minerals from each of the four sacred mountains. And the four pouches have to be made of deerskin from a doe killed without bloodshed."

Joe was silent but met Lamar's eyes as the man grinned at him. Lamar didn't appear to know that Joe's gesture was a rude one, that a Navajo only looked another man in the eye to show that he thought he was lying, or a fool. The FBI man tossed the sparkling crystal in the air and caught it with a swift, sure movement.

"Well," he said, "from what I've seen, I can't recommend it for personal protection."

The photographer, back from his explorations, gave a snort of laughter.

"You said there was a third man," the FBI man said. "I'd like to look for him. This guy fell from up there," he nodded his head toward the cliff, "and if we can, I think we should see what's up top."

The sheriff said, "Think you can find a way up, Joe?"

"I was there many years ago," Joe said, "and I know a way that is not too hard. The path we have been following leads in that direction."

"Okay." The sheriff turned to his deputy. "Get Matt and a stretcher, and take these remains down to the boats." He grinned tightly. "And try not to mess them up." The deputy nodded and hurried off. The sheriff looked at Joe. "After you," he said.

Joe set a steady, moderate pace, and soon all but Lance and the sheriff were strung out some distance behind. The path skirted large boulders, climbed in and out of ravines, and then became a serious struggle up a wash that cut deeply into the cliffs. It ascended in a series of waist-high steps, and again, where many years back Joe had climbed with some difficulty, he now found ladders. The others fell farther behind as Joe, Lance, and the sheriff labored steadily toward the top.

Over an hour later, Joe clambered from a dry stream bed to stand atop the Kaiparowits Plateau. He wiped his face with a sleeve and surveyed his surroundings while waiting for the others. The grasses and brush were brown here, and grew low to the earth. Huge boulders, rounded and pockmarked with erosion, were scattered across the terrain. A lizard with bright white stripes dashed from the shade of a rock near his feet and disappeared into the brush.

Joe gazed after it, and when he looked up, saw a coyote sitting beside a rocky outcropping an easy stone-throw away. The animal appeared at ease, its tail wrapped around its

27

feet, intelligent eyes watching him with no sign of fear. The animal was healthy and well fed and its sharp-nosed muzzle opened in a grin, red tongue lolling.

"Hello Trickster," he said in Navajo. For another moment they regarded each other, then from the arroyo at his back came the sound of movement, and the coyote trotted lazily away between the bushes. Joe turned as Lance arrived beside him, and together they gave the sheriff a hand up. The big man was breathing heavily and his uniform had lost its sharp creases. Sweat ringed the shirt beneath his arms, spread a dark stain across his chest.

"Man," he gasped, "I forgot that when you say it's an easy path, you're talking about mountain goats and Indians."

Joe smiled faintly. "It is easier going down."

"I hear that." The sheriff looked toward the arroyo. "Guess I'm not the only one that had a hard time; the others got quite a ways behind." The difficulty the others were having reassured him and he squared his shoulders. His gaze strayed to the canteen Lance carried and he swallowed and licked his dry lips. "I could sure use a sip of that water you're carrying, Lance."

Lance unslung the canteen and handed it to him. The sheriff took a few conservative swallows, capped it, and handed it back.

"Christ, if I'd been thinking I would've brought my own," he said. "Guess I'm tryin' too hard to figure out what's happened here to keep my mind on practical matters. Which way does the trail go?"

Joe pointed where the coyote had been sitting. A moment later the BLM man dragged himself from the arroyo and sat panting as the FBI man and the photographer arrived, slapping dust from their clothes. Joe and Lance passed their canteens around and let them rest five minutes. Then Joe started on across the plateau.

The path was easy to follow in the soft dirt, and down its center were the paw prints of a coyote. But soon the soil gave way to wind-scoured stone and boulders. Massive spires of Entrada sandstone thrust up from the bare rock over which they traveled, a place where the only tracks were long, ser-

28

pentine grooves in the stone, the tracks of the wind.

No bird called, no lizard scurried from the shade. No plant grew. Rock surrounded them, rock baked beneath them, and after a few hours of fruitless searching the FBI man decided they should turn back. Dust covered his gray suit and his face was beaded with sweat. Joe handed him the canteen and saw the beginning of a bad sunburn on the man's face. He gulped the water greedily and handed the canteen back nearly empty.

"Okay," he said, "we'll try this again when we're better prepared. Let's get back to the boats."

No one argued the decision. Joe motioned for Lance, and his son arose from the shade of a boulder. Without a word he started off across the stone. At the arroyo he stopped to wait and grinned as his father joined him.

"I wasn't walking very fast," he said.

"I know." Joe's lips twitched with a smile. "They will be here in a minute. You stay in the lead. I will come last in case someone has trouble.

The others were panting when they arrived, but so eager for the shade of the arroyo that they paused to rest only a moment before following Lance down. The BLM man was last. Joe gave him the canteen.

"Drink it all," he said. The man eagerly complied, face shining with sweat, gasping between swallows. When the water was gone he continued to hold the canteen above his open mouth, tongue extended, catching the last few drops.

"Thanks." He handed it back and his hand was shaking.

"Okay." Joe slammed the cap home with the palm of his hand. "You go down now. Take it nice and easy; we are in no hurry."

The man nodded and let himself over the lip, slid down in the soft dirt, his belly red with soil when he stood. He waited below as Joe paused for a last look across the plateau. A locust rasped monotonously, the only sound on the hot, still air. Joe shaded his eyes and saw a gray shape appear beside a rock outcropping; a coyote, red tongue hanging.

"Walk in beauty, Trickster," he said in Navajo.

They arrived back at the houseboat in late afternoon. The

29

bodies, anonymous in zippered plastic bags, were loaded aboard Harold's Bertram. It took another two hours to extract the houseboat from the narrow canyon, and though it was dark when they arrived at the marina, the dock was alive with reporters, lights, and cameras. Sheriff Nathan Andrews spoke quietly as Joe maneuvered the Whaler into its slip.

"Oh boy," he said, "we're about to be famous."

Two

"What do you mean?" Harold Lowtah glared at the telephone clutched in his fist. "It's October already! Isn't there anyone in the office with any authority? Yes, you do that, you have him call me as soon as he gets in!" He slammed the phone down and the dewlap of flesh beneath his chin was quivering.

"Nobody has any balls," he said to Joe, "nobody has any balls any more. But they've all got fingers to point."

Joe nodded absently as he gazed at a painting on the wall behind Harold's head. It hung between his M.B.A. degree and a photo of him shaking hands with a famous actor at the marina dock. Joe laced his fingers around his knee, narrowed his eyes, and tried to remember how the painting was supposed to be.

It was a copy of a Rain Ceremony dry painting by some unknown artist, small, only a foot square, smaller than it would be on the floor of a hogan. Some *bellicanos* would call it a sand painting, but sand was only one of the materials used by the artists. The painting depicted Pollen Boy, an important Navajo deity, but the ceremonial colors had been altered and certain key elements left out so the power of the picture would not be achieved. A flicker of unease crossed Joe's face as he looked away from this religious figure imortalized behind glass, a design that should properly exist only for the day of a ceremony and be brushed away at sunset.

Harold lifted a buttock from his chair, removed a white handkerchief from his hip pocket, and wiped the sheen of sweat from his face. He looked up at the air-conditioning grill where the streamers he had fashioned from a piece of magnetic recording tape were flapping. The air conditioner was running with its rhythmic tick-tick-tick that never

31

ceased to annoy him, but the unseasonable heat was invading his office anyway. Then he noticed Joe studying the painting and smiled.

"I got a bargain on that painting," he said. Joe grunted in reply and Harold's features collapsed into their usual dour expression. He clasped his hands on his desk and stared at them.

"It was a good Sing we had for you and your son," he said in Navajo, "and many people came that I seldom see. Many years had passed since I last heard the Blessingway."

"A good ceremony," Joe agreed, "everyone enjoyed it. The young men still come for a Sing, but I think it is because they know the women will be there, and the young women because the men will be there."

"That is so," Harold laughed, "I have known many marriages that were arranged at ceremonies. You felt better afterward?"

Joe shrugged. "I felt fine before, but a Sing always makes me happy. The chants and the sweats, the people, the food, the gossip . . ." He waved his hand and smiled while Harold nodded.

"Yes, I know what you mean; I am always happiest in the crowd of my relatives. Maybe because our grandfathers and grandmothers spent so much time wandering alone, across *Dinetah* —." He waved his hand vaguely and his gaze passed beyond Joe to focus in empty space. "Out there, with their flocks. They say a Navajo should never be alone, but we are alone. We always have been and always will be."

"Perhaps."

The telephone rang and Harold's face hardened as he lifted the receiver. He spoke briefly in English and hung up.

"That was Brian Thornton of the FBI returning my call," he said. "We have our boat back. They've decided they aren't going to find the third man and won't need the boat for evidence in a murder trial. And it only took two months." There was sarcasm in his voice as he uttered the last sentence and Joe glanced at him quickly, looked away. Harold sighed and held out his big, flaccid hands in a gesture of helplessness.

32

"Two-thirds of the homes in Dinetah are substandard," he said. "Half don't have running water or electricity, and still we'll have to beg the government to reimburse the loss we've suffered from their investigation."

"Some of the people prefer hogans," Joe said.

"What else can they afford, Joe?"

"Is that what is really bothering you Harold?"

Harold looked startled, then his eyelids drooped. "No." He shook his head and pursed his thick lips. "There has been talk about the boat, about the whole affair. Mostly the old people." He shook his head again, his sad features managing to look even more mournful than usual. "The old people," he repeated. "Keeping traditions alive is fine, but I'll be glad when some of these foolish old ideas die out. They want us to sell the boat for what we can get and be done with it. I told them we can't get a good price for it this time of year, but they don't want to hear about the economics." He growled deep in his chest as anger began to replace sorrow on his face.

"That damn boat's only been rented part of one season! If we can keep it in service for the next several years we'll make enough in rental fees and depreciation to justify unloading it. But do you think they can listen to reason? No, they don't want to wait. And I always thought old people were supposed to be patient."

He slapped the desk with his hands and shook his head. "I can't justify selling, no way. I won't win any popularity contest with this decision Joe, but I can't see any way around it. If the profit-and-loss statement is in the red at the end of the year, it's my neck on the block, not theirs. We need that boat back in operation before the end of the season. See to it, will you?"

Joe looked up slowly and his gaze returned to the phony dry painting. He nodded. "I will see to it." He stood and walked to the door. As he opened it he heard Harold speak in a soft, exasperated voice.

"Think about it, Joe. If the rest of the country abandoned a building every time somebody died inside, for fear of their evil spirit causing mischief, why, there'd be a chain of empty

33

hospitals covering half the continent." He chuckled, and there was derision in the sound. "The year 2000 is almost upon us. We can't be dragging our ghosts behind us forever. I'm glad you and I, at least, have some sense of perspective."

Joe stared down at the thick, brown legs protruding from his canvas shorts. His legs, bowed and funny looking. When he was certain Harold had finished, he nodded again and closed the door quietly behind him.

From high in the shadows of the metal building came the sound of sparrows quarreling and a small flock of the drab little birds tumbled from their perches and swooped through the open doors into the sunlight.

Hector Garcia hawked and spat into the oily water. He was short and slight as a boy, with a boy's lively movements, but years of manual labor had left lines in his face that betrayed his age. He pushed the baseball cap up his forehead and grinned. When he grinned, the lines deepened.

"Shit," he said, "I'll do it if nobody else will. But you get Chris to help me." His dark eyes sparkled as he gave a leering wink. Joe smiled.

"Your wife would like that," he said, "you and some young girl alone on that fancy houseboat. I will tell her you suggested it." He raised his clipboard and crossed off the houseboat repair.

"*Cabron!* Don't tell Lucille!" Hector laughed and ran a hand through his hair. "She'd cut off my *cojones!* I'm not kidding, you don't know what trouble is until you've had my wife on your case. When she's mad at me I'm afraid to sleep. As soon as I close my eyes I think she might . . ." He drew his hand across his throat and made a hissing sound.

"I will find someone to help you," Joe said, "but not Chris. We need her in the office. How about the new kid, the one from Salt Lake City?"

"Leonard?" Hector looked thoughtful. "Yeah, he's okay, knows which end of a wrench to hold. When do you want me to start?"

"Today if you can, when you get caught up with the shop

34

work."

"Caught up!" Hector twisted his face into a look of incredulity.

"When you can fit it in, then," Joe said.

"Okay. Yeah, I can start today. After I get Mr. Crandall's boat back in the water." He jerked his chin toward the speedboat suspended from the dry-dock slings. "He came by yesterday asking about it, said he wants to take his brother fishing tomorrow. Somebody told him the rainbows are biting. Man, in this hot weather they'll be catching poached trout."

"Somebody is always sending poor Crandall on a wild goose chase," Joe said, "but he never catches a thing." He walked across the metal flooring and stood beneath the boat, ran his hand over the smooth patch, only a faint outline remaining where a log had punched a hole big enough to stick his head through. "Nice job on the hull. What is left to do?"

"Install the shaft and the prop, and check for vibration. No big deal." Hector wandered over and thumped the hull with his fist, nodded, then grinned and said, "So, you Indians afraid to go aboard that houseboat? Think maybe the boogeyman'll get you?"

Joe smiled faintly and flipped a page on his clipboard. "Have you followed any *chanecos* into the forest lately?"

Hector gave a nervous chuckle as he crossed himself, trying to conceal the gesture by scratching his chest.

"Ghost stories," he said, "what do you know about the laughing voice that makes people vanish in the woods? Stupid Mexican fairy tale."

"I have heard all the stories," Joe said, "I probably have as many Mexican relatives as you. Your people and mine were stealing each others' wives and horses before the *bellicanos* even dreamed there was anything west of the Mississippi. Every feast I attend, the tamales are right there beside the grilled mutton." He traced a column of figures with his finger and frowned.

"Today is October twenty-fifth," he said, "almost the end of the busy season. Because of the way the feds dragged their

35

feet the boat has been out of service sixty-one days. 350 dollars each day. The corporation has lost a possible 21,350 dollars."

Hector whistled. "Can't you make the fed pay it back?"

"Who knows?" Joe said. "Not my department. And even if the fed does pay it back, we always come up short somehow."

"Por seguro!" Hector laughed. "Remember the Alamo!"

"The Long Walk, Canyon de Chelly, all the Alamos," Joe said, nodding his head. "I will send Leonard to help you. How long do you think it will take?"

"One, maybe two days. I already looked it over and there's not much damage. Some repairs to the gunwale, spread a little gelcoat, check the outboards. God damn, they sure screwed up the props, didn't they? But we've got spares. Cleaning is mostly what it needs, after sitting so long."

"Okay, I will get out of your way." Joe crossed the floor of the cavernous building to the corner where his ancient oak desk hunkered beneath its usual layer of clutter. The chair creaked as he lowered himself into it, and when he cleared a spot for the clipboard, pushing aside a pile of technical books and service manuals, the wood beneath was as scarred and oil-stained as any of the workbenches. From a discarded piston that served as his pencil holder, he plucked a pen and flipped pages on the clipboard until he came to his inventory sheet.

Beyond the desk, row upon row of metal shelves extended out from the wall, each laden with dispenser boxes, plastic-wrapped spare parts, bins of nuts and bolts. Joe scowled at the shelves, then sighed and hoisted himself to his feet. He wandered between the shelves with his clipboard, counting, making entries on the sheet. When he reached the last shelf he glanced at his watch to find more than two hours had passed. He tacked the inventory sheet to the large bulletin board on the wall behind the desk.

The board was mostly obscured by bills, notes, and order forms, but interspersed were a few photos and he noticed one in particular as he stabbed the thumbtack into the cork. A small, blond-haired girl, holding a fish on a string and smiling so broadly that her eyes were squeezed shut. Her feet were bare and she wore jeans rolled up just below her knees and a white T-shirt two sizes too big.

Joe unpinned the picture and cradled it in a calloused hand. A gentle smile creased his lips. From the building at his back came the clang of metal striking metal, followed by Hector's swearing. He turned to look, but whatever he might have said was drowned out by the whine of Hector's pneumatic wrench. He laid the picture on his clipboard and rummaged atop the desk until he uncovered his rolodex. In the S's he found Sanders, Jonathan and Lucy; and their Phoenix address and telephone number. He dialed and listened to the phone ring a dozen times before hanging up.

A silence had fallen upon the shop as Hector laid his wrench aside, and into the silence Joe announced, "I am going to lunch."

"Thought you were on a diet," Hector replied. "Don't you got no will power?"

"Diet does not mean a man should not eat," Joe said as he stepped through the door. It closed on Hector's reply. He paused at the main walkway and leaned against the gate, looking across the marina. There were few people at the lake this late in the season, despite the unseasonably warm weather. A flop-eared puppy panted past, dragging two young girls at the end of its leash. The girls wore frilly one-piece bathing suits and their chins dripped with red juice from the half-melted popsicles clutched in their fists.

"Hi there," Joe said, "it looks like that dog is taking you for a walk." The girls giggled and began to skip, much to the puppy's delight. It broke into a clumsy run and the trio scampered along the walkway, turned at one of the fingers with much leash tugging and many high-pitched yells of encouragement, and clambered aboard a cabin cruiser.

Joe continued to gaze toward the boat where they disappeared, his features dull from the heat. He closed his eyes and crossed his arms on his chest, drew a deep breath, and let it out slowly. A fish leaped nearby with a loud splash and faint music drifted from one of the boats. Then, from among the docks, a man's voice yelled angrily, and Joe opened his eyes and found himself staring across the rows of docks toward the houseboat.

It was silhouetted darkly against the bright water, tied at the very end of the farthest finger. Solitary and neglected, it rose above the other, smaller houseboats. A yellow police barricade ribbon still fluttered from its lifelines and even at a distance the boat looked dirty.

A hot wind, a wind that sucked the moisture from his eyes and lips instead of refreshing, a wind that carried the smell of something rotting in the heat, swept in from the lake, and Joe swung the gate shut and walked toward shore. At the administration building he straddled his motorbike and noted the bulge of his waistline as he bent toward the ignition. He gave a grunt of disgust and decided to walk. He started up the gentle slope toward the RV park and, despite the heat, or perhaps in defiance of it, broke into an easy jog. A couple in a station wagon towing a fancy trailer approached and he stepped off the pavement and lifted a hand in greeting. The man driving lifted a finger but the woman beside him stared rigidly ahead.

Joe labored up the final grade to find Anna on her hands and knees in the herb garden. He clasped his hands behind his head and walked in circles, puffing and sweating, waiting for the hammering of his heart to slow, moisture trickling down his chest and sides.

"Hi!" Anna said, looking up with a smile. "Somebody chasing you?"

"Yes, ten extra pounds was right on my heels, but I think I gave it the slip." He lowered his hands and rolled his head and his neck made small popping sounds.

"Ten pounds huh?" She arose and stood, feet apart and hands on her hips, and gave him an appraising look. She had not gotten heavy, like so many of her friends, and she was smooth skinned and brown. "I think maybe you only outran five of them." She grinned and wiped her forehead with the back of her hand. "But not bad for a fifty-year-old man. Your lunch is on the table. Lance has already been here and gone."

"Forty-nine-year-old man," he growled.

Joe climbed the steps and entered the blissful coolness of

the trailer, went to the bathroom and splashed cold water on his face and the back of his neck. A thick ham sandwich was on a plate on the counter. He opened the refrigerator and poured a glass of iced tea and seated himself at the table. Anna came in pulling off her gardening gloves.

"So how was your morning?" She poured herself a glass of tea and joined him.

"All right. Harold says the investigation is over and we can put the big houseboat back in service, so I asked Hector to get it ready. With Leonard helping him it should not take more than two or three days. Of course, the season is almost over, so we probably will not see much rental money coming in." He took a bite of sandwich while Anna studied him.

After a time she said, "Sure, I guess you have to do that don't you?"

"Why not? It is important revenue."

"Aunt Ida was talking to me about it." She waved a hand vaguely and took a swallow of tea. "There's talk that we should sell that boat before it brings trouble."

"We have lost a lot of money," he said. "We need to get it rented and no reason not to. Oh, I tried calling John and Lucy but nobody was home."

"They never are. Jonathan spends twenty-four hours at his car dealership and Lucy has jazzercise, volunteer nursing, golf, bridge club, all her social activities, not to mention taking Rebecca to school and dance class."

"Where does she get all her energy?"

"Where does she find the time?" Anna smiled and shook her head. "I'm looking forward to their visit. It'll be quite a crowd with Norm and Jude and their baby along. Oh, and Martha's coming too. How they talked her into it I don't know; a Mediterranean cruise is more her style. Wonder if we'll see much of them this trip."

"Depends on John," he said around a mouthful of sandwich, "he is the one that always takes charge."

"You're right, he *is* pushy."

"I did not say that."

"It's what you meant."

"He is the natural leader of the group, is all I meant." Joe drained the last of his tea and wiped his mouth with the back of his hand. "When he was serving under me in the service, nobody every questioned any order he gave. And speaking of being under orders, the investigators had our boat tied up for almost two months, and if they discovered anything at all I have not heard about it. Have you heard anything?"

"Nooo," Anna said slowly, shaking her head, "but I understand the university is busy studying all the artifacts they recovered." She set her glass down and rubbed her face with her hands. "I still get a queasy feeling when I think of how that man died. Do you think he lived for long after he . . . after it happened?"

"No, he died quickly," Joe said. "I told you what I heard about the coroner's report. The cerebrum was all messed up, lots of hemorrhaging. And there are no pain receptors in the brain so he would not have felt much once the wire was in. At least that is what the coroner said. But the coroner did not try it himself to find out." He grimaced. "A man would have to be crazy to do that to somebody, and even crazier to do it to himself."

Anna's eyes widened. She swallowed and said, "How can they call something like that suicide? It's unthinkable."

"Hector says a deputy told him the coroner determined it by the angle of the wire, the force it had exerted, and so on, but I do not know how they could tell the difference if he had been murdered."

"I'm sorry I brought it up," she said. "But you should be grateful for the Sing we had, or that might have been you or Lance. A *chindi* is nothing to mess with."

"We were talking about John and the others," he said. "Do you want to invite them for a meal while they are here?"

"Sure, if they'll come. You know how they are, always in a hurry to start their relaxing vacation."

"In a hurry to relax is a good description," he said. "It will be nice to see Rebecca though."

She smiled, reached across the table and patted his hand. "You sure love that little girl, don't you?"

He hunched his shoulders. "She is a good kid; we understand each other." He squeezed her hand tightly for a moment before he arose and carried his plate to the sink.

"Well, back to the salt mine," he said. "With Hector on the houseboat, I will be working in the shop the rest of the day. See you tonight." She smiled and lifted her face so he could kiss her cheek.

He stepped outside into the heat. It seemed worse after the coolness of the trailer. Pausing a moment on the small front porch, he looked toward the western horizon, where streamers were breaking free from a greater mass of storm cloud roiling up above the Kaiparowits Plateau, big, businesslike clouds moving quickly on a high wind, sliding toward the lake on a single, unbroken plane, their lower surfaces flattened atop some unseen atmospheric barrier like raindrops on a windowpane. The wind and clouds meant a fall storm was brewing, which might mean relief from this hot spell, but might also mean rough conditions on the lake and in the marina. He descended the steps and began to jog down the road, his pace quicker than it had been on the way up.

At the marina he walked the docks, checking the lines mooring the boats to their slips. He reached the office and stepped inside to find Lance and Chris holding hands across the counter. Lance turned toward him and grinned foolishly, thrust his hands in his pockets, and Chris flushed as she ran a hand through her hair.

"Hi Joe," she said, "the radio says we've got a big storm coming."

"Sure looks like it," he said. "Is this guy bothering you?"

"Not really, I kind of like having him around." She winked and Joe laughed.

"Well, sorry to disappoint you," he said, "but I need him right now. I will send him back when I am through with him."

"Okay, but don't keep him too late, he promised to take me in the boat to the Sunlight Marina restaurant for dinner."

"A boat ride with Lance? Alone?" He cocked an eyebrow and turned to his son. "She has not heard about your reputation?"

41

Lance gave Chris a pained look and followed his father out the door.

"Nice girl," Joe said as they paused outside the office, "pretty too. I guess you noticed though, huh?"

"Yeah, she's kind of cute," Lance said, staring down at the dock. A gust of wind whipped his hair across his forehead and he raised a hand to brush it back, saw his father's smile, shuffled his feet and said, "Well, yeah, I like her, all right? Listen, let's tend to the boats. That's what you dragged me away for isn't it?"

"Right. I have already worked the transient slips."

"Okay," Lance said, "I'll take the south side." They began to work their way toward the end of the marina, making sure that no cleats were working loose from the floats, that lines were not frayed, that fenders were properly placed.

By the time Joe reached the big houseboat the wind was kicking the tops off the waves in plumes of white and boats were coming in off the main lake. Hector was standing on the dock with a screwdriver in his hand, attaching an aluminum rub rail to the gunwale.

Joe stopped a few feet away, behind Hector's back, and surveyed his handiwork. "How is it going?" He asked. Hector jumped and spun around, dropping a screw into the water between the boat and the dock.

"*Que verga!* Don't do that Joe!"

"Do what? Something wrong?"

"Nothing! I just . . . you damn Indians can sure sneak up on a man."

"Sorry. How is Leonard working out?"

"Oh fine, fine, he's one hell of a good housemaid. He's inside running the vacuum." Hector's dark gaze flicked back and forth as he jiggled the screwdriver in his hand. He glanced at the foredeck. "They put that fingerprint powder everywhere," he said, his voice still agitated. "It's hard to get off some surfaces, and not one of those guys has ever heard of deck shoes. Scuff marks all over. And this paint—," he gestured at the cabin with the screwdriver, "it really should be rubbed out and waxed. But that's a couple of extra days."

"Can it wait? If not, you can have more help."

"What, you gonna climb aboard and lend a hand?" Hector snickered.

"If you need me," Joe said.

"No, it can wait. Just kidding. We'll finish tomorrow, or the day after. *Gracias Dios*, it's all plastic. But screw this *pinche* heat." He tossed the screwdriver in the air, almost missed his catch, glanced over his shoulder again at the boat.

"What is the matter, Hector?" Joe asked. "Been drinking too much coffee? You seem jumpy."

"What, coffee in this weather? You crazy? Beer maybe. No, I think it's this storm coming in. A change in the weather always makes me nervous. I'm tuned in to mother nature, at one with my environment, a natural man. I can tell when a bad storm's coming. Like a coyote, you know?"

"Sure." Joe rolled his eyes.

A gust of wind whipped their clothes and Hector flinched, searched his pocket for a screw. He stuck it in a hole in the rub rail and screwed it down tight. As he moved to the next hole Lance hurried toward them, his shirt clutched in hand, sinewy arms and chest bared to the wind.

"All through?" Joe asked.

"Yeah. Had to replace a couple of lines on private boats, but ours were all good. I wrote the slip numbers down so you can bill them for the lines." He handed Joe a matchbook cover with the numbers scrawled in ballpoint.

"Good job, thanks." He waved a hand at the lake. "Do you think you want to be out on the lake in this? Forty miles each way. The Whaler can handle it, no problem, but it would be a rough, wet ride, more of an adventure than a pleasure cruise. Not much good for . . . ah . . . holding hands."

Hector snickered and Lance gave him an irritated glance. "Yeah, guess you're right. We'll have to do it some other time."

"You can take the truck if you want. Maybe drive her to Blanding or Mexican Hat?"

"Hey, that would be great. Thanks a lot!" He smiled and hurried toward the office.

"You're all right, *Jefe*," Hector muttered. He looked up

43

from his work and grinned. "Can I borrow the truck some night?"

"Are you kidding?" Joe said. "I know how you drive. I am going to the shop to work on that outdrive overhaul. Maybe I will see you later."

"See you *Jefe*." Hector's gaze followed Joe's retreating figure along the docks until the slam of a door made him jump. He turned to see Leonard standing on the foredeck, staring at the sliding door, a confused look on his face.

"Hey, what are you trying to do?" Hector shouted. "That's glass in that damn door, you know?"

"I . . . I just gave it a little push," the skinny, blond-haired boy said. "The darn thing slid so easy, like the wind caught it or something."

"Well, be more careful." Hector rubbed his eye with the back of a hand, blinking to clear a bit of wind-borne dirt. "You all through in there?"

"I think so. You want to come in and take a look?"

"No, if you say it's done, that's good enough for me."

The boy stepped to the dock. "Is there anything else you need me to do?"

"That's it for today. Get here early tomorrow though and we'll try to finish this job."

The boy squinted and leaned into the wind as he walked off down the dock.

Hector worked quickly, turning the screws in with sharp snaps of his wrist, and he swore softly as the first drops of rain struck. One of the screws stripped out, and three holes later, another. Normally he would have replaced them with larger ones or glued them in with epoxy. But today he just swore a little louder, hurrying to finish, and when the last screw was tightened he gathered up his tools and climbed aboard. He could work inside now, repairing damage done by the feds during their search. If he worked quickly, he would be done shortly after dark, and Lucille was fixing *sopapillas* for dessert.

When the truck came over the rise and its headlights

dipped toward the bottom of the gulley where the road should have been, Lance saw a rushing, swirling violence into which the white centerline vanished. He had only an instant to react, jamming the brake pedal hard against the floor. He and Chris were thrown against their seat belts as the tires squealed on wet pavement and the truck stopped with its front bumper awash. They looked at each other, eyes wide; then Lance shifted into reverse and backed a safe distance up the road.

"My God," Chris said, "I'm glad you weren't speeding."

Lance shook his head in wonder. "I've lived here long enough to suspect we might have a flash flood tonight, but I've never heard of this arroyo flooding before."

"How deep do you think it is?"

"Hard to tell. I bet it's deep enough to carry off a truck though, especially moving as fast as it is."

"God, I've never seen a flash flood before. We could have been drowned!"

"A few people are every year."

"It's kind of awesome," she said, staring at the dark water in fascination. In the truck's headlights she saw a small tree carried past, and a tire that surfaced like some thick, dark serpent, the glistening curve of its diamond-tread visible for an instant before it vanished beneath the turbulent surface.

"So, what do we do now?" Chris slid across the bench seat to press against him.

"Not much we can do; take us most of the night to drive the long way around. Guess we'll just have to wait it out; these things don't usually last too long." Lance's teeth flashed in the darkness of the cab. "But first, I'm gonna get us off the road so somebody doesn't plow into us from behind." He cranked the wheel around and the power steering pump squealed in protest. At the top of the rise they left the pavement and wove a course between the mesquite bushes and yucca. A short distance from the road he turned off the ignition.

"I should put out a flare," he said.

"Good idea."

They climbed from the truck and Lance reached under

45

the seat for the emergency kit. He removed the cap from a road flare and struck its tip on the igniter. The flare sputtered, then caught and burned fiercely, bathing their faces in red light.

"Be right back," he said. He walked to the road, his shadow dancing weirdly across the ground. He laid the flare atop the hill, where it was clearly visible to oncoming traffic, and returned to the truck. Chris had her head buried in the toolbox mounted behind the cab.

"What are you looking for?" he asked.

"Oh, I don't know. Maybe something like this." She turned toward him cradling a sleeping bag.

"Dad keeps that in there in case one of us is stranded during the winter."

"Suuure, he does," she said, "why else would it be there?"

"No, really —"

"Don't be so defensive!" she laughed. "Come on." She walked away from the road until she found a patch of desert grass. She opened the bag on the grass, sat down, patted the fabric with her hand.

"Care to join me?" She held out her hand, and when he laced his fingers with her own, she drew him down beside her. Her face was mysterious in the darkness, illuminated only by the stars. With a teasing smile she brought her lips to meet his, slid her arms around his neck. Several minutes later she drew away gasping for breath. "My goodness, that's nice. Now I know what your dad meant about your reputation; you're quite a kisser."

"Me? What about you?" His arm around her shoulders pulled her down until they lay facing each other, bodies pressed together, his hand resting on her hip.

"You're something else," he said. And, "God, you're beautiful."

"Like me?"

"I like you."

"I like you too. More than like."

A car approached the rise and slowed, stopped near the flare, swept the desert with its headlights as it turned around. A minute later it was gone back the way it had

46

come.

"Road's still flooded," Lance said in a quiet, abstracted voice.

"Could it be all night?"

He studied her face in the starlight, fingers touching her hair.

"Could be." After a time he added, "I should call my folks so they don't worry."

"How long until they start worrying?"

He smiled and looked at his watch, pushing the button that made the little light come on inside. "A couple of hours."

"That's plenty of time." She laced her fingers behind his neck, drew his mouth to hers, and as her lips parted she lay back and felt the length of his body molding itself to her. Overhead the last of the clouds vanished into the east and the stars glittered sharp and clear in the clean desert air. The storm was over.

It was dark by the time Hector finished his repairs aboard the houseboat. The sounds of the storm were muffled by the cabin as he packed his tools into the battered metal toolbox. But when he stood and lifted it with a grunt, he heard the sound of something scampering the length of the roof. It began at the bow and traveled toward the stern, a pattering like footsteps, or scrabbling claws, or perhaps just a handful of windblown pebbles.

He craned his neck to follow the noise as it passed, then shook his head and walked down the hall, out on deck, and stepped to the dock. He peered up at the top of the houseboat, and a flash of lighting granted him a brief moment of illumination during which he seemed to see something.

He blinked his eyes as the dazzle of the lightning left him momentarily blind. And when he looked again he saw nothing. Just the lounge and a locker, both permanently attached to the sun deck on top. Nothing crouched darkly beside the locker, peering down with green, reflective eyes. He set the box aside and started to climb aboard for a closer look, but a squall of warm rain drenched him and he grabbed his tools and hurried, cursing, along the deserted docks to the parking lot. He threw the box into the back of his old Nova and drove the three miles to the Winged Rock employee housing tract.

The house was small and plain, a stucco box identical to those on either side. A swamp cooler the size of a refrigerator hunkered atop the otherwise flat roof. The darkness concealed most of the discarded toys and auto parts littering the yards, the old boats and appliances and worn-out tires.

Lucille came smiling from the kitchen to welcome him, then scolded him for being late without calling, then fetched him a beer from the refrigerator and a chilled glass from the freezer and told him dinner would be ready in five minutes and he just had time to wash up.

They had dinner in front of the television as usual.

"Another car chase," he said in Spanish around a mouthful of refritos. "I think the entire budget of this movie went to Ford Motor Company." He took a big swallow of beer. "I've seen it before, you want to know how it ends?"

"No, you dummy! Can't you let me enjoy it? You have to know everything?" Lucille glared at him, but the trace of a smile played at the corners of her mouth. She was plump, no denying that, but her face was pretty as ever. He ran a hand up her leg beneath her skirt and she gasped with feigned indignity, batted his arm with her fist. He laughed as he returned his attention to the plate balanced on his knees, and to the TV where the big white Lincoln Continental was smashing its way down a San Francisco street.

Later they made love, and Lucille, who was twenty-two, said in Hector's ear, "Maybe this year, maybe no more pills, yes? Maybe this year a *nino?* I can scrimp a little, and you have a raise coming. A child would fill our home with happiness."

"Possibly," Hector said, already half-asleep. "Or possibly next year. We have to do things right. I don't want to raise some kid to collect aluminum cans for a living."

Lucille turned away from him and tugged the covers up around her face, and Hector sighed deeply and buried his head beneath the pillow. It seemed he had just fallen asleep when Lucille screamed and he lunged up and stared about the room with wild eyes. He took her shoulders in his hands and shook her, his fear making him act angry, and her babbling became coherent.

"There!" she shrieked, "he ran out the door! His hands were on my throat!"

Hector leaped from bed and ran into the living room to find the front door swinging slowly shut. He howled with anger and ran into the street, saw a figure running awkward and bowlegged beneath one of the street lights. Clad only in his shorts he chased after it, his small, hard hands balled into fists. He was so enraged that growls came from his throat with each breath.

He gained on the intruder swiftly, and as he closed the distance separating them Hector saw something odd. The arms were too long, the legs too short, the torso grotesquely broad-shouldered and elongated. The heavy head appeared attached directly to the shoulders without benefit of a neck. Hector slowed his pace and looked about for something he could use as a weapon.

Already they were approaching the turn where the road doubled back along the other side of the block. At the turning of the road was a brightly lit, fenced enclosure that housed a metal utility building, and beyond that was the desert. Hector saw nothing he could use as a club or knife, nothing useful in the yards he passed, and he swore softly as they approached the desert where the intruder might lose him. Instead, it leaped at the chain link fence and stuck like a cat, arms and legs outstretched, the wire rattling from the impact of the blow. Then it heaved itself up and over with an impossible movement and vanished into the shadows.

He stopped at the fence, his face filled with uncertainty. A sign on the fence read, "Danger — High Voltage," and another, "No Trespassing — Property NTC." Inside the building was the diesel-electric generator that provided the houses with power, and the drone of its engine drowned all other sounds. He walked completely around the enclosure, but the intruder had vanished. Then he saw something and stopped; someone had left the padlock on the door open.

He clambered over the fence and paused at the door, opened it slowly. The drone became louder. He reached inside, felt along the wall, and found one of the wrenches he knew was hanging on the pegboard there.

Clutching the heavy length of forged steel, he stepped inside and switched on the light. It was only a single bulb above the big engine, and seemed to enhance, rather than dispel, the confusion of wire and pipe and machinery, the heat and stink and noise.

"Come out of there you son-of-a-bitch," Hector shouted. He cocked his head and listened to what sounded like a faint cackle.

"*Hijo de puta!*" he yelled angrily. "Son of a whore! Touch my wife will you! I'm gonna bash your God damned skull!" Again there was a sound like a wheezing laugh, and with a muttered curse he raised the wrench and stepped inside.

To his right the yellow Caterpillar engine throbbed and whined. To his left, lining the entire wall of the building, was a heavy wire grate that protected a profusion of wiring, transformers, and terminal boards. Several white placards bearing red lightning bolts were attached to the wire mesh, as were more signs warning of high voltage. The air smelled of oil, diesel fumes, and ozone. Big hoses led from the engine to the roof, where the radiator and fan added their whir to the general din.

Down this narrow corridor Hector stalked slowly, carefully, keeping as far from the wire grate as he could, glancing at it nervously from the corners of his eyes as he strained to hear or see some sign of movement in the shadows ahead. He had often been in the space on the opposite side of engine and generator, an access area for cleaning the injectors and changing the transmission and engine oil. If the intruder was inside the building, he had to be crouching there, waiting . . .

Hector drew a deep breath and let it out shakily as he reached the far end of the building. He shifted the wrench in his grip and wiped sweat from his face with the back of his wrist. Slowly, placing each bare foot very deliberately on the concrete floor, he crept between the front of the engine and the metal wall.

Something dropped from the ceiling and landed behind him with a thump. He shrieked as he spun about and his elbow struck the massive cast iron engine block. Desperately he raised the wrench in the tight confinement and swung, unable to see clearly through his terror and pain. And nothing was there when the wrench descended in a sweeping blow, nothing but a white placard with a red lightning bolt. The wrench drove the placard, and the wire mesh to which it was attached, against an anodized gold transformer terminal.

There was a thunderous crack and blinding blue light as several thousand amperes of alternating current sizzled through the wrench into Hector's body, through his rigid body into the floor. The street lights outside flickered as the electricity ceased to power the lights and refrigerators, the air conditioners, the water pumps and stereos. The electricity left its normal circuits and chose instead the less resistive path through Hector's flesh and bone. The scream never had a chance to leave his lips as heart and lungs were instantly paralyzed. His hand blackened around the wrench and his feet smoldered. The violent river of electricity poured down his arm, through his chest, out his legs, and a wisp of smoke issued from his open mouth as total darkness descended over Winged Rock employee housing.

Lance was awakened by the tremulous call of a screech owl. He opened his eyes, blinked, then sat up abruptly and the sleeping bag fell down around his waist. There was a trace of chill in the air and a faint rose tint on the eastern horizon.

"Oh shit," he said.

"Whaaa . . . what is it?" Chris said, rubbing her eyes with her fists.

"We overslept," he said, "it's almost sunrise." He looked at his watch. "Christ, 5:15. I hope my folks don't have the cops out looking for us."

He was already groping for the clothes scattered on the grass at his side. Chris dressed quickly, her back modestly turned. By the time she was finished, he had the sleeping bag rolled up and stored in the truck and the engine running. She climbed into the cab.

"My dad is going to be some kind of pissed," Lance said as he turned the truck onto the highway. A layer of mud and debris deposited by the flood remained at the bottom of the draw. "Hold on, I'm going to hit it fast so we don't get stuck." He stabbed the throttle as the truck sped down the hill.

The mud was deeper than it looked and the truck slewed sideways as the tires plowed wide furrows. Lance turned the wheel in the direction of the slide and the truck straightened out, just made it to the other side before they ran out of momentum, wheels spinning. But the tires dug through and chirped and the tread contacted pavement, and Lance drove the truck hard, both hands clutching the wheel.

"Can't you slow down a little?" Chris asked.

"Sorry, but I know what I'm doing," he said tightly.

"What are you so worried about?"

"You don't know how my dad is when he's mad."

"What's he going to do?" she asked in exasperation. "Beat you?"

Lance glanced over at her and she gave a small, hopeful smile. He eased his foot off the throttle.

"It's not that," he said, "it's just . . . responsibility to my family. I guess the worst thing you can say about a Navajo is that he acts as if he has no family. And one of the best you can say is that he's generous to his relatives. A real Navajo owns nothing he would not share with his family, and does nothing without thinking of their feelings."

She looked at him curiously, then smiled and slid up close against him. She pried his hand from the wheel and draped his arm around her shoulders.

"You're a good man, Lance Redhill," she said. "I don't think I've ever met anyone quite like you."

He tried to keep a straight face, but her compliment brought a smile of pleasure. He drove the remaining miles to the marina at a reasonable speed, her head on his shoulder, brushing her hair now and again with his lips. And all too soon they arrived at employee housing, where she shared a house with another woman. The street was jammed with emergency vehicles.

"What's going on?" he said. "Isn't that Hector's place?"

"Yeah, it sure is," she said. "Jesus, look at all the cop cars Lance. Something bad's happened."

They continued up the street until a sheriff's deputy stopped them. Lance rolled down the window and said, "I'm Joe Redhill's son, Lance." The deputy glanced in at Chris, then down at the NTC logo on the door of the truck, and waved them past.

Lance parked the truck behind a sheriff car. Two state patrolmen, holding cups of coffee and conversing in low tones, gazed at them suspiciously as they approached Hector's house. But Joe was just coming out the front door and met the young couple on the sidewalk.

"Dad!" Lance called, "what's happened?"

"There has been a terrible accident." Joe rubbed his eyes with the back of a hand, then looked up the street toward the generating station where men in uniforms were moving slowly about, staring at the ground, inspecting the fence, taking photographs. "Hector is dead," he said in a tired voice.

"Oh, no," Lance said slowly. "How can that be, Dad? He was fine yesterday. I was talking to him, at the houseboat."

"Accident," Joe said, "it was an accident. That is what the officials are saying." He gestured toward the generator station. "Electrocuted. Late last night. Lucille says he was chasing an intruder, but they can find no trace of one. No fingerprints but Hector's, no footprints but his. So I guess it was some kind of crazy accident. Either that, or . . ." He shook his head, eyes narrowing, "No, I do not know."

"Dad, look . . ." Lance stared at his father, concerned at the lines of weariness and the way Joe continued to gaze up the street, as if he had forgotten they were standing beside him. "Dad, I'm sorry, sorry I didn't call —." He thumped his fist against his thigh. "Dad, I'm sorry about Hector, I don't know what to say. . . ."

53

Joe turned to them and put an arm around each of their shoulders, urged them toward the truck.

"You were gone all night," he said, "your mother worried. What will you tell her?"

"There was a flash flood and we couldn't get through."

"Then tell her that." Joe nodded and released them.

"Go now, both of you. Lance, tell your mother I will be home in an hour or so."

"You're sure there's nothing I can do here?"

Joe shook his head, lifted a hand in a gesture of farewell as he turned, and they climbed into the truck and drove away. Lance stopped the truck in front of Chris's house and they kissed, but their eyes opened while their lips were still touching.

"Chris, about last night —," he started to say, but she laid a finger on his lips and reached for the door handle.

"It was fine," she said, "really fine. But . . . I don't want to talk about it now, okay? Everything's so crazy this morning, and last night was so perfect. Poor Hector, and poor Lucille." Then she was crying and she opened the door and stepped out. "I'll see you at work," she said quickly. She closed the door and Lance watched until she disappeared inside the nondescript stucco box; then he drove slowly toward the RV park.

Already the sun burned above the horizon, red as an angry wound, and the morning sky was a strange mustard yellow. The pools of rain on the pavement were drying quickly, steaming like ponds of acid. Small flowers had blossomed during the night, colorful confetti thrown carelessly across the landscape, but by the time Lance made peace with his mother and left the trailer for the ride to the marina, the tiny, pale blossoms had withered from the merciless heat.

Three

Now came Norman Sanders and wife Judy, crossing the blistering landscape in their three-year-old Chevy wagon, with baby Stephen in the car seat between them. Norman, sandy-haired and overweight, habitually nervous, eyed the temperature gauge as his fists clutched the wheel. The gauge was steadily climbing but he ignored it and continued to drive fast.

Perspiration beaded his forehead and upper lip, and his face was more pallid than usual, making him look like a faded photo, a pale outline; nothing remarkable about him whatever. He stepped on the brake as they came upon the arroyo where the flash flood had occurred the previous night. Several vehicles had plowed the mud aside by now, and the way was rough but passable. Over the next rise they passed a sign.

"Thirty miles to Winged Rock," he read, "thank God we're getting close. When did we leave last night, seven?"

"Seven-thirty," his wife said quietly, careful not to wake the baby. Her head was turned to watch the passing landscape, and after a moment she added, "It's beautiful, don't you think?"

"Desolate, Jude," he replied, "just desolate. What the heck do you do out here if your car breaks down? I mean, we've only seen one other car since we turned off of 163. Give me Los Angeles any day; it may be crowded, but if you get into trouble AAA is there in ten minutes."

"Oh, you're such a worrier, you're worse than an old lady." Judy smiled at him, reaching across the sleeping child to touch his shoulder.

"And us with a ten-month-old baby in the car. I may worry," he growled, "but it helps me anticipate things that

55

could go wrong. We've never had any major problems because I anticipate them in advance."

"Shhh," she scolded, "do you want to wake him?" When he didn't reply, she added in a thoughtful tone, "I forget, you're perfect at whatever you do."

"Perfect enough."

"A perfect worrier." She chuckled and rummaged in her purse, producing a comb which she ran through her short, brown, pageboy haircut. Her jaw was a little too wide to be called beautiful, but her lips were full and sensual and she was wholesome-looking, slender in tight jeans. Her T-shirt showed her small, firm breasts to advantage. And now the baby, disturbed by their voices, opened its eyes and made an inquiring sound.

"Oh, look who's awake!" she said brightly. "How's my baby boy?"

"Hey Bruiser," Norman said, "get a good night's sleep buddy?"

The baby, chubby and rosy-cheeked, looked at each in turn, blinking sleep from his brown eyes, then yawned and burped. His parents laughed, and Steve scrunched up his face and emitted an angry howl. Judy reached into the cooler on the back seat and produced a bottle. As soon as he saw it the baby took it from her hand.

"What a cute baby," she sighed as he sucked greedily. "Don't you think he's the cutest baby in the world Norm?"

"Yeah," he said, glancing fondly at his son, "he's okay for a rug rat." The Chevy chugged to the top of the next rise and Norman sighed with relief, rolled his head to ease the stiffness in his neck.

And now also, not far behind and closing fast, came Jonathan, Lucy, and Rebecca Sanders, accompanied by John and Norman's mother, Martha. John and his daughter Rebecca were playing a game with simple rules—whoever spotted a car and yelled 'car' first earned a point, and if they could identify the make before the other did, earned another point, and another for the model, and another for the year. Rebecca only won when John let her, but neither was racking up many points this morning.

"How much further Daddy?" Rebecca asked.

"That's the hundredth time you've asked," John said, "and I answer — five minutes sooner than when you asked the last time." He was taller than his brother Norman, blond, bearded, with broad shoulders and a flawless tan.

"But when, Daddy, whennnn?"

"When we get there!" he barked.

"Oh, now Jonathan," Martha said, "you used to do the same thing when you were a boy." She pushed a wisp of white hair from her face, gave his reflection in the mirror a wry smile. Her eyes were lively, an electric blue in color, and her face darkly weathered from years of outdoor activities.

"Thanks for the history lesson, Mom," he drawled, "but I think I can deal with Becka without the heavy burden of parental wisdom."

Martha didn't answer, but turned her attention to the passing landscape.

"John, we're almost there," Lucy said. "Since you won't let me spell you at the wheel, can I pour you a cup of coffee?" She stretched her long legs and sighed, cramped from hours in the car. Her eyes were a luminescent emerald green, almond-shaped. Her long blond hair was pulled severely back from a face with high, unlined forehead, prominent cheekbones, and thin nose. The hair hung in a thick braid over her shoulder. Even with her elegant body folded into the front seat of the wagon, it was obvious she was a strikingly beautiful woman.

"Sure," he said. "Sorry Mom. Sorry Becka. I've been driving too long."

"So how long—" Rebecca started to say and he interrupted her with, "An hour, hour and thirty minutes, okay honey? Think you can wait that long?"

"Do I have any choice?"

"Whoa, eight years old and sharp as a whip already," he said. "No honey, that was a dumb question and you called me on it. You don't have any choice; we get there when we get there." He sipped noisily from the cup his wife handed him. "Ahh, that's good. Thanks babe."

"You're welcome. Martha, would you like some?"

"Hm? Oh, no thanks dear. Not unless there's a restroom in sight."

"There's always the porta-potti in the boat." John gestured over his shoulder with a thumb, toward the boat and trailer towing behind the big Silverado station wagon.

"Oh Daddy! You can't go to the bathroom on the boat when it isn't in the water!" Rebecca laughed. Green-eyed, blond Rebecca. Gangly, happy, a spray of freckles across her nose.

"Why not?" John asked. "The porta-potti works just the same."

"It does?" Her face furrowed with thought, then brightened as she said, "Yeah, I guess so, huh? Do you want some coffee now Grandma?"

"No thanks Becka," Martha said, chuckling. "Not right now anyway."

John touched the brakes as they began the descent into a canyon where they could see the road winding back and forth below, appearing and disappearing among great upheavals of sandstone. He turned the air conditioner up a notch now that the engine wasn't working as hard, sighed as the cool air hit his face. He searched the twists and turns below, but there was nothing except miles and miles of empty road crossing an empty land.

Even as Jonathan and family reached the bottom of the canyon and began their climb up the other side, Anna Redhill was answering her doorbell to find Norman, Judy, and Stephen Sanders on the front porch. For an instant she could only stare in surprise, her hand holding the door frame.

She recovered herself and said, "Why, hello! Goodness, I . . . I wasn't expecting you today. I must have gotten the date mixed up. Come in, come in out of the heat. My, look how big Stephen's gotten." She herded them into the living room and closed the door, leaning against it with her hands behind her.

"Well, make yourselves at home, won't you?" she said. "How was the drive? Can I get you some coffee? How about some breakfast, have you had anything to eat?"

"Anna," Judy said, "what's wrong? You look beat."

Anna sagged and rubbed her face with her hands. "Pretty obvious, is it?" She smiled a tired smile. "We've had quite a night around here. One of the workers at the marina, a good friend of Joe's and mine, had a fatal accident last night. I've spent part of the night and most of the morning with his wife. And there was a big storm yesterday afternoon and a flash flood last night. The road was blocked and Lance couldn't get home from his date, so I was worrying about him, and we had a big fight when he finally showed up a few hours ago. All in all it's been one huge mess."

She took a deep breath and closed her eyes. When she blew out the breath and opened her eyes, her face had lost some of its strain and her smile seemed to come more easily. "But let's talk about more pleasant things. Come on in the kitchen and I'll fix you some breakfast."

"Oh Anna no," Judy protested, "we didn't stop by to turn your place into a restaurant."

"Nonsense," Anna said. "I've been stumbling around in a haze and thinking too much. Come in and sit down at the table." Norman started to add his voice to the protest, but Anna shook her head and turned away. And when they saw her carrying dishes from the refrigerator to the counter beside the stove, they exchanged a helpless look and seated themselves at the table. The baby made an inquisitive noise as Judy balanced him on her knee.

"Do you both like French toast?" Anna asked. "I've got a fresh loaf of sourdough bread, and it's something Stevie can eat if we soak it with some milk."

"We've got plenty of the new dehydrated foods for the Bruiser," Norman said. But Judy countered with, "That sounds fine Anna; I've been starting him on regular foods. So far the only thing he really doesn't like in any way, shape, or form is apples. Apple sauce, apple juice, you name it."

"Really?" Anna looked over her shoulder, a dripping eggshell in her hand. "Well, don't be too surprised; it seems they all have something they don't like. With Lance it was bananas."

Norman fell silent as the two women talked of children

and foods, his gaze exploring the kitchen and what was visible of the living room.

"Excuse me," he said after a time, "where's the bathroom Anna?"

"Through the living room, second door on the right."

"Thanks."

He used the toilet, then ran the sink full of hot water. He sighed as he lifted handfuls to his face, almost too hot to stand and making his skin tingle. When he finished toweling dry, the face in the mirror looked refreshed. Or at least not as hangdog as it had. On the floor beside the toilet was a scale. After a moment of hesitation he stepped onto it, shook his head and grunted with disgust as the needle passed 200 pounds.

But his disgust didn't prevent him from wolfing down seconds of Anna's delicious French toast, made with nutmeg and cinnamon, covered with powdered sugar and real maple syrup. He was just mopping up the last of the syrup with the final bite of toast when the tramping of feet sounded on the steps and someone knocked at the door.

"Anna!" John shouted as she opened it. "How the hell are you? I see my little brother beat us here."

"John! Lucy! Well hel-lo there Martha! And Becka, look at you! Goodness how you've grown! Come in, all of you. Come in, come in."

Norman and Judy greeted them as they entered. Rebecca hurled herself into Norman's arms.

"Uncle Norm! Uncle Norm!"

"Hey Beaker! Boy am I glad to see you! Did ya bring your fishing pole?" She laughed and bobbed her head up and down, then struggled free from his arms.

"Where's Uncle Joe?" she asked.

"Down at the docks, dear," Anna said.

"Oh." Rebecca slumped into a chair and pouted, head in hands.

Judy and Lucy cleared dishes as Anna returned to the stove, insistent that everyone be fed. Norman retired to the opening between the kitchen and living room.

Five minutes later John lifted a forkful of French toast and said, "Hey Anna, I read something a few months ago about some guy found dead on a houseboat. What the hell was that all about?"

Judy looked at Norman and rolled her eyes. But Anna, standing at the sink, seemed undisturbed by the question as she turned and said, "Yes, it was a few months back, at the end of August. Three men rented the marina's biggest boat and didn't return it. When Joe and Lance finally found it up a canyon of the Escalante River, it was full of plundered Indian artifacts. The men that rented it apparently had some kind of big-money pot-hunting operation going on."

She carried the coffeepot to the table and poured the cups full. "They only found two of the men. Apparently the third man, well," she glanced at Rebecca who was listening with wide eyes, "he's wanted in connection with the other two, if you know what I mean."

"They think he killed them and split with the loot?" John asked. Rebecca gasped with excitement at the mention of murder.

"That's right," Anna said evenly. "And there's something else; the professor studying the recovered artifacts found some of the burial sites they raided. And you won't believe what he's claiming the prehistoric inhabitants were doing."

Those at the table looked up from their breakfast, and even Norman, seated in Joe's chair in the living room, eyelids drooping, showed a sudden interest as she spelled out, "c-a-n-n-i-b-a-l-i-s-m."

"What's that mean, Grandma?" Rebecca asked.

"It means some ancient people were being . . . were doing mean things to each other," Martha said, "sort of like war."

"You don't say." John glanced sharply at Anna. "What's his evidence?"

"Bone fragments that show evidence of human tooth marks." Anna nodded and returned the pot to the stove. "And the Navajo community is up in arms, let me tell you. Some of our older people don't like his ideas at all. They feel it's an insult to the Anasazi, the 'Ancient Ones'. And I can't blame them; they've had everything else taken away but their heritage."

61

John looked thoughtful. "No, guess you can't," he said. Then, enthusiastically, "Well, that was a damn fine breakfast Anna, thanks a million. Really hit the spot. Hey, where'd you say Joe was?"

"Down at the marina. At the shop probably." Anna turned to the sink and rinsed out her cup. "As I told Norm and Judy, we had some problems last night and he's trying to get things sorted out."

"Okay, we'll look him up. Listen Luce," he wiped his hands on the napkin and stood, "if you want to help Anna clean up, Norm and I'll take the boat down and launch it. That is, if Norm doesn't fall asleep." He grinned and winked.

"That's fine, if we aren't keeping Anna from something." Lucy looked at Anna for confirmation.

"Go," Anna waved at him, "don't worry about us."

"We're gone. C'mon Norm, I've got a surprise for you." The two men stepped outside and John pointed proudly at the boat. "What do ya think?"

Norman whistled. "Man, that is some fancy rig. When did you get it?"

"Couple of weeks ago." John descended the steps and crossed the drive, ran his hand along the gleaming chrome rub rail. "Twenty-eight feet of greased lightning, fuel-injected, turbocharged Chrysler V-8, three hundred horsepower, jet drive. A low freeboard, three-point suspension hull, designed purely for speed. I don't even know how fast she'll go, but the dealer promised I'd see six-oh without opening the throttle all the way. Haven't had it on a lake big enough to find out yet."

Norman shook his head. "Must have cost you a pretty penny."

"Shoot, Bro', it's only money," John waved a hand dismissively. "And car sales have been fan-fucking-tas-tic. C'mon, climb into my land yacht and we'll haul this baby down to some aich-two-oh."

"Listen, John," Norman said as they drove toward the launching ramp, "Anna didn't get a chance to tell you, but some guy named Hector died last night."

"What, Hector?" John glanced at him in disbelief. "That leathery little Mexican? Shit, he looked like he'd live forever. What happened?"

"Anna didn't say; some kind of accident. Apparently Joe is pretty upset. Why does Becka call him 'Uncle'?"

"Just a sign of affection. He's always called her 'Daughter,' like he probably would any Navajo girl remotely related to his clan. And so she calls him 'Uncle.' "

"I see." Norman rubbed his eyes and yawned. "Well, Anna looked beat when we arrived this morning, but she seemed fine by the time we left, don't you think?"

John nodded and fell silent. A truck was just hauling an aluminum fishing boat up the ramp when they arrived and he waited for it to pass before turning the wagon across the slope, pointing the stern of the boat toward the lake.

"Be right back," he said. He walked to the trailer and unfastened the tie-downs, then returned to the car and backed the trailer into the lake until the stern of the boat began to float free.

"All right!" he shouted, stomping on the parking brake. "We is all set. I'll climb aboard and fire her up. Once I get her running you can release the winch and drive the rig up to the parking lot. I'll meet you over at the fuel dock. Questions?"

"Nope, sounds easy enough to me."

"Right." John kicked off his deck shoes, removed his socks, and rolled up his trousers. "Christ, should have worn my shorts," he muttered. "Hot already this morning, be able to fry an egg on the road by noon." He rummaged beneath the front seat and found a pair of thongs, slipped them on. "Well, the hotter it gets, the better the beer will taste and the water will feel." He grinned and slid from the car.

He hoisted himself aboard the boat easily, the muscles in his big arms bunching as he swung his legs over into the cockpit. He switched on the bilge fan and let it run several minutes to clear any gas fumes before turning the ignition switch. The engine responded with a throaty roar, then subsided into a rhythmic rumble. He glanced at the gauges and signaled for Norman to release the winch.

The boat slid smoothly into the lake as he pulled the control lever into reverse. He swung the boat around and idled out beyond the "wakeless speed" buoys, sitting atop the seat back to remove his shirt and tie it around his waist. He then dropped into the seat and pushed the lever forward. With a muted roar the boat gathered itself beneath him and climbed up onto plane. As the whine of the turbocharger mounted higher and higher, the wind whipping his face began to make his eyes water.

"Oh boy," he said with a grin. Glancing shoreward, he saw his car and trailer already on the road to the parking lot, and with reluctance he throttled back and turned toward the marina entrance. As he passed between the breakwaters and idled along the dock, he saw a large houseboat with a skinny teenager waxing its topsides. His gaze lingered on the streamlined cabin and spacious beam, not failing to notice the NTC logo. "Nice," he murmured.

Norman and Lance were waiting for him at the fuel dock. He passed them the mooring lines, then slung a pair of fresh white fenders between the boat and the dock and leaped out. His massive upper torso rippled with muscle as he stretched and grinned at Lance.

"Well Christ Almighty, is that you Lance?" he boomed, gripping the younger man's hand. "Damn, you've turned into a handsome devil. Got the women fighting over you, I bet. Where the hell's your old man?"

"Nice to see you sir," Lance said, wincing as John crushed his hand. "Dad's at the maintenance building." He nodded his head.

"Good enough, we'll go pay him a visit." He gave Lance's hand another squeeze that elicited a moan and a painful smile.

"Need to work on your grip, Lance my boy. Choke your chicken a little more often." John roared at his own humor. "Good to see you! Fill 'er up, would you? C'mon Bro', let's go find that old Indian." He bounded off along the dock with Norman hurrying to keep up. At the maintenance building, John pounded the door once with his fist, then flung it open and strode inside.

"Hah! Scare you, did I?" he said as he spotted Joe at the desk. "Sergeant Jonathan Sanders reporting for duty, Captain!" He gave an exaggerated salute and snapped to attention.

"Hi John." Joe arose with a smile. "Hello Norm."

John's grin faded at Joe's subdued response, and as they shook hands he said, "Shit Joe, I'm sorry to hear about Hector. What the hell happened?"

"Some crazy accident," Joe said with a shrug. "Lucille claims somebody came into their house last night and Hector chased him outside. Next thing anybody knew, the electricity went out all over the neighborhood, and Hector was found dead in the generating station. Electrocuted."

"Jesus Christ! Electrocuted!" John paused, pondering, then said, "That sounds pretty suspicious Joe; Hector knew what was what about machinery and such."

"I know." Joe nodded solemnly, "I know it. And what you say about his mechanical knowledge, well . . ." He gestured helplessly with his hands. "This may sound mercenary, but besides missing him as a friend, I do not know what I am going to do about replacing him; he was the only good mechanic the shop has had since I have been in charge."

"Yeah, that could be a real problem couldn't it?" Norman said. "I guess it's not easy to find people willing to live and work out here in the middle of—out here away from everything."

"No," Joe agreed, "not easy at all."

"Listen Joe, I saw some kid working on a big, sharp-looking houseboat with your brand on it," John said. "How much to rent that sucker?"

"It is not ready yet."

"Not ready, what do you mean?"

"You saw the boy working on it; we are still getting it cleaned up after the last charter."

"Shit, Joe, I don't care if the paint doesn't blind me. How much?"

Joe fixed his gaze on John's chest, said, "Did you hear anything about some deaths we had here a few months ago?"

"Yeah, sure. I was just talking to Anna about it." Then

65

understanding illuminated his features and he said, "That's the boat! That's the one they were using for their home base, isn't it?"

Joe nodded slowly.

"Well hell, that's better yet! Kind of exciting. Shit, wait'll I tell my salesmen I rented the same boat that . . . Joe, I want that boat. How much?" John's voice was dead serious now, all kidding aside, and Joe sighed and said, "Three-fifty a day."

"Done." John reached out his hand and Joe, after a moment of hesitation, shook it.

"All right! Hey, thanks Joe. My new toy's gonna look good towing behind that floating condo. Listen, I know that with Hector . . . with things the way they are, you're probably pretty busy right now, so we'll just get out of your hair. We'll move our stuff aboard and catch your act a little later, okay? Got to visit though, talk old times, fight the good fight one more time. Promise?"

"Fine." Joe gave a faint smile. "Anything else you need, just tell Lance."

"John," Norman said when they were outside, "I thought we were only paying two-twenty a day for a boat. I wasn't counting on anything this expensive. Jude and I really can't afford—"

"Don't worry about it," John interrupted, "I'll take care of it. Business is good, Bro', business is good. Hell, how often do you get to take a vacation like this? Come on, let's look at this boat. Here's the office, we'll get somebody to show us around."

Chris checked the two men out on the houseboat and its systems, and when she was satisfied they were capable of handling it, led them back to the office where they filled out the contract and paid the deposit. She sighed with relief when the door closed behind them and the big blond man's eyes were no longer slyly watching her every move.

"Cute little number, huh?" John asked as they unhitched the trailer from the car.

"What's that?" Norman looked up in confusion from unhooking the safety chains.

"The blond chick in the office."

"Oh. Oh yeah, pretty nice looking."

"You're hopeless," John said as they drove to the RV park. "The day I miss a pretty ass when it walks past is the day I'll be pushing up daisies." He swung the car to a halt in front of the trailer, and a few minutes later the women and children were climbing aboard.

"Come by for dinner when you get back," Anna said as her guests filed out to the car.

"We will Anna," Lucy said, "wouldn't miss it for the world."

"See you in a week," Martha added. "And thanks for the hospitality."

"Oh, my pleasure," Anna beamed. She waved them out of sight.

A short time later they were aboard the floating home they would occupy for the next seven days.

"Hot damn, Bro'!" John crowed, waving his beer. "Stereo, microwave, double ovens, ice maker, fresh water maker, this baby's got everything but a jacuzzi."

Norman raised his bottle in acknowledgment and said, "Amen. Listen to those women oohing over the bathrooms."

"The heads, little brother, oohing the heads. We are now seamen, so's we best talk like 'em."

"Ay, ay, Bro', seamen it is." Norman laughed but the sound was ragged, his eyes red and tired. "Whew, before I have any more beer, I better get our gear aboard or I'm going to pass out. Why don't we see if we can get the women to lend us a hand."

"Sure. Jude! Luce!" John roared, "Mule train time! C'mon and let's get our gear aboard."

Lucy and Judy entered the salon. "Do you have to yell so the whole marina can hear?"

"Martha," Judy said, "would you mind watching the Bruiser while the rest of us fetch the luggage?" She passed the baby to his grandmother. "It's his nap time and he'll be ready for a bottle. Just mix up some of the powdered formula with warm water, the directions are right on the package."

67

"Not to worry dear, I've already raised a few myself."

"I forget," Judy chuckled. "Okay, he's all yours."

"Thanks Mom," Norman said. "We'll be right back. And don't worry, we have no intention of making you permanent baby-sitter this trip."

"Norman, Norman, do you think you could trap me into anything I don't want to do? After all these years?" She tsked and shook her head.

"No," he laughed. "No, I guess not. It's been a few years since anyone made you do anything you didn't want to."

"You're right there, Son," she said. "Okay, see you. And don't forget my mask and fins under the seat; I want to see if the snorkling is as nice here as in Hawaii." Norman nodded. Out on the dock Lucy was waiting for him as Rebecca raced up ahead of John and Judy.

"Norm," she said, falling into step beside him, "I wanted to say something to you and I hope you won't take it wrong, but we don't call Rebecca 'Beaker' any more."

"Oh?" he said with surprise. "Okay, that's fine. Should I call her Becka?"

"Sure," she said, smiling. "It's just . . . we decided it was kind of demeaning. It was different when she was younger and didn't really understand about test-tube babies. But she asked about it one day not long ago and John had to explain how a beaker is a kind of big test tube, and that she was conceived outside the womb because I couldn't get pregnant. And about how that was why we started calling her 'Beaker.' We're not sure how much she understood, but at this point in her life we'd just as soon cool it."

They stepped aside to let two fat men in bermuda shorts puff past with an ice chest. The men nodded their thanks, too winded for words, faces florid and sweating.

"I'm glad you told me," Norman said. "Becka it is. How is she, by the way? Have the bad dreams stopped?"

"Pretty much." Lucy waggled her hand. "She still has one every now and then, climbs in bed with us. But nothing like when she was younger, thank God." She wiped her forehead with the back of a hand and shuddered.

"So the therapy helped," he said.

"Oh yes. Good thing too; I don't know how much more John and I could have taken. You remember . . . ?"

"Yeah, I remember." Norman nodded his head firmly.

"Where are you parked?" Lucy said, deliberately changing the subject.

"Second row."

"Oh, yeah I see it. Okay, meet you back at the boat."

Forty minutes later all their gear was loaded aboard and the smaller boat tied to the stern.

"This is great," Judy said to her husband as she arranged their cabin. "Walk-in closets, reading lights, private bathroom, the works." In a corner Stephen slept in the crib they had brought along.

"Hey lady, looks pretty cozy. Feel like a little nooner right now?" Norman approached her from behind as she bent over the suitcase open on the bed. He put his arms around her and cupped her breasts in his hands.

"Nor-man San-ders," she hissed, "do you want to wake the baby?" She waggled her bottom against him as he kissed the back of her neck.

"God, no, it's a sin to wake a sleeping baby," he whispered.

"Darn right. Now you get out of here and let me finish putting things away."

"Okay." He released her and wandered from the cabin, pulling the door closed quietly behind him. He found John in the salon. "Hey," John said, "let me buy you a beer."

"You got a deal."

A few minutes later, with beer in hand, John stood at the helm and pushed the throttles forward slightly, turned the ignition key. The twin 150 horsepower Johnsons started instantly.

"I'll let them warm up a minute," he said to Norman. "When you hear a quick blast on the horn, cast us off."

Norman nodded and stepped out on deck to prepare the mooring lines, and spotted Joe approaching along the dock.

"Hello Joe," he said.

"Hi Norm. I meant to get here earlier to say hello to Becka and the ladies, but things kept coming up. It looks like you are heading out."

"I think so, yeah."

"Well, you have a good time. I will try to get down the lake and visit later in the week."

"That'd be nice," Norman replied, "we'll look forward to it. And say, it's really a beautiful boat."

Joe swept the boat with his gaze, nodded slowly. "Well, enjoy it." He waved toward the bridge.

John waved, stuck his head out to yell, "All aboard Joe! Want to go?"

"Some other time my friend."

"Uncle Joe! Uncle Joe!" Rebecca ran out on deck, waving and laughing. Before anyone could protest she leaped to the dock and hurled herself into his arms. He laughed and picked her up, hugged her, set her down.

"I thought you weren't going to come to see me," she said, frowning.

"Of course I was, Becka! Would I miss seeing my favorite girl?"

She wrapped her arms around his neck and hugged him.

"Well, I am a lucky dog." He chuckled and his weathered features creased with a smile, teeth gleaming against his dark skin. "Now, you get aboard and I will see you later in the week. I will take you fishing." He handed her up to Norman, then called after her, "You have fun Becka, and be careful like your daddy and I taught you around boats."

"I will Uncle Joe."

Joe nodded and returned her wave. He stood on the dock as the horn sounded and Norman released the lines. The houseboat turned ponderously, pointing its bow toward the marina entrance. Rebecca ran to the stern and continued to wave as the boat left the marina, and only when her tiny figure disappeared from sight beyond the dark, ragged stones of the breakwater did Joe turn and walk slowly down the dock toward the empty maintenance building, his smile dissipating in a cloud of unease.

On board the houseboat Norman stepped into the coolness of the cabin as John eased the throttles forward. Slowly the big boat picked up speed. A few minutes after clearing the marina they entered Lake Powell's main channel and

John said, "We're underway!"

Rebecca jumped up and down with shrill cheers, almost trampling her young cousin who was now loose on the salon floor. On hands and knees he followed her across the carpet, echoing her excitement in his own babbling fashion.

"Okay, okay you two, calm down." Lucy mussed her daughter's hair affectionately. Judy plucked Stephen from the floor, bounced him on her knee as she sat on the couch watching immense walls of red sandstone glide past on either side. Norman had put a tape in the stereo and the eerily harmonious strains of Hovhaness's "Mysterious Mountain" played from the hidden speakers.

"Air conditioning, good music." She sighed and nuzzled Stephen's fine hair. "Isn't this great?"

"Not too bad, Jude," Lucy said, "I think I can handle it."

"Look Becka," John said, "there's the first marker buoy. Mile one-fifty."

"One *hundred* fifty?" she said with awe. "Is that how long the lake is?"

"It's actually longer. The book says one hundred eighty-six miles. More than two thousand miles of shoreline. So we actually started partway down. I'm not sure how far upstream a houseboat can go before it gets stuck." He winked at Norman, standing beside him at the helm.

"Then let's not go upstream Daddy; I don't want to get stuck."

"Okay, we'll go the other way. The way we're going."

"How far?"

"All the way honey, all one hundred fifty miles to Wahweap."

"Wah weep? That's a funny name Daddy. What's it mean?"

"It's a Navajo word, means Bitter Water. Here, you can take the wheel."

Rebecca whooped with delight. With great seriousness she guided the vessel downstream, keeping to mid-channel, her father at her side.

"Three hundred feet of water underneath us," he said, pointing at the depth sounder, "so you don't have to worry

71

about getting stuck."

"Wow," she said, "that's a lot, isn't it Daddy?"

"That's a lot," he agreed.

For the rest of the afternoon they moved serenely down the lake, taking turns at the wheel, sitting on the foredeck in folding chairs sipping cocktails and gossiping, enjoying the respite from the heat offered by the breeze of their passage. And the lake enchanted them, intrigued them, delighted them. The great walls of stone towered three hundred feet and more above their heads, majestic and eternal, humbling in their immensity. Then the cliffs receded and the lake spread out like some great inland sea, islands of stone upthrust from its sparkling surface.

Twice they came upon enormous flocks of ducks that churned the water white as thousands of wings and feet thrashed to avoid the boat, then settled back into a floating blanket after it had safely passed. John insisted on a brief detour up Ticaboo Creek, where he pointed out the floating grave marker of Cass Hite.

"You mean somebody's buried under the water?" Rebecca asked, watching her father carefully to see if he was lying.

"That's what it says in the book honey. 'Prospector, ferry operator, and shopkeeper, 1880–1914.' The buoy is connected to his grave by a chain."

"You're macabre," Lucy said, shaking her head. But Rebecca was delighted.

"Keep your eye peeled," John told her as she gripped the wheel, kneeling on the seat in order to peer over the instrument panel. "When you see the buoy marked 'M' we turn to port into Good Hope Bay. We'll camp there tonight. Remember what port and starboard are?"

She nodded. "Port-left-red, starboard-right-green; all the big words go together and all the little words go together."

"That's very good Becka," Norman said.

She nodded again, biting her lower lip as she watched for the buoy. A moderate headwind had begun to blow, slowing their progress slightly and creating short, choppy waves that slapped the pontoons and sent spray onto the foredeck. Judy, sitting outside with Stephen on her lap, retreated inside and slid the glass door closed. The baby, half-asleep after a bottle, roused and looked about when Rebecca cried out at spotting the buoy, then drowsed as they entered the quieter waters of the bay.

By the time they found a sandy beach, dark clouds had begun to gather and the air was noticeably cooler. John took the helm and ran the bow onto land; then he and Norman led lines from each stern cleat to the beach at forty-five-degree angles, planting the anchors in the meager sand and piling large stones atop them for good measure.

It began to drizzle, a warm mist that plastered their T-shirts to their skin. They secured the speedboat to the port cleats of the houseboat and hung fenders to keep it from grinding against the steel pontoons. There, protected from the wind and waves, the smaller boat rode easily.

"What's the matter with you boys?" Martha asked as they entered the salon dripping water on the carpet. "Didn't either of you have the sense to bring a raincoat?"

John shrugged. "Sure, I brought one. But hell, I needed a shower anyway."

"You sure did," Norman said with a grin. "And if your rain gear's packed like mine, it's not worth the trouble of digging it out."

She shook her head and tossed them each a towel from the galley. "Well then, I guess you won't mind standing outside cooking the steaks for dinner will you?"

"Well, uh, maybe we better flip a coin." Norman looked to John for support but his older brother had suddenly developed a great interest in the contents of the cupboard above the sink.

"Better dig out your raincoat," she said.

"Yeah," Norman said. "Guess I had."

He found his old yellow slicker at the bottom of his duffel bag and returned to the galley, where Martha handed him a platter of thick steaks. The drizzle had become a pelting rain that drummed steadily on the deck as he cooked. The drops hissed to steam as they struck the gleaming stainless steel cover.

During dinner the storm increased its force, and by the

time the dishes were cleared, rain and wind were lashing the starboard windows. Later, after brandy and coffee, the women went to bed while John and Norman went out to check the anchors and the speedboat. The anchors were holding well, and the smaller boat seemed to be secure in the lee of the houseboat. A gust of heavy rain chased them back inside and they shed their dripping rain gear just within the empty salon. A murmur of voices came from the cabins, but soon the only sound was the drumming of the rain.

"Glad we're not out on the main lake right now," Norman said with a yawn. He raised his glass to his lips and tossed down the last of his brandy.

"You and me both," John agreed. "I never cease to be amazed how fast a storm can come up on the lake."

"Yeah. One thing I learned sailing on the West Coast is respect for the weather." Norman closed his eyes, rubbed his face with his hands. "Well, hate to leave you alone, but I am beat. See you in the morning."

"I'm right behind you Norm. G'night."

Norman shuffled down the hall and let himself into the cabin as quietly as possible. He stripped to his shorts, wandered into the head to brush his teeth and pee. It seemed he had just lain down when the baby awoke and started crying. Quietly at first, then louder. Soon a full-fledged howl. Norman moaned and pulled the pillow over his head. A minute later Judy stirred and muttered, got up to fetch a bottle.

Many, many minutes later, Norman tossed the pillow irritably aside. "What's the matter?" he asked as Stephen continued to wail.

"I wish I knew," Judy said in a tired voice, "probably just upset at the unfamiliar surroundings. And maybe the storm. I don't think he has a temperature." She crooned to the baby as she sat holding him, illuminated by the dimmest setting of the lamp on the nightstand. Norman lay on his side and gazed at them, his eyes closing, opening, closing. A look of pain contorted his features and he massaged his temples.

"I've got a feeling it's going to be a long night," he said as the headache began to pound behind his eyes.

Fifteen miles up the lake at the RV park, Joe entered the trailer and forced the door shut against a blast of wind-driven rain. Standing on the entry rug he removed his bright yellow foul weather gear, hung it on the hook beside the door to drip dry, then tugged off his boots and walked the few steps across the linoleum to the dining table. As he seated himself, Anna brought him a cup of hot coffee.

"Where's Lance?" she asked.

"With Chris."

"Rough night for you two, huh?"

He nodded and wiped his forehead with a napkin, then sipped noisily at the scalding brew.

"A young couple with three kids caught out on the lake trying to bring their houseboat in. Suppose you were listening on the scanner?"

"Yeah. They sounded pretty scared."

"They were, but we got them in all right. We are sure getting a bunch of fall storms all of a sudden. It is kicking up out there; three-foot swells in the main channel."

"Oh my. I hope the Sanders are safe."

"I would not worry about them; John is as competent as they come. And Norman used to do lots of ocean sailing. They will have anchored up hours ago."

"I'm sure you're right." Anna went into the living room and turned off the television, then returned to ask, "Do you want your dinner now, or wait for Lance?"

Before Joe had a chance to answer, the front door burst open and Lance rushed in, slammed it behind him.

"Guess I will wait," Joe said with a smile.

"Wait for what, Dad?" Lance asked.

"For you to get home for dinner."

"Oh." He laughed. "Yeah, well, I had to take Chris home. Boy, something smells good."

"I'm sure you did," Anna said with a sly glance, "and what you smell is roast beef. Now get those wet clothes off and sit down at the table. All appearances aside, I'm not running a cafeteria here."

Lance shrugged off his windbreaker and kicked off his soggy sneakers and socks. He joined Joe at the table and Anna handed him a cup of coffee, then took the roast from the oven.

"Dad, the Sanders took the big houseboat huh? I didn't think it was ready yet." Lance gulped his coffee, eyes bright above the rim of the cup. The pan holding the roast hit the top of the stove with a bang as Anna stared at Joe, who had developed a sudden interest in his empty cup.

"You let them take *that* boat?" she asked.

"John insisted," he said. "You know how stubborn he is."

"What's wrong Mom?" Lance asked. "Worried about ghosts or something?"

"You stay out of this!" she shouted. He recoiled as if she had struck him. Thin-lipped and shaking, she pointed a finger at Joe and said, "If anything happens to them Joe, if anything happens . . ."

"What?" he said. "What is going to happen? They are just another family taking a vacation on the lake. Two able men, three able women; we send out thousands of less-qualified people every year with no problems at all." Joe continued to toy with his cup as Lance shifted his gaze from one to the other. For more than a minute each was silent.

Then Anna drew a deep breath and let it out slowly. She opened the utensil drawer and removed a knife and a steel, began sharpening the blade.

"All right Joe," she said. "All right. I'm sure you're right."

"Of course I am, Anna," he said. His words sounded certain, but a flicker of doubt crossed his blunt features.

"I put Lucille on a bus today," she said as she served slices of roast to the men, slices crispy brown on the outside and pink inside. "She's going to stay with her mother in Texas for awhile."

"That is a good idea," Joe said. "She has no one here. Nobody she knows well."

"Yes." Anna joined the two men at the table. She picked up her fork, set it down, took a sip of water. "What are you going to do about finding a replacement for Hector?"

"Harold is running an ad in the local papers. And I called

76

some people I know in Moab and Green River. Somebody will turn up."

"But probably nobody as good as Hector." Her face was sad, her eyes suddenly moist.

"No," Joe said. His mouth was dry and he had to wash the delicious roast down with a swallow of coffee. "Not as good as Hector, no."

And later, as they lay in bed together, Anna turned to him and said, "I wish you would go check on the Sanders, Joe. Sometime soon."

"I have already decided to Anna. Tomorrow, or the next day."

"Good, now I know they'll be all right and I can sleep."

"Yes, they will be fine. Good night Anna."

"Good night."

Her lips brushed his, and she snuggled against him as he put his arm beneath her head. But Joe didn't sleep. He lay gazing at the ceiling until his arm began to ache and he gently eased it out as she muttered and rolled away. And the rain, usually a soothing sound, drummed endlessly against the roof, on and on and on. The rain buzzed and spattered, hissed and sizzled, angry as flies driven from a carcass, flinging themselves against his home, trying to find a way in.

Four

The eastern sky was blooming with pale light by the time Stephen was well and truly asleep and softly snoring. Enough light entered the room for Norman and Judy to exchange a weary glance across the crib where he slept. Norman opened his mouth as if he might say something and Judy's eyes widened in alarm. Her hand darted from the sleeve of her robe and touched a finger to his lips.

Martha, John, and Lucy looked up from the table as the weary couple shuffled into the salon. "You two look exhausted," Martha said. "Where's Stephen?"

"Sleeping," Norman said, "fell asleep at the first light of dawn, up the whole rest of the night. I got about three hours, and . . ." he yawned and pawed at his eyes, "how many'd you get Jude?"

"I dunno," she said. "One or two."

"Ain't fatherhood wunnerful?" John asked with a sympathetic grin.

"You poor dears, why don't you go back to bed?" Martha said. "There's no reason you shouldn't sleep in. If we decide to get underway, we can handle it ourselves."

"That's right," John said.

"I'm afraid to go back in the room," Norman said. "Afraid I might wake him."

"Use our room," Lucy said.

"Naw, hell, I'm awake," Norman said. "Might as well enjoy my vacation instead of sleeping through it."

"I heard the baby crying," Lucy said. "Poor little guy sure sounded upset. What was the problem?"

"We don't know," Judy answered. "He just wouldn't sleep. It's the longest tantrum he's ever had. I don't think he quit crying for more than ten minutes the whole night. We took turns holding him, tried leaving him alone, gave him a bottle, sang to him," she made a helpless gesture with her hands. "Nothing helped."

"Poor little thing must be exhausted," Martha said. "Not to mention you two."

"I've felt better," Judy admitted.

Lucy brought them each a cup of coffee. "Here, maybe this will help."

"Bless you, kind lady," Norman said as he cradled his cup in his palms.

"Speaking of exhausted," Martha said. "Becka is still snoozing."

John produced a bottle of Irish cream liqueur from one of the cabinets and added a stiff dose to his coffee cup, held the bottle out and cocked an eyebrow questioningly at Norman. Norman shook his head no. John shrugged, returned the bottle to the cabinet and said, "Hell, let 'em sleep. They both had plenty of excitement yesterday."

"Tell you what," Martha said. "Since Norman cooked dinner, I'll fix everybody breakfast. Here's the catch, we're having what I want, that being crepes, and somebody else has to do dishes.

"Oh, twist my arm," Lucy said. "I'll do the dishes."

John and Norman retired to the salon and talked quietly while their wives and mother cooked. Fifteen minutes later Martha said, "Belly up to the bar, boys," and began tossing thin, golden crepes onto plates. Lucy added a platter of thick, crispy bacon from the microwave, and there were glasses of ice cold orange juice, jars of jams and preserves, fresh-sliced melon, even a bottle of champagne Judy opened to spike the orange juice with.

John pulled up a stool at the breakfast bar and loaded his plate. He took a bite of crepe and moaned.

"Dear gawddddd! I feel like I done died and gone to culinary nirvana."

"I feel like you could sell me down river for two bits," Norman said. "But the breakfast is outta sight."

Soon the only sounds were clink of fork against dish, and afterward Judy and Lucy cleared away the dishes.

"Martha, that was superb," Judy said. "I think one more cup of coffee might bring me entirely into the world of the living."

"Help yourself, dear," Martha said. "It's such a nice morning you should take it outside."

"Oh, that's a great idea! Norman, care to join me honey?"

"Sure." They carried their cups to the stern deck and leaned on the railing.

"Spectacular," he said.

"Yesterday it was desolate." She gave him a teasing smile.

"Yesterday it *was* desolate, but look." He waved a hand toward the east. The lake glowed like molten gold, reflecting the morning sunrise. A mile distant the rugged line of bluffs dividing lake and sky played a trick on the eye, reversing itself to become a dark chasm, a fracture in the fabric of the world where one could peer into infinity, and then reversed itself again to become a towering obsidian mountain range. And overhead, high, thin wisps of cloud streamed toward the north, moving visibly, writhing from the turbulent winds.

"Spectacular," Judy said. She snuggled close and leaned her head on his shoulder. "Glad we came?"

"Last night I wasn't so sure, but this morning—" he put his arm around her waist and smiled at her upturned face, "yeah. I'm glad. We're going to have a nice time." He kissed her lightly on the lips.

"Good." She hugged him. "I think we are, too."

Silently they enjoyed the morning, content to hold each other and feel the cool, clear desert air on their skin, to gaze upon the endless play of light and shadow, of changing colors, to absorb the stillness within themselves, suspending time for a moment. A brief moment.

And then Judy stirred. "I better go check on the Bruiser."

Norman sighed and drained the last of his coffee. "What did the great man say? 'Don't just do something; stand there.'"

He leaned on the railing and continued to enjoy the view after she left.

"So," John said, appearing suddenly at his side. "Tough

night huh?"

"Yeah. Not much fun."

"Well, he'll be okay after a day or so. Kids can get pretty upset when their routine is interrupted. By the way, I was listening to the National Oceanic and Atmospheric weather broadcast this morning on the radio. And NOAA says," he paused dramatically and lifted a finger, lowered his voice, "the five-day forecast looks in-fucking-cred-ible."

"Trying to cheer me up?" Norman asked with a grin.

"Not my job," John said, shaking his head. "Everybody's responsible for their own good time. Or bad. Ya pays your nickel, ya gets your ride. Speaking of which, what would you guys like to do today? We don't have to be anywhere and we don't have to stay. The world is our —" he held up his hand and belched, "oyster."

"You got class, John." Norman gazed across the bay and rubbed the stubble on his chin. "Hadn't really thought about it. Judy mentioned trying her hand at fishing, and I'd like to find some Indian ruins, maybe some rock paintings, stuff like that. But you're the official Lake Powell guide and expert."

"Let's just relax this morning, just kind of laze around, and when Becka and the Bruiser wake up we'll take the speedboat out for an excursion. Fish, cut bait, whatever."

"That sounds fine with me."

Suddenly, a dozen yards from the stern, a large fish exploded from the lake and hung suspended a moment in midair, dripping silver water, then plunged back out of sight with a loud splash.

"Santa Maria!" John exclaimed. "Did you see that?"

"How could I miss it?" Norman said. "What kind of fish was it?"

"Striper I think," John called over his shoulder, already disappearing inside. Moments later he returned with a fishing rod and a large tackle box that he opened to reveal glittering multitudes of carefully organized lures.

"I'm gonna guess the striped bass are eating little froggies this morning," he said, selecting a casting plug from its compartment. He clipped it to the swivel already attached to the

81

line and cast with a smooth, easy motion past the spot where the fish had jumped, then began retrieving it with quick jerks, twitching the rod tip up abruptly to make the plug dart toward him, letting the tip down as he reeled line onto the spool, bringing it up again, down, up, down, twitch, twitch, twitch.

He tried several times, then switched to a different lure. No luck. Another lure, and more casts, and again no strike.

"Well, no harm in trying," John said as he replaced a silver spoon in the tackle box. "I'd been itching to wet a line and that big old fish just set me off."

"Do you catch many?"

"To be honest, not that many. But sometimes enough for supper."

"Daddy, are you fishing?" They turned to find Rebecca rubbing her eyes, still clad in pajamas covered with Big Bird and Cookie Monster.

"Good morning, sweetheart. I don't know if you'd call it fishing exactly; I'm not catching anything. Let's just say I'm practicing my cast."

"Daddy." She fixed him with a stern look. "You said you wouldn't go fishing without me."

"I'm sorry, honey," he stooped to hug her, but she stood stiff-armed within his embrace. "A big fish jumped while your uncle and I were standing here talking, and I just couldn't help myself. Forgive me?"

"Ohhh, okay." She smiled and kissed him on the cheek. "But next time I want to fish too."

"Sure. Now how about some breakfast? We got lizard's gizzards and steamed swamp rat on toast."

"Ohhh yuuuck! That's disgusting! I want frosted flakes. And cocoa."

"You don't know what you're missing, that swamp rat's fresh this morning." He took her hand and led her toward the galley. Norman saw the door to their cabin open as Judy emerged, and met her in the passageway.

"How's the Bruiser?" he asked.

"Still sleeping. Norm, what if this is his routine the whole vacation? Crying at night and sleeping all day?"

82

"Worst possible scenario," he said with a mock scowl. "Never happen. Don't worry, he'll do fine. Remember, it's the first time he's been away from his own house for more than a day. Once he settles in he'll be happy as a clam."

Judy smiled and put her arms around his neck.

"Well, let's hope so. He's sure cute when he's asleep."

"All babies are cute when they're asleep."

"He's cuter."

"I know."

"I love you, Norm."

"I love you too, sweetheart. We're going to have a good time.

"Oh, we are, I know we are."

Anna was up before sunrise and Joe's breakfast was waiting for him when he arrived at the table. He was dressed in jeans and T-shirt and smelled faintly of skin lotion. The sweet aroma mingled with that of oatmeal and toast.

"Good morning." He kissed her cheek and seated himself at the table.

"G'morning. I'll be going into town today. Shopping, in case you've forgotten. Any special requests?"

He nodded and swallowed a bite of toast. "Yes, stop by and see if Sam has finished reworking the spare set of props for the Whaler, would you? He said it would take about a week and it has been that long and more."

"Okay. Anything else?" She mopped up the last bit of oatmeal from her dish with toast, washed it down with grapefruit juice.

"One thing." He glanced up almost shyly, head lowered to meet his spoon. "Licorice?"

"My goodness." She sighed mockingly, eyes rolling toward the ceiling. "You are a licorice junky." Then her eyes became soft and warm. "But I'll see what I can do."

"Thanks Anna."

"Big favors you ask, old man, big favors. By the way, that lazy boy's still sleeping after being out most of the night with Chris." Her voice became brusque. "They've been seeing a

lot of each other lately and I hope they're taking suitable
. . . precautions. He knows all about the birds and the bees,
so it's up to him, and she is a very nice girl. You like her?"

"Mm," he swallowed hastily. "Yes, I do."

"Good. Anyway, you should wake him soon, and I better
get moving." She thrust herself up from the table and carried
her dishes to the sink, rinsed them, and put them in the
dishwasher rack.

"Have you checked the oil in the pickup lately?" she asked
as she searched her purse for the keys.

He looked up from his cup, face thoughtful. "I had not
thought about those two. But I suppose they are, well, they
are both old enough."

She cocked an eyebrow and asked, "The oil? In the
truck?"

"Yes, a few days ago. It was fine; I think replacing those
leaky valve seals helped plenty."

"Good. Okay, see you this afternoon." She leaned over to
peck his cheek on the way to the door.

Joe finished the last of the oatmeal, gulped his coffee, and
added his dishes to the dishwasher. With a glance at the
stove clock, he hurried to the bedroom and pulled on a
denim shirt, fastening its imitation pearl snaps as he walked
to the door. He stepped into his moccasins to find them still
damp, opted for a pair of sneakers. Though he doubted he
would need it, he grabbed a jean jacket from the hooks
beside the door and thrust his thermos of coffee under his
arm.

"Lance," he called into the darkness of his son's room,
"time to get up. Breakfast is on the stove." Lance mumbled
as his head appeared from beneath the blankets. "See you at
the marina," Joe said.

Outside, he straddled the little Honda trail bike, kicked it
to life, tossed the jacket and thermos into the luggage basket
atop the rear fender. The exhaust muttered quietly as he
drove to the marina, the sound almost drowned out by the
singing of the knobby tires against the pavement. The cool
wind caressed his face as he leaned into the turns, the hand-
grips cradled easily in his strong hands. He propped the

kickstand in the dirt beside the administration building and slung the coat over a shoulder and the thermos beneath an arm.

Far across the bay several fishing boats carved glistening wakes across its surface. He found the right key on his cluttered ring and let himself into the rental office to check the daily calendar; only four houseboats going out, gas delivery due, Lance and a boy named Oscar on dock duty, Chris working the desk. He pursed his lips and initialed the page.

He left the office and locked the door behind him, went to the maintenance building and let himself inside. His movements echoed from the high, corrugated steel walls, and when he turned on the lights the harshness of their illumination served only to accent the starkly functional nature of his surroundings. Mornings like this Hector would often be at work before him, head buried in some difficult mechanical problem. Joe stood for a minute undecided, staring about as if unfamiliar with the place, and then crossed slowly to the desk. He eased into the chair, uncapped his thermos, and poured a cup of coffee.

One hour later, as he struggled with the endless paperwork, he heard a sound at his back. He swiveled in the chair to see a slight figure silhouetted against the bright rectangle of the open door. He arose from his desk and his eyes widened, his lips forming a name that his paralyzed breath could not pronounce. His hand clutched the edge of the desk.

"Beg pardon?" a distinctly southern voice drawled. "I was told I could maybe find a part for my trolling motor here. It's a little four-horse Johnson, model number . . ."

Joe sat heavily back in his chair, staring as the man approached him, holding a piece of paper. Not Hector—not a visitation from the spirit world, of course. Just a tourist looking for an outboard motor part.

"Something wrong, Mister?" the man asked. "You look like you seen a ghost." He chuckled, then fell silent when Joe failed to share his humor.

"No," Joe said, "nothing wrong." He continued to stare, then abruptly dropped his gaze and asked, "What model did you say?"

"Man, what a beautiful day!" Norman said as they sped down the lake. The sky was clear and the sun was shining and it was not too hot.

"Yessir," John said. "Not too shabby. And can you believe how this baby moves out? Even with . . . what have we got here . . . five adults and two kids aboard. Hey, check it out." He jerked a thumb over his shoulder and Norman turned to look back. The women and Rebecca, relaxing in the comfortable wraparound stern lounge, followed his gaze to see a sleek ski boat overtaking them.

"Hang on boys and girls!" John shouted happily. "I'm going to open her up." He shoved the lever forward and the engine responded with a growl, thrusting them back in their seats. The whine from the turbocharger mounted higher and higher as John pointed at the speedometer where the needle hovered just above fifty. The other boat began to fall astern and John's boat was really bounding along now, gathering itself and leaping into the air, landing with a loud 'whump,' engine howling each time the jet drive came out of the water. Roarrrr whump! Roarrrr whump!

"Hey!"

John jerked his head around as his wife grabbed his shoulder, a look of anger on her face. She pointed at Judy holding Stephen who was crying and said something he couldn't hear over the engine. He eased the throttle back until the boat was cruising smoothly.

"Sorry," he called toward Judy and the baby. She waved her hand, searched the bag near her feet for his bottle. With the nipple firmly plugged into his mouth he became contentedly silent. Norman took a sip of his beer, watched the wall of sandstone pass to his right.

"That cliff is somewhere between three hundred and six hundred feet high," he said, studying the Lake Powell guidebook in his lap. "It's sure hard to judge by looking. There's nothing to compare anything with, except us and the boat, and we're so small in comparison to even the littlest cliffs."

"Alien," John said, nodding firmly. "Alien is the word that came to mind the first time we were here. I thought it looked like a mistake, like maybe the Old Man in the sky was practicing, designing a world for some race of lizard people, or maybe cyclops. Yeah, I could imagine a cyclops, some big fella a couple hundred feet high, stalking these canyons with a petrified tree trunk over his shoulder for a club."

"You're getting kind of poetic in your old age John," Norman said with a smile. "I like it. But you know who I think this place was designed for? The wind."

"Wind?" John grinned at him.

"Just look around you. The way the rocks are all polished or eroded, the plant growth twisted and stunted. Even the tops of the plateaus are sheared right off. I read that waves striking the California coast sometimes come from halfway around the world, generated by huge storms off the coast of China. Well, there's an ocean of air, too, full of uncharted currents endlessly circling the planet. Maybe this is one of the places where the waves of wind crash on the shore."

"I like cyclops better," John said. "If we're gonna spin tales, I like to have an old-fashioned, cold-blooded, one-eyed monster clomping around. Hell, look at the cliffs, everything here's oversized, exaggerated, built for a goliath."

Norman, studying the illustrations of Anasazi rock art in the book, looked up and nodded.

"Sure John, I can visualize it. Those cliffs streaked with minerals, like the dark tears of a weeping giant. You can sure see how the Anasazi came up with some of their images; the pictures were already there, in the rock itself. These things, for instance." He held the book out and John glanced at it and nodded.

"These paintings are so unique they have their own name," Norman said, "called 'Barrier Canyon Style.' Nobody knows how old they are, or their origin. But they've all got these huge shoulders, long tapered bodies with decorations like tattoos on them. They don't have arms or legs, look sort of like gigantic mummies with skulls for heads."

"Well, we're almost to the pictures I wanted to show you," John said, "but they're nothing quite that spectacular. Hope

87

nobody minds a short walk."

They arrived at Moki Canyon a short time later, beached the boat, and Norman shouldered Stephen's backpack. The day was quiet and the air was still as Rebecca led the way to a sandstone cliff where two animal figures were pecked into the rock. A mourning dove called softly as the group studied the petroglyphs. They appeared to be mountain sheep with long, rectangular bodies, and there were a few fainter designs beside them.

"Kind of uninspired, aren't they?" John asked, seeing his brother's lack of interest.

"Yeah," Norman said, "sort of a 'Bob Smith killed two sheep here' billboard art. I'll tell you what is interesting though." He pointed high above where a small dwelling was tucked into a pocket in the cliff face. The walls were crafted from native stone and it blended so well with its surroundings as to be almost unnoticeable.

"What do you suppose they were hiding from?" he asked the others as they stared upward.

"Marauders, according to the experts," his brother answered. "That house, or whatever you want to call it, looks to be about fifty feet above us, and whoever lived there climbed up and down every day using those tiny hand-and-footholds pecked in the stone. Probably several times, and it's almost vertical. Christ, how'd you like to haul a bag of groceries up those steps?"

"I'm glad we don't live like that," Rebecca said, "I'd afraid of falling."

"You and me both, honey," John said, turning to her with a smile and a wink.

"They must have been hellacious climbers," Martha said quietly.

"Would you climb up there Grandma?" Rebecca asked her.

"Not on your life."

Norman nodded his agreement.

"Those hand-and-foot holds look like they would hardly support a fingertip or a toe, but they've probably eroded over the centuries. Still—"

"Not for me," Judy said, "I'm afraid of heights."

Stephen squirmed and whined in the backpack and Norman slid his hands under the shoulder straps to ease the strain.

"How about some lunch?" Lucy said to nobody in particular. Immediately Rebecca shouted her agreement, and led the way back to the boat, where sandwiches and paper plates were quickly handed around. Soon, with sodas or beers in hand, they sat quietly eating and enjoying the afternoon. The canyon was peaceful, isolated, a private world all their own. High overhead a jet contrail was the only interruption of endless blue sky.

But the trip back up the lake was a pounding, jarring ride, and they were all tired from exposure and the rough motion when they arrived at the houseboat. Stephen was crying again as Judy handed him aboard to Norman, who winced as the baby gave a high-pitched wail directly in his ear.

"He needs a nap," he said.

"So do I," Judy agreed.

"Me too," Lucy added. In fact everyone echoed the sentiment, except Rebecca, who said, "I don't waaaant a nap."

"Okay," John said. "But if you stay up you've got to be quiet. Promise?"

"I promise."

"All right." He and Lucy drifted into their cabin and closed the door, and Martha disappeared into hers. A minute later, Rebecca yawned and followed her grandmother, pulling the door shut behind her. Judy put Stephen in his crib, then lay down on the bed as Norman sighed and fetched his briefcase from the closet.

"Oh honey," she said. "You're not going to work today are you?"

"Sorry, but I've got to do it sometime, and you know I can't work with distractions. Believe me, I'd rather goof off."

"I'm sorry too," she said. "Sorry you've got to work so hard."

"Gotta pay the bills." He closed the door quietly and walked to the salon, opened the briefcase on the coffee table,

89

and removed the tools of his trade; flow charts, coding forms, pen and pencil, a COBOL Standard reference book, and several thick computer printouts. Massaging his temples with his index fingers, he studied the printout until he came to a row of asterisks and an error message.

Fifteen minutes later he was still trying to find a way around the logic problem when the door to John and Lucy's cabin opened and John shuffled along the hall, yawning.

"Couldn't sleep," he said as he saw Norman sitting on the couch. "What the hell are you up to? Work?"

"Yeah, I've got a project I was supposed to finish last week." Norman leaned back and laced his fingers behind his head.

"It's basically just an accounting program, see, a general ledger system for the Tiara Corporation. Basically. Except that the Tiara Corporation has dozens of subsidiaries, and foreign affiliates, and branches, and investments. And each facet of the corporation employs personnel to key the data my program collects. And the program inspects the data for errors and sorts it to determine which hole it fits into. And then juggles the data and determines which accounts to credit and which to debit and eventually tells them whether they're winning or losing. Financially."

"Sounds like bullshit to me," John said. "Want a beer?" He opened the refrigerator and looked at Norman.

"No. Wait. Yeah, why not. I usually don't drink when I'm working, but I usually don't work on vacation either."

"Here you go," John said as he seated himself across from his brother and handed him a beer. "What's the deal anyway? I thought you were the hotshot programmer that finished in a day what it took the rest of your buddies a week to figure out."

Norman tipped the bottle to his lips, then said with a pained smile, "I was the hotshot. The guy that wrote the shortest, most efficient routines, the cleverest logic, the cleanest flow charts. Norm Sanders, wonder boy, the guy everybody came to when they had a problem they couldn't solve." He shook his head. "But lately, I don't know. I can't keep track of the logic any more. The programs are getting so damned complicated, so sophisticated." He ran a hand through his hair.

"Once upon a time I would have done a page of coding in five minutes, solved this problem," he tapped the printout with a finger, "and been on to the next without missing a beat. Know how much programming I did in the fifteen, twenty minutes I've been sitting here? Five. Five lines. I don't know what the hell has happened; sometimes I think I've got a brain tumor."

"Jesus Christ, Norm, that's no way to talk." John shook his head and eyed his brother with a worried expression.

"Aw, I know it John. I know it. But look, here I am thirty-six years old, making forty-eight-grand a year, and never a dime left at the end of the month. Every raise eaten up by cost of living increases, by insurance and doctor bills, food bills. Mortgage payments . . . do you know what mortgage means, literally? 'Dead pledge.' I feel like I've pledged myself to death, that's for sure. And I don't know what I'm going to do if I can't get back on top of my work."

"Norm, I thought you came on this trip to relax and get away from all that."

"I did." Norman sighed. "But this one program has been kicking my ass and I thought bringing it with me I might have some sudden, brilliant insight that would help me see the light at the end of the tunnel."

"And—?"

"Nothing." He tossed the pencil onto the coding sheet and rubbed his face. "I think I'm burned out John," he said, staring from red-rimmed eyes. "Burned out. I always thought the term was a cheap excuse for people too weak or dumb to make the grade, but lately I've had a change of heart. I work ten to twelve hours a day, seven days a week, haven't exercised or taken a weekend off for over a year. I'm carrying thirty extra pounds and feel like shit and I'm still falling behind on this project. Please don't think I'm whining, it's just the way it is. I chose it, nobody else to blame, but lately it's been hard."

"Yeah. Well, I haven't said anything but you don't look so hot either. Have you thought about trying something else?"

91

"Like what?"

John shrugged. "I don't know," he said. Then hesitantly, "Ever think about sales?"

"You mean, like car sales?" Norman gave his brother a wry smile.

"Yeah, car sales," John said. "And don't give me that holy look. I know what you think about being a car salesman, but God damn it, I've made a good living at it. And listen to you. So you're some kind of brain, what good is that if you don't enjoy what you do any more and your job's killing you?"

Norman stared at him for a moment, took a swig of beer.

"Thanks, John. I appreciate the offer, I really do. But I couldn't sell water to a man dying of thirst. You know that."

Again John shrugged.

"We're all salesmen after a fashion. You sell your programming abilities to your employer, he sells the programs to a consumer, and so on down the line. Everybody that makes a buck is selling something."

As Norman started to reply, Rebecca wandered in rubbing sleep from her eyes, and Lucy was a few footsteps behind. He gathered up his supplies and returned them to the briefcase.

"Think about it," John said.

"I will." Norman set the briefcase on the floor beside the couch.

"What are you guys talking about, Daddy?" Rebecca asked.

"Business, honey, just business."

"How borrrring," she said.

"My dear Becka," Norman said, "you are right."

It was Judy's night to cook dinner, and she opted for hamburgers. Huge, juicy ones accompanied by homemade French fries. A short time later, pleasantly stuffed and sipping their coffee, the adults watched Stephen play with an empty paper towel tube and a dishcloth on the floor, ignoring the bright red rattle, the soft teddy bear, the clear plastic ball that made music when rolled.

"I keep thinking about these rock paintings," Norman

92

said. He had the guidebook open again and was idly flipping pages. "They're really interesting, but kind of sinister too. Almost malevolent looking, especially this one with horns on its head."

"Interesting, huh?" John said, stifling a yawn with his hand. He came over and looked at the book. "That's probably the devil, Bro'. An Indian devil, specialized sort, come and scared off all the Anasazi. And then there were none."

"Hush Jonathan," Lucy said, "there are ears to hear."

"You're right. Sorry."

"Time to get your PJs on, Becka," Lucy said.

"But Mommy, I don't wannnnt to."

"Yes dear, I know. Do it anyway."

"Come on Becka," Judy said, cradling Stephen in her arms, "after you get your PJs on, you can help me get the Bruiser into his."

"Okay," she said. Lucy gave Judy a smile and a wink.

"Hey," John said, "how about some cards?"

"Sure," Lucy said, "sounds fun."

"I'm in, if anybody's got money they want to lose." Martha narrowed her eyes and smiled slyly.

"C'mon Norm," John said, "how about a little poker."

"Sure." With reluctance he laid the book aside as John opened a box of cards.

"Chips," John said, "we don't have any chips."

"We'll use matches." Martha got a box of stick matches from the galley and counted out twenty for each player, including Judy, who returned shortly with Rebecca.

"Come here and give Mommy a kiss," Lucy said. "Then off to bed with you."

"Oh Mommy! Daddy, can I stay up?"

"You heard your mother."

"Come on Becka," Martha said, "I'll tuck you in." Rebecca allowed herself to be led away by her grandma as Norman asked Judy, "Is the Bruiser actually sleeping?"

"He's drinking his bottle, but it looked like he'd probably drop right off. He should, with all the fresh air today."

"God, I hope so."

Martha returned and they cut for the deal. John won and

called for seven-card stud. An hour later they were playing jackpots, it was Lucy's deal, and Martha had amassed a large pile of matches. And then Rebecca screamed.

John came off his stool in a leap and met her as she ran down the hall. He wrapped her in his arms and picked her up, smoothing her hair with his hand.

"There, there honey, it's alright. Everything's all right, Daddy's got you."

"What happened sweetie?" Martha asked quietly.

"There's someone else on board!" she sobbed as John hugged and patted her.

"Who else is on board?" Martha asked gently.

"I don't know *who* it is Grandma," she said, hiccuping now. "Just *somebody*. Somebody scary. He came into my room and looked down at me in bed. He was short and big and his face was all *horrible!*"

"You've just had a nightmare, sweetie," Martha said. "Just a nightmare; there's nobody else on board. But just to be sure I'll have your daddy and Uncle Norman look around. Okay?"

"Okay." Rebecca nodded, face buried against her daddy's shoulder. She didn't protest as John passed her to Martha, but clung to her and hid her face against Martha's bosom. She looked up to be sure that John and Norman were actually leaving the room to do as promised, then burrowed against Martha's sweater.

"Another nightmare," John said to Norman as they entered the cabin. There was desolation in his voice. "Man, I hope this is just a normal kid's scare and not a recurrence. Do you remember the nightmares?" He made a pretense of checking the closet, looking under the bed.

"Yeah, I remember," Norman said.

"There's nothing here," John said. "Of course. You see anything?"

"No," Norman shook his head. "Of course." But for some reason he hurried to be the first out of the room as John nodded absently and turned toward the door. They returned to the salon where Rebecca was curled in Martha's lap, breathing deeply, and Lucy held a finger to her lips. Though

94

Rebecca's face wad hidden, she surprised them by saying, "I'm not asleep, Daddy."

"Okay, honey. Do you want to talk about it?"

She shook her head very slightly. "No. I want Grandma to come to bed with me."

"But honey, grandma can't do that because—"

"Sure she can," Martha interrupted. "And she will. Poor Grandma was getting tired of taking all her foolish children's money. Here we go, give me a hand Jonathan." John helped her to her feet.

"You know Daddy won't let anything, anything hurt his little girl, don't you Becka?" he said.

She nodded her head as he stroked her hair. Martha carried her down the hall, pausing at the door of her cabin to say quietly, "Tally my winnings Lucy; I'll collect in the morning."

"Okay Martha. And thanks."

Martha's cabin door closed and the four adults breathed a collective sigh of relief.

"I know it sounds selfish," Judy said, "but I'm glad Stevie didn't wake up."

"Oh, that's not selfish at all," Lucy said with a wave of her hand. "You and Norman weren't married yet when Becka was having her nightly nightmares. A child that won't sleep can be an awful, awful experience, for both the kid and the parents. Did Norman ever tell you about it?" Judy shook her head no and Lucy continued.

"Well, you probably know that for many years the Sanders family always gathered at Martha and John Senior's chalet near Vail for Christmas. Always, no matter where they were, they made the journey to be together for the holidays. Christmas four years ago was different, though, because that's when we found out John Senior was dying of lung cancer."

"He didn't tell us," John interjected. "I found out accidentally."

"That's right," Lucy said. "He wanted to keep it from everybody so it wouldn't ruin the holiday."

"But we all found out," Norman said.

"Right. Anyway, we all were at the chalet by noon on Christmas eve, and I guess we all knew about it by dinner. Except Rebecca, we kept it from her. At least we thought we did. John Senior didn't look too bad, and he acted cheerful enough, and Rebecca seemed happy as a clam. God, how that man spoiled that little girl.

"So she talked us into letting her open a present before bedtime, I remember it was a teddy bear she'd been wanting for, oh, a long time. One with a cassette player inside it that made it sing and tell stories. And we put her to bed with the teddy bear, and about an hour later she woke up screaming."

"Just like tonight," John said.

"Right. And you asked her what was wrong."

"Yeah." John took a sip of whiskey and stared at his glass. "She told me she'd had a bad dream. 'Baddeem', she called it. Said she'd been talking to grandpa and a big black spider poked its legs through his chest and ate its way out."

"Oh my God," Judy said, face paling.

"Yeah," John agreed, nodding solemnly. "Terrible thing for an adult to dream up in their head, much less a four-year old girl. And after that she was afraid to sit on his lap. It broke his heart. She'd walk with him, hold his hand, but she wouldn't sit on his lap. Poor Dad. Poor little Becka, bless her."

"It went on for almost a year," Lucy continued as John fell silent, gazing at his hands. "Every night, as soon as she drifted off to sleep, she'd wake up crying that the spider was getting grandpa, getting bigger. She said it was hurting him, and that when it was done with him it was going to come after her. Terrible, terrible time in her life, and ours too. Pretty soon she was afraid to go to bed. We ended up taking her to a child psychologist, who suggested telling her the truth, which didn't do any good at all. And then we took her to the pediatrician, who prescribed a sedative that just made her thick as a brick the day after she took it."

"I remember that," Norman said. "Poor Becka was like a zombie."

"Right. Nothing worked. John and I were starting to yell at each other all the time. That June, as I guess you know,

John Senior died. He was buried at a small mountain cemetery where he and Martha had purchased adjoining plots after learning of his condition. We took Rebecca to the ceremony. I was pretty worried about how she was going to handle it, let me tell you. Neither one of us was sure it was a good idea, but she and her grandpa loved each other so much that we couldn't do otherwise. And she did fine. It was odd . . ." Lucy fell silent as her thoughts wandered.

After a moment John said, "She had more nightmares after that, but they weren't as bad. And in about a year they stopped completely. She's been okay ever since."

"She is very bright isn't she?" Judy said.

"Yes, she is," Lucy said with a smile. "She really is. And I'm sure Stephen will be too."

"I'm sure," Judy echoed, returning her smile. Then, turning to Norman she said, "Well, I'm about all done in, honey. Guess I'll have to win back my matches some other time."

"Hey, I'm beat," he said. "Especially after last night."

"I think we'll be right behind you," Lucy said, glancing curiously at her husband. He continued to hold his empty glass, silent, face thoughtful. He felt their eyes on him and shook himself, looked up and said, "Yeah. Man, I is whipped like a dog even though we didn't do a damn thing today. Go warm up the bed for me, woman."

"Dream on." Lucy stood and pecked him on the cheek. The four wandered down the hall to their cabins, said final goodnights. For a few minutes the sounds of flushing and running water were heard, then silence.

Five minutes later Stephen awoke for a repeat of the previous night's performance.

Five

A big wave tossed the Whaler into the air and Joe clung to the wheel as the boat pounded through the crest of the next. Though his knees bent to absorb the impact, the force still made his teeth chatter. The steering console was barely protected by a windshield and the rest of the boat streamed with moisture. He stuck his head around the windshield for a clearer look at something glimpsed momentarily atop a wave and a blast of spray hit his face hard enough to sting. He veered slightly to avoid what turned out to be a styrofoam cooler lid.

But the morning wind was comfortable, as long as he stayed out of the spray, and he wore only jeans and a T-shirt beneath his flotation vest. The waves were running several feet in height and the few boats he saw were motoring slowly, throwing bursts of foam from beneath their bows. The Whaler handled the weather easily but not necessarily comfortably, thrown this way and that by the confused waves.

The helmsman's seat was folded out of the way and he was standing, wearing a wide nylon belt around his waist. The belt had a stainless D-ring on each side shackled to short lengths of heavy nylon line that were attached to eyelets on the center console. Thus secured he could stand at the helm absorbing the pounding with bent knees, in no danger of being thrown from the boat.

Already he had investigated two of the spots he knew John liked to stay and was now passing channel marker buoy 123 just past the confluence of the main lake and SEVEN MILE CANYON. It was an especially narrow section of the lake, with great vertical walls on either side that tended to increase the size of the waves and the force of the wind. He found the houseboat around the next turn.

Norman was groggy as he stood at the helm, staring at the cliff on his right. The sleepless night had done nothing for his mental state, and the black mineral deposits on the cliffs loomed like the shadows of giants. One in particular seemed to stare down at him from glittering green eyes. He shook his head and looked again. It was a ray of sunlight striking patches of verdant moss growing from the moisture trickling down the cliff face. The sound of an air horn caused him to jerk his head around and spot the boat beside him.

"Hey, there's somebody next to us," he said. "It looks like Joe from the marina."

"Yeah, it sure is," John said as he appeared at Norman's side. He smiled and waved and the man in the other boat waved back, teeth gleaming white against his dark skin. "Throttle back Norm, but not so much that the wind can push us around."

Norman nodded and slowed their progress. Rebecca ran onto the foredeck, waving and shouting. John joined her, pointing toward the stern, and he and his daughter followed along the side deck as Joe dropped back. Joe eased the Whaler past the speedboat and gently touched his bow against the houseboat to toss John a line. He waited until John made the line secure to a cleat before shutting down the outboards. After unclipping his safety harness, he strode to the bow and stepped through the gate onto the houseboat, swinging it shut behind him with a clang.

"Uncle Joe!" Rebecca jumped up and down beside him in her excitement, seizing his hand with both of hers.

"Hi Becka," he said with a grin. "I am glad I found you." He put an arm around her shoulder and hugged her, then they watched John play out line so the Whaler rode safely, just ahead of the other boat. He secured it with a series of figure-eights wrapped around the cleat and pulled tight, then coiled the excess line neatly on deck before offering his hand.

"Welcome aboard," John said. "Decide to get out of the

office for a few hours did you?"

"I sure did, but I did not count on getting my teeth rattled out of my head. I have to say, you folks are sure taking your time this trip. I thought you would be past Will's Crossing by now."

"Naw, we're taking it slow and easy."

"Are you going to stay for dinner?" Rebecca asked, tugging his hand to draw him inside.

"It is not even lunch time yet, why are you worrying about dinner?"

"I just want to know." She stuck out her lower lip, face stubbornly set. "I don't want you to leave."

"I will not leave for a while," he said. "But Anna is expecting me for dinner, okay?"

"Okay. I guess. Are you going to take me fishing?"

"Not today Becka, too windy. I will take you another day though. But you know what I would really like?"

"What Uncle Joe? What?"

"I would like you to take me inside to say hello to your mother. I was wondering if she is still as pretty as you are."

"She is, Uncle Joe! She is!" Rebecca dragged him by the hand as he exchanged a grin with John above her head.

"Well hello Joe!" Lucy said as the trio entered the salon. "What a nice surprise! Let me introduce Judy, my sister-in-law, and of course you know Martha."

"Nice to meet you Judy, hello Martha." Joe shook their hands gently.

"Hi Joe." Norman swiveled the helmsman's seat and waved.

"Hello Norman," Joe said. "Are you getting the feel of driving one of these big boats in the wind?"

"I sure am. And I've decided it wouldn't be much fun if the wind really decided to blow."

"You got that right," Joe agreed. "When the wind gets serious, the best thing to do with a houseboat is run it up on the beach and dig in the anchors. With their windage and shallow draft they become completely uncontrollable. John knows what I'm talking about."

"Man, I'd rather not go through that again," John

agreed, voice muffled as he inspected the contents of the refrigerator. "Hey, how 'bout a beer?"

Joe shook his head, a look of surprise on his rugged features. "No, thank you John."

"I've already put a pot of coffee on," Lucy said. "It'll be ready in a minute."

"Shi— er, shoot, I forgot Joe. Sorry. Norman, how about you?"

"Yeah, sure."

John took his brother a beer, then joined Joe and Rebecca on one of the couches while Judy and Martha sat on the other.

"Your boy is sleeping?" Joe asked Judy.

"Yes. He doesn't want to want to sleep at night. I don't know why, we've never had this trouble with him before."

"Is that so?" Joe's face appeared grave as he considered her words. Perched erectly on the edge of the couch, he held Rebecca on his knee and bounced her gently up and down.

"Does he sleep during the day?" he asked.

"Falls asleep at first light." She nodded her head.

"I see." He ran his free hand over his bristling gray hair, frowning. "Well, I am certain when he becomes used to the boat things will get back to normal."

"I'm sure they will."

"What do you think of the lake?"

"Me? I love it. It's some of the most spectacular scenery I've ever seen."

"Here you go Joe." Lucy brought him a cup of coffee. "Strong and black, right?"

"Ah, how well you remember." Rebecca slid from his knee and inserted herself between them as Lucy sat on the couch. He took a sip and sighed. "Delicious. I feel refreshed already. What are your plans for today?"

"We'll put in at Will's Crossing for fuel," John replied, "and take the speedboat across to the restaurant at Sunlight marina for lunch. Then we're heading on down the lake. Tomorrow I want to take everyone up the Escalante. Norm's taken a sudden interest in the rock art and I think he should see the paintings in Davis Gulch."

"Good idea," Joe agreed.

"How about some more coffee?" Martha asked, already rising from the couch.

"No, thanks Martha. It is excellent, but I drink too much caffeine these days. You are enjoying the boat?"

"Oh yes, it's lovely. And the lake's most impressive." Her smile was slightly uncertain as he refused to meet her eyes, though she knew its cultural significance.

"Well," he said suddenly, "I must go." He set the cup on the table and stood.

"Oh no, Uncle Joe!" Rebecca cried. "But you just got here."

"Yeah, really Joe," John said with a puzzled smile. "Can't you even stay for lunch? Hell, we're only a few miles out of Will's Crossing."

"I am sorry. There are too many demands waiting for me back at Winged Rock, and even this little trip down the lake is stolen time. No, but I will get away later in the week perhaps. Judy, nice meeting you. And Lucy, Martha, thank you."

"Oh, heck Joe," Lucy said in exasperation, "don't thank us. You came all the way down the lake just to say hello? Thank you!"

"Becka," Joe said, "would you like to help me cast off?"

"Oh I would Uncle Joe! I really would."

"Good. Come on then." He waved to the others and allowed her to tow him along the hallway to the stern, with John at their heels. John seized the tow line and began to pull the Whaler in hand over hand, waving off Joe's offer of help. Joe shrugged. Rebecca tugged his hand until he kneeled, cradling her delicate shoulders in his powerful hands. Her face was pinched tightly, unsmiling, and her lips moved as if she was trying to find words.

"Yes?" he said gently, "what is it you wish to say Rebecca? You know you can tell me anything."

She nodded and swallowed. "Uncle Joe, there's someone else on the boat." Her voice was a whisper and her eyes were large. Joe didn't reply but a cloud of concern settled across his features. The lines in his face deepened, and his mouth turned down even more at the corners than usual.

"I see," he said. "Was it someone you know?"

"No." She shook her head solemnly.

"What do you think they wanted?"

"I don't know Uncle Joe, but it's somebody bad."

"Man or woman?"

"It was a man. I think."

"Here." He reached behind his neck to untie the leather thong, and withdrew his Four Mountains bundle from within his shirt. Holding it before her, one end of the thong in each hand, he showed her the small doeskin pouch.

"What is it Uncle Joe?" she asked, staring in fascination at the swaying bundle.

"It is . . . it is a kind of medicine, Little Daughter." He tied it loosely around her slender neck. It hung almost to her stomach.

"It goes inside," he said, "next to your skin."

She slipped it inside her sweatshirt. "Should I take it off when I swim?" she asked.

"No. Wear it always. And do not tell anyone else; it is our secret."

Her face filled with excitement and she threw her arms around his neck and hugged him. "Oh, I love you Uncle Joe."

"Yes," he whispered. "Yes Little Daughter. I think we understand each other, hm?"

"Oh, we do Uncle Joe. And I won't take it off, I promise."

"Here you go Joe!" John said.

"Thanks John." Joe stood and opened the stern gate. "If I do not see you until your return, have a good time. And take care of yourselves."

"Sure will Joe." John's forehead furrowed as they shook hands. "Is there something you aren't telling me, old buddy?"

Joe smoothed Rebecca's hair with his hand, studied her upturned face. "No," he said after a moment. "You know

103

the boat's history. Just be careful this trip. And Rebecca," he said as he kneeled, "you know that if you ever, ever need me all you have to do is call. Toward the east, like I showed you."

"Okay Uncle Joe."

"Right. John, see you." He stepped through the gate and boarded the Whaler. After securing the safety belt around his waist he started the outboards and John tossed him the line. Immediately Joe backed his boat safely away from the speedboat and its towline, spun about, and waved as he opened the throttles and sped back up the lake with the wind and waves at his back.

"He didn't stay long," Rebecca said with a long face.

"No." John gazed after the boat with a thoughtful expression. "He sure didn't, honey. But he's got lots of work to do lately. Come on, let's go inside."

John joined his brother at the helm and Rebecca begged Martha into playing a game of old maid.

"That was a strange visit," John said quietly.

"What do you mean?" Norman glanced at him. "I was under the impression he liked to chase you down for a visit. Doesn't he show up like this often?"

"Oh, at least once every trip." John waved a hand dismissively. "But he comes for a *visit*, you know? This was something else. I've known the old fart long enough to know when something's bothering him. I think he came to check up on us for some reason. Did you see the way he was watching everyone, or were you too busy at the wheel?"

"No. I mean yeah, I noticed. But I thought it was just my imagination, or maybe just the way he is."

"Huh-uh. He's been acting funny since we got here; first about letting us have this boat, then coming all the way down the lake to look in and see how we were doing. Hell, he knows I can handle myself on the lake; there's never been a single scratch on any boat I've rented."

"So what's the deal?" Norman asked.

"I think the old Indian's worried about what happened aboard this boat," John said. "You know, I really think that might be it. They're pretty superstitious about certain things. But not Joe. At least, not till now. Joe's never shown anything but common sense in all the time I've known him."

"So? He just lost his mechanic, and scavengers are digging up the bones of his ancestors in his own backyard. I think I'd be acting kind of funny too."

"Yeah, maybe you're right. But Joe's the kind that usually gets tougher under pressure."

"What's the deal about these pot hunters anyway, John? Is the market for artifacts really attracting the big money people?"

"Norm, I can show you a pot in a museum that's insured for a quarter-million."

Norman whistled and shook his head. "Jesus, I didn't know the stuff was worth that much!"

"Let me tell you the financial story behind these scavengers." John took a swallow of beer and wiped his mouth with his hand. "The pot hunters come out here and find a village site or burial mound, dig it up, steal these historical artifacts and scatter the bones. No conscience, no reverence for the past, just simple profit motives. There's no serial number, no description, they've got a valuable piece of merchandise that's virtually untraceable because it's never been seen before. An original work of art that can be verified as authentic by an expert.

"So what does the pot hunter do with it? He's still got to be careful because there're laws against what he's doing, even though the laws don't have much in the way of teeth.

"So, what the looter does, he sells his finds to a dealer. The dealer sells the piece to a collector, a patron of the arts. Well, federal tax law lets your average philanthropist write off the value of a donation to a museum. Okay, the dealer knows that, so he gives the piece a much higher value than the patron pays, testified to in writing by a certified 'expert.'

"And the patron, this noble philanthropist, takes the write-off. And he, along with the IRS, subsidizes the pillage of Native American burial grounds, and nobody's the wiser. The museum is happy, the dealer and the scavenger get their money, and everybody pats this wealthy jerk on the back for his generous contribution to the our national heritage."

Norman gazed blankly through the glass, shaking his head. "Man, that's pretty bleak. I had no idea all that was going on out here. It looks so barren, so desolate. Who would guess there were millions to be made digging up old pots and baskets?"

"Historical artifacts," John corrected. "Irreproducible and irreplaceable. To the Navajos it's a terrible sacrilege. At least, the old timers. I've heard rumors of pot hunters vanishing in the desert, never to be heard from again."

"You're quite an authority," Norman said. And a minute later, "Is that Will's Crossing ahead?"

"Yeah, and the bay to starboard is Bullfrog Bay. That's Sunlight Marina way across there." He pointed and Norman nodded as he saw reflections from the cluster of buildings, boats, and cars.

"Reason I know so much about pot hunting," John said, "is because I've had a chance to buy some of the stuff. Good price, too."

"But you didn't?" Norman asked.

"Naw. I couldn't face Joe if I did something like that."

The two fell silent, their faces thoughtful as the houseboat seemed to barely crawl toward distant Will's Crossing Marina. But suddenly the buoys marking the harbor entrance were off the bow, and a minute later the boat was approaching the dock. Norman spun the wheel this way and that, working the throttles back and forth as he attempted to maneuver the houseboat alongside the fuel dock.

"Want me to take over?" John's voice said at his side.

"No," Norman said with irritation, "I can do it."

The water was calm but he had to fight the wind, and they struck the dock hard enough to send a shudder through the boat but not hard enough to do any damage. When at last the attendants had the bow and stern lines secured to the dock Norman shut down the outboards and

106

gave John a shrug.

"Nothing to it," he said, then smiled. "Call it a five on the one-to-ten scale."

"Hell, Bro', I'll give you a six." John slapped his brother's shoulder and turned to the salon where he began rousing everyone for a trip across the bay. It was a wet ride on rough water. John paid for lunch at the Sunlight restaurant, so when they returned to the houseboat, Norman insisted on paying the fuel bill.

John had the helm as they got underway once more, and during the next two-hour shift everybody except Norman retired to their cabin for a nap. Even Rebecca, fussy and rubbing her eyes, was tempted back to the cabins, and soon slept soundly.

The two men watched the canyon drift pass, sipping their beers, the boat quiet but for the muted drone of the outboards from astern. The time passed quickly, and John turned the helm over to Norman as they approached a buoy swaying in the waves.

"That's the marker indicating the entrance to the Escalante River," he said. "We turn to starboard."

"Aye aye, Captain." Norman turned the wheel and said, "If you hadn't told me, I'd think we were still on the main lake. Be easy to get lost."

"You're right there. I guess the lake wasn't as well marked in the early days. Boaters got lost for days."

"I can believe it. So what's our program here?"

"About five miles up the Escalante on your left we'll come to Davis Gulch. That's where we want to stay tonight. If it's rock art you want, you'll like this place."

They beached the houseboat on what John referred to as a 'pocket beach,' a tiny delta at the mouth of a gully barely wide enough to admit the boat's pontoons. They secured the mooring lines to rock outcroppings, since there was no place to bury an anchor. Judy appeared on the foredeck with Stephen.

"Hi," Norman said as he spotted them. He stepped aboard and wiped the clinging red soil from his shoes with a towel. "Sleep well?"

"Fine. Bruiser's in a good mood. Aren't you kiddo?" She tickled him under the chin and he wrinkled up his nose and giggled. Norman wrapped them both in his arms and hugged them, kissed his wife.

"Did I tell you today how much I love you?" he asked.

"Yes," she said, "just now."

"Hey hey hey." John sprang from a rock ledge beside the bow and landed with a thump on the foredeck. "Hi, sleepy heads."

"Say 'hi, Uncle John'," Judy said to Stephen, waving his tiny hand with her own. "Hi, Uncle John. Hi. Hi. Oh well, guess he doesn't want to wave today."

"They never do those things when you want them to," John said. "Feeling ready for a little sightseeing excursion?"

"Sure. Where to?"

"Just up the canyon here."

"That sounds good. Is there somewhere to get out and walk around?"

"Sure is, but wear tennies or boots instead of thongs; it's kind of steep walking until you get up top where it flattens out."

"Okay."

When Lucy and Martha were awake, and Rebecca running in circles yelling her enthusiasm, they loaded a cooler aboard the speedboat and headed up the canyon. The rumble of the engine was loud between the enclosing walls of rock, walls that gradually closed in upon them like huge hands, shutting out the light, seeming to compress the very air until they traveled through a narrow, twilight world where no sound or movement occurred save their own. John drove the boat carefully, engine idling as he glanced continually around at the dark water beneath the hull.

There was a faint chill in the air and a pungent, cloying odor reminiscent of mushrooms. The water looked cold, impenetrable as agate, the bow wave curling back as precisely as steel shaved on a lathe. Stephen whimpered and Norman turned to look at his son cradled on Judy's lap. The baby's eyes were large and watchful in the shadows.

The boat moved beneath a cliff that was hollowed out, looming over the water to cast a pool of deeper shade beneath it.

John shifted to neutral and killed the engine. "This is the place," he said.

The ensuing silence was profound, broken only by the lapping of tiny wavelets against the hull as they drifted into the shade toward the canyon wall. Now they shifted in their seats, craning to see the paintings, and every movement echoed from the natural amphitheater of stone, magnified and distorted. As John unclipped an oar from its bracket it boomed like a huge fist pounding on an iron door, and when he maneuvered them closer the splashing seemed to come from all around, from every hidden pocket of darkness, from the unseen gloom of the canyon beyond.

"Wow," Norman said quietly, staring upward. "Man what an impressive setting." The paintings were tall torsos, limbless, heads only suggested by a line or rectangle, bodies decorated with bold, primitive designs of a few thick lines running vertically or across. Heroic in proportion, the ghostly images loomed above the boat's occupants. A swirl of smaller, curious designs surrounded them, hinting at unknown meanings, inviting recognition, but defeating any attempts to make sense of them.

One in particular that caught Norman's attention was a small figure rendered in negative within a white circle. Its body was roughly triangular, the shoulders extremely broad and the hips and legs tiny by comparison. Its arms were slender and bent downward at the elbows. The exaggerated, splay-fingered hands dangled limply, and two curving horns sprouted from the neckless head.

Rebecca began to sob quietly. In moments it became actual crying and Lucy drew her close to comfort her as the others stirred, awakening from the trance imposed by the spirit of the place.

"I've seen enough," Judy said as Stephen began crying. "I say let's find a sunny spot and go for a walk."

"Seconded," Martha said, stroking Rebecca's hair.

"I'm scared, Grandma," she wailed.

"I don't blame you a bit honey," Martha said, "it's a gloomy place."

"It's the bad man, Grandma, it's the man I *saw.*"

"Where Becka?"

Rebecca raised a trembling finger and pointed at the small, horned figure.

John put the oar away and started the engine. He turned the boat around and they left the paintings behind in the eternal shadow of the deep canyon. A short time later John nosed the boat gently onto a muddy shore. The passengers clambered out, hiked up the sloping stone into the sun.

"Oh yeah!" John shouted. "The sun feels great!"

"Hey!" Judy yelled, "Look at this!" She stood spread-legged atop a small stone arch that looked too delicate to bear her weight. But when Norman joined her he found it was strong enough to support him also, and the others when they wandered over.

Rebecca gave squeals of delight as she skipped across the smooth sandstone. She returned with both fists clutching handfuls of round, polished black stones.

"Look Grandma, look Daddy!" she shouted. "Marbles!"

"Boy, those are nice," Martha said. Rebecca joined her where she rested in the shade, leaning against a boulder. "Where ever did you find them?"

"There's all these little, like, bowls in the rock, and there are marbles in some of them. Maybe lots of them. How come, Grandma?"

"Well, I don't know. Let's think about it for a minute."

Rebecca nodded, rolling the stones between the palms of her hands.

"I've got it!" Martha said. "I bet what happens is the wind blows these little stones across the rock and they fall into the holes. Then, when the wind continues to blow, the stones roll around and around in the hole until it becomes shaped like a bowl and the stones get polished into little balls."

"Oh. You're smart, Grandma." Rebecca poured the

stones from hand to hand and one fell out, rolled down the slope and took a little hop to disappear into the lake. "Good thing there's more," she said as the ripples spread outward. The sun dropped behind a pinnacle of stone directly to their west and Martha stood, reaching for Rebecca's hand.

"I don't know about you, but I'm ready for some dinner," she said.

"Me too, Grandma, what are we having?" She put the rest of the stones into her pockets and took Martha's hand.

"Well, I don't know, what would you like?"

"Hot dogs!"

"This child says she wants hot dogs for dinner, Daddy," Martha said as they approached John and Lucy, standing hand in hand watching the sunset.

"Hot dogs huh? I suppose that could be arranged." John turned to them with a smile.

"Come on Uncle Norm, Aunt Judy," Rebecca called, "it's time for dinner. Come on Stevie."

When they were back aboard the houseboat, Martha tried to tempt Rebecca with the spaghetti everybody else was having for dinner but she remained adamant.

"Hot dogs you said." Her jaw was set, her eyes hard as flint.

"Just like her father," Martha sighed. "Stubborn as a mule." She tossed two hot dogs in a pan of water and set them on a burner beside the pot of pasta. By the time the noodles were tender and the hot dogs cooked, a hungry crowd was gathered at the breakfast bar and in the salon.

They consumed the spaghetti to the last strand and the garlic bread to the last crumb. Even Stephen managed to wolf down a large portion of mashed noodles. He and Rebecca went to bed without protest, and both were asleep moments after the covers were tucked around them.

The adults sat on the aft deck looking out at a glass-smooth lake, its surface broken only by the expanding rings of leaping fish. The air was still and pleasant, neither too warm nor too cool, as stars began to appear overhead.

"This is how it should be," John said. "Any objections if

111

we just float around like this for a few years?"

"None here," Martha said. "But let's spend part of the time in the Mediterranean; I love Saint Tropez this time of year. And Nice would be nice."

"The jet-setter," Lucy said. "Is there any place you haven't been lady?"

"Oh, plenty. Want to explore some of them with me?"

"God. Would I. Can Rebecca come?"

"Sure, we'll make it a girl's trip. You in Judy?"

"You bet. I'll just leave Bruiser with Norm for a few weeks; shouldn't be a problem."

"Supposed to be some good fishing up Willow Creek Canyon to the west of here," John said. Norman grunted in reply.

"Want to try it in the morning?"

"Sure."

"Okay." John cocked an eyebrow at his brother, but Norman yawned and stared at the lake from half-lidded eyes. John turned to Martha and said, "Tell me about Athens."

"Oh, that's a wonderful place," she said, "it's my idea of what a city should be. It's got . . ." she waved her hand, spoke at length of ruins and museums, of the Acropole Palace hotel where she and her late husband had stayed, of the Gerofinikas Restaurant where they had eaten.

"Norm." He started as Judy shook his arm, turned to find her staring at him, the two of them alone. "The others have gone on to bed; you were asleep in your chair."

"I wasn't asleep," he said, "just thinking."

"You were thinking pretty loud; they could probably hear your snore clear across the lake."

"Oh? Well, whatever."

"Are you coming along to bed?"

"Sure." He stood and slipped an arm around her waist, walked her to their cabin. After closing the door, he tumbled her onto the bed fully clothed and kissed her passionately as his hands sought beneath her blouse.

"Hey," she whispered, "is this an invitation?"

"Sshh," he said, touching her lips with a finger. "You'll wake the baby."

"God forbid."

They undressed quickly and quietly and Judy slipped into the head for her diaphragm. She returned to Norman and he pulled her down and rolled atop her, penetrating her roughly. She moaned and her hands sought his shoulders.

"Oh God!" she whispered fiercely. "Oh God, don't stop!"

Norman responded with vigor, pounding into her, and guttural sounds escaped his throat as she moaned, gave tiny cries of pleasure. It went on and on as he delayed his pleasure to make hers greater. When at last they collapsed, shuddering, the blanket moist and rumpled from their efforts, Norman fell immediately asleep.

And was awakened an instant later by the muffled, terrified scream of Rebecca from the cabin across the hall.

Norman sat bolt upright in bed, Judy beside him gripping his arm. The sound was one of total, unmitigated fear, as if someone or something was attacking the little girl in her bed. Norman's feet hit the floor already moving and he jerked open the door, burst into the other cabin and fumbled for the light switch. As the room was bathed in light he saw John's naked form kneeling beside Rebecca's bed as he tried to comfort her. Lucy was beside him, round-eyed and pale, a sheet clutched across her breasts.

Norman covered his nakedness with his hands and backed up a step, his foot landing on something small and hard. He gave a shout of pain and danced back into the hall.

"For God sake, Norman!" Martha said, obviously upset by her granddaughter's screams. She pushed past him into the cabin as he returned to his for something to wear.

"Nightmare?" Judy asked as she stepped aside to let him in. He nodded, grabbed a pair of hiking shorts from the chair, then stepped to the crib and glanced at the baby.

"Don't know why he's still sleeping," he whispered as he returned to the door. He stooped to retrieve the object he stepped on a moment earlier; a round black stone. He thrust it into a pocket and put his arms around Judy, kissed her forehead, said, "It's all right Jude, go back to

113

bed. I'll be in in a minute."

He returned to Rebecca's cabin. John was now wearing pajamas and Lucy a nightgown as they comforted their daughter.

"But it wasn't a dream," she sobbed, shaking her head. She put her hands against John and pushed him away. "I threw my marbles at him! I hit him, Daddy, I made him go away or he would have hurt me!"

Norman reached wordlessly into his pocket and pulled out the stone, tossed it to John, who missed the catch. As he stooped to the floor to retrieve it Rebecca pointed and Martha, seated on the foot of the bed, gasped and clutched her robe at the throat.

"See?" Rebecca said. "He was here!"

Smudged, but plainly visible, two muddy red footprints stained the carpet beside the bed.

"That . . . that's nothing," John said doubtfully. "One of us made them, forgot to wipe our feet." He peered closely at the footprints, touched one with his finger, then stood and made his voice authoritative. "You can see that, can't you honey? We've been on and off the boat all afternoon; we forget to wipe our feet lots of times."

"He was *here*, Daddy!" Rebecca pounded the mattress with her fists, her tear-streaked face now angry as well as frightened. "He was here he was here he was here! I saw him! I wasn't asleep because I remember waking up and he was looking at me standing right where those muddy feet are!" Then she started crying again as she repeated, "He was here, he was here."

Norman stepped casually closer and squatted, brushed a footprint with his fingers. He lifted his hand and rubbed the moist soil between his fingertips. John shook his head no as Norman looked up and met his gaze.

"Well," Norman said, "guess I'm not doing any good standing around in your room. Think I'll go back to bed. Good night Becka. I'm sorry you had a bad dream, honey." He turned away as she continued to weep, her face buried against Martha's shoulder.

"It wasn't a dreammmm," Rebecca moaned.

"I believe you," Martha said. "Grandma believes you, honey. Don't you worry, you can come and stay with me in my bed tonight."

"Is she all right?" Judy whispered as Norman climbed into bed.

"Yeah. Just scared is all."

"Okay. G'night." She turned away from him and her breathing deepened.

"Night, honey." He lay on his back staring at the ceiling. Gradually the houseboat became still, and soon the only sound was the faint, almost indiscernible sound of an owl hooting somewhere out in the desert. He closed his eyes and sighed.

A moment later his eyes flew open and he lay listening in the darkness. Something had roused him. A noise, or a movement of shadow and light, a scent in the air. His heart thudded heavily, a drumming in his ears. Judy pushed up against him and moaned, tugged the covers around her neck. The beating of his heart slowed and he drew a deep breath.

He slipped quietly from the bed. The shorts he had worn earlier lay crumpled on the chair where he had tossed them and he put them on, then moved cautiously to the hallway. There was nothing. He turned his head and looked both ways; there was nothing. The boat was silent, dark, and empty of uninvited guests.

Quietly he padded along the hall to the salon, fingers brushing the wall, his gaze searching the shadows until his touch encountered a table lamp and the bright light chased the darkness from the room, exiled it beyond the windows. Nothing.

He sighed and turned toward the hallway. But the refrigerator fell beneath his gaze and he went to it and removed a carton of cold orange juice, poured himself a glass, and carried it out onto the foredeck. He gulped the juice greedily, tipping his head back and closing his eyes. With a gasp of pleasure he lowered the glass. He froze, eyes wide and staring.

A figure stood on the shore gazing toward him. It was

broad shouldered, with skinny hips and waist, and a broad face with eyes that glittered in the starlight. Its wide mouth parted like a frog's as the figure grinned. It lifted a huge hand at the end of a long, stringy arm, and reached out toward him, fingers bent like claws, and Norman jerked as if he had been struck. Slowly the hand turned and beckoned him with a finger, beckoned him to follow. Then it took a few shuffling steps and vanished into the darkness.

The glass slipped from Norman's fingers and hit the deck, bounced without breaking, rolled over the edge and into the water. He stood rigid, breathing shallowly, mouth open, a trickle of orange juice dribbling from his chin. He lifted his right foot and plopped it forward, followed by the left, then the right again. He clutched the railing and paused as a shudder shook him, then leaped over and landed heavily ashore.

Now he began to jog. Through the darkness his feet found the way, following a path unseen, hands outstretched before him like a blind man's. Though a crescent moon had risen, clouds racing past high overhead periodically obscured its light and Norman stumbled, fell, climbed to his feet and hurried on.

And the thing stopped now and again to wait for him, weaving the air with its fingers, stroking the deep stillness of the night, summoning him, demanding his obedience. He saw it as he topped a rise, saw a darker shadow against the night, the flash of green from its eyes like an animal glimpsed in the headlights of a car, and its gaze filled him with a fear so great that his belly twisted and emptied its contents in wracking heaves.

When he was able to move again, on into the night he went, now walking, now breaking into a slow jog, now slowing and feeling carefully with his hands as the path led along the face of a cliff. How far the drop beneath him? He could not see. Fear of what lay ahead twisted his features, and compulsion to keep moving drove his legs, though he did not know how far he traveled or what route was taken.

He only knew of small round rocks that rolled under his bare feet, causing him to stumble and dance about for balance. Soft dirt that puffed up between his toes and coated his ankles. Brittle branches that scratched his legs. Hard, smooth rock still warm from the day, his feet slapping against its surface. Something that fluttered past his face uttering high-pitched squeaks and his hands coming up instinctively to ward it off as he felt something dry and leathery brush his fingers.

Lowering his hands, he stepped forward and encountered empty space beneath his foot. With a cry he spun about as he fell and threw his arms out to strike heavily against the ground. His legs hung over the edge, his feet encountering nothing but smooth cliff as he sought for purchase. He knew he could not hang there long; already he was slipping backward, backward, toward an abyss that could be one foot deep or one hundred.

He groped forward with his right hand and found a minute depression that would just fit a fingertip. Pulling, straining, he gained an inch and reached out with his left. A narrow crack beneath his fingers, scant purchase, but enough to pull far enough up to raise a leg, get a knee over the rounded edge. No time to slip now, balanced precariously, right hand creeping forward like a spider searching for another grip as his entire weight hung from the fingers of his left.

His touch revealed a knobby projection and his fingers wrapped around it, tugged gently, then harder. It held. Carefully, carefully, he drew himself forward, got his knee beneath him, raised his other leg, stood and stumbled forward away from the sheer drop at his back. Just then the moon shone through a break in the clouds and Norman, still breathing heavily, saw the squat image standing before him only a few yards distant and recoiled, caught himself, trapped between one terror and another.

"What are you?" he shouted. "What do you want?"

In answer it beckoned again, turned away and started on into the night, its gait awkward but swift, knees bent outward, hands flapping limply at the end of long arms. It

117

made no sound and raised no dust. Norman swayed, took a step, then another.

He stopped and turned to look back the way he had come and his mouth opened. Far away was the place he had left. Far, far away. The moonlight glistened on the distant water, a thread of silver in the black and wrinkled fabric of the landscape. Towering pillars and precipitous canyons lay between him and that furtive glimmer where his family was sleeping.

A small frightened sound escaped his throat as he was jerked like a fish on a hook, jerked away from the lake and his family and all he loved and held dear and forced to follow the elusive shadow that waited just ahead. He ran quickly now while the moon shone through the rift in the clouds and the shadow scampered easily across the slope below. Smooth bare rock, his footing sure, the way easy to see, the destination unknown.

Descending. Down and down, the slope steady and limitless, the shadow ahead appearing and disappearing, never altering its stride. Norman's breath coming in gasps, flesh jiggling with each jarring step, mind numb and eyes staring straight ahead. The odor of decay hung in the air, of deep damp places, of things living beneath rotting logs, in ancient cellars where nobody goes, the odor of lurking death.

He cried out as his feet plunged into soft sand and he fell forward helplessly, landing on hands and knees as the moon vanished behind the clouds and the black silence enfolded him. A sob arose in his chest as he panted and tears gathered behind his closed eyelids. Then a sound made him raise his head.

There was a small fire, flickering brightly, and its light revealed a tall, shallow cave. The creature stood beyond the fire and its shadow was thrown quivering and leaping upward over the naked stone at its back. Its shadow danced among others of its kind, huge images, broad-shouldered, limbless torsos. Monsters dark against the stone, a writhing chaos of insane creatures, emblazoned with snakes and diamonds, with spinning suns and sting-

118

ing scorpions, titanic and frightening, eyes staring sightlessly down at him crouched in the dirt.

The figure raised a hand, a hand huge and misshapen, the fingers bent like claws as it beckoned and he lurched to his feet. It twitched a claw and he took a step toward the fire, then another. It looked at him through the flames and its eyes glittered coldly green. He stared rigidly ahead as he took another step forward. One more and he would be in the fire. The hand fell and he collapsed to the ground like a puppet whose strings have been cut.

Now it began to speak, a muttering drone full of harsh consonants and clicking sounds and Norman's bowels released their contents warm and stinking on his paralyzed legs as it came up beside him and reached out with its hands with those horrible hands the fingers splay-tipped and bent, quivering, poised now on either side of his head.

He stared at its face and his mouth opened in a scream that caught in his chest so only a hollow croaking issued from his throat. The face, the face, so twisted and cold, so almost human but not quite for the total lack of emotion on its weathered wrinkled features with skin like leather like mud that baked for years in the desert sun until buckled and split and cracked. The fleshless skin that clung to a skull broad and flat, thin dry lips that moved over yellow teeth and a tongue that flicked forth to lick them with a sound like dead leaves scraping together. And the eyes.

Oh the eyes! The cold ancient reptilian gaze from those green, glittering, malicious eyes, as if all the spite and hatred of a thousand murdered souls clotted its brain and seeped out through those evil festering eyes. Norman's face trembled with effort as he tried to close his own eyes but it held his gaze and the long lizard fingers fluttered on either side of his head and he could neither turn away nor strike out as the face came closer and closer while a deep droning began to issue from the hollow cliff, from the very stone where the shadows scampered, where the images twisted and writhed, and the thrumming filled the night as the fingers touched him.

Now the scream that had been trapped in his chest burst

119

forth high and shrill as a woman's and filled with an agony of terror as the creature's thumbs, its hard and leathery thumbs like bones clothed in dirty gloves, sought the corners of his mouth and inserted themselves. And pulled. Tugged. The fingers following, creeping along his jaw, slipping inside to pry at his palate and compress his tongue so the scream became a burbling, gagging, strangling lament as its face drew closer to his own.

The terrible remorseless gaze filled his vision and the mushroom smell, the decaying fungal musty smell, filled his nose and lungs, the guttural muttering of its voice now a growl like a cat rumbling deep in its throat as it stretched his mouth wider and wider and now came a tearing as he felt the flesh at the corners of his mouth part and the hot metallic taste of blood on his tongue filling his throat, choking him, but still the hands pulled harder and harder.

Norman's jawbone creaked and his eyes rolled upward in the sockets as he hovered near unconsciousness from the pain and a roaring filled his ears like the waters of some thunderous river plunging down and down into the deepest bowels of the earth as the creature thrust its head into his gaping mouth and churned its legs, pushing and pushing as Norman's throat expanded with poppings and snappings, and he swelled like a balloon, ribs cracking as its head entered his chest and its broad shoulders forced between his jaws, torn impossibly wide and the fingers wormed their way down into his groin, clutching for purchase, dragging itself into him, raping itself into his body, its toes seeking purchase against his teeth and the world a blaze of red pain and horror and ugly sounds as his body expanded to accept the thing into him.

His head tipped fully back and the thing came like a skewer driven into his mouth all the way down into his belly as it writhed and kicked and forced itself ever deeper into him and he toppled to his side on the ground. The sounds were those of something feeding, and the sharp crunch of bone and soft juicy tearing of flesh as it was almost all the way in now, curling itself inside his body like a fetus, its feet making ripping sounds as they kicked against his throat while his throbbing jaw hung useless. With a last convulsive thrust it squirmed into his chest and he lay swollen and huge as it settled itself inside, and the throbbing that filled the night died away and away until it was a faint hiss like a phonograph needle endlessly scratching around and around some forgotten recording, or papers skittering through abandoned graveyards in a cold midnight wind, or, perhaps, snakes slithering across the sand in the darkness.

Six

When Judy shook him in the morning Norman was slow in responding. His eyes fluttered open and he stared at the ceiling, pale with the light of dawn. Across the room, the baby cried for its bottle.

"Your turn Norman," she said wearily, "I was already up with him at three o'clock this morning. Please."

She shook him again and he sat up without answer and swung his legs over the side of the bed to stand stupidly swaying, gazing about him like a man awakening from a dream only to find he is still dreaming. His eyes flicked back and forth in their sockets and alighted on Judy, strayed to the baby.

"Go on!" she whispered. "It's already made, in the refrigerator."

He jerked his head toward the door and she nodded. He shuffled toward the galley, right hand touching the wall for guidance until he reached the breakfast bar. He opened every drawer and cupboard and swept its contents with his gaze, coming last to the refrigerator. The bottle seemed to puzzle him and he turned it this way and that before suddenly nodding and returning to his cabin.

Stephen grabbed the bottle from his hands and thrust it greedily in his mouth, sucking and staring past his father with unfocused eyes. For a minute Norman stood watching, face blank, legs bent slightly at the knees. Then a quiet knock sounded at the door and his brother's voice whispered, "Norm, you awake?"

He grunted a reply, stepped to the door and opened it.

"We're going fishing this morning, remember?" John peered at him curiously. "You about ready to go?"

Norman's eyes darted in panic, lips moving soundlessly,

searching for the words. . . . "Sure," he croaked. "Minute."

"Okay. Hurry up." John grinned crookedly and yawned, turned toward the galley. Norman closed the door as Judy said sleepily, "Thanks, honey. You going fishing?"

"Mm."

"Be gone long?"

"Mm."

"Oh. Well, okay. Have fun." She rolled over and pulled the covers up under her chin.

He paused as if deep in thought, or perhaps listening to a voice none but he could hear, eyes closed, head tipped to the side. Suddenly he jerked and scampered to the closet and stripped off the shorts. He pulled on clean underwear and socks, a pair of jeans, a flannel shirt. Stiff and clumsy, it took three tries to tie his shoes and he scowled, shook his head and bared his teeth. On the way out of the cabin he grabbed the fishing pole leaning against the wall beside the door.

"Hey," John said, "coffee sound good?"

"You bet." Norman seated himself at the dining table, pole still clutched in his fist. John brought him a steaming mug and looked at Norman saying, "You going to stir it with that or what? Hey, you awake yet?"

"No." Norman leaned the pole against the table and burned his mouth as he took a gulp of coffee. Blowing out through pursed lips, he stared at the cup with slitted, glittering eyes, then glanced at his brother with a dull expression.

"Hangover," he murmured.

"I don't know why," John said as he seated himself. "We didn't have that much to drink last night. Maybe it's because of Becka's nightmare. Speaking of which, why don't you put our gear in the boat while I rouse her? She'll kill us if we go without her."

Norman stood without answering, reached for his pole, and turned toward the hallway.

"Well for Christ sake, you can finish your coffee," John said in exasperation. "I didn't mean right this instant." He shook his head as he went down the hall to the cabins and

123

knocked on Martha's door.

Norman took another swallow of coffee and grimaced, set the cup aside. He walked around the outside of the houseboat to the stern where a cooler and several tackle boxes and fishing poles were haphazardly piled beside the railing. After arranging the gear carefully in the stern, he clambered into the front seat and waited, his sharp gaze appraising the instruments and controls, his hand touching the vinyl upholstery while his tongue darted out to moisten his lips.

"Hi, Uncle Norm!" Rebecca said as she appeared from the hallway. Her smile faded when he didn't return her cheerful greeting, merely lifted a hand lethargically and waved.

"All set?" John asked.

Norman nodded as they climbed aboard. Rebecca seated herself in the stern and John slid behind the wheel.

"Get the lines, would you Becka?" John said. "I think your Uncle Norm's still asleep and it'd be a shame to wake him."

Rebecca eagerly complied and John started the engine and turned them out onto the lake. The air was brisk as they motored into the breeze with small wavelets slap-slap-slapping the hull. The Escalante River twisted and writhed between its high walls, and they traveled one minute in sun, the next in shadow, out in the sun again, back into shade. At the buoy marking the confluence of Willow Creek Canyon and the Escalante, John turned up the smaller tributary.

They went more slowly now as John switched on the electronic fish-finder. Even on this relatively small, narrow branch of a branch of the main lake the depth was one hundred feet in places. But John was looking for something else, dividing his attention between the small screen and the water ahead, and when he spotted it he shifted to neutral and turned off the engine.

"Right here is what fishermen call a break, or breakline," he said in an authoritative voice. "Fish stay in deep water most of the time, moving into the shallows to feed. Where there's a sudden change in depth caused by some underwater geographical feature, they congregate. Depending on the weather and other conditions of course. There's a sort of underwater cliff here and it's a hotspot for striped bass this time of year."

Norman grunted and reached for his pole, causing John to stare at him with a mixture of resentment and curiosity.

"You're a real talkative guy this morning aren't you?" he said.

"Sorry," Norman muttered. "Hang . . . hangover." He seemed to have difficulty making his mouth pronounce the words, twisting his features in concentration.

"Okay." John shrugged and glanced at him uncertainly, then turned to help Rebecca prepare her line. "We're using waterdogs this morning, honey. Stripers love 'em." Rebecca squealed her disgust as he removed one of the larval salamanders from the bait bucket and threaded it on her hook.

Soon all three were sitting quietly, waiting, a thumb on their lines to feel the first tug of a bite. The boat rocked gently and faint breezes chased across the water of the cove, making V-shaped disturbances as if invisible beings were skating lightly on the surface. A pair of ducks appeared over the bluff and descended toward the water, saw them and veered off up the canyon.

The morning sun crept across the water and the colors of the cliffs became vivid, the sky electric blue. The water undulated like a living thing as Norman stared into its depths. From his lips came a word, a sound, a series of harsh consonants and clicks that made his brother and niece turn to him with curious gazes.

"What did you say?" John asked. Norman looked up with a startled expression, but before he could answer, John jerked the tip of his fishing pole skyward as it bent sharply. The drag clicked, then began to buzz as the fish headed for deep water.

"Got him!" he said with delight as he reeled. "Feels like a big one!"

"Don't let it get away Daddy!" Rebecca said, her own pole forgotten on the floor of the boat as she peered over the side where the line disappeared into the water. John tightened the drag slightly and began to regain line, then the fish made a run and the reel sang as Rebecca danced about yelling instructions.

"Keep the line tight," she said. "Keep the rod tip up. Don't get the drag too tight or you'll break him off."

"Becka, would you shut up and get the net?" he said. "He's tiring; I'll have him at the boat in a minute."

"I can't Daddy, it's under Uncle Norm's seat."

"Norm, would you mind?"

But Norman continued to sit as he had since the fight began, pole in hand, watching the antics of the other two with a curious expression and glittering eyes.

"Norm? Come on man, I can see the fish! If he spooks he'll break off."

Norman stirred, set the pole aside, began searching slowly for the net as his hands fluttered over the tackle box, paddle, his eyes blinking rapidly as he examined the objects.

John and Rebecca were unaware of Norman's odd behavior, their attention on the fish as it made another run. In a minute John turned the fish and began working it toward the boat again, pumping the rod, speaking to the fish with Rebecca echoing his words.

"Come on, buddy," John said.

"Come on, come on," Rebecca said.

"Here we go, nice and easy, nice and easy."

"—Nice and easy—"

"Just a little bit closer."

"—Closer—"

"Okay Norm, get the net!"

"The net—"

Norman's hands fell on the aluminum handle with sudden recognition, tugging the net from its spring holders. He leaned over the side and thrust its hoop clumsily into the water.

"Not yet Norm," John growled, his exasperation becoming more and more apparent. "Don't let the fish see it. Christ, they're not that stupid."

126

Norman lifted the net so that water ran down the handle onto his shoes and pant legs, seemed not to notice. But when John yelled, "Now!" he plunged the net beneath the fish and hoisted it aboard.

"It's a beauty, Daddy," Rebecca said solemnly when the prize was safely landed. The fish was exquisite with its iridescent silver body and delicate tracery of dark stripes, but already the colors were fading as it gasped out its life on the floor of the boat. John inserted the hook remover into its mouth, and as the hook came free the fish flapped frantically once, twice, then lay quivering on the bottom of the boat as blood oozed from its gills to mingle with the water pooled about its body.

Rebecca wrinkled her face in disgust and rose abruptly, started to turn away. At that moment, Norman, facing the bow, brought his pole casually back over his shoulder and began a powerful cast. He seemed not to notice as the bait fell free, and the wicked treble hook whistled through the air and caught Rebecca in the scalp just behind the left ear. The tip of his pole bent backward as he continued his motion, lunging forward against the sudden resistance, still apparently unaware of what had happened. Rebecca screamed as the point sank all the way to the shank and scraped bone.

"Jesus Christ!" John shouted. He moved with lightning speed and grabbed the tip of Norman's pole, yanked so savagely that it shattered in his hand and Norman tumbled backward to land heavily atop a tackle box that burst beneath him, strewing its contents across the bottom of the boat.

"You asshole!" he shouted at Norman as he took Rebecca in his arms, attempting to comfort her and at the same time determine how badly she was hurt. One glance told him the hook was deeply embedded, and though he shuddered at the injury to his daughter, his lips moved in a silent prayer of thanks that it hadn't been an eye. Or her face. She cried hysterically as he stroked her head with his hand, holding her to his chest.

Norman stared blankly, blinking his eyes in confusion,

then seemed to realize what had happened and covered his face with his hands.

"Sorry," he moaned. "Sorry."

John was too concerned with his daughter to see Norman peeking between his fingers like a naughty child, or to notice the faint upturn at the corner of his lips.

"Forget about that Norm," John said, forcing himself to speak calmly. "We've got to get her back to the houseboat. She's fine. Yes, you're going to be fine honey. She's all right but we need to get this hook out of her. Come on, you drive. Get this boat headed back down the canyon."

Norman bobbed his head up and down and clambered into the driver's seat while John used his pocketknife to cut the line attached to the hook. Rebecca sobbed as he held her, smoothing her hair, carefully avoiding the area of the hook, crooning softly to her. Norman started the engine and steered the boat back the way they had come, making erratic corrections despite the calm water and lack of any other boats.

The women appeared on deck as the boat arrived. Martha held Stephen while Lucy and Judy stood by to catch the line. Lucy was the first to notice something wrong. She called to John in a fearful voice, "What is it? What's happened?"

"We had a little accident," he said, "nothing serious. Here, give us a hand." He passed Rebecca up to the two women, who immediately enfolded her in their arms and ushered her inside. Martha waited for the men, her arms cradling the baby protectively, and as they stepped aboard she fixed them with a stern but worried look.

"Is she hurt badly?" she asked.

"No, I don't think so," John replied. "But the hook will probably have to be cut out, and it might need stitches."

"Tell me what happened," she said.

"M-m-my fault," Norman said in a dull voice. "I hooked her, here." He pointed behind his ear and hung his head, shook it slowly. "Stupid," he said, "stupid, stupid." His eyes filled with tears.

"It was an accident Norman." She laid her hand on his

arm and darted a quick, meaningful glance at John. "It wasn't your fault, dear, you mustn't blame yourself."

"Nobody else to blame."

"Even so."

John jumped back aboard his boat and rummaged through his tool chest. He came up with a pair of wire cutters and hurried forward to the galley, where Rebecca had been taken. Martha and Norman followed to find Lucy and Judy carefully washing the blood from Rebecca's hair in the sink as she sniffled and gave occasional sobs.

"Here," John said, "let me make this easier." The two women stepped aside to give him room and Rebecca looked up at him from reddened eyes.

"What are you going to do, Daddy?" she asked in a quavering voice.

"Just get rid of the other hooks honey. I won't hurt you at all, I give you my most solemn promise."

She regarded him a moment before saying, "Okay. If you promise."

"That's my girl." He gently tipped her head forward while he lifted her wet hair out of the way. Now he could see the hook clearly, and he winced. Two of the inch-long points were entirely embedded in the flesh, and two bleeding half-inch furrows led to where the points had entered the skin. The hook was barbed, of course, which meant it could not be withdrawn without causing more damage. He positioned the remaining point between the jaws of the cutters and snipped it cleanly, caught it in his palm and tossed it in the trash with a look of disgust.

"We're going to have to take a little trip up the lake Becka," he said as he released her head. "We'll see if we can't find a doctor. I'm afraid you're going to need a couple of stitches."

She began to cry again and he patted her gently as he exchanged a look with his wife.

"In that case we better get going," Lucy said sharply. "How long will it take?"

"It's only about thirty miles from here to Bullfrog Bay; if the lake's smooth we can make it in half an hour. An hour

129

if it's rough. Why don't you get this girl some aspirin and I'll grab a couple of jackets."

"Okay. Come on, sweetheart." Lucy led Rebecca to the head and helped her swallow two tablets, then took her to the stern. As they started to climb into the boat Rebecca suddenly turned and cried, "I want Grandma. Come with us, Grandma. You and Stevie. Pleeease."

Martha leaned forward and planted a kiss on her forehead, smoothed her brow with a hand.

"I think I better stay here, honey. If it gets rough you'll be better off without me. Tell you what, while you're gone I'll fix you a treat."

"Nooo, come with me Grandmaaa." She cried mournfully for a moment, then sniffed and said, "What kind of treat?"

"A surprise, but you'll like it."

"Cookies?"

"Mmmm, maybe. You hurry back and find out."

"Okay."

John, watching this scene with obvious impatience, started the engine and motioned for Norman to throw off the lines. The moment the boat was free he backed clear and roared down the canyon toward the main lake.

Judy and Martha watched the boat out of sight. Norman stood gripping the railing, head bowed, eyes dull. The women noticed his misery and exchanged a glance. Stephen started squirming, raising his voice in protest at being held so long, and Martha carried him inside to free him on the salon floor. Judy laid a hand on Norman's arm and gave a smile of encouragement.

"Hey," she said, "I know you must feel awful about what happened, Norm. But moping around won't help and Becka's going to be fine."

Norman continued to stare at the dark water and she added, "Come on Norm, these things sometimes happen; it was an accident."

"Was it?" Two words, spoken in a flat and sullen voice, that caused Judy's hand to drop away from his arm and her eyes to widen in surprise.

130

"Are you saying that it wasn't?" she asked.

He turned his gaze toward her and a cruel smile twitched his lips, there and gone again so quickly she might have imagined it. She backed up a step and reached a hand to the railing. He raised a hand toward her, dropped it, and when he spoke again his voice was utterly lifeless.

"Don't know Jude. Think I'll walk ashore. Be alone. Sort things out." He puffed out his chest and pursed his lips after this, the longest speech he had made all morning. The longest since—.

"Okay Norm, if that's what you need to do." She looked at him with sadness and confusion.

His face contorted and he shivered, reached for her and drew her into his arms. He hugged her tight and breathed the scent of her hair as its softness brushed his cheek. But after only a moment his body jerked and he thrust her away as his face hardened. He shuffled along the side deck toward the bow without another word.

"Be careful," she called after him. "Please Norman, don't get lost."

He sprang to the shore and walked quickly up the dry creekbed. Some time later he found himself atop the mesa, looking down at the houseboat beached far below, tiny as a toy. He stretched and his joints creaked and popped.

He started across the mesa, walking briskly, then broke into a jog. His pace became swift and steady as he descended washes, climbed steep slopes, and a short time later arrived atop another mesa and paused to look back. Several miles at least. The sky was pale blue without a cloud and the sunlight warm on his skin as he removed his shirt and tied it around his waist. A speedboat cut the surface of the lake, but the sound of its motor was lost in the distance. From overhead came a raucous cry and he looked up to see a large, black bird flying above him. His left arm arose, hand outstretched as if to beckon.

The bird plummeted and swooped past him with a scream, the sound of wind booming from its broad wings. The light glistened blue-black from its feathers as it flapped, circling his head.

"Raven," he muttered as his gaze followed its flight. But it had another name also and his lips formed the sound, a name as harsh and guttural as its cry. As if in answer, the bird set off to the west and he followed.

The going became rougher now and he panted and sweated heavily as he pursued the bird, a dark blot against the bright sky ahead. Several times he was forced to stop and rest, and each time it returned and screamed as it circled, its call an ugly rasping filled with urgency. And he clambered to his feet and plodded onward. The earlier vigor was gone from his movements and he no longer jogged, but walked doggedly onward looking neither right nor left.

His jeans were soaked with perspiration, and the sleeves were of the shirt cinched tight around his waist were chafing the bulge of his belly hanging over its confinement. He reached a hand to loosen it, stumbled and almost fell, raised a hand to shield his eyes against the bright sunlight as he sought for sign of his winged guide. The sky was empty.

He spun to look back the way he had come; nothing there either. His breathing was labored and his legs quivered with weariness as he stepped from foot to foot to ease the throbbing caused by the pounding of stone through his thin-soled shoes. He stared down at his body and snorted in disgust. Through slitted eyes he squinted at the sun, turned his back on it, and had taken several steps when he heard the croak of the bird.

He grunted and turned and shaded his eyes again, searching for the source of the sound. The dark bird was perched instead of flying, perched on the limb of a twisted, naked tree not far ahead. The image shimmered in heatwaves from the earth and he hurried toward it. It waited, unmoving, and when he reached the tree it cocked its head so one cold, gleaming, black eye peered down at him.

He stared up at the bird and the limb beneath it swayed with its weight. Its beak was massive and glistened like polished steel and its feet were gnarled and long clawed. It returned his scrutiny, tipping its head this way and that, then began to bob its heavy beak and make curious little bows. It dropped almost lazily from the branch into the chasm below, spreading its wings and flapping around a bend out of sight.

Norman's gaze followed its flight downward and he saw the reflection of water. He swallowed hard and rubbed his eyes with the back of his hand, squinted at the reflection of sky in the canyon below, and began shuffling along the rim. He came to a path that descended through broken stone and thorny brush, and followed it down toward the water. He dropped to his knees in the soft sand and plunged his hands into the water, raised them dripping to his mouth.

The water was warm and green and tasted sharply metallic, but it was wet. He drank deeply, choking in his haste, and when his thirst was slaked he sprawled backward into the shade of a rock and lay staring upward. His stomach rumbled and gurgled and he belched loudly. After a minute he raised himself to a sitting position and peered about.

He was in a shallow canyon, fifty or sixty feet deep and just as wide. The canyon floor was green with brush and grass and he heard the chuckling call of an unseen quail from somewhere to his right. The bird that had guided him was gone now and he climbed to his feet and began to explore his surroundings.

A large lizard dashed across the sand near his feet and his gaze followed it until it disappeared. His lips moved soundlessly and his eyes darted back and forth in their sockets. He lifted each foot carefully and placed it toe first, making no sound as he moved up the valley. He walked bent forward at the waist with his arms dangling at his sides, fingers cupped.

His foot almost landed on the stone blade lying in the dirt. His hands trembled as he stooped to retrieve it from the soil, rubbed the dirt from its surface. It was fashioned from a green, glass-like material and was longer than his hand, so artfully wrought and shaped that its razor edge knicked his palm and drew blood despite his extreme care.

He wiped the blood on his jeans, and for a time stood turning the blade over and over in his hands. And when he looked up his eyes widened in excitement, for there was a dwelling not twenty feet from where he stood, built into the sheltering overhang of the canyon wall. The walls were of tightly mortared stonework joining the ledge on which it rested to the cliff that formed its roof.

Something rustled through the grass at his back and he whirled about, the spear point clutched in his right fist. But what sounded like some animal moving through the grass was only the wind. A strange wind, cool and damp, a wind that darted about, twisting and turning and doubling back upon itself, its progress revealed in the bending of the grass and shaking of the brush. The wind, the seeking wind . . . his lips muttered a sound.

Like an animal stalking its prey the wind cast back and forth in the confines of the canyon. It found him and slid over his face like cold fingers, probing, intimate. He welcomed its touch and lowered the blade. And the wind withdrew and died away. He stood motionless but for the swiveling of his head as he looked for it to return. A column of dust arose into the air at the bend of the canyon, spiraling higher and higher, whistling as it spun faster and faster.

It swayed back and forth, a towering conical shape now that resembled those dark figures drawn on stone by centuries-old hands. Limbless, headless, a whispering writhing torso that pulsed and sighed and suddenly collapsed downward, bending the grasses flat as it hurtled toward the stone dwelling. Dust and dry grass were carried along with it as it streamed into the dark, T- shaped doorway, howling through the stone confinement, suddenly gone as the canyon fell deathly silent.

He stood staring, mouth open, and a drip of blood fell from his fist to the dry soil. He glanced down at the red blot, then approached the dwelling slowly. Unlike most of the Anasazi dwellings, this one offered no protection against intruders. The doorway was at head height on the low ledge, high enough to avoid flood waters but easily reached even by a child. Indefensible.

He mounted the ledge and paused at the low doorway. There were chisel marks in the stone above it where a human figure had apparently been obliterated. His lips moved and a derisive sound came out, then he laughed.

As he squeezed into the opening a clammy breeze oozed out past him, a faint odor of mushrooms, or decay, its touch like cobwebs clinging and parting as he entered the small, dark room. He squatted, immobile, breathing shallowly as his eyes became accustomed to the shadows. Little by little, his surroundings revealed themselves.

It was a small space. He could almost span its width with his outstretched arms, and the length was perhaps a yard greater. In the center of the floor was a blackened depression where a fire had burned, and at the top of the wall was a small sooty opening for the smoke to exit. In one corner lay a stack of sticks broken into regular lengths, and beside it, where the wind had blown the dirt aside, he could see the outline of a stone block set in the floor. It was about a foot square, and could not have been plainer if there had been a sign directing him to it. He set the blade beside him and tried to pry the stone loose, but there was not enough edge showing for his fingers to grip. It was loose though, and when he tapped it with the blunt end of the blade it sounded hollow, as if there was a space beneath it, but it would not budge.

He inserted the blade and worked it around the perimeter. The drifting sand wedging it tight seeped down with a faint hiss and he began to attack it more vigorously. It started to move, coming up a fraction of an inch at a time as he pried, first one side, then the other, holding it tightly with his fingertips that were beginning to ache.

He almost had enough of the block exposed to get a hold on when the blade snapped. He swore and tossed the broken piece of flint aside and pulled with all his strength. It came slowly, grating with reluctance, and he slid it out of the way and looked in.

135

There was a shallow depression, barely big enough to hold a pack of playing cards, that appeared to be filled with a pile of small white pebbles. He crooned with delight as he lifted them out and it became apparent it was a necklace, the string stretched tight between his fingers. Teeth. It was teeth. Human teeth. Roots and all, precisely and carefully drilled through the center, strung on some twisted fiber, a small knot separating each one.

Hands shaking with excitement, in one smooth motion he dropped it over his head to hang around his neck. The instant it was in place his body convulsed as if he had been struck in the stomach and a grunt escaped his lips, a guttural sound that echoed within the confining walls.

The shadows fluttered and rustled as a wind fled through the doorway and he gripped his head and growled, teeth gritted. Bulges appeared in his body, sharp peaks and deep hollows, as if his very bones were rearranging themselves, and he dropped to hands and knees and crawled into the light, gulping the fresh air. His body writhed on the ground and saliva dribbled from the corner of his mouth and his eyes were dull and glazed.

Slowly, awareness returned to his gaze, and the brightness of the day made him blink. He clambered to his feet and swiveled his head, looking for something, for something that came now, rustling the grass, a wind that poured over him and snatched at his shirt as he tugged it on. He raised his arms over his head and howled and the wind responded by increasing until its moan filled the canyon and he stumbled beneath its force.

He turned his back to the wind and began to jog and it propelled him until he seemed to fly over the ground and he was not tired. The necklace hung inside his shirt and the fabric pressed the teeth against the skin of his chest, teeth that nibbled, that tasted his flesh, teeth of those who once lived and breathed, lusted and hungered, loved and mated . . . and died.

The teeth touched and caressed him and whispered against the thin fabric of his shirt. His hands rose to his throat as he ran and his fingers played across the necklace

136

lovingly as a cackle of laughter came from his lips.

And upon the crest of a hill the bird appeared, swooping down upon him so closely that a wing brushed his head. He called a single word after its disappearing shadow and it responded with a harsh scream, and at dusk he arrived back at the houseboat, dirty and tired.

"Norman!" Judy cried as he stumbled into the salon. "My God, where have you been? We've been worried to death about you! We thought you were lost."

"I was uh . . . I was uh . . ." he stammered, looking around at their tense faces. "I was hiking," he said. They stared at him. John shook his head in disbelief.

"Becka," Norman said suddenly. "Are you all right?"

"I got three stitches!" she announced proudly. "Wanna see?" Before he could answer she bounced across the floor and presented her injury for his inspection, head bent, holding the hair away from a shaved spot with her hand. He leaned forward and saw puckered tissue and black sutures, narrowed his eyes and covered a smile with his hand.

"I'm sorry Becka," he mumbled. "Sorry it happened."

"It's okay," she said cheerfully. "I got to go out for lunch, and grandma made me a cake. Chocolate with fudge icing; my favorite. You can have a piece if you want."

He didn't answer and Judy peered at him. "You look pale. Here, sit down while I get you something to drink." As she uttered the last sentence her eyebrows shot up. "You must be dying of thirst; you didn't have a drop with you did you?"

"No," he said. "But I found some."

"Jesus, Norm," his brother said. "You didn't drink lake water did you?"

"No, I found a spring," he said.

"Oh. Well, that's probably okay. Christ, no telling how many kinds of bugs you'd get drinking lake water. Giardia at least."

"Here you go, honey." Judy handed him a glass of beer as Stephen crawled across the carpet toward him. The baby clawed himself upright on Norman's jeans and swayed, saying, "Gaw, gaw gaw gaw," his tiny hands reaching for the glass. Norman laid a hand on his fine, soft hair and stroked his head.

"Hey, I think he wants a drink," John chuckled.

Norman gave a weary smile and glanced around the salon; the others were watching him while trying not to be obvious about it.

"This tastes good," he said. He raised the glass to his lips and drained it in two huge gulps.

"Drink a couple more like that and you'll be feeling no pain," John said. "No pain at all."

"Yes, you're right. Maybe I better take a shower while I can still stand."

"We waited dinner for you, so make it a quick one, okay?" Judy cocked an eyebrow at him.

"Sure." He stood and walked unsteadily to their cabin, stripped, and stepped into the shower. He sighed as the hot water pounded against his back, and it was many minutes before he took the bar of soap from its dish and began to scrub himself. The water swirled brown and dirty at his feet. By the time he joined the others, dinner was already on the table and places set.

"Honey, are you going to eat dinner in your robe?" Judy chided him.

"Why not?" he said.

"Why not," she echoed, looking around the table for support. Nobody else said anything and she shrugged. "Okay. Why the heck not."

Dinner was a beef stew Lucy had prepared, a glutinous mixture with large chunks of meat and vegetables. Norman picked at it and took a few bites washed down by several glasses of water.

"Honestly Norm," Judy said, "I'd think you'd be famished. Usually you'd eat two or three helpings."

He shook his head. "Just tired I guess," he said. "Sorry. It's not the cook's fault."

"I know," she said. "Everybody else has cleaned their plate, and John's on seconds."

"You don't get any cake if you don't clean your plate,"

Rebecca chanted.

Norman shrugged and smiled wearily, nibbled at a crust of French bread. And afterward he went almost immediately to bed, eyes closing as his head touched the pillow. Even Stephen's crying didn't awaken him as Judy sat holding the baby and rocking him late into the night.

"Grandma!" a voice whispered sharply and Martha started, giving a cry as a hand touched her arm. She sat up in bed to stare at the small pale face beside her.

"Becka! What is it child?"

"Sshhh! He's here again, Grandma."

"Who's here again?" she asked as her eyes darted back and forth, searching the shadowy corners of the room.

"You knowwww. The one everybody said is a nightmare. But he's not a nightmare, Grandma. I know because I just followed him around the boat and you can tell I'm awake can't you?"

"Yes. Yes Becka, you're awake. Is anyone else up?"

"No Grandma. Nobody else believes me so I came to get you."

"Do you want to get in Grandma's bed?"

"No, Grandma, I want you to see him."

"Goodness sake child. It's—" she squinted at the travel clock on the night stand beside the bed, "it's 3:30 in the morning. You should be asleep."

"Please, Grandma. Pleeease."

She snorted her displeasure as Rebecca waited beside her bed, small and alone. After a moment she sighed and swung her legs from beneath the covers.

"All right Becka. All right. Then back to bed we go." She clicked on the lamp and slipped her arms into the sleeves of her robe, her feet into the slippers beside the bed.

"After you Sherlock," she said. Rebecca was already waiting at the door and Martha followed her into the hall. The little girl moved silently ahead, her hand brushing the wall for direction, footsteps sure and stealthy. The hallway brightened as moonlight streamed into the salon, then darkened as a cloud obscured the light. At the salon Rebecca paused and her head swiveled from side to side as she searched the room; then without so much as a backward glance, she waved for her grandmother to follow.

Martha went to her and took her hand, allowing herself to be led across the salon and out through the sliding doors, which were already open. Standing at the bow railing they stared into the night, Martha's arm around the girl's shoulders, and after a time she patted her and said, "Well, they must have left. Come on, let's go back to bed." But just as she started to turn away Rebecca stiffened.

"There!" she whispered, pointing.

"What?" Martha turned back, looked where the girl's slender finger pointed, and clutched the throat of her nightgown tightly.

Someone or something was out there in the night. Something dark, something in shadow, something that was moving slowly, rhythmically, with a droning sound rising and falling like the moaning of wind through a ruined building. Martha squinted to see as her breath came in short gasps and she held Rebecca tight around the shoulders. Then the clouds cleared away and the moon shone down and bathed the figure in cold white light.

Rebecca grabbed Martha's arm and held on as if fearing to be swept away by the sudden breeze, a breeze that became an icy wind tugging at their clothes, tangling their hair, chilling their flesh. And as her granddaughter clung to her, Martha filled her lungs and bellowed into the night, "Who are you? What do you want?"

It looked up, twenty yards away on the shore, and Martha gasped as Rebecca whimpered and huddled against her side. The eyes glowed green like some nocturnal animal. They could not see its body clearly, standing in deep shadows as clouds again streamed across the moon, but there was something familiar about it. One of its hands appeared to be holding a small object, and it was doing something to it. Martha tightened her arm around Rebecca.

"Come child," she whispered hoarsely. "Come back in-side." She tried to keep her voice calm, but knew it was quavering. They backed into the salon, and once inside Martha shoved the door with sudden strength and snapped the lock as it banged shut.

"See, Grandma?" Rebecca said, excitement in her voice. "See? Didn't I tell you so?"

Before she could answer, from the hallway came the sound of shrill crying as Stephen awoke, his distress filling the night, infant terror. A cloud covered the moon and for a moment they stood shrouded in darkness, listening, wait-ing. Then the cloud passed and they stared out into the night to where it had stood upon the shore. Nothing.

Martha backed to the couch and collapsed onto it, hand on her chest. Rebecca was still standing at the door, nose pressed against the glass.

"Becka!" Martha called. "Come away from there! And bring me a glass of water. Please."

Reluctantly Rebecca turned and wandered into the gal-ley, found the light switch and a glass, brought the water. As Martha sipped it, Rebecca asked, "Who was that out there, Grandma? Do you think Daddy will believe me now?"

Martha shook her head as her breathing began to slow.

"I don't know," she said. "I don't know who it was. But your daddy will believe you now, yes. Especially after I tell him." The hammering of her heart was easing and she passed her hand across her face, surprised at the terror the mysterious figure on the shore had inspired. Even now her hands were shaking. She looked at her granddaughter curi-ously. "Were you afraid?"

Rebecca looked down at the floor, crossed the pajama-booted toes of one foot over the other, hands clasped be-hind her back.

"Sort of," she said in a quiet little voice, "but not like before. Not like with . . . with Grandpa, and the night-mares." Then she looked up and thrust out her lower lip and her voice was steady as she said, "I don't want to be scared any more Grandma. I'm too big to be scared . . .

of monsters and nightmares and make-believe stuff any more. I don't like it. And you know what else? If I had a gun, when that man came up to my bed, I'd shoot him! I would!" And though she glared defiance and nodded, her lower lip trembled and Martha reached out her hand and drew Rebecca to her.

"I know you would child," she soothed as Rebecca choked back a sob. "I know you would. You're the bravest girl I know." She stroked the girl's hair. "It's true Becka. The bravest girl I ever met."

"Jesus." John shuffled into the salon rubbing his eyes, half-awake. "Sounds like Stephen's gonna have another one of his nights. What are you two doing up? Did he wake you too?"

Martha stared at her son, and Rebecca stared at her, waiting to see what she would say.

"No," Martha said. "Rebecca woke me because there was someone aboard the boat."

"What?" He paused, hand outstretched toward the refrigerator. "What are you talking about?" The sleepiness was gone from his voice. "Another nightmare?"

"No." Martha shook her head firmly. "No, John, I saw it too. Whoever it was, I saw plainly in the moonlight. On the shore."

John opened the refrigerator and reached inside, removed a beer, closed the door, and walked into the salon. He popped the can and set it on the table untasted, stood looking from his mother to his daughter and back again. As he opened his mouth to speak, the door to Norman and Judy's cabin opened and she stepped into the hallway with a squalling Stephen, saw them, and walked to the salon.

"Guess we woke up everyone huh?" she said in a tired voice. "Have you seen Norm?"

"He's not with you?" John asked.

"No. I got up to tend Stephen and he wasn't in bed."

"Well," John said with a satisfied smile easing himself into a chair. "That solves the problem. He must've stepped ashore, and spooked Mom and Becka when they saw him."

He lifted the beer and took a swallow.

"No," Martha said firmly. "Whoever we saw, it wasn't Norman."

And at that moment Norman stepped from the hallway into the salon. His face was blank and his eyes dull, but when John spoke to him he turned toward him and answered plainly.

"You been outside Norm?"

"No, I wasn't ashore," he said. "Why do you ask?"

"Mom and Becka thought they saw somebody. What were you doing?"

"Out on the stern for some fresh air. Until I heard Bruiser crying, that is."

They fell silent, John still staring at Norman, when Lucy appeared pulling a shawl around her shoulders.

"Christ Lucy!" John said, half-rising from the chair. "What happened to your hair?"

"What do you mean?" She raised a hand to her head and felt with her fingers, eyes widening. Spinning so her nightgown swirled around her bare legs, she ran to the head and screamed as she looked in the mirror. John hurried after her, returning several minutes later with his arm around her shoulders as she sobbed, head bent. Her beautiful, long blond hair had been crudely chopped off so it stuck out in ragged clumps from her head, only a few inches at the longest.

"What the hell is going on here?" John shouted angrily. "Just what in the hell is going on?"

"Somebody came into our bedroom and cut my hair!" Lucy wailed, looking up at the others with fear in her eyes. Stephen continued to bawl and Rebecca began to sob loudly.

"Everybody shut up." Martha spoke firmly, clearly, and coldly.

The effect could not have been more immediate if she had threatened them with an axe. All except Stephen ceased their crying, staring at her in surprise.

"Now!" she said. "I suggest you get on the radio and try to raise somebody, John. It's obvious we've got some nut

143

trying to frighten us and we need to get the sheriff, or the Coast Guard, or whoever is in charge around here, out to investigate."

"Yeah. Sure, I agree." John nodded his head firmly and stood, walked to the radio. "But I doubt it'll do any good; these marine transceivers are strictly line-of-sight. If we can't see them, we can't talk to them."

"Try anyway." She sat down with Rebecca, who gave her a look of admiration. Patting her granddaughter's hand she said, "Don't worry Becka, we'll get this straightened out. Whoever it is is going to be sorry they started it."

"They'll be sorry they messed with you, Grandma," she said.

"Darn right."

"Shit," John muttered after several minutes. "Nothing. Nobody around."

"Why?" Lucy moaned. "Why would anyone want to do this to me? My hair . . . that they could get so close − ." She buried her face in her hands and sobbed.

Stephen's crying was subsiding as he tired out, now a monotonous "unn-unn-unn" repeated with little enthusiasm. Judy went to the refrigerator and got a bottle which he eagerly grabbed and plugged into his mouth. In the ensuing silence she said, "Well, I think the two of us will try to get some sleep. Are all the doors locked?"

"They will be," John said. "And I'm going to sit up for a while; I've got a little folding .22 rifle on my boat. It's not much of a weapon, but a small bullet in the right place will drop an elephant. I haven't forgotten how to shoot. You go on to bed, and the rest of you too. Nobody else will be disturbed on this boat tonight, I promise."

Judy nodded, hesitating a moment before asking, "Norm, will you come with me?"

"Yeah." He shifted his fascinated gaze from Lucy's head. "I'm beat." He followed Judy to the cabin and closed the door. Martha's and Rebecca's voices murmured outside for a moment before the closing of a door silenced them. Judy tucked the blanket around the baby as he continued to suck at the bottle, eyes closed. Then she climbed into bed beside Norman and was instantly asleep.

In the salon John sat with his arm around his wife.

"I still can't understand it," she said. "That anybody could get so close to me without our knowing. I'm so scared John, and I don't know why. Why? Why is this happening?"

"Got to be some kind of crazy loose," he said, pulling her tighter against him. "When I go to bed I'll leave the rifle under the bed where you can drop your hand and grab it. Okay? God, I can't believe this shit!" He scowled and clenched his fist.

"We've never had even a hint of trouble before in all the years we've been coming down here. And now this. Norm and I could stand watches, but that brother of mine—." He shook his head. "I'm not sure about him all of a sudden. Half the time he's been acting like some kind of fucking zombie. I thought he would get better after we'd been out a few days, away from the hustle and bustle. But instead he seems to be getting worse. I'd like to think I could count on him. But I don't know."

"Ssshh," she said. "You'll wake the children." Then she paused and nodded. "You're right; he is acting strange. But you don't think that he . . . you know. I mean it's really odd about Becka. And now my hair."

"What?" He looked at her hard. "Oh, hell no! Norm's a little weird, but he'd never hurt a fly. If he tried anything with you, it'd be to hustle you into the sack."

She sniffed, looked up with a timid smile. "Think so?"

"Any man with the proper equipment would make a play for you," John said.

"Really?"

"I give you my word on it."

"Your word," she said sleepily. She yawned, covering her mouth with her fist. Her head became heavy against his shoulder and her breathing deepened. John reached his free hand and switched off the light, then sat with his arm around her and stared out into the night. After a time he yawned and moved his arm, letting her head settle into a more comfortable position.

145

"Well, guess I better get you to bed," he whispered, gazing at her peaceful face. He reached beneath her legs and lifted her easily as he stood, turning for a last look through the glass doors. There was nothing he could .see. Nothing ashore. Ashore.

His forehead furrowed in thought as he carried his wife to bed, but not until he had fetched the rifle and was almost asleep did his eyes suddenly widen as he muttered, "Norman said he wasn't ashore, but I asked him if he was outside, not if he was ashore. Didn't I?" He couldn't remember now, and it was late, and the boat was quiet. He closed his eyes. Tomorrow would be time enough to think about it.

Seven

"No," Lucy said firmly, "we're not going to ruin our vacation because some yahoo is playing sick jokes on us." She planted her fists on her hips and thrust out her jaw. It was morning now, the sun was shining, and the fear was gone from her eyes.

"I'm not saying we should abandon our vacation," John said. "Just that we should contact the sheriff or somebody and have them look into it. It would take a half a day, a day at the most."

"And what's the sheriff going to do about it? They won't find anything because there's nothing to find. My hair will grow back, we'll keep the boat locked at night, and we won't have any more problems." She patted her scarf-bound head and looked around at the others gathered in the salon.

"Don't be noble," Martha said. "This is no joking matter."

"She's right, this is nothing to make light of." Judy reached for Norman's hand. There were bags under her eyes and her hair was still mussed from what little sleep she had gotten. Norman regarded Lucy with half-lidded eyes, though his face was alert. His skin was darker than when the trip began, tan from his time in the desert. His eyes, too, appeared a shade darker, and somehow cold.

"While you argue what to do, I'm going for a walk," he said, then let himself out before anyone could comment. John's hand caught the door as Norman started to close it and he joined his brother on the foredeck.

"I'll go with you," he said.

"Fine." Norman hopped lightly to the beach and John landed beside him. He gave Norman a sharp look and said, "Have you lost some weight?"

"Don't know."

"Well, you look like you have. I wouldn't be surprised, little as you've been eating, and running around in the dirt out here like you've been doing."

"Yeah." Norman strode up the gradual incline of sandstone with John at his heels, then stopped so abruptly that his brother bumped into him.

"What the hell is that?" Norman asked.

John gasped and grabbed his arm. "Christ! That looks like . . . that's Lucy's hair!"

The two men stood looking down at a small figure fashioned of brown clay. It was human and crudely female, and thrust into its head and between its legs were long clumps of blond hair.

"Jesus Christ, Norm — ." John's face had gone completely absent of color as he stared at the thing near his feet. With a grimace he poised his heel to grind it into dust, but Norman's hand seized his shoulder in an iron grip that made him gasp.

"I wouldn't do that if I were you," Norman said in a chilling voice. John looked up in amazement and Norman returned his gaze from eyes emotionless as a snake's.

"Yeah," John said, lowering his foot with a look of frightened confusion. "Okay Norm, you're right. Yeah."

"Come on, Big Brother. I think we better get back to the boat."

"Yeah, you're right." He followed Norman back down the slope and they clambered aboard. Twenty minutes later the houseboat backed slowly away from the beach and turned down the lake, with John at the wheel. He had told nobody what he and Norman had found and he was still shaken by it. His shirt and trousers had reeked of fear-sweat when they had returned from the beach and he had changed into a bright red T-shirt and a baggy blue swimsuit. Lucy joined him now and laid her head against his shoulder.

"You okay, honey?" she asked.

"Sure. Yeah. Glad to be getting out of there."

"Me too," she said. He rubbed his cheek on the scarf binding her head. The silk felt pleasant, cool and slippery, and its reddish copper color against her golden skin was quite attractive. Much more so than her stubbled coiffure.

"How far are we from Wahweap, Daddy?" Rebecca asked from the couch. She was still in her pajamas, reading a book open on her lap.

"About sixty miles, honey. That's Hidden Passage Canyon we're passing on our right."

"I remember Hidden Passage," she said, "I remember the name anyway." After a pause, turning a page of her books she added, "It's a good name."

"It is, isn't it?" Lucy said. Judy entered the salon with Stephen and put him on the floor, sat beside him, and tried to interest him in a pink plastic rattle. He pulled himself upright on her arm and grabbed for her gold chain necklace, ignoring the rattle.

"Daddy, what are some of the other names?" Rebecca asked.

"Oh, there's a lot of them," he said. "How about Dangling Rope Canyon?" He consulted the map lying on the chart table. "Or Dungeon Canyon, or Last Chance Bay?"

"What was the canyon where you found the rattlesnake that time?" She crossed the salon to look at the map as he said, "Iceberg. You still remember that, do you?"

"Sure. I never saw one before. Hey, here's a funny one, 'Lab, labie, ri . . . enth.' "

"That's labyrinth," Lucy said, mussing her hair.

"What's a labyrinth, Mommy?"

"It's like a maze."

"Amaze? Like to surprise me?"

"No, honey. Like a . . . like a puzzle," Lucy said. "You know, one of those puzzles where you take a pencil and try to follow the trail in or out of a bunch of passages, and there's only one right path?"

"This whole lake is a labyrinth," John said, "and without the buoys and maps you'd be just as lost as a man in the wilderness."

"You could just ask another boat." Rebecca said.

149

"Touché," he laughed, "if there were other boats. But if there weren't, then you'd *really* be lost wouldn't you?"

"Yeah," she said doubtfully, "I guess so."

"You've never been really lost, otherwise you'd know what I'm talking about. It's one of the scariest feelings you can ever have."

"Nowww," Martha said, setting aside her knitting, "you stop that talk. There's been enough talk about scares and fears on this trip already."

"You're right, Mom. I'm sorry. Hey, tell you what, in an hour or so we'll be at Rainbow Bridge Canyon. We can take the speedboat to the bridge and hike around, give us a chance to stretch our legs while they refuel the houseboat at the marina. Lunch and ice cream bars are on me."

Norman snorted derisively, as if in reply to his brother's forced cheerfulness. He had been staring blankly at a sheet of computer coding for some time without making so much as a note. Now he tossed his papers in the briefcase and snapped it shut. "I'm going to take a nap," he said to Judy. "Wake me when we're there." Without waiting for an answer he stalked down the hall to their cabin and slammed the door.

Martha gave Judy an inquiring look, arched one eyebrow, but said nothing. Rebecca returned to the couch and picked up her book. Judy simply shrugged and plucked Stephen from the floor and kissed him on both fat cheeks.

The marina was deserted when they arrived except for a sullen-looking teenaged boy who helped John tie up.

"Fill the gas tanks, would you?" John said. "And you might check the propane too while you're at it."

The boy nodded without speaking and sauntered over to the fuel pump. John watched him drag the hose across the dock and plug the nozzle into the fuel fitting. As the pump began to whir he returned to the salon. Norman and Judy were arguing in the galley as Martha and Rebecca came down the hall with their outing bags.

"Let's get loaded into the speedboat," he said. Norman glanced at him angrily, then nodded and hoisted a cooler onto his shoulder. He stomped out through the front doors and along the side deck to the stern.

"What's the matter with him?" John asked.

"I don't know," Judy sighed, her face looking even wearier than it had in the morning. "Just woke up cross I guess."

John shrugged and helped carry her things to the speedboat while she slung Stephen on her hip. When they were all aboard, he started the engine and they made the five-minute trip to the Rainbow Bridge trailhead dock. There were no other boats and John tied up right at the walkway to shore.

The day was hot and still, with a fishy smell in the air from the thick accumulation of weeds and algae at the end of the canyon. Norman carried Stephen on his shoulders, a hand gripping each fat leg, his eyes on the ground as he followed the dusty trail toward the stone arch. When they came into its shadow he eased the baby down and cradled him in his arms.

"Three hundred nine feet," John said quietly as he pointed toward the top. "Two hundred seventy-eight feet." He spread his arms to point at the stone columns of the arch base. "Largest natural span of stone on earth." Norman grunted his acknowledgment.

"I'm going to climb to the top," John announced to the group.

"Can I come?" Rebecca asked.

"No!" Lucy said, tugging the scarf from her head. She ran her fingers through the stubble of her hair and her eyes were suddenly wide with fear. "And why do you want to climb up there John? We'll all have to sit here and wait."

"Won't take long," he said. "When I get up top, take a picture of me waving. You want to come Norm? Feeling brave today?"

"Sure." And even as he spoke Norman started off, leading the way.

"You be careful!" Judy called after him.

He lifted a hand in acknowledgment, didn't break his stride, and John was soon panting as he struggled to keep up.

"Hey Norm, what's the story? Are you taking up jogging?"

"Sure."

"One word vocabulary," John muttered. "Christ Almighty, you have lost weight Norm. Wait up." But Norman kept going as if he hadn't heard.

They couldn't climb the steep leg of the arch on their side of the creek, so it was necessary to cross and hike alongside a cliff for almost a mile. There, a fracture in the cliff and its resultant rubble field made a giant stair to the top, several hundred feet above the canyon floor.

Norman never paused, either during the hike along the cliff or the ascent up it. His movements were sure and steady as he climbed, and when he reached the top John was still a third of the distance below the summit. It was high and exposed where he stood, nothing but wind-scoured stone, wind that stirred his hair lightly, playfully.

"Come on," he murmured, staring down at his brother, who could never have heard so quiet a voice. Then he uttered another word that John would not recognize even had he heard it. The wind snatched at the sound and carried it away up the canyon. Norman turned and walked toward the arch. He didn't look down until he stood at the highest point of its span.

Far below, the women and children looked up, tiny bright specks of color against the desert landscape. He stood easily, hands on hips, breathing deeply of the warm air. Air that smelled faintly of a foundry, the smelting of metals, sun so bright it could blister a lizard. He turned his head at the scrape of movement and saw his brother approaching.

John moved carefully, hands held out from his body for balance, though the stone bridge was wide enough to drive a car across, wide enough for five men to walk abreast. He stopped beside Norman and grinned, but his face was beaded with sweat and his eyes nervous.

"Wow," he said. "What a view!"

"Sure is," Norman agreed. He glanced at his brother from the corners of his eyes, eyes that glittered as he

152

smiled a thin smile.

"Christ, they're small as ants," John said as he spotted his family. He held both arms over his head and waved them slowly. "Hope they remember to take the picture."

Norman was waving now, too, but facing the opposite direction. Head thrown back, eyes closed, his lips moved silently as he spiraled his hands in the air. A breeze caressed his face, plucked at his wet shirt, and the hidden teeth of his necklace moved against his chest, clicking and chittering, nibbling his flesh. High overhead a black speck appeared in the sky, growing slowly as he lowered his arms. He moved several steps away from his brother, crossed his arms, and watched John waving at the others on the canyon floor.

John never saw the bird as it came out of the sun at his back. It was a big raven, a male, well over two pounds and diving with wings folded as it whistled through the air, a black feathered missile, its target the back of his head. John lowered his hands and was turning toward his brother when it struck.

With a look of surprise he pitched forward, twisting as he fell so that he landed face first against the slope of stone and scrabbled with arms and legs as he slid down its smooth surface until it curved away from beneath him and then there was only air for his limbs to claw and kick against as he fell screaming, screaming, falling a long time before he hit the rocks below.

Lucy saw the figure plummeting through the air, bright red shirt unmistakable in the sun, and her camera clattered to the stone at her feet. Its back sprang open, vomiting film across the ground as she echoed her husband's scream, shrill and maniacal. Her fingers gouged clawmarks in her face as she shook her head and screamed and screamed. Then she began to run toward where the body had disappeared, shouting his name at the top of her lungs.

Rebecca tried to follow, bawling, tears streaming down her face, but Martha caught her in her arms and hugged her to her bosom as she, too, sobbed and stared at the

153

remaining figure atop the stone arch. Judy swayed, clutching the baby in her arms, and Martha looked at her pale face and yelled, "Sit down!"

Judy obeyed without question, and a moment later toppled to her side unconscious as the baby spilled from her arms and added his cry to the others. Martha urged Rebecca toward the mother and child and pulled her down to her lap, scooped up the baby with one arm as she held Rebecca with the other. Crooning softly to the children, she closed her eyes until her breathing slowed and her heartbeat steadied. When she opened her eyes again, Norman was no longer visible atop the arch.

Martha waited, holding the children, speaking quietly to them as their crying became whimpers. After a time Judy roused and sat up, then turned away and was sick. When she regained control of herself she crawled over beside Martha and took Stephen into her arms. The four of them were huddled together when Norman ran up the slope and slid to a halt in front of them.

"Oh Norm!" Judy cried. She struggled to her feet and reached out a hand and he enfolded her and the baby in his arms. His face was dusty and streaked with tears or sweat, and his chest heaved as he tried to catch his breath.

"I . . . I don't know what happened," he gasped. "We were just standing there, and then this bird, this God damned bird—." He burst into sobs and buried his head against his wife as Martha stared up at them from the ground. Rebecca had not yet opened her eyes, merely sat leaning against Martha saying quietly, from time to time, "Daddy, I want Daddy."

Norman's tears didn't last long, and with a sidelong glance at Martha he gripped Judy's shoulders and said, "We've got to get you and Martha, and the kids, back to the boat. Then I'll go find Luce . . . Lucy, and . . . and John."

Judy nodded without speaking, and Norman reached a hand to help Martha but she ignored it and stood, drawing Rebecca with her. With Norman in the lead they retraced their path to the boat and climbed in.

"I'll be back," Norman said. Judy again nodded, but Martha and Rebecca seemed not to hear. Stephen appeared to be sleeping.

Norman jogged easily back up the trail. A smile played at the corners of his mouth and his hands hung limply at the ends of his arms and he ran with a curious, bowlegged gait. He ran directly to where he had seen John fall as he watched from above.

The body was lying on its back, jackknifed over a boulder, pelvis thrust unnaturally and obscenely toward the heavens. Lucy was seated beside it hugging herself and moaning, eyes closed, and gave no notice as Norman approached.

"Lucy," he said quietly, squatting beside her. She moaned louder and buried her chin against her chest. He reached out and gently shook her shoulder and her eyes flew open as her hand lashed out, narrowly missing his face with its curved nails as he dodged the blow.

"Don't you touch me!" she hissed. Her face was distorted with rage, mottled and quivering. Spittle trickled from a corner of her mouth. "Don't touch me you monster!"

"Lucy. Luce, it's me, Norman."

"I don't know you," she said in a high, thin voice. "I don't know who you are but you aren't Norman Sanders. Norman Sanders is pale and fat and timid as a mouse and you . . . you . . . you stay away from me!" She crouched protectively above the broken, bloody thing that had been her husband and her eyes burned with a wild, dangerous light. Norman's eyes shifted slyly and his tongue flicked across his lips.

"I guess you think I'm trying to fool you," he said quietly. "But it's not me, it's that other guy next to you." He jerked his chin and directed his gaze to her right. She automatically glanced in the same direction and he cracked her on the jaw with a bony fist. She swayed for an instant as her eyes rolled upward in their sockets, then she collapsed unconscious across John's corpse.

Norman lifted her with a grunt and slung her over his shoulder. He staggered the first few steps, but when he reached the path he was able to trot slowly back to the dock.

"Mommy, Mommy!" Rebecca cried as Norman carried Lucy's limp body to the boat.

"What happened?" Martha barked. "Is she all right?"

"She was hysterical. I had to slug her." Norman slipped her gently off his shoulder into the passenger seat, then cast off the lines and started the engine. Martha held Rebecca and stared at her son with confusion.

"What about John? What are—," Judy started to ask, but he interrupted her sharply.

"He's not going anywhere." He shoved the throttle forward and roared down the canyon. "I'll have to get help to haul him out of there," he called over his shoulder, sitting atop the seat back. Martha and Judy both stared at his back with shock as the meaning of what he was saying sunk in. Lucy was beginning to moan and roll her head as they arrived at the marina, and Norman carried her aboard the houseboat, herding the others before him. The teenager shuffled from the snack shack and watched with a crooked grin on his pimply face.

"You owe ninety-six dollars and fifty cents," he said as Norman came back out on deck.

"Do you have a telephone here?" Martha asked.

"Nawww. Shoot, lady, where do you think you are? Salt Lake City?"

"There was an accident," she said, her voice thickening as she fought back a sob. "My son . . . we left him up the canyon. Beneath the bridge."

"You mean he's dead?" The boy's mouth hung open, a look of joyful awe on his face. "Gawd damn! What happen? He fall off from up top?" His eyes sparkled with fascination.

"Don't you have some way to contact somebody?" Martha shouted angrily.

The boy recoiled from her rage, but the excitement still smoldered in his eyes as he said, "Nawww. Ain't no way unless somebody shows up with one of them long-distance radios. Otherwise, I'm here till the boss picks me up at eight tonight." Then he brightened and looked up. "Want me to help you drag him down here Mister?"

"You're no help to anyone!" Martha shouted.

"She's right," Norman said quietly. "Wait on the boat while I pay the boy, Mom."

He walked toward the boy, whose eyes widened as he backed toward the shack. The doorway was hidden from the houseboat on the opposite side of the dock and as Norman and the teenager disappeared behind it, Norman grinned and pulled the fillet knife hidden inside his shirt, the knife he had taken from John's tackle box.

"Aw shit!" The boy moved surprisingly quickly and dashed into the shack like a mouse down a hole. Norman slammed into the door with a furious strength that made the whole corrugated steel building resonate, but the door was locked tight. For several long heartbeats he stood absolutely motionless, head tipped to one side as he gazed at the door. Then he slipped the blade back into his shirt and strode to the houseboat.

Martha, Rebecca, Judy, and the baby were in Lucy's cabin as Martha pressed a wet washcloth to Lucy's forehead. Norman walked through to the helm and started the outboards and cast off the lines. By the time the women appeared in the salon, the houseboat was out on the main lake.

Rebecca and Lucy went immediately to the couch and huddled together. Lucy's face was pale, and her eyes, which darted back and forth like those of a cornered animal, were sunk deeply in their sockets. She drew her knees up under her chin and wrapped her arms around them as her daughter leaned against her, staring at Norman.

"Where are we going?" Martha asked. Norman turned from the helm and she flinched at the intensity of his dark gaze.

"Wahweap," he said. "We're headed into bitter water." He stared at her and laughed, the sound low and ugly. She put her hand to her mouth and stumbled backward into the couch, sat heavily, put her arm around Judy, who was cradling Stephen as he sucked on a bottle.

"Norman?" Judy said. He didn't reply, staring straight ahead, hands on the wheel. The outboards were barely idling as the houseboat drifted down the main channel.

"Norm?" Still he gave no sign that he heard her. She paled and exchanged a look with Martha. But Martha shook her head and there was fear in her eyes as she gripped her daughter-in-law's hand with both of her own.

"Why don't you give me a hand with Luce," Martha said, looking Judy in the eye. "I think we should get her to take some rest, don't you?"

"Yes, that sounds like a good idea," Judy said woodenly.

"Come on Lucy, come on Rebecca." Martha stood and grasped Lucy's hands, pried them loose from her legs, drew her to her feet. Lucy allowed herself to be led to the cabin but gave no sign of recognizing her surroundings. When they were all inside, Martha closed the door and eased Lucy down on the bed.

"Mommy, wake up, Mommy," Rebecca cried wearily as she clung to her. Martha beckoned Judy into the head, closed the door and spoke in a whisper.

"Judy, dear, I'm afraid that Norman may have been . . . pushed too far by witnessing his brother's death."

Judy nodded her agreement, holding her baby and looking small and lost. Martha drew a deep breath and placed her hands on the younger woman's shoulders.

"Now, dear, you're going to have to be strong, all right?"

Again Judy nodded, though there was uncertainty in her eyes.

"We need to get off this boat. And that means getting everyone into the speedboat without Norman finding out. We'll have to be very quiet, understand?"

"Yes." Judy felt the baby's diaper. "I better change him first; the diapers are across the hall in our cabin."

Martha started to shake her head no, then sighed and said, "Okay, I'll get them. You stay here with Lucy and Becka." Judy nodded and Martha went to the door, turned the knob gently, and pulled. It wouldn't open. She tugged and it budged, ever so slightly, but that was all.

"Norman," she said softly.

Out in the hall Norman smiled, crouched beside the door. A paddle spanned the door opening and was lashed to the knob with many turns of monofilament fishing line.

"I hear you, Mother," he said.

"What are you doing Norman?"

"Keeping you safe, Mother."

"Safe from what Norman?"

"Keeping the women safe, until tonight."

"Then what Norman?" Her voice had begun to quaver. The answer from the other side was unintelligible, a series of harsh consonants and clicks, then mirthless laughter. She turned her back to the door and leaned against it, slowly slid down until she was sitting on the floor. Judy looked at her hopelessly, and the baby began to cry, and there was nothing she could do.

Several hours later, Martha laid her hand on Lucy's brow and frowned.

"How are you feeling, dear?" she asked.

"Tired," Lucy said. "Headache and kind of . . . fuzzy."

"Bring us some more aspirin, would you Becka? Careful not to wake Stevie." Martha patted the girl on the arm and she hurried to comply.

"These'll make you feel better, Mommy," she said as she handed her the tablets. Lucy smiled and held Rebecca's hand for a moment before swallowing the aspirin.

"I think I feel better already," she murmured as she lay back on the bed.

"Good, you just rest a bit now." Martha stood and tossed a blanket over her. She pursed her lips in thought, then switched on the table lamp at its lowest setting.

"Goodness, is it evening already?" Judy blinked her eyes as she awoke in the chair beside the dresser. "I must have nodded off."

"You've been sleeping for almost an hour, dear," Martha said.

"Stephen—" She came out of the chair but Martha held up a hand and said, "Becka and I made him a bed in the

159

bathtub. He's been asleep almost as long as you."

"Oh, thank you, both of you."

"It's all right Aunt Judy." Becka touched her shoulder hesitantly. "We won't let anything happen to you or Stevie. Or Mommy. Will we, Grandma?"

"No, of course not, dear."

"Have you heard from Norm?" Judy asked.

"No, not since—" Martha started to say, but Lucy interrupted her in a cold, sepulchral voice.

"Norman's gone."

"What?" Judy looked at her in confusion.

"I don't know who it is but it's not Norman." Lucy's eyes stared blankly at the ceiling.

"What are you talking about?" Judy said. "You're scaring me."

"I . . . I'm sorry." Lucy looked at her sister-in-law and awareness returned to her face. "I don't know. My mind . . . I'm not thinking straight. Sorry."

"It's all right, Lucy." Judy went to the bed and seated herself lightly on the edge, took her hand. "We'll be out of this soon," she said.

"Sure." Lucy closed her eyes and drew a deep breath, let it out with a shudder.

"Well, I can still hear the motors running," Martha said. "So I guess we're headed somewhere."

"This is crazy!" Judy said in a voice suddenly angry. "If Norm's flipped out, let's smash the damned window and make a run for the speedboat."

"We already talked about that, remember?" Martha shook her head slowly. "If he has gone off the deep end, and we're agreed that he has, he'd hear the glass breaking and who knows what he might do? No, it's too dangerous for the children."

"I'm not afraid," Rebecca said, thrusting out her lower lip.

"I know you're not, honey," Martha said with a proud smile. "It's Stevie I'm worried about."

"Oh. Yeah, he's pretty little."

"Well then what are we—" Judy began and Martha

hissed, "Ssssh!"

"What is it?" Judy asked.

"The motors have stopped!" Martha said. An instant later a loud boom filled the room as the hulls struck shore and the houseboat lurched to a halt. They waited motionless in the ensuing silence, straining to hear. From the head came a cooing sound and Judy climbed to her feet. By the time she reached the baby he was making little hiccups of crying, and by the time she returned with him he was wailing at the top of his lungs.

"He's hungry," Judy said in a frightened voice. "Oh my God, what am I going to do?"

She didn't have to wait for an answer as the door burst open and Rebecca shrieked. Norman stood in the doorway, naked but for a pair of underpants. He was shadowy, indistinct in the dim lamplight that barely reached beyond the bed where the women were huddled. Judy called out, "Norman?"

"Norman's gone," he said, imitating Lucy's deep voice. Then he gave a burst of ugly laughter and said something unintelligible. The women pressed closer together as Martha drew Rebecca between her and Judy, who clutched the wailing baby to her breast.

He sprang to the center of the room and landed in a crouch with the fillet knife extended toward them, eyes glittering. The tip of the blade glistened darkly red and three fresh cuts bled on each side of his face, sliced precisely from the cheekbones just below the eyes, angling down and in to the corners of the mouth, giving his face the whiskered, predatory appearance of a cat.

His tongue oozed out between his lips and licked a drip of blood. Lucy moaned and he opened his other hand to reveal the crude clay doll. Slowly, his gaze fixed on the terrified women, he brought doll and blade together. Lucy shrieked and clutched at her stomach.

Before Martha could stop her, Rebecca burst free of her grasp and ran at him yelling, "You leave my mommy alone!"

He swung the knife hand backward in a lazy gesture

that caught her on the side of the head with his knuckles and she stumbled past to collapse limply in the doorway.

"She's a brave one," he said with a chuckle. "Who's next?" He touched the blade to the doll again and Lucy screamed, high and shrill, as the baby wailed and Martha began to sob.

"Norman!" Judy shouted. "For God's sake Norman stop! What are you doing?"

In answer he tipped back his head and howled like an animal as he brought the doll and blade together. The clay crumbled in his hand and fell to the carpet. Lucy reared up from the bed with a gurgling cry, her body arched in agony. Slowly, slowly, eyes already glazing, she fell back onto the bed and her breathing stopped.

"Noooo!" Judy screamed and ran toward the door, bent protectively over the baby. He grabbed her as she tried to run past, and as she screamed frantically and hurled herself against his grasp, Martha stumbled toward Rebecca with tears streaming down her cheeks. His back was turned and she dragged the unconscious girl out into the hall with a strength born of desperation.

"Come on!" she gasped. She pulled Rebecca's arm around her shoulders and staggered toward the stern. The speedboat had drifted so its bow was against the houseboat and Martha draped Rebecca against the railing as she clambered over. Rebecca began to regain consciousness, but was still groggy as Martha hauled her over the railing. She lost her footing and they both tumbled into the bow of the speedboat, with Rebecca landing on top of her.

Martha dragged herself from under her granddaughter and scrambled behind the wheel, eyes wide with panic as she looked at the unfamiliar controls. The key was obvious enough and she grabbed it and turned. The engine caught and sputtered after a few seconds of grinding, then died.

"Please God," Martha whispered. "Oh please God, help me."

"Give it some throttle," Rebecca said quite clearly from where she lay in the bow. "That lever on your right."

Martha nodded and turned the key again, shoved the

lever forward. Immediately the engine roared and the boat leaped forward to the limit of its towline which snapped it around, throwing Martha across the cockpit and Rebecca against the hull.

Martha looked up in a daze and saw him appear on the stern, shadowy and terrible in the dusk. The bow of the speedboat was against the shore, engine straining as it tried to climb the beach and fight the restraint of the towline at the same time.

"The line!" Martha yelled as she crawled back into the driver's seat. Already he had leaped the railing and was splashing toward them and she jerked the lever into reverse. The boat roared backward and a wave came over its stern and spilled across the upholstery until once again the towline stopped it and it zigged and zagged against the restraint.

He was up to his waist when he began to swim and Martha yelled again, "The line! Becka untie the line!"

"I'm trying!" she cried. "It's too tight, Grandma! I can't!" Then she screamed as a hand came over the bow and his face appeared. Martha shoved the lever forward and the hand and face disappeared as something bumped beneath the hull. She dragged the lever back to its stop and the engine roared. The boat sped backward and hit the end of the line, hung suspended for the barest instant, then the cleat pulled free of the bow and a big wave came over the stern, almost swamping them.

Martha pushed the lever forward again and turned the wheel, pointing the boat out across the dark water of the lake. Rebecca made her way to the passenger seat, saw the water in the boat, and pointed at a switch on the instrument panel.

"You better turn on the pump, Grandma."

Martha flipped the switch, then glanced over her shoulder toward the houseboat. Already it was a mere outline against the darker shore, dwindling, soon to be lost in the night.

"Mommy," Rebecca cried softly. She crawled into Martha's lap and sobbed, and Martha's tears fell on her fine blond hair as she stroked the girls head, unable to speak for the tightness in her own throat. Slowly the stern of the boat rose as the pump evacuated the water, and when its whine indicated the bilge was clear, Rebecca reached out and turned it off.

"Where are we going, Grandma?" she asked. She sniffled and wiped her nose on her sleeve.

"I wish I knew. Is there a map on this boat?"

"I don't think so."

"Look and see, would you dear? Here, I think there's a flashlight somewhere." She rummaged in the pocket next to her seat, found it, and handed it to Rebecca. Rebecca searched the glovebox and shook her head, then started looking in the various storage compartments as Martha strained to see what might lie ahead. She turned on the running lights, then the spotlight, but it only illuminated the path directly before them without giving a clue to their general surroundings. After a time she switched it off and found she could see better without it.

"Grandma!" Rebecca shouted. "I found it! I found a map!" She hurried forward clutching a damp chart in one hand and the flashlight in the other, momentarily blinding her grandmother.

"Here, spread it out here," Martha said. They unfolded it across her lap and some of the strain left her voice as she said, "Good, Becka, very good. Now all we have to do is find a buoy to tell us where we are."

"Then we won't be lost, will we, Grandma? In the labyrinth."

"No dear." She pulled Rebecca's head against her bosom as her vision clouded once again with tears. "No, we won't be lost in the labyrinth now." And she prayed, so quietly that Rebecca didn't hear, "Please God, help Judy and her baby. Free them from the labyrinth too, make them safe. Sweet Lord Jesus, help us all."

But on the houseboat Judy was not free, and the baby was not free as she cowered in the salon holding him while he kicked and squalled. And the man who had once been Norman raged through the houseboat, howling and leaping, terrifying the woman who had been Norman's wife and the baby who had been Norman's son.

Then a silence settled over the houseboat and Judy crept into the galley and prepared a bottle for the baby with trembling hands, spilling half of the milk on the floor, and returned to the couch with it. But the baby wouldn't drink and thrust the bottle away with its tiny hands as it bawled and bawled. She cried soundlessly and the bottle fell from her hand and rolled across the cushions. She reached for it, and looked up and saw him, and her mouth opened in a scream that wouldn't come.

His face and chest were smeared darkly red and an acrid, metallic smell filled the room. The baby's cries became even more shrill and piercing and the man's head snapped around with a quick, jerky motion like a lizard. Or a snake.

Judy held the baby against her and shook her head back and forth as he approached. But he didn't touch her, merely gestured with his big limp hands, and she stood and preceded him onto the foredeck. Again he gestured and she climbed, with difficulty, the ladder to the roof as he followed close behind. He pointed at the sun lounge and she sat.

Now he began to stamp his feet, slowly, staring at her, then turned his back and stamped faster as a resonant grunting came from his throat. The big hands ascended slowly upward and he stamped in a circle, turning and turning, weaving an intricate pattern as the hands floated higher and higher, until he was staring up toward the stars with fingers fluttering and the sound mounted to a shrill and dissonant ululation.

The stars wavered. The sky was clear and the moon was not yet up and the stars shimmered as if seen by reflection on the water. The stars flickered and an instant later the wind struck. He flung his hands toward the stars and shrieked and the wind came down, down out of the clear sky. He shrieked again and the wind answered in kind, pouring over him, dropping out of the heavens, pounding the waves flat around the houseboat in a widening circle of

165

white froth.

He flung his arms toward the west and shrieked, and now the wind turned and poured its torrent across the waters. Again and again he repeated the ritual, and with each gesture the wind mounted in intensity until Judy was forced to turn her back against its fury and shield the baby with her body. The houseboat moved, grating on the beach, bobbed as it came free and the wind began to blow it across the water.

Still he shrieked and whipped his arms and the wind began to moan and the waves to build until their tops foamed and turned to spray, spray that reached the roof and soaked Judy where she crouched, whimpering. The baby's screams were carried away by the wind and she was shivering, incapable of movement against its force, leaning into it with her feet firmly planted to keep from being swept away, eyes squeezed shut, and so she never saw the hands that lifted her and pushed.

And the wind snatched her up, as she still clutched her child with all her remaining strength. The wind took them and carried them out across the lake carried them out and out before at last dropping them down, down into the eternal embrace of the cold midnight waters.

The wind piled great waves over the place where woman and child vanished. It whipped the lake into a frenzy and the figure atop the houseboat howled and the wind echoed the cry and turned its fury across the water, seeking and slashing the surface, seeking a solitary boat in the night.

The wind had not yet reached them when Rebecca sighted the buoy and called out, "There Grandma! I see one!"

Martha shifted to neutral and switched on the spotlight. "Fifty-one!" Rebecca cried as she read the number. "That means fifty-one miles, Grandma!"

"Quick now, hold the flashlight for me." Martha found the number on the chart. "We're on the main lake near Twilight Canyon." Then the chart was snatched from her hands by a gust that struck with no warning. The blow was like a huge hand pressing down on them and suddenly the boat was moving sideways through the water.

"Sit down!" she yelled at Rebecca. As the girl crouched on the floor, Martha crawled to the stern and got two life jackets. Even while they struggled into them, waves were appearing and the boat was beginning to rock, broadside to the swells. Martha slid behind the wheel and shifted the engine into forward, brought the bow into the wind.

The boat steadied, then began to pound as the waves continued to increase in size. Though they were barely making headway, just enough to maintain steering, the stinging spray made it difficult to see. The bow rose with a wave and slammed down, then another, another, and water was breaking over the boat now because it had not been designed for seaworthiness.

Martha gasped as the cold water struck her, blinking spray from her eyes. She didn't know what else to do so she pushed the throttle forward. The boat lunged forward, climbed atop the waves and smashed its way across the surface, each wave pummeling it like a fist. It was a jarring and dangerous ride with the wind getting beneath the hull and trying to flip it, and the waves bashing against it.

Martha wiped her face with the back of her hand and blinked, saw the rugged black silhouette of rocks, turned the wheel recklessly toward them. The boat almost broached as it quartered the waves. It breasted one, two, two more, then struck with a shuddering crunch and flipped.

Martha went down, down into the cold dark water, unable to tell which way was up. Then her feet touched bottom. She pushed off with all her strength and a moment later her head broke the surface as she gasped for air.

"Rebecca!" she yelled. A wave swept over her but the life jacket kept her from going under a second time. "Rebecca!"

"Grandma!" She turned in the direction of the sound and paddled frantically, felt her hand strike something soft and she grabbed Rebecca's jacket.

"Hold onto me Becka!" she shouted. "Hold tight!" The girl's arms went around her neck, and as the next wave broke over them and they descended into its trough, she pushed off against the soft mud of the lake bed, pushed toward the sound of breaking waves and stroked as she had learned long ago on the girl's swim team in college.

When they reached shore she was almost knocked unconscious by the wave that pummeled them against the smooth sandstone. But Rebecca, arms still around her neck, tugged and shouted so that she crawled groggily up, out of reach of the pounding water. And after a time she stood, shaking, took Rebecca's hand and sought shelter from the wind.

It was nothing more than a pocket in the stone. They could find nothing better because they were in a cove from which there was no escape. The cliff rose precipitously behind them and its arms curved out into the thrashing lake. There was no beach, just a smooth slide down into the waves, and the trunk of a tree that bobbed slowly in the water like the severed limb of a giant, trapped with them in the cove.

The hollow was barely large enough for the two of them to huddle together, and offered little protection. The wind was blowing cold and they were both shivering. Rebecca's teeth chattered. Martha clasped her hands and prayed, stuttering as chills shook her.

"Dear G-G-God, please w-wa-watch over us."

Rebecca was crying weakly, her arms around Martha's waist and her head buried against her bosom. But when her grandmother began to pray, she sat up and reached into her pocket and pulled out a small compass.

"Where d-d-did you get that?" Martha asked.

"It was with the map," she answered in a small voice. Still holding the compass, she tugged at the string around her neck and pulled the soggy bundle out from under her sweatshirt.

"What is that?" Martha asked, coughing.

"Uncle Joe's medicine." Rebecca leaned over the compass, squinting to see the little blue needle. She turned her hand until it hovered over N. Then she faced east and held the bundle up and scrunched her eyes tightly shut as her

168

lips moved soundlessly.

Martha watched without comment, her eyes opening and closing, opening and closing, head nodding toward her breast. After a time Rebecca pressed against her and they waited, shivering, lost in the labyrinth.

Eight

Anna had just stepped from the shower when Joe came through the front door, and she greeted him in her robe, still toweling her hair dry.

"Hi!" she said. "How was your day?"

"Not too bad." He removed his jean jacket and hung it on the hook beside the door. "Harold and I interviewed a mechanic from Salt Lake today. He is young, but he seems to know his way around a shop. We decided to hire him."

"Good for you!" She smiled happily. "That should be one less problem for you to worry about."

Joe smiled faintly and shrugged. "Ask me after he has been on the job for a few weeks."

"Oh, don't be such a pessimistic old man."

"Pragmatic middle-age man. Did you attend that lecture today?"

"Yes." She frowned and slipped into the bathroom to hang up her towel, returned with a brush, and seated herself on the couch. Joe went to the kitchen and poured himself a cup of coffee as she brushed her long, lustrous hair.

"So," he said, blowing on the hot liquid. "What did the professor have to say for himself?"

"Well," she paused, seemed hesitant. "He says the newspapers and television blew the story all out of proportion. Like they always do. He said there was only one person involved in the cannibalism, and probably out of dire necessity. Starvation, in other words. But Joe, he said there was something strange about the tooth marks; they weren't normal. Pointed, as if the teeth had been filed." She shook her head and gazed at him with a thoughtful expression.

"And the bones were crushed with a force most human jaws couldn't generate. Whoever, whatever was doing it, it had the jaw muscles of a wolf." She cocked an eyebrow at him. "The professor had two theories about why the cannibalism occurred, but starvation seemed to be the one that made the most sense."

The door burst open and Lance rushed in, hurrying as usual, bright eyed and already talking as he tossed his jacket aside.

"Hey Mom! Hi Dad! I finished painting the inside of the office today, and cleaned the brushes and left them on the workbench in the maintenance building. And listen, I've got a date tonight with Chris and wondered if I could use the Whaler. Looks calm enough. We thought we'd try to make the cruise down to Sunlight I've been promising her. What do you think?"

Joe, standing in the doorway between the kitchen and living room, exchanged a glance with Anna, who gave him a wry smile.

"Sure," he said. "Why not."

"Thanks, Dad! Mom, we'll have dinner at the restaurant so I hope you didn't fix too much. I've just got time to shower and change my clothes; she's expecting me in half an hour."

He disappeared into his room, and Anna stared after him with a mixture of amusement and irritation.

"I don't know why he couldn't have told me earlier," she said.

"Young men are always in a hurry," Joe said.

"I suppose." She arose from the couch and put her brush away, tugged the robe tighter, walked to the kitchen and pecked him on the cheek as she passed. "I hope he's got enough sense not to get Chris . . . not to get them both into trouble." She carried a chicken from the refrigerator to the counter and expertly dismembered it with a carving knife.

"She is on the pill," Joe said.

"What?" She turned to him with a look of surprise, knife suspended in midair. "How do you know that?"

"Lance told me."

"Oh." The knife descended and removed a thigh. "Well. It's good he can talk to his father. So. Now I don't have to worry about my son, and my husband's found a mechanic, and since your trip down the lake I don't have to worry about the Sanders. What am I going to do with my time now that every-

171

thing's taken care of? Here." She thrust a plate piled with raw chicken at him. "Your turn to cook. I already lit the grill."

He took the plate and turned toward the door. As he opened it he paused and said, "What was the other theory?"

"Mm?"

"You said the professor had two theories."

"Oh, yes. The cannibal might have been practicing homeopathic magic. Eating his victims to gain their virtues, like the Aztecs eating the hearts of their bravest enemies." She raised her eyes to his.

Joe's face looked like he had been struck, but he met her gaze and said calmly, "Really?" He stepped outside and pulled the door closed behind him. A few minutes later he stood in the smoke of the sizzling grill as Lance left the trailer and pounded down the steps, skidding to a halt in the gravel.

"Hey, Dad, thanks again. I should be home by eleven or so."

Joe stared past his son toward the lake with a troubled expression and nodded.

"What's wrong Dad?" Lance threw a leg across his motorbike and kicked it to life.

"Nothing." He forced a smile. "Have a good time."

Joe raised a hand as Lance disappeared down the road astride his bright, pollen yellow motorbike with its little motor straining at full throttle. The evening was calm, with a touch of chill in the air, not unusual for the end of October. Far out across the Kaiparowits Plateau a thin band of black divided gray earth and dark orange sunset sky. There was always the possibility of a squall sweeping down on the lake this time of year, but Lance was at home on the water, and the Whaler was practically bulletproof. He shrugged and forked the chicken off the grill and carried it inside.

Several hours later Anna muttered irritably as Joe tossed in his sleep and dragged the blankets off her. She grabbed and tugged until she was covered, but a moment later he rolled the other way and elbowed her in the back.

"Joe!" She pushed him and he snorted, opened his eyes.

"Joe, why are you so restless?"

"Sorry Anna," he sighed. "Bad dream I guess."

"Well, if you can't calm down, one of us is going to have to sleep on the couch."

"Sorry." He rolled over and pulled the covers under his chin. Then the wind began to blow. He listened for a minute, waiting for it to die down. When it didn't he sat up and swung his legs from beneath the blanket, walked to the window, and looked out. The sky was cloudless. Anna watched him, head resting on her arm.

"West Wind," he said in Navajo.

"Lance?"

"He can handle it." Joe returned to bed but did not sleep, lay with his hands behind his head staring at the ceiling. The wind continued to gather strength and one of the big, metal trash bins outside in the RV park blew over with a loud crash. Joe got up and walked into the living room, where he switched on the radio scanner and keyed in the frequency of the NOAA weather station. As he listened to the broadcast, Anna came in tugging her robe around her and sat on the couch beside him.

" — a high wind warning in effect immediately from southwestern Utah west through Nevada and into California, including the Lake Mead and Glen Canyon recreation areas. Winds in excess of one hundred miles per hour have been reported, and drivers of high-profile vehicles should be aware that an extreme hazard exists below canyons and along interstate Highways 40 and 15 across the southern portions of the states. Boaters are warned that dangerous localized conditions may exist and are urged to take appropriate precautions. Current temperatures being reported are —"

"I don't like the sound of that," Anna said above the placid voice of the NOAA broadcast. Joe switched the radio off and put his hand on her arm.

"No need to worry about Lance; he has a good, seaworthy boat, and there are more places to hide from the weather on the lake than a bird has feathers. He is as competent as I am."

"I'd worry about you, too," she said.

The telephone rang and Anna sprang from the couch to answer it.

"Hello? Oh, Nathan." She stiffened. "This isn't about Lance is it? What? No, he's out on the lake. Yes, I'm sure he will be too. Okay, just a minute." She held the receiver out to Joe. "He

173

wants to talk to you."

"Hi Nathan," he said as he pressed it to his ear. "What can I do for you?"

"Joe, I just got word of a problem that might concern you." The sheriff sounded worried and Joe frowned.

"Yes?" he said.

"I got the story in a roundabout way. Seems there was some trouble at the Rainbow Bridge marina today, but you know they've got no way to contact anybody there. So we didn't hear about it until this evening, after the manager picked up his employee. Then he called the state police, and eventually they called me."

"So?"

"Joe, the folks on this houseboat, well, apparently one of the party fell from the bridge."

"Oh no."

"Yeah. They'd left their houseboat at the marina for refueling, and when they returned for it, one of the fellas chased the marina employee into the shack with a knife. They left without paying."

"Who was aboard?" Joe asked in a flat voice.

"The kid said it was two men, three women, a little girl and a baby that went out. One of the men didn't come back."

Joe stared unseeing toward Anna, telephone clutched in his fist, a look of shock on his face.

"Joe? You there?"

"Yes."

"What is it Joe?" Anna asked. He shook his head slowly and said, "I think the Sanders are in trouble."

"You know them Joe?" the voice said on the phone.

"Yes. Have you checked the other marinas Nathan?"

"Yeah, I have Joe. Nobody's seen them."

"Okay." The wind buffeted the trailer as Joe closed his eyes in thought. "Nathan, Anna told you my boy is out on the lake in the Whaler. As hard as it is blowing, he probably holed up somewhere. I will have to use Harold's Bertram. Think you can put any other boats on the water?"

"I don't know Joe. In the morning, yeah. But it's blowing like hell over here in Mexican Hat, so I can imagine what it's doing down on the lake. Doesn't seem like it'd do much good tonight."

"Okay, I understand. If you do find somebody willing to go out, I will be monitoring channel sixteen."

"Right Joe. Good luck."

He hung up and told Anna what had happened. Her face registered disbelief, then shock, then anger.

"Damn it Joe! Damn it! I told —"

"Shut up," he snapped. She did, and looked like he had slapped her. "There is no time for that now," he said. His voice was hard and so was his face. Already he was dialing the telephone, and a moment later he said, "Harold? Joe. I need your boat." He told the story in a few words, nodded, and hung up.

"I will need a fresh pot of coffee," he said over his shoulder as he went to the bedroom. He pulled on jeans and a flannel shirt, moccasins over bare feet, and fetched his foul weather gear from the closet. Anna had the water heating when he entered the kitchen.

"I'm sorry," she said without turning. He put his arms around her from behind and hugged her, touched his lips to her head.

"You are a good woman Anna," he said quietly. "And I am just a man, who sometimes makes mistakes."

She nodded without speaking and pulled away, measured the grounds into a filter, and poured the hot water through. When the thermos was full she capped it and handed it to him.

"Be careful, Husband."

"I will do what I can." He kissed her upturned lips, turned to the door, and was gone.

The wind tore at him as he descended the front steps. He considered a moment, then struggled into his rainproof clothing instead of tossing it into the basket. The wind shoved the little motorbike back and forth across the road on the way to the marina and knocked it over when he tried to prop it on its stand, so, he drove down the walkway and out onto the dock and left it wedged between the rental office and a piling.

He searched the stern locker where Harold had told him he would find a hidden key, opened the cabin and stowed his thermos, then climbed to the flying bridge and started the engine. The cabin cruiser, unlike the Whaler, had a single prop which, combined with its tall superstructure, made it much more difficult to control in the wind. It took all Joe's skill to get it safely out of its slip and into the channel, and even so he careened off the stern of a boat on the opposite dock.

He switched on the radio and punched up 16 on its glowing digital readout. There was no audible traffic, nothing but static. Out on the main lake he pulled the drawstring of his hood tight as the wind and spray lashed him. It was rough, the waves running three feet, but the Bertram was designed to handle offshore ocean conditions and was ruggedly built. He traveled down the lake into the teeth of the gale. The twisting path of the lake made wind and waves unpredictable, a confused melee where mountains of dark water suddenly arose to port or starboard without warning, without rhythm, tossing the boat this way and that.

Time was measured by how long the boat hung on a wave that tipped it thirty degrees to starboard, by how many heartbeats until it righted itself. By how many times he wiped his face free of stinging spray, squinting to make out the channel, by how many times he swerved to avoid rocks that loomed up and suddenly disappeared.

But no man knew the lake better than Joe. After two hours of fighting the wheel, he sought the shelter of a protected cove in Good Hope Bay and drank a cup of coffee. Several hours later he stopped for another in Knowles Canyon. By then the wind had begun to die.

Now he was able to apply full throttle and shortly he passed Bullfrog Bay as the Bertram pounded down the lake at twenty-five knots. He yawned and threw back his hood, letting the cool air refresh him. He ran a hand over his thatch of gray hair and rolled his head in a circle. His neck made small cracking sounds.

The radio hissed and sputtered, but messing with the squelch only produced more static. He plucked the microphone from its clip and thumbed the switch.

"This is Joe Redhill aboard the boat 'Harold's Hogan,' is anybody receiving me?" Nothing but the hiss of static from the speaker. He thrust the mike into its holder. He was passing Iceberg Canyon to port, which told him he was about halfway down the 150-odd miles of the lake. His watch said 2:15.

At 3:00 A.M., he reached the confluence of the San Juan River with the main lake, and arbitrarily decided to begin his search. He turned the cruiser starboard into Reflection Canyon, working the spotlight with one hand as he drove with the other. The cliff walls plunged vertically into the dark water; there were very few places here where a boat could beach, much less hide. In about a mile the canyon forked, Reflection continuing to port and Cottonwood Gulch to starboard.

He followed Reflection to its end, then sped back to the fork and turned up Cottonwood. Nothing. He ran at full throttle back down the canyon to the main lake, slowed to search a few small coves on the northwest shore, then turned up Hidden Passage Canyon. His watch said 3:20.

There was no sign in Hidden Passage Canyon. Nor Music Temple, Anasazi, or Twilight Canyons. Oak Canyon took longer, as the lake made a great sweep to the southeast, creating a bay almost two miles across with many small coves. It was 4:30 by the time he returned to the main channel. He was only a mile from the Rainbow Bridge buoy.

There was a faint blush in the eastern sky as Joe halted the boat in mid-channel and climbed down to the cabin to pour a cup of coffee. He cradled it in his hands and savored its warmth, for the morning was cold and his exposure on the flying bridge had taken its toll. He climbed back up top and blew across the cup, his gaze searching the passing shoreline as the boat drifted.

And on the shore, Rebecca opened her eyes and saw the boat. She was too cold and stiff to move, could only whisper, "Grandma." But her grandma was breathing slowly and shallowly and her lips ware blue. A few minutes earlier she had shivered and awakened and now she shivered again. But her eyes didn't open and she didn't speak. After a minute Rebecca also closed her eyes and drifted back to sleep. Comforting sleep.

Joe pushed the throttle forward and cranked the wheel to straighten the boat down the channel just as the sun broke above the horizon. Something flashed near the shore and he squinted and swung the bow around. When he got near

177

enough he saw the chrome nozzle of a jet drive projecting above the water, and the white gleam of a hull floating just beneath the surface.

He cupped his hands around his mouth and yelled, "Rebecca! Lucy! Hello!" There was no answer. He put the boat in a fast idle and searched the shore, the cup of coffee forgotten as his eyes strained to pierce the shadows.

It was the pale blot of Rebecca's face within the gloom that caught his attention. He shouted and pulled the wheel hard over, gently ran the bow right up onto the rock. His heart was hammering as he sprang to the shore, threw a coil of line around a rock, and ran to the huddled figures.

"Oh, Becka," he whispered. "Oh Becka, Little Daughter." He lifted her gently in his arms and carried her to the boat. Her eyes drifted open as he set her on the settee and she whispered, "Uncle Joe." Then they closed again.

He returned for Martha and laid her on the V-berth in the bow of the boat, then put Rebecca beside her and covered them both with every blanket and towel and jacket he could find. He lit the burners of the stove and turned them all the way up, then hurried to the bridge and tried the radio again. No reply. He swore and motored out into the channel, then returned below to check on them.

Rebecca's hands were balled into fists, and as he stroked her head she opened her eyes and looked at him, though she didn't have the strength to speak. But her fist nudged his leg, and he looked down and saw her hand had opened. His Four Mountains bundle lay in her palm. He swallowed against a tightness in his throat.

"Yes, Little Daughter," he said. "Yes. Hold it tight." He folded her fingers back around the bundle. "Rest now, and I will take you to a place where you will be safe and warm." He opened Martha's eyelids delicately with his thumb and she moaned as he checked her pupils. He frowned and stood. The cabin was becoming very warm and he turned the stove burners down for fear of asphyxiation. He closed the cabin door behind him and climbed to the bridge, eased the throttle forward to its limit, and turned the radio all the way up.

"Mayday, Mayday," he said into the mike as the boat sped up

the lake. The radio hissed like a snake. Clutching the microphone in his fist he shook it at the sky and bared his teeth, but no sound came from his throat. Then his face became icily calm again and he repeated, "Mayday, Mayday, anybody listening?"

He was passing the canyons he had searched only hours earlier, and the sun was well above the horizon now. A channel marker buoy drifted past all too slowly, marked with the number 56. The nearest marina with an airstrip was Will's Crossing, almost forty miles up the lake. An hour and a half at twenty-five knots. He shook his head and tried the microphone again.

Seven miles later he still held it clutched uselessly in his fist as he passed the confluence of the San Juan and entered the narrow stretch of canyon below Llewellyn Gulch. A big, sleek cruiser swerved to avoid him and swept past in the opposite direction not twenty feet off his beam. It slowed, turned, caught up easily as its driver hailed him.

"You Joe Redhill?" The woman at the helm was big, but not sleek. She looked enormous beneath her red rain gear, and her voice carried easily above the rumble of the engines.

"Yes. You have come to help?"

"Yeah. Name's Mavis Delaney."

"Do you have a single-side-band radio, Mavis?"

"No. Just VHF. What's the problem?"

"I have a little girl and an old woman below, both suffering from hypothermia. How fast will your boat go?"

"Sixty-five knots flat out."

"Can you follow me to shore and transfer them?"

"God damn right I can."

"Okay. I'll leave this boat so I can tend to them aboard yours."

"Get going."

Joe pointed the boat toward a relatively gentle slope of shoreline and raced toward it, throttled back and ran the hull aground. He sprang from the bridge and took a line ashore, which he secured to a knob of stone. The other boat pulled alongside and the woman yelled, "It'll go faster if I just hold her here with the engines. You bring 'em aboard and get 'em below."

179

Joe was already moving as she spoke. He brought Rebecca over first, then Martha, careful not to bump or jostle them. He called to the woman that he was ready, then climbed into the queen-size bunk. Hugging them close he gave them his warmth as the water sizzled past the hull and the muted roar of the engines filled the cabin. The driver kept her boat going hell-bent, and several times its entire fifty-foot length was airborne, but the race-bred hull settled gently as the V-12's howled and the props sang, slicing white water.

Neither Rebecca nor Martha had spoken or opened their eyes when they arrived at Will's Crossing thirty minutes later. The engines continued wide open, it seemed to Joe, until an instant before the boat touched the dock. As he slid from the bunk the woman hurried down the companionway steps and said, "I radioed ahead a few minutes ago; they're calling in a chopper from the Moab hospital and trying to find a doctor at the campground."

As if in response to her announcement, feet thumped on the deck and a man came below, while two others stared down through the companionway. He was bearded and wearing shorts and a bulky sweatshirt, and carried a black bag in his hand.

"Dr. Mathieson, here on vacation," he said as he squeezed past the woman and Joe. "Excuse me." He felt Rebecca's pulse, pulled back an eyelid and looked at her color, did the same with Martha. "How long have they been this way?"

"I found them at 4:30 this morning."

The doctor nodded and glanced at his watch.

"They're both suffering from hypothermia," he said. "We've got to start warming them immediately. Don't want to move either one of them too quickly or we could send the heart into fibrillation, especially the older woman. We'll wrap them in the quilts and carry them to the car I have waiting at the end of the dock. No time to wait for the helicopter." He turned to the men waiting on deck and called up to them, "You got bathtubs here?"

"Sure do, Doc."

"Good. Okay, let's get them up to the car."

The big woman proved strong as a man, cradling Rebecca

180

protectively in her arms and refusing help from the two men on deck as she carried her to the car. Joe and the doctor carried Martha carefully between them, and a few minutes later the doctor was supervising the filling of tubs at the resort manager's home while Joe and the woman waited in the kitchen.

"Thank you for helping, Mavis," Joe said.

She waved her hand. "Poor things, I wish there was more I could do. They friends of yours Joe?"

"Yes." He gazed blankly at the plate of toast and scrambled eggs the manager's wife had prepared, but he was unable to eat a bite. He sipped coffee instead and waited. The woman, unlike most *bellicanos*, did not seem disturbed by silence and went to stare out the window at the lake. The doctor came in wiping his hands on a towel and scowling.

"I think they're going to be okay," he said cautiously. "Of course, the older woman is still at much higher risk than the girl, but her heart is starting to sound a little stronger. The little girl, ah, Rebecca is her name? She's already alert and responsive. It's best they be taken to the hospital for observation after they've warmed up some more. How did this happen?"

"I wish I knew," Joe said. The doctor cocked an eyebrow, waiting for him to continue. When he didn't, the doctor said, "Well, it's a good thing you found them when you did; their core temperatures were quite low. If they'd gotten any colder it —"; he was drowned out by the thump of rotors as the helicopter passed low over the house.

"That'll be our ride," he said. "But they can wait a bit."

"Would it be all right if I spoke to Rebecca?" Joe asked.

"Sure. Be good for her." He strode down the hall to the bathroom and entered without knocking.

Rebecca was lying in the tub, looking small, pale, and lost, her wet hair a tangled mess. A woman was kneeling beside the tub as the men came in and she draped a towel across it so Rebecca had a semblance of modesty. The doctor reached into the water and checked the thermometer, nodded, went out.

"Uncle Joe!" Rebecca said in a hoarse voice. Then she was crying and he went to her as the woman excused herself and joined the doctor out in the hall.

"I am here, Becka." Joe knelt beside her and stroked her head gently with his thick and callused fingers. She scooted closer to him and laid her head against his chest as he put his arms around her frail shoulders. The towel fell into the water and settled over her.

"I am here, Little Daughter," he crooned. "Do not be afraid any more." She sobbed weakly for several minutes, and then Joe produced his bandana from a pocket and wiped away her tears, wiped her nose.

"I'm not afraid now, Uncle Joe," she sniffed. "I'm not afraid but I want to go home. I want my mommy and daddy, Uncle Joe. Where's my grandmaaaa?" She started crying again and he held her until it passed.

"Becka, listen to me Little Daughter." She looked up into his face and nodded, lower lip trembling, large green eyes reddened from crying and sunken in her pale face. He swallowed and said, "I am going to go and find them now, and you must be braver yet and take care of your grandma. She got very sick last night and she will need you. Can you do that?"

She nodded solemnly. "I'll take care of her, don't worry." She sniffed and looked across the room. "You better take that if you're going after Waaa-weep." She pointed at the soggy pouch of his Four Mountains bundle on the towel stand beside the tub. He eyed her curiously, head tipped to one side.

"Who is Wahweap?" he asked.

"I don't know," she said as a flicker of fear crossed her face. "Maybe Uncle Norm. Norm was nice. This one looks like him, but it isn't. He said so. And he really doesn't look much like him. He would have killed me if you hadn't given me the medicine."

"How do you know?"

"Because he had a knife and it didn't cut me. And later, when we fell in the water and got so cold, I held it and it kept me warm and I called for you like you said. And you came and saved me. You better take it Uncle Joe, if you're going after Wa-weep."

He nodded and ran his hand over her head again, then bent and touched his lips to her forehead as he arose.

"Okay." He lifted the bundle and tied it around his neck, put it inside his shirt. "I am going to see your grandmother now. There are good people here who will take care of you until I get

182

back. You go with them and do what they tell you to do, right? And stay close to your grandmother like I asked."

"I will Uncle Joe, I promise and cross my heart." She drew an X on her chest. "When will you come see me?"

"As soon as I can, the very first thing when I return. I promise, and cross my heart." He nodded and ran a thick forefinger across his shirt. "Okay?"

"Okay." Her tired gaze followed him as he went out into the hall.

"Can I see Martha now?" he asked the doctor. The man nodded and led him to the master bathroom upstairs. The shower curtain was drawn so only her head and shoulders were visible.

"Hello Martha," Joe said.

"Hello Joe." Her voice was weak, and quavered. She looked old, like one of the stick figures seen in wheelchairs outside rest homes. Her eyes stared from dark hollows where the skin was flaccid and wrinkled, and her cracked, dry lips were surrounded by fissures like a crater on the moon.

"How are you feeling?" he asked. There was no sparkle in her eyes as she stared at him blankly and shook her head.

"Not good," she said.

"I am sorry Martha." He seated himself on the toilet lid and gazed at his feet. "Can you tell me what happened?"

"Yes." She drew a shuddering breath and let it out slowly. "Norman went insane."

His eyes widened but he did not look up. The doctor said, "Excuse me," and squatted beside the tub to take her wrist, gazed at his watch and checked her pulse.

"He started acting strange," she said. "The baby cried all night from the first. They weren't getting any sleep. He was worried about his job." She sighed and closed her eyes. The doctor lowered her wrist gently back into the water and turned on the hot water tap for a moment, then turned it off and drew the curtain so only her face was visible. "You're doing fine Martha," he said.

"Thank you, Doctor." Her eyes remained closed as the doctor retired to the master bedroom. From downstairs came the sound of feet and voices as the helicopter crew arrived.

"It's all mixed up now," she said, opening her eyes to gaze at

183

Joe with a lost and puzzled expression. "I can't seem to remember what happened first. I'm not even sure some of it happened at all."

She told him of Rebecca's night visitation, of Lucy's hair, Norman's 'accidentally' hooking Rebecca in the head. Of how Norman stopped eating, spent most of his time alone ashore, lost weight, and turned dark from the sun.

The voices were in the master bedroom now and she spoke more quickly, sounding almost feverish.

"It was a big black bird that hit John," she said. "My eyes are still good and I saw it clearly. It hit him in the back of the head while Norman stood right beside him. Norman took us back aboard that boat and out on the lake where we couldn't get away, locked us in the cabin. He came for us after dark and there was a doll—"

"Mrs. Sanders?" The doctor came in accompanied by a woman who wore a one-piece jumpsuit with a winged heart over the left breast. A stethoscope hung around her neck. "I think it's time for you and your granddaughter to take a quick trip into Moab; these good people have just gotten another call."

"Thank you Martha," Joe said as he stood.

"But you haven't heard it all," she protested, reaching out a hand to push the curtain aside exposing her withered body, oblivious to such trivial matters. "You don't know what he did! What a monster—."

Joe averted his gaze, embarrassed by her nakedness and stunned by what she had already told him.

"Please Mrs. Sanders," the doctor soothed. "We need to get you ready to go and you mustn't excite yourself. It could be dangerous in your—"

"Do not worry Martha." Joe took her hand in both of his though he would not look at her. "I will hear the rest of your story when you are rested. And you have my word that I will take care of everything personally. But for now, you must do as the doctor says so that you can care for Rebecca until I return. Please."

She lay back in the tub and closed her eyes, the strength gone from her grip. He released her hand as she said, "You're right,

184

I must think of Becka. But Joe, even though Norman is my son, I want to warn you." Her eyes popped open and she gave him an intense look as she whispered, "Be careful of him Joe; he isn't right. Not just crazy, Joe, but . . . evil." Her whisper ended in a hiss and he turned abruptly and strode from the room.

He stayed until they were loaded aboard the helicopter. It rose into the sky with a big noise and a cloud of dust, then dwindled rapidly toward the northeast. He used the manager's telephone to call Anna.

"Joe, I've been worried to death," she said. "There are some terrible stories going around here. What's happened?"

"Martha and Rebecca are safe. I just put them on a helicopter to Moab hospital. Is Lance home?"

"Yes, they hid in Cedar Canyon until the winds stopped. They got in around four this morning."

"Okay, good. Listen Anna, I will be gone the rest of the day. Please get ahold of Harold and let him know. If I cannot get home tonight I will call you."

"Yes, all right. Is there anything else I can do?"

"No. I am sorry Anna, sorry about all this."

"Oh Joe, Joe." He heard her struggle to control her voice. "It's not your fault, you know that. Don't blame yourself."

"I must go," he said.

"Goodbye Joe. Joe . . . I love you."

"Yes," he said. "Yes, and I you." He hung up the phone and stood silently for a moment, head bowed. Then he seemed to shiver, turned to thank everyone for their help and walked down to the docks where Mavis waited aboard her boat. He boarded and joined her in the bridge. She was bent intently above the instrument panel and turned to him with a stricken expression.

"They've found your houseboat," she said. "I'm afraid you're not going to like it Joe; I've been sitting here listening to the radio traffic between Will's Crossing and Sunlight."

"What? What has happened?"

"It's on the rocks in Dungeon Canyon. And there's a dead woman aboard."

Joe sat down heavily on the passenger seat and passed a hand

185

over his face.

"Oh no," he said quietly.

"I'm so sorry Joe. Really, I don't know what to say."

"There is nothing more to say." He stood, his face like stone. "Please, take me back to my boat; I will cast off the lines."

She nodded and started the engines. She didn't babble or try to make small talk as Joe stared rigidly ahead, and forty-five minutes later he was aboard the Bertram heading down the lake; it was 11:20 in the morning. He reached Dungeon Canyon just before 2:00. The houseboat was listing, bow-down in shallow water, its stern pointing toward shore. The floor of the galley and part of the salon were under water. A swarm of smaller boats surrounded it and lined the shore, and a helicopter passed overhead and settled on shore as Joe beached the Bertram. He stepped ashore and Sheriff Nathan Andrews detached himself from a group of men and came to meet him.

They shook hands solemnly.

"The girl and her grandmother all right?" the sheriff asked.

"Rebecca probably, the old woman maybe. What have you found Nathan?"

"Oh Christ, Joe, it's another ugly mess." The sheriff shook his head. Though the day was still cool, he pulled off his Stetson and swiped his forehead with his sleeve, settled the hat back in place.

"There's just one body aboard, identified as Lucy Sanders. No trace of the others. God damn, Joe, I'm sorry to have to be the one to tell you this. But you might's well hear it from someone you know I guess." He pulled off his sunglasses and polished them on his shirt, staring at the ground.

"What else Nathan?" Joe asked.

The whine of the helicopter's turbine died away as it disgorged its occupants. The sheriff hooked the sunglasses behind his ears and crossed his arms with a sigh.

"She's been cut up pretty bad Joe. We can't even find part of her. I've seen plenty of highway accidents but . . . well, we've got a real loony on our hands as near's I can tell. I don't think you want to—"

"Joe? Joe Redhill?" One of the passengers from the helicopter approached them. "I didn't think we would meet again so

186

soon. Brian Thornton, FBI." He wore a gray suit and sunglasses and didn't offer his hand. "Sheriff Andrews."

"Mr. Thornton." The two men nodded at each other.

"So what have you got this time, Sheriff?"

"A definite homicide aboard the houseboat, a possibly accidental death beneath Rainbow Bridge, a woman and a little girl on their way to the hospital, and a man, woman, and baby missing."

The FBI man pursed his lips and whistled.

"When it rains it pours down here, doesn't it?" he said.

"Yessir, I guess it does." The sheriff frowned and hitched his equipment belt higher on his hips. "We're just getting a search party organized now. Figured to work the area between here and where Joe found the others."

"Fine. My pilot and helicopter are at your disposal. Joe, I'd like to know what, if anything, the woman or the girl told you."

Joe shrugged, staring past the man's head at the looming bulk of Navajo Mountain. "Martha told me her son Norman went crazy. She also said a bird knocked her son John off Rainbow Bridge."

The FBI man waited for Joe to continue. "Is that it?" he asked after a minute.

Joe nodded, still gazing at the mountain. It was twenty miles inland yet towered above them as if they stood at its foot. There was not a cloud in the sky but for its summit, hidden in swirling mist. Joe's eyes were slits, and his face so unmoving it might have been carved from the same dark flint that littered the ground at his feet.

"That's not much to go on," the FBI man said.

"It's all we've got." The sheriff turned away from Joe and waved a hand. A man in uniform hurried over. "Get those boats out on the water deputy, and tell the men to please stay alert; the lives of a mother and her child depend on it. None of those volunteers are to engage Norman Sanders if they spot him, they're to call for an officer. You got that?"

"Yes sir." The deputy hurried back to the group and repeated the sheriff's instructions. A few minutes later the boats began heading out onto the lake.

"What's your plan Joe?" the sheriff asked.

187

"I will refuel at Rainbow and search until dark. I will go up the lake."

"Okay." He turned to the FBI man. "Mr. Thornton, if you don't mind, I'll accompany you in your helicopter. I know this country pretty well."

"Fine. Good luck Mr. Redhill," Thornton said.

Joe grunted and lifted a hand, and the trio moved toward the helicopter. He waited until its noise and wind had moved off across the lake, then stretched his hands over his head and arched his back. His joints creaked and popped. He drew a deep breath and let it out slowly. Then he started jogging slowly toward Navajo Mountain.

When he was a quarter mile or so inland he turned northeast. He ran bent forward at the waist, hands swinging free at his sides. After several miles he moved inland another quarter mile and turned back the way he had come. The terrain was rugged and it was more than an hour before he cut the tracks.

He squatted beside the barefoot prints in the dusty soil. Delicately he traced the outline of a foot and his face furrowed in thought; it did not look like a white man's foot. The toes were splayed, the sole broad and flat. It was the print of a foot that had never known the confinement of a modern shoe. He stood and looked once again toward Navajo Mountain, then turned his back and jogged down to the shore.

He spent the rest of the day working the Bertram slowly back up the lake, talking occasionally over the radio to other searchers when they passed close enough; nobody had found anything. The lake was in shadow and a chill was in the air as he passed the San Juan River. He yawned and rubbed his eyes; it was time to go home.

Anna had dinner waiting when he came in.

"Lance called and said he was eating out," she said. "He'll be home in an hour. Do you want to shower before you eat?"

"I am too tired to shower."

She served him mutton stew and corn bread, a large tossed salad. He ate like a machine taking on fuel, with no trace of enjoyment, as she picked at her dinner. When he was finished she brought him a cup of coffee.

"I called the hospital this afternoon," she said. "Rebecca

sounded fine. Well . . . as good as a frightened little girl can be expected to sound. But the doctor was a little worried about a scalp wound that she must have gotten after you visited them. It had stitches. He said it was infected from the lake water." She put her fork down and laced her fingers under her chin. "And Martha doesn't seem to be doing so hot. The doctor said she is experiencing confusion and he's worried about her coming down with pneumonia."

He stared at the cup cradled in his hands. "What will become of them?" he asked in a tired voice. "They were out there all night. Martha has had a terrible experience, but I hoped the thought of caring for her granddaughter would cause her to grow strong. . . ." He sighed and shook his head. "We can only hope."

"Yes, of course. I spoke to her on the telephone, she even laughed. It's a miracle you found them in time." Her voice held a forced lightness, and she looked away when he glanced at her. The telephone rang and Joe went into the living room.

"Joe, it's Nathan." The sheriff's voice sounded utterly exhausted. "Joe, we found Judy Sanders's body just before sunset. It was washed up on the rocks near Mazuki Point. She was . . ." his voice pitched up an octave and he coughed, clearing his throat. "The baby, Stephen Sanders, was still in her arms."

Joe said nothing, just moaned and ran a hand over his face.

"Joe, uh, Anna's there huh? You doing okay?"

"Yes."

"All right. Listen Joe, we're going out after this guy in the morning. Nobody knows this back country like you do, and if there's a better tracker I haven't heard about it. Even the Navajo Police speak highly of you. We could sure use your help. I'd like to deputize you."

"Certainly."

"Okay. Thanks Joe. Thornton's coming out in his chopper, we'll pick you up at the airstrip around seven. Okay?"

"Yes, fine."

"Yeah. G'night Joe."

"Good night." He hung up. Anna was in the doorway watching him.

"More bad news," she said.

"Yes. They found Judy's body. And Stephen's."

"What?" her mouth hung open in disbelief. Then it snapped shut and her face went pale as she struggled to control herself. "There!" she shouted. "There! You see? What did I tell you Joe? Everybody tried to tell you. You and Harold. But would you listen? No! How many have to die Joe? Your friend Hector! Jonathan!" She counted on her fingers, folding them over one at a time, face quivering. "Lucy! Oh yes, I know about her! News travels fast around here, especially bad news! Judy! And . . . and . . ."

"Stop it!" he shouted. He stood and picked up the telephone, threw it across the room so hard that it made a gaping hole in the imitation pine paneling. He stared at what he had done with a look of bewilderment, his hand outstretched as if by grasping at the air he could reverse the telephone's flight, erase the damage.

Anna was speechless. For a moment neither of them moved. Then he slowly lowered his hand and she fell forward against his chest, her arms around him as she sobbed. He held her.

"Oh Joe, Joe," she sobbed. "I am so sorry. I don't know what I'm saying. So much death, Joe. So many. Why so many?"

He shook his head slowly. "The man went insane, Anna. Now he has vanished into the desert. That is all I know."

"No. On no, Joe. You still don't see it do you? What about Hector? What about those pot hunters you found? It is not a man you are after, Husband. It is a *chindi.*"

"Anna. I know what I am doing." He squeezed her hand. Then he gently brushed a strand of hair from her face and spoke in Navajo. "As surely as morning follows night, with morning my feet will follow the enemy's path. He walks on the earth like a man, and he kills like a man. As a man I will follow him, and as a man I will bring him to justice."

Anna looked at him, and did not speak, but lowered her head as tears fell from her dark, thick lashes, and she went into the kitchen so that he would not see. Joe moved lethargically into the bedroom and fell asleep fully clothed.

She awoke early and slipped out of bed, put on her robe, and padded silently into the kitchen. She prepared a breakfast of eggs scrambled with *chorizo*, fried potatoes, sliced melon, and homemade flour tortillas kept warm in the oven wrapped in a moist linen towel. Joe came in as she was having a cup of coffee.

"Good morning," she said.

"Good morning." He bent to kiss her. "This looks like quite a meal."

"I wanted you to remember what good cooking tastes like, so you'll be sure to come home." She smiled, though there was no humor in her voice. "It seems to be the only chance I have."

"Anna," he caught her wrist as she served him. "I am going to help the sheriff find a lunatic in the desert. One man, Anna, and he is not even armed. I will come home, I promise."

"He's more than one unarmed man. You know that. He may not even be a man anymore. If you were concerned about coming home, if you wanted to ever see me again, you would at least take the time for a Sing. There are men who still know the Evilway ceremony. Let the sheriff go after him, let the *bellicanos* track him. If they don't find him before the Sing is over, then you can help them. Then you will be ready."

"I am not tracking a ghost, Anna. I saw his tracks."

"You're wrong, Joe. Why won't you see it?"

"Please, Anna. Not this morning. We went through all this last night."

"You have become just like them, Joe!" Her face was pale with fear and anger. "You believe the world is just how you think it is, there is no room in your mind for anything that doesn't fit what you know. Do you have the slightest idea how stupid that is? Especially out there," she flung her hand toward the window, "out there where you're going?"

"Anna, please. I do not want to talk about it anymore."

Lance came into the kitchen, poured himself a cup of coffee, and gazed from one face to the other with a groggy expression.

"Hard to sleep with all the yelling," he said.

"We weren't yelling," Anna said.

"Loud talk, then. Lots of loud talk. You going with the sheriff today, Dad?"

Joe cocked an eyebrow at his son. "How do you know of it?"

"Oh, you know." He fluttered his hand through the air like a bird. "Word travels fast, the drums have been beating. Can I

191

come with you?"

"No." He shook his head firmly.

"Why not?" Anna asked in a ragged voice. "Why not Joe? It's just one man, unarmed. Sure, take your son. Maybe I'll come along too, pack a picnic lunch."

Joe glanced at her with alarm. "There is no reason for that kind of talk."

"Sure there is!" she shrilled. "You've got all the answers. There's nothing for your silly wife to worry about! So why shouldn't Lance go with you?"

"You could use another searcher, Dad," Lance said cautiously, watching his mother. "Even though I'm not as good a tracker as you. They were my friends too."

"Okay Lance," Joe said suddenly. He pushed his plate aside, tossed his fork on it with a clatter. "If the sheriff will have you, you can come. But you'll have to eat fast, we leave in five minutes."

"I'll be ready," he said around a mouthful of eggs.

Anna stared as Joe left the room, her mouth open. Slowly she raised her hand to her face. She turned to speak to Lance, but before she could say anything he vanished into his bedroom.

Joe searched his key ring until he found the one that fit the lock on the heavy wooden chest on the floor of the closet. On top was a uniform, neatly pressed and folded. He lifted it out and it smelled of mothballs. He rubbed the fabric with his thumbs and stared at the row of medals, then set it aside. A pair of boots followed, and some worn but clean fatigues, and then he found what he wanted.

First was a heavy canvas belt, rolled tightly and encircled by a rubber band. A black-handled knife with a slender blade in a handmade sheath of darkly gleaming steerhide. And, in a cotton drawstring bag, a well-oiled .357-magnum Colt Python revolver in a leather holster. It was silver-worn in places, but the cylinder clicked precisely when he spun it with his thumb. He threaded the belt through the loops of the holster and sheath and buckled it around his waist, found a box of ammunition in the trunk, and thrust it in his pocket. After replacing the uniforms, he locked the trunk.

Lance was waiting for him at the front door, while Anna rinsed dishes and put them in the dishwasher, her movements mechanical and wooden.

"We're going," Joe said softly.

"Go." She didn't turn. Joe jerked his chin, opened the door and stepped outside, with Lance following. They mounted their motorbikes and kicked them to life, rode out of the RV Park through the chilly morning air.

In the kitchen, Anna gripped the edge of the counter with both hands and hung her head.

"What have I done?" she whispered. "Oh, what have I done?"

Nine

Six men rode in the helicopter including the pilot, a mild, quiet young man who wore glasses. As they approached Dungeon Canyon, Joe tapped him on the shoulder and pointed down. He nodded and the powerful Aero Special LAMA dropped from the sky. The skids touched earth and the rotors coasted to a stop as the whine of the turbine faded. The passengers climbed out. The sun was barely above the eastern horizon and Thornton pulled the zipper of his parka up tight under his chin.

"It's a little cooler than the last time you took us hiking Joe. How cold do you think it is?"

"Not bad," Joe said. "Forty-five maybe."

"Man, that's cold enough. Seems like there's only two temperatures here; too hot and too cold."

"That's good!" the man with the rifle chuckled appreciatively. Thornton had introduced him as special agent Walt Chase, and hinted at various 'jobs' Chase had assisted with. He was carrying a sleek, walnut-stocked rifle, wore a daypack, a nylon ski jacket over a thick sweater, and jeans and hiking boots. Both his face and his blue eyes were unusually pale, and when he spoke it was in a loud nasal voice.

"Nice rifle," Joe said.

"Thanks." Chase smiled proudly and hefted the weapon in his hands. "Yeah, Weatherby Mark V, seven- millimeter with a Zeiss variable-power scope."

"You oughta be able to reach out quite a ways with that," Sheriff Andrews said. "Hope you aren't planning on doing any shooting this trip."

"Not unless I'm asked to." Chase's smile turned frosty, and his eyes looked through the sheriff.

"Hey, what do you say we get moving?" Thornton said

194

quickly. "It's cold as a witch's tit standing around like this. Joe, are we ready? I don't want to start out half-assed like last time."

Joe glanced at the others. He and Lance were dressed alike in denim jackets over flannel shirts, blue jeans, and thermal underwear. Lance wore a bulky down vest over his jacket, and low-topped hiking boots. Joe wore a coil of climbing rope over his shoulder. The sheriff had on a green nylon jacket with the San Juan County logo on the sleeve, but instead of his usual crowded equipment belt he wore a simple canvas belt holding a pistol, a canteen, and a two-way radio in a leather holster. Lance and Chase were the only ones not wearing sidearms.

"Ready enough," Joe said. Thornton nodded and returned to the helicopter, leaned in the door, and spoke to the pilot. A moment later it lifted off as he ducked his head and hurried over to join the others.

"Freeman's going up toward the mountain and setting it down to wait for us."

The helicopter dipped its nose and clattered away toward the southeast, and Navajo Mountain.

"Okay, let's head out." He motioned for Joe to start, who led them to the place he had found the tracks the day before. He followed the trail inland setting a brisk pace, but one that would not tax the others too greatly. They had not been walking long when Lance came up beside him.

"Hey, Dad, I thought we were after Norm Sanders," he said quietly.

"We are." Joe glanced at him.

"But these aren't his footprints," Lance said with a puzzled expression. "I've seen his prints, wet on the dock. I'm not the world's greatest tracker but I notice things like that. He's got a high arch, and skinny toes all pressed together like most *bellicanos*."

"Tender feet," Joe said. "They are swollen from going barefoot. That is why they look strange." He glanced again at his son, face impassive, and Lance nodded uncertainly.

"Yeah," he said. "I guess that could be it." He dropped back until he was at the end of the line of men strung out behind Joe. The tracks led across soft soil where they were easy to follow, and across bare rock where Joe had to cast about until he found them again. Lance wandered up beside Chase as he watched Joe search and asked him, "What do you make of the footprints?"

"Looks like we're on his trail all right, boy." He eased the rifle sling with his thumb and spat into the dirt. "But I sure wish that Indian daddy of yours would hurry things up. I got business back in town tonight, if you know what I mean." He gave Lance a leering wink. Lance smiled thinly, then Joe found the tracks and they started on.

The ground rose steadily as they moved away from the lake, and the sun mounted higher in the sky and bathed them in its warmth. Soon they began to shed their coats, then their sweaters. Canteens were opened. The ground was hard and the vegetation sparse, and dust rose from their feet.

Time and again they descended into arroyos and climbed back out as the tracks made no accommodation for obstacles, going over or through them rather than finding a way around. The distance between the men increased as the group found its natural order, with Joe in the lead, followed by the sheriff, then Lance, Chase, and Thornton last.

Joe no longer cast about when he lost the tracks; their direction was obvious. Now when the thin soil gave way to windsmoothed stone he continued straight toward Navajo Mountain, and sooner or later found the tracks again. The sun was standing overhead when he called a break for lunch. He chose a place where the wind had carved a hollow in the stone, a sort of natural amphitheater a dozen yards across. The men seated themselves on the sun-warmed stone, and they ate their food.

"How far do you think we've come Joe?" Thornton asked.

"Seven or eight miles."

"Is that all? You couldn't prove it by my feet; they're claiming twenty."

"It's hard walking," Lance said. "On easy trails we would've done ten or twelve."

"Makes you think about the pioneers that came out here with nothing but horses and wagons," the sheriff said.

"Some came without wagons or horses," Joe said quietly.

The sheriff pulled off his Stetson and wiped his forehead

with his sleeve. "You're right Joe. Damned if I don't think just like a white man." He combed his hair back with his fingers and shoved his hat on. "Speaking of which, any idea where Sanders thinks he's going?"

Joe nodded and raised his hand toward Navajo Mountain. "Up there," he said.

The sheriff squinted. "Christ, I'm glad *he's* not an Indian. We'd need an army to flush him out of there."

"You got that right," Joe said. "Nobody follows the *Dine'* up Navajo Mountain."

"Well, if he's not up there, I hope your people have the roads bottled up tight." Thornton arched an eyebrow at the sheriff, who scowled back.

"He won't get out on the roads," he said. "Don't worry about that. My people aren't all expert trackers, but between them and their relatives, they know if a dog crosses the road between here and Arizona."

After lunch they continued across the arid landscape, and as their altitude above the lake increased, the vegetation also increased. Trees became more numerous, gripping the stony soil with twisted roots like rheumatic fingers, their branches tortured into curious shapes by the desert winds.

Joe had been walking quickly but now he slowed, bent forward at the waist, and stalked slowly into the shade of a tree at the edge of the bluff that they were crossing. A sharpened stick was thrust into the soil and beneath it was a pile of ash. Small bones were scattered about, and the ends of half-burned twigs.

"Hey, now we're getting someplace!" Chase said as he arrived. "Damned if he didn't get a rabbit."

Joe sifted the ash through his fingers. Cold. "He cooks like an Indian," he muttered. His words were not lost on the sheriff, who squatted beside him, eyes narrowing. He licked his dry lips.

"Now where would a Los Angeles computer programmer learn to cook rabbit like an Indian?" he asked.

"What I want to know is how he killed it," Thornton said. "I thought he was unarmed."

Joe stood and considered, face furrowed in thought. "John's .22 was under the bed in their cabin," he said. "I do not think

197

Norman would have a gun of his own. John told me his brother hated guns. He was a conscientious objector during the war."

"Being C.O. twenty years ago doesn't mean he isn't armed now," Chase said. "He's a murderer, and probably insane, isn't that the picture? I'm gonna have to consider him armed and dangerous."

"I think that's reasonable," Thornton said. "Better to assume he's armed when he's not, than to think he isn't when he is."

The sheriff snorted. "We'll keep our heads down," he said.

"Well, we better step it up if we want to find him today," Thornton said.

"I am afraid we will be slowing it down," Joe said. "Look." He stepped from beneath the tree and swept his hand in the direction they had been traveling. The bluff on which they stood descended steeply into yet another rugged canyon. Beyond, the land was heaved up in ridges and carved by gulleys, littered with boulders, riddled with erosion, studded with yucca and prickly pear, with thorny bushes.

"Oh great," Thornton muttered. The descent was a skidding, arm waving slide to the bottom, and when he reached it he stopped to remove his boots and dump out the gravel as the others started up the next slope. Except Chase, who waited. A bird hovered above the next hill, too far away to be seen clearly but soaring on broad wings like a hawk or a crow. Chase raised his rifle to his shoulder.

"Crow," he murmured. "A hundred bucks says I can take him out. Another hundred says it'll be a head shot."

Thornton stood and gripped his arm. "I believe you, I've seen your work."

"Just kidding," Chase said, lowering the rifle. "But I am beginning to wonder what I'm doing on this little outing."

"Insurance," Thornton growled. He tugged at his laces and winced. "I want this case wrapped up. The media has gotten ahold of this like a dog with a rotten piece of meat and they're spreading stink all over the place. Nothing like a sensational murder to set them howling." He stood and brushed at his pants.

"See, the bright boys have already linked these deaths with the ones from this summer. A case that was never solved, if you'll recall. The third man is still missing. I don't want that to happen this time. Bad for our image. We're going to get Sanders, one way or the other."

"You're bucking for promotion aren't you?" Chase asked.

Thornton ignored the jibe and jerked his head at the others nearing the summit. "What are these guys, mountain goats? Come on, let's see you climb."

Joe was making allowances for nobody now, setting a pace that had even Lance breathing deeply and left Thornton and Chase farther and farther behind. When he paused to study the tracks there was a thoughtful look on his face and he clucked in his throat.

"Bet I know what you're thinking," the sheriff puffed as they walked three abreast across a low mesa.

"Hm?" Joe glanced over at him.

"The trail is too clear, too easy. Sanders wants us to follow him."

"You would have made a good Indian," Joe said. "Yes, that is what I was thinking."

"Maybe it's just because he's crazy," Lance said.

"I don't think so Lance," the sheriff puffed. "Brought in a few. Courts call 'em criminally insane. Mean as rabid coyotes. Crazy mean." He took a few running half-steps and panted, then said, "No. Crazy is not stupid. Sanders is leading us."

They climbed and descended a half-dozen rugged hills before the trail entered a narrow canyon and the walking became easier. The tracks were sharp and clear in the soft sand and led to a wall of sandstone, where they ended abruptly. A line of ancient Anasazi hand and footholds dotted the vertical cliff face.

"Looks about seventy, eighty feet," Lance said, craning his neck. "Guess we better find a way around."

"I will climb," Joe said. He unslung the rope and tied one end to his belt.

"It can't take that long to go around, Joe," the sheriff said. "That looks like a mighty serious climb."

"This is Rainbow Plateau," Joe said. He pointed right. "Three miles." He pointed left. "Four miles. I will climb." Before they could protest he started up.

The holds, gouged with primitive stone tools by the Anasazi many centuries earlier, had become shallow as the surrounding stone was eroded by wind and rain. They did not ascend straight up the cliff, but angled to Joe's right, utilizing whatever natural irregularities there were in the cliff itself to aid the climber. He hugged the cliff with his whole body, sliding hands and feet along the stone carefully, never losing contact, fingers splayed for purchase, toes gripping through the thick bullhide soles of his moccasins.

It was slow, agonizing work, and when he reached a point about fifty feet up, he found the ancient builder had prepared a surprise. The cliff bulged outward and the holds continued up its underside, but he was forced to shift to the right in order to reach his next grip. The holds were "keyed" to a proper sequence, an Anasazi trick, and he had lucked out. If he had started up the cliff with his left foot first instead of his right, he could not continue, but would have had to back all the way down and start over.

"The steps are keyed," he called over his shoulder. "Right foot first."

"Got it," Lance said quietly.

Joe closed his eyes and crept his right hand across the stone, feeling with his fingers. But the hold was too shallow and would never support him. He returned his hand to the previous grip and risked leaning out for a look. There was a crack in the stone just above the hold, and it seemed to continue upward around the bulge.

He stretched to his limit and inserted his hand in the crack. By cupping his fingers, he was able to support his weight and pull himself up hand over hand with the enormous strength of his arms as his legs swung free in the air. When at last he was past the bulge, the cliff began to slope inward more and more the closer to the top he came. Now his feet sought what purchase they could find, and his aching arms got some relief, and a few minutes later he stood atop the cliff and stretched, breathing hard.

He waved at Lance and the sheriff. His headband was soaked and he removed it and wrung the sweat from it. He searched for a place he could sit and brace himself, then nodded and stepped to the edge of the cliff. He gathered a few coils of rope and said, "Okay Nathan. Tie a bowline beneath your arms. Yell when you are ready."

He removed his jean jacket and tied it around his waist for protection against the rope, then seated himself in the place he had found, a small hollow with a ridge of stone where he could brace his feet. He draped the rope around behind his back, gripping the free end with his right hand, and holding the other, where it disappeared over the cliff, in his left.

"Okay!" the sheriff called.

Joe took up the slack and put enough tension on the rope to hold the sheriff should he fall, but not so much as to hinder his movements. In five minutes he was sweating with exertion, and in ten the sheriff joined him atop the cliff.

"Tough climb," he said. He removed his Stetson and wiped his forehead. His hand shook as he removed the rope and sent it down to Lance. Lance was tying it around himself when Thornton and Chase appeared.

"Ready," Lance said, stepping to the cliff.

"You've got to be kidding," Thornton said, staring upward.

"It's no problem," Lance said, glancing at Chase. "Watch." He swarmed up the cliff with a lithe grace, finishing faster than either his father or the sheriff had.

"I don't know about you, but I've never liked heights," Thornton said quietly. "Think I'll go around and try to cut Sanders's trail farther on."

"Whatever you say." Chase shrugged. Though the voices of the men atop the cliff were clearly audible, Thornton cupped his hands to yell, "We're going around!"

The sheriff looked at his watch.

"We've only got about three hours of daylight left," he said. "By the time you get up top, we'll be long gone." Joe and Lance stood beside him, Lance dangling the end of the rope and grinning.

"I'll go up," Chase said suddenly. Lance lowered the rope and he tied it around himself, slung his rifle across his back.

"Let me." The sheriff took the rope from Joe. "You've already pulled two men up, now it's my turn." He seated himself as he had seen Joe do and put tension on the rope.

Chase was stronger than he appeared and only slipped twice on the way up. The sheriff held him easily both times, and as he dragged himself erect he smiled coldly at Lance and said, "No problem, boy."

Thornton was a bad climber. He slipped many times, and each time he cried out. The sheriff pulled him most of the way and he arrived on top pale and shaking, bleeding from scrapes on his face and hands.

"This is stupid as hell!" Thornton swore as he stood and brushed himself off. He dragged his radio from its holster. "I'm going to call in the chopper and have it pick us up. It can drop us right at the mountain and we'll continue on from there."

"We can't be sure Sanders didn't turn aside," the sheriff said. "And we can't be sure of picking up his trail again. I'm walking." Joe and Lance nodded their agreement. Thornton looked at Chase.

"Most of my hunting's been done in the cities," Chase said. "But one thing I've learned is that once you've found a warm trail you stay with it. I'll walk too." He held Thornton's gaze a moment, then turned his attention to inspecting his rifle for any damage that might have occurred during his climb. Thornton sighed and holstered the radio.

"Right," he said. "Let's get moving."

"The walking will be easier from here," Joe said, then set off across Rainbow Plateau without a backward glance. He walked hard and fast and was soon well ahead of the others. The mountain loomed above the shadows of the plain, catching the rays of the sun low in the west, and a breeze began to stir. High overhead a crow glided past, a mere dot against the sky, its cry drifting faintly to his ears.

The land was mostly flat except for occasional conical hills topped by stone spires taller than a man. The pillars held silent vigil over the parched soil, and the plants grew low to the earth, hoarding their life in tough branches, thorny stems. Joe no longer looked down to follow the tracks. The rhythm of the trail was within him, leading him on, leading them all on toward the mountain, lofty and immortal, its summit piercing the sky.

Joe stopped to wait for the others beside one of the hills, standing in the shade of its spire. He laced his fingers behind

202

his head and stretched and his spine popped. He drew a deep breath and gazed back the way he had come.

The sound of a polite cough caused him to spin about. An old man climbed stiffly upright from the shade of a boulder at the base of the hill. His hair was long and silver, his face wrinkled, and he gazed calmly past Joe into the distance with a gentle smile. He leaned upon a wooden staff held at his throat with the same hand that clutched the blanket around his shoulders. His other hand was raised in greeting.

"Ya aat' eh, Grandson," he said in Navajo.

"Ya aat' eh, Grandfather," Joe replied. The blanket was a lovely yellow color, tightly woven and in very good condition. "Is that a Chin Lee?" he asked.

The old man chuckled. "You have eyes that see well, Grandson. Yes, I traded my cousin, Sits-In-Water for it. Two fine horses and a silver bracelet."

"You are a clever trader," Joe said. "It is worth more." Lance arrived and stood a respectful distance behind his father, as did the sheriff a moment later.

"You follow someone," the old man said.

"You have seen him?" Joe asked.

"I have not *seen* him." The old man waved his fingers in front of his eyes, which did not change their focus, and they understood that his distant stare was not simple politeness; he was blind. "But I have *seen* him." He touched his fingers to his forehead.

"Which way was the man going, Grandfather?" Joe asked.

"Man? I have seen no man." The old one shook his head. "In the night a shadow came walking darkly in my dream, and dark clouds swirled about it, and a wind blew darkly at its heels. Is this not what you seek?"

"Perhaps," Joe said quietly. "Where did the shadow travel, Grandfather?"

He raised a hand toward Navajo Mountain, fingers curled so they would not point impolitely. Thornton and Chase arrived panting and sweating and shuffled to a halt beside Joe.

"Who is this?" Thornton said. "Did you ask him if he's seen anything?"

Joe ignored him and said, "Thank you Grandfather. We are

203

sorry to have disturbed your rest."

"Walk in beauty, Grandson." The old man moved to the sunny side of the pillar and seated himself in the afternoon warmth.

"Walk in beauty, Grandfather." Joe waved and started on. The others followed, except for Thornton, who remained standing and called angrily, "What did he tell you?"

Joe stopped and turned. "Nothing we did not already know," he said.

"Oh." Thornton looked puzzled. "You could have just said so." He limped slightly as he walked. But the sun was settling in the west and Joe was in no hurry now.

"What the hell is that old guy doing out here in the middle of nowhere?" Chase asked.

"This isn't nowhere," the sheriff said, "it's his backyard." He swept his arm toward the south. "Navajo Land, far as the eye can see. Twenty-five-thousand square miles."

"But what's he doing out here?"

"Tending his flock," Joe said. "Did you not smell sheep?"

"Sheep," Thornton said with a snort of amusement. He wrinkled up his nose and sniffed. "I don't smell anything."

"What do they eat, rocks?" Chase laughed.

"This time of year most of the grass is dried up," Joe said. "There are places up here where water comes from the rock, and the grass is green and tender. He knows all of the places, and their names." The wind had begun to blow harder and he buttoned his jacket. Chase pulled a stocking cap from his pocket and tugged it down over his ears.

"I can't believe this," Thornton said. "We've been walking all day and we're not even close yet. We should've started at the base of the mountain."

"Perhaps," Joe said. "But the trail was there to follow. Tomorrow will be different. Night is coming, and with it the wind. Tomorrow there will be no tracks."

"How far to the mountain?"

Joe stopped and turned his back to the wind. He shrugged, eyes narrowing as he judged the distance. "Not far. Three miles maybe."

"Anybody have any objections to calling it a day?" When

nobody spoke, Thornton called the pilot on his radio.

"Come and get us Freeman. We're about three miles north-west of the mountain. When you get close enough I'll guide you in."

"Yes, sir. On my way."

A few minutes later the helicopter thudded toward them from the western slope of the mountain, and as Thornton spoke to the pilot it lurched earthward through the buffeting wind. They piled inside and the helicopter lifted off immediately. It was a rough ride home.

Anna was quiet and withdrawn during dinner, and Lance excused himself as soon as he finished and left to meet Chris. Joe was tired from the long walk and he showered and went to bed. He lay on his back with his eyes closed, listening to the wind prowling around the trailer. Anna climbed in beside him.

"I have been thinking," she said quietly. "About the man you found aboard the houseboat."

"Mm?" Joe turned his head and looked at her, but she was staring at the ceiling.

"There were some stories about him in the papers," she said. "He was a hardened criminal, starting as a child. The toughest jails in the country couldn't break him." She turned to look at him. "I think that's why he did it."

"Did what?"

"Killed himself like that. Because he was so tough."

"What are you talking about, Anna?" Joe gave her a puzzled look.

"The *chindi* tried to get to him, inside his mind, and he killed himself that way to prevent it."

"Oh." Joe sighed. "That again."

"Yes. And it tried Hector too but he was even tougher. He fought for everything he ever got and had the scars to prove it. So the *chindi* just killed him. Or tricked him into killing himself. But Norman Sanders was weak, Joe. You could see it in his face. Weak and smart. Just what the *chindi* needed."

"You talk like Norman is dead," Joe said.

"Norman Sanders is dead," she said. "You know it. In your

205

heart you know. It's only his body you're following, and what's inside that body you don't want to find out!"

"Anna—." He laid his hand gently on her arm but she pushed it away.

"Don't try to soothe me!" she hissed. "You're just like Harold Lowtah. You've turned your back on everything, your people, your beliefs, your heritage. You're empty, Joe, can't you see it? If you weren't, you would know the danger you're in!" Her eyes narrowed. "No, you're not like Harold. He believes in the almighty dollar. You don't believe in anything but Joe."

"Is that so bad?" he asked gently.

"Oh Joe. You think things you don't believe in can't hurt you. Because you're so brave and strong. You're the bravest man I've ever known, but it's not enough. I'm afraid I'm going to lose you, and I'm not strong enough or brave enough for that." She began to cry and turned away when he tried to comfort her. He sighed and pillowed his head on his arms, and she cried, and the wind moaned, and sleep was a long time in coming.

She had breakfast waiting when Joe and Lance came into the kitchen. Lance was cheerful and his eyes sparkled and he didn't seem to notice his parents' solemnity. Joe and Anna exchanged only a few words while they ate, but she hugged them both at the door.

"Goodbye Anna," Joe said. "We'll be back tonight."

"Goodbye." She closed the door, and she leaned against it, and she cried.

The helicopter rocked and lurched as they flew above the glittering ribbon of the lake. The pilot called over his shoulder, "It's gusting to about fifty, Mr. Thornton. I'm going to have to get in and out again in a hurry. Even so it's going to be touchy."

Thornton swallowed and wiped beads of sweat off his pale face.

"Tell you what you do then," he said. "Drop us off and find some place you can hole up where we can make radio contact. If you don't hear from us by late afternoon, come looking."

"No problem."

Joe and Lance were the first ones off when the skids touched down, followed closely by Thornton, then Chase and the sheriff. Immediately the whine of the LAMA's turbine shrilled as it fought for altitude against the downdrafts pouring from the mountain. It sped away toward the lake and its sound was quickly lost in the howling wind.

"Come on!" Joe shouted. He jogged toward a thicket of piñon trees and the others were quick to follow. The forest was filled with the sound of creaking branches and thrashing leaves as the wind rushed like a river through the tops of the trees.

"So, is everybody in agreement about our plan?" Thornton asked.

"Fine with me," the sheriff said. "You and Chase are working south and we're working north right?"

"Right. If you find anything, give a call on your radio." He patted his belt. "And we'll make routine radio checks every hour. Get into trouble, fire three shots, evenly spaced. Any questions?" Nobody spoke. "Okay. We're gonna get him today and wrap this up."

"Sure," the sheriff said.

"Good. Let's go, Chase." Thornton turned away and Chase winked at the others.

"Good hunting," he said.

"Same to you," the sheriff replied. He hurried to catch Joe and Lance making their way along the slope beyond the trees.

Thornton took the lead and pushed himself hard. The wind made his eyes and nose run and he wiped them on his glove. They tried to stay on the game trails that cut the slope every five or ten feet of elevation, but the footing was meager, being only a hand's width and requiring a heel-to-toe walk.

Soon they came to a broad slope littered with loose soil and fist-size stone, and even the game trails seemed to despair of finding an easy route through. Thornton swore as a seemingly solid rock shifted beneath his foot and he slipped, his boot cutting into the throbbing rawness of a broken blister.

But they crossed the slope, and the next, and the one after that. In an hour Thornton made radio contact with the sheriff, and again an hour later, though the signal was erratic. The third time he couldn't raise him at all. The wind beat at them relentlessly and each slope seemed steeper, each step harder. Finally Thornton glanced at his watch and said, "We've been walking for almost four hours and it doesn't seem like we're getting anywhere."

"This mountain is a big son-of-a-bitch," Chase said in agreement. "Hostile too, don't you think?"

"This whole damn canyon land is hostile. No wonder the Indians out here are such sullen, quiet bastards. How'd you like to spend your life chasing a bunch of stupid sheep from water hole to water hole?"

"Not me."

"Me either."

They fell silent as they worked their way down a gulley and back up the other side, only to find their path blocked by a rock slide.

"Why don't we work our way uphill a ways," Thornton said. "If we can get above this mess, up there in the trees, it'd probably be easier going."

"Fine with me." Chase winced as he eased the strap of the rifle on his shoulder. "Especially since we don't have a choice."

It was a steep climb and they stopped every twenty or thirty steps to catch their breath. The gully widened near the top but the brush became thicker and soon they were forcing their way through branches that clawed and clung, protecting their eyes with their hands, sweating, slipping on unseen stones. At a flat-topped rock the size of a truck they found they could go no farther; the brush was impenetrable.

"Oh Christ. Don't tell me we're going to have to go back." Thornton's eyes widened as he turned and stared. His face was scratched and soiled, dust mingling with his sweat, running in rivulets down his cheeks like dirty tears. Chase scrambled atop the rock and looked at the trees and open slopes only twenty yards ahead.

"Yeah, well, I've about had enough of this," he said. "If that county sheriff has got the roads bottled up like he says he has, I vote we call the chopper in and wait for the weather to drive this asshole out of the woods."

"Right now I'm inclined to agree," Thornton said. He looked at his watch. "But first I'm going to try to reach Andrews again and see if they've found anything." He pulled out his radio, looked up, and froze. Beyond the thicket was a grove of sparse trees, and beyond the trees a gentle slope. The slope led to the base of a cliff several hundred feet high. Atop the cliff stood a man.

Thornton shaded his eyes and stared, and Chase followed his gaze. He gasped and raised his rifle.

"Yesss," Chase crooned. "Oh yes, that's him all right. I've got him right in my crosshairs, Thornton." His finger eased the safety off with a quiet snick of metal on metal.

"Hold it! You don't know that's Sanders."

"Who else would be running around up here half-naked? All this idiot's wearing is a pair of pants. If that's not crazy you tell me what is."

"You can't just shoot him down for God sake!" Thornton hissed. "We need a cover story!"

"Make one up, you've done it before! I thought that was why you brought me along!" Chase snapped, still sighting his rifle. "Damn it man, at least let me take out a knee! Do you want to spend the next two weeks busting your ass all over this fucking mountain!"

"I said you can't shoot."

Chase hesitated, then slowly turned to Thornton without lowering the rifle. His face was flushed with excitement and his eyes glittered icily.

"I say I'm taking this guy out," he said.

But Thornton was gazing upward in fascination as the figure atop the cliff danced slowly, shifting its weight from one leg to the other. Its hands were raised above its head, shaking at the sky imploringly. The wind brought the sound of its voice, guttural and harsh. Then it flung out its arm and something black and slender fell toward them.

It spiraled as it fell and the wind carried it this way and that with jerky motions. It spiraled and spun as it dropped, whirring, faster and faster until it buzzed like a maddened hornet, the sound growing louder as it approached the men. Chase looked up at the sound. The object quivered and paused in its flight. Then a wind current appeared to seize it and it plunged suddenly downward and buried itself in Chase's eye.

He shrieked and clawed at his face and his rifle fell to the rock at his feet. Its thunderous explosion echoed from the mountain and Thornton staggered and clutched at his neck. Chase fell from the rock into the brush and thrashed about madly, shrieking and howling, as Thornton stared curiously at his hand.

There was blood on his fingers. His mouth worked soundlessly and the radio dropped from his other hand. His knees buckled beneath him and he fell back into the brush, staring upward. A great black bird launched itself into the air from atop the cliff and its scream was the last thing Thornton heard.

Many miles to the north, Joe stopped and held up his hand. "One shot," the sheriff muttered. They waited a full minute, listening intently, but heard only the wind.

"I don't like that at all," the sheriff said. He switched on his radio.

"Thornton, this is Andrews, do you read me?" Static hissed from the speaker when he released the transmit button. "Come on Thornton, answer me!" Again no response. He tried several more times before shoving the radio back in its holster.

"Radios are usually worthless around here," Joe said calmly. "I am surprised he was able to reach you earlier."

"Yeah. Damn! I don't like it Joe. What does one shot suggest to you?"

Joe shrugged. "Hard to say. Could be somebody else shooting. I know people who will take a deer out of season when they are hungry. And *bellicanos* sometimes shoot just for the hell of it."

"Sure," the sheriff said, shaking his head no. "That Chase fella, he's the kind that sleep with their gun. Joe, I better go take a look." He gazed toward the south as he considered, then unbuckled his belt and slipped the radio off.

"You hang onto this," he said. "When I find Thornton I won't need it, and maybe I'll be able to contact you. And we'll stick with the same signal, three shots, okay?"

"Fine, Nathan." Joe cradled the radio in both hands and stared at it. "Maybe we should come with you."

"No, no," he waved a hand. "It's probably a poacher or something, like you said. Better that you should keep looking, then I won't feel like such an idiot when Chase and Thornton laugh at me. And Lance, you be careful. I'm responsible for you, and Anna will have both your dad's butt and mine if you get hurt.

Okay, I'll see you." For a big man, he moved with surprising agility as he bounded back the way they had come. "Well, looks like it's you and me, Dad," Lance said, drawing a deep breath. "And this is a good time to tell you something."

"Yes?" Joe said.

"Chris and I have decided to get married."

"What?" Joe looked shocked.

"Oh, not right away," he added quickly. "After I finish school. We've been talking about it for a while but we hadn't really decided until last night."

"Well good for you! Good for you!" Joe said happily. He grabbed his son and hugged him, thumped him on the back. "She is a fine woman, Lance. I think you have chosen well." He held him at arms length and said, "And I think she has chosen well also."

"Dad . . . thanks Dad." Lance blinked rapidly and swiped at his eyes with his sleeve. "I wasn't sure how you'd feel about it. I'd made up all sorts of reasons why you might disapprove. You know. School. Different cultures. Too young. Everything you can think of."

"Hah. A good man and a good woman is all that matters. I am happy."

"That's great. You can't imagine what a load that is off my chest." He scuffed the ground with his boots and said, "How do you think Mom will feel?"

"She will be proud, Son. Have no fear."

"Think so?" He looked up and smiled.

"I am certain of it. Married. Hah! Soon I will be a grandfather."

"Whoa!" Lance said. "Not right away, Dad. Let's hope not."

"But sooner or later there must be grandchildren," he said over his shoulder. "Someone for me to spoil in my old age."

"Sooner or later, Dad," Lance laughed. "Hopefully later." They dropped over a waist-high ledge of stone and in its lee found soft soil, tender plants, and Sanders's footprints. Joe exchanged a glance with his son, and wordlessly they followed the tracks up the slope into the trees. There the signs became harder to read and Joe moved slowly, focused entirely on the ground before him.

The trail led them uphill through the trees to the base of a high cliff, part of the same geological formation that encircled this whole side of the mountain.

"What is this?" Lance said. "Two sets of tracks?" And there were, where there had only been one. A path to the right, and a path to the left.

"He is playing games with us," Joe said.

"Yes, but which way do we go?"

Joe sighed. "I suppose we should split up. What do you say?"

"Makes sense to me."

"You are not . . . uneasy?"

"Uneasy, yes," Lance said with a smile. "But not afraid."

"Okay. Here." He undid his belt and gave Lance the pistol. "Put this on."

Lance took the well-oiled leather holster and put it on his belt.

"Now, if you see Norman Sanders, or have any trouble, you fire three shots just like we keep saying, okay?"

"Right Dad, no problem."

"I will go south, you go north. If you lose the trail, meet me back here. And even if it keeps going, meet me here before sundown."

Joe started north, and Lance turned south. Lance's hand rested on the pistol, and the weight of it pressed against his thigh, heavy and reassuring. He rubbed the serrations on the hammer with his thumb, the steel cool and smooth to his touch. After a time he unsnapped the holster and drew the pistol, pointed it and said, "Boom, boom, boom," making the barrel kick up as if from recoil. He shook his head and thrust it back in the holster and snapped it shut.

He walked more than a mile before he came to a rubble field where part of the cliff had crumbled away strewing huge hunks of stone and gravel down the mountain side. He followed the tracks into the midst of it, and lost them. For a time he searched, wandering slowly between rocks the size of houses, rocks the size of cars, rocks the size of peas. There was no sign.

He climbed atop a car-size rock, and leaped from it to a house-size rock. No matter which way he faced, the wind seemed to blow right in his eyes as he surveyed his surroundings.

The helicopter had dropped them on the western slope, but he found he had worked his way around to the northwest. Directly below him, beyond the rockslide, was a stand of piñon trees lining the lip of a steep drop. Beyond, more canyons. Then the deep blue water of Oak Canyon Bay, and farther yet, the sweeping bands of color which were the Straight Cliffs and the Kaiparowits Plateau.

He looked at his watch; almost two o'clock. He found a protected spot on a ledge and ate his lunch. He had almost finished when a shadow passed across him and a crow landed on a rock opposite where he sat. It seemed entirely unafraid as it cocked its head to watch him from one beady black eye.

"Check this out." Lance tossed a piece of bread crust which landed not a foot from where the bird sat. It didn't seem to notice, but continued to study him.

"Fine, be that way," he said. He finished his lunch with the crow as an audience, then put on his pack and stood. "See you later," he said. He climbed back on top of the rock and crossed it, prepared to jump down. The crow leaped into the air, flapping frantically and cawing, and Lance turned and watched it fly up the slope, battling the wind, to land atop an outcropping that had once been part of the cliff above. Something red was at the base of the outcropping.

He leaped to the ground and scrambled up the slope to find an expedition-type backpack propped against the rock, as if its wearer had just shrugged it from his shoulders and taken a stroll. But it was patinaed with dust, and leaves and other debris had piled up in its lee. And there were no tracks near it anywhere. A lightweight sleeping bag was strapped to the top, and a foam backpacking mattress to the bottom. Tied to either side were a folding shovel and a collapsible pick.

He went through the pockets. Matches, compass, toilet paper, Swiss Army knife, flashlight, eating utensils, cookware, more gear than Lance would carry, but all of it sensible and useful.

And then he opened the map pocket and found the notebook. It was a cheap, cardboard-cover, spiral job, fifty cents at any drug store, and inside were notations of a sort he had seen before, aboard the houseboat, when a man lay dead with a wire in his brain.

"The third man," he said, voice trembling with excitement. "But what happened to him?" He shoved the notebook in his pocket, stood, and looked around. He searched for fifteen minutes before he found the cave.

It was well hidden, little more than a place at the base of the shattered cliff where dirt had crumbled away to reveal an opening. When he stuck his head inside, his body blocked most of the light, so he crawled in and found there was room to sit up. There was a faint musty smell, almost unpleasant, but not quite. After a minute his eyes adjusted and he found he could see quite well thanks to the light streaming through the opening.

It was an unremarkable cavern, round, about eight feet in diameter and four high. The floor was rock covered with fine dirt, and a rat had built a nest of sticks in a pocket near the opening. Not until he looked up at the ceiling was he certain he was not the first to find it.

There was a white circle painted on the stone, and in its center, rendered in negative where pigment had not been applied, was a figure. It had broad shoulders and narrow hips, crooked legs that bowed outward, a heavy, neckless head. A horn sprouted from each side of the head. Its arms were long and skinny and ended in huge hands. One hung at its side, the other pointed toward the back of the cavern. Lance peered more closely at the stone where the figure pointed, and saw that what he had mistaken for shadow or discoloration was actually another opening.

He peered inside, but again his body blocked the light and he could see nothing. He swore softly, thinking of the flashlight in the backpack outside. Then he remembered and reached into his pocket. Matches, a whole book of them. Joe had taught him well, never to go into the wilds without the ability to make a fire.

He tore a match out and struck it once, twice, three times before it sputtered to life. Its light revealed a narrow passageway four or five feet long, large enough for a man to crawl through, and beyond it, impenetrable darkness. The match burned down to his fingers before he dropped it.

He sat on the floor of the cavern and blinked his eyes, momentarily blinded by the match. The odor was stronger near the opening. He breathed shallowly, all his senses alert. He stared into the darkness, straining to see or hear anything that might be lurking within, waiting for him to crawl through that tight passage and emerge into its lair, arms and legs helplessly trapped as he thrust his head and neck forward, vulnerable.

"Come on," he muttered. "It's just a cave. I've been in caves before."

Just to be sure, however, he lit another match and looked again. There was nothing threatening at all, no sign of animals or . . . or anything. He shoved the matchbook in his pocket, drew a deep breath, closed his eyes, and slithered in. It was tighter than it looked and he had to back out, put his arms in first, then pull with his hands while he pushed with his legs to squeeze through.

Firm rock was beneath his hands as he emerged but he sensed the presence of the low roof, mere inches above his head, causing him to lie on his belly within this inner chamber. The smell was cloying, musty, so thick it was almost a taste in his throat. He wiped some clinging strands of web from his face and squirmed to retrieve the matches. He lit one and gasped.

It was indeed a low cavern, almost as wide as the other, and roughly rectangular, and the walls and ceiling were extraordinarily beautiful. Black and glistening as obsidian, laced with flecks of brilliant red, reflecting a thousand points of light from the flickering match that dimmed, dimmed, reached his fingers and went out. He swore softly and thrust his burned fingers in his mouth.

As he tore another match from the book there was a sound gentle as a sigh and he cocked his head to listen.

"Just the wind blowing outside," he murmured. He struck the match and turned his head to the other side. The lovely walls and ceiling were revealed again and he reached out a hand to stroke the glistening surface, but before he could do so his attention was distracted by something lying against the cavern wall and he squinted, one hand holding the match, the other raised toward the ceiling.

215

It was rounded and almost as long as he was, pale ivory, gleaming, and seemed to be moving ever so slightly, like a sheet in a gentle breeze. He stared at it in fascination as the match burned down. Something black and glistening thrust its way through the whiteness and swarmed upward to merge with the seething mass on the ceiling and walls. Just before the match went out he saw the toe of a hiking boot protruding from one end of the whiteness. Just before it went out in his shaking fingers, he saw a tremor of agitation sweep across the walls and ceiling as the black widow spiders reacted to the hated light. Just before it went out, he saw their pendulous bodies sway, clinging to each other in their thousands, layer upon layer, suspended by their spindly legs. And then it did go out.

A scream welled up in his chest but only a strangled sound escaped his lips. His breathing was rapid and shallow as he lay with his head against the cool stone listening to the rustle of tiny movements. Something landed beside his face with a soft plop and he jerked his head back. His whole body twitched and he screwed his eyes shut, queasy with nausea, listening to the rustle on the ceiling at his back, inches away, writhing with the angry spiders.

There was another plop, and another, and one landed on his back, one on his leg. He gritted his teeth and whimpered. The patter of falling bodies was all around him now and they were on him crawling and trailing their slender webs.

He tried to keep perfectly still. Because if he moved, the spiders would feel threatened. And if the spiders felt threatened . . . they would start to bite. He absolutely mustn't move. But they were on him, with that web. And he did not, did not want to become a participant in whatever horror was taking place beneath that shroud of web. He had to get out. Slowly he slid backward along the stone, pushing with his hands. Two inches. Three. Four and his feet touched the wall. He felt for the opening and shifted his hands to push another inch, another two inches, and his feet were inside the opening.

He shifted his hands and felt the stinging prick of a spiders fangs in the tender skin of his wrist and the scream exploded from his lungs as he scraped the spider off on the rock floor. He reared up against the ceiling and pulped hundreds of spiders, thrashing and screaming as hundreds more took their place clinging and biting. His hands slipped in their juices as he thrust himself backward along the passage.

He fell out into the main cavern shrieking and clawing at his head and neck, throwing himself furiously about, scrambled toward the light and emerged at the base of the cliff. He stumbled to his feet and brushed wildly at his hair, swatted his shirt and pants where the spiders were crawling inside. His cries were incoherent, his eyes mere slits between the swollen lids. He gasped for breath.

His hands fumbled the holster open and grasped the pistol. He swayed and moaned weakly, clutched it in his fists, raised it into the air and fired once, twice, three times. The pistol fell from his hands and clattered across the rocks and he cried, tears forcing past his eyelids. For another moment he remained standing, crying from the pain and the sadness within him. He took a staggering step and went down on one knee, slowly toppled to his side with a shuddering gasp, and lay still as a solitary spider crawled from his sleeve and dragged itself jerkily across the ground toward the darkness of the cave.

A short time later a figure came down the slope, weaving in and out between boulders, its movements swift and furtive. It stopped and knelt beside Lance, observed his shallow breathing, cackled and leaped to its feet. Its face was a distorted mask of indecision and greed, Norman Sanders's face, tongue protruding between cracked lips as he glanced warily about. He reached out and touched Lance's face, then paused and cocked his head. His eyes narrowed and he sprang back into the concealment of a boulder, growled low in his throat, and disappeared back the way he had come.

Sheriff Andrews held his Stetson to his head as the wind gusted. He leaned forward, head bent, and waited for the gust to pass before starting on. A hundred yards back he had come across the print of a deep-lug boot and been encouraged, but now the way seemed blocked by a rockslide and his shoulders sagged.

"Well hell," he muttered. "Some Indian I would be; I couldn't track an elephant across a sand box." He climbed atop a rock and gazed about dejectedly. Below him was a steep drop, above was a brush-choked gulley. He chose the gulley.

Right away he began to see broken branches and trampled weeds that seemed to indicate he was on track again. And when the wind brought a high-pitched keening to his ears he started bulling his way through the brush, intent on the sound, which came and went and seemed to have no definite source.

"Thornton!" he shouted, cupping his hands to his mouth. "Chase!" The wind snatched at the names and carried them away without answer. He struggled on. The brush became thicker and the wind grabbed his hat. He watched it sail away, borne upward across the slope only to fall spinning out of sight. He swore and pushed through a snag of interlocking branches, and almost tripped over Thornton's legs.

"Oh Christ!" The sheriff recoiled and threw out his arm to brace himself against the rock. Thornton lay supported by a bush as if he were sitting in a reclining chair, arms at his sides, his open eyes glazed and unseeing. There was a hole in the right side of his neck and the front of his parka was covered with blood. The sheriff quickly recovered from his shock and knelt to check for pulse though it was obviously useless. A moment later he shook his head and stood.

The weeping started again and he listened for a moment, head tilted, then forced his way through the brush growing up against the rock and found Chase huddled in a ball, rocking back and forth.

"Chase!" He knelt and took the man's arm. "Chase, it's me, Nathan." He shook him but Chase continued to cry and chitter through clenched teeth, arms wrapped around his knees and face hidden. He was shivering violently, and when the sheriff turned him over he saw blood but could not tell where it was coming from.

"It's all right," he said. "You're gonna be alright, Chase. Got to get you out of here though. Come on." He tried to get Chase on his feet but he only wailed louder and hugged himself tighter, and the sheriff had to drag him from behind the rock into the small open space beside Thornton.

As he stripped Thornton's corpse of its parka he said, "You

won't be needing this, old buddy." He pried Chase's arms off one at a time and managed to wrestle him into the parka and zip it. His face wrinkled with distaste as he wiped the blood from his hands on the grass and leaves. Then he looked at the object he had found clutched in Chase's hand. It was a feather. The vanes were crushed and the shaft broken from Chase's fist. The end of the shaft had been sharpened like a quill pen, but instead of ink, this had been dipped in blood. Chase's blood. He peered more closely at it and gave a snort of surprise when he noticed that two small, detailed eyes had been scribed into the shaft just above the sharpened point. After opening his jacket and tucking the feather in his shirt pocket, he retrieved Thornton's radio and switched it on.

"Freeman, Freeman, this is Andrews. Do you copy?" He had to concentrate to hear the faint voice from the speaker.

"Freeman here — ," the signal broke up, then, " — for you?"

"Freeman, your signal's fading. Can you move toward the mountain?"

"Ah, Roger, Sheriff. Winds here are — ," hiss of static, " — five minutes."

"Freeman, did you say you will be here in five minutes?"

"Affirmative, Sheriff."

"Okay Freeman. I'll be waiting." He threaded the radio holster on his own belt. "Chase," he said, "you aren't gonna make me carry you down this mountain are you?" He squatted beside him and pulled his head back to gently slap his face. The sight of the sunken eyelid, and the blood and clear jelly streaming down Chase's face, made him wince and reconsider. The injured man was not shivering as badly as he had been a few minutes ago, but neither did he show any awareness of his surroundings. The sheriff tried several times to pry his arms loose, but Chase shrieked and curled up again.

He sighed, drew back his fist, and cracked him firmly on the jaw. Chase went limp. He seized a wrist in each hand and stood, drawing Chase up onto his back, started down the gulley.

"I'm glad we're going downhill, old buddy," he gasped as he struggled through the brush. Twice he had to put his burden down and rest, swinging his arms to restore circulation. He was still in the brush when he heard the helicopter. He eased Chase down again and got out the radio.

"Freeman, I hear your chopper. Can you read me?"

"Yes sir, Sheriff, loud and clear. What's your situation?"

"Not very damn good Freeman. Thornton's dead, and Chase looks like he lost an eye somehow and he's curled up in a ball and doesn't even know what planet he's on. I'm tryin' to get 'em both somewhere you can land and get us the hell out of here."

"Oh, dear God. Yes, okay Sheriff. How long do you figure?"

"Give me ten minutes. You just hang around, okay?"

"Yes sir, Sheriff, I'll be waiting."

"Okay." He shoved the radio in the holster and dragged Chase's arms over his shoulders. Chase began to moan when they reached the bottom of the gulley, and by the time the sheriff found a low ridge free of obstacles he was conscious enough to curl up again. And that was how the sheriff left him; curled in a ball beside a mesquite bush.

"I can see you off to the southwest," the sheriff said into the radio. "If you'll rotate in a slow circle I'll tell you when you're facing me." The helicopter did as he asked and he said, "Whoa! Right there! Now you come ahead on." As it approached it bobbled and lurched in the wind. He waved his hand as he said, "Can you see me?"

"Roger, Sheriff, I see you."

"Okay. Don't you land yet. I've got to go back for Thornton. But you stick around."

"Will do, sir."

He brought Thornton down the same way he did Chase, giving the Weatherby rifle a longing look, but too tired for the added burden. When he arrived beside Chase, he let the body slip to the ground and moaned, rolled his head to ease the stiffness in his neck. His face was scratched and bleeding from the branches and he rubbed at his eyes, which were red and irritated from the wind and dust. Gripping the radio in one huge fist he said, "Okay Freeman, bring it in."

"Yes sir. It may take me a few tries in this wind, so stay clear."

The helicopter came in slowly, bobbing up and down, touched its skids and lifted away again, circled and touched.

He saw the pilot wave and grabbed Chase in his arms, ran bent at the waist and deposited him unceremoniously on the floor, sprinted back for Thornton. A gust of wind poured over the ridge as he dragged the body toward the helicopter and it tilted, its rotors whistling just above his head as he threw himself face down on the ground. The machine lifted into the air and its tail rotor whipped past, then it settled again and he raced toward it and hurled himself and the body into the open door.

"Sorry about that, Sheriff!" the pilot shouted as they climbed away from the ridge.

"S'okay. But I'd rather not lose my head right now." The sheriff propped Chase in a seat and buckled him in, did the same with Thornton's body, then fastened himself in the copilot's seat.

"All right, let's see if we can find Joe and Lance," he said. He unclipped the microphone and depressed the button. "Joe, this is Nathan calling, do you read me?"

The helicopter bucked and lurched and the speaker hissed. The sheriff tried again and again as the pilot guided them in a broad sweep of the mountain, but there was no reply.

"Can we get in any closer?" the sheriff asked. "Maybe we can spot them."

"I sure wish we could, Sheriff, but the winds coming off the mountain are getting real bad. I've already taken more chances today than I ever have before in my life. We're running low on fuel and short on daylight, and Walt Chase doesn't look good at all to me. I'd advise that we head back. Sir."

"Yeah. Damn!" The sheriff slammed his fist on the armrest and the pilot flinched. "I hate to leave them out here! Why can't I contact them? That crazy bastard probably won't use the radio."

"Sir, our fuel—"

"Yeah, yeah, I know." The sheriff scowled, squinting toward the mountain. He waved his hand. "Okay Freeman, take us home."

The pilot sighed with relief and set his course toward the northeast.

"Well, it won't be the first time you've slept under the stars Joe," the sheriff muttered. "I'll see you in the morning."

He turned to watch the mountain recede and saw the last rays of the setting sun bathe its summit in red light so that for an instant it looked like a volcano, simmering with molten violence. Then the light faded and the mountain became a dark silhouette, solitary and immense amidst the expanse of the plateau it dominated, stark, dark, and brooding.

"Good luck, old friend," the sheriff whispered.

Ten

Joe found his son where he had fallen, outside the mouth of the cave, the pistol by his side. He knelt beside him and lifted his head. Gently he stroked the hair out of Lance's face, a face swollen beyond recognition and covered with circles of reddened, feverish skin where the spiders had bitten him. He saw the broad, flat footprints in the soft soil at his side.

A crippled spider dragged its sagging abdomen across Lance's shoulder and dropped on Joe's hand. With a strangled cry of horror and rage he grabbed the spider in his fist, squeezed until his whole arm trembled and his nails gouged into his palm and drew blood.

He hugged his son to his chest. He closed his eyes, and tipped back his head, and his mouth opened but no sound came. The wind swirled about them and the sun went into the west and darkness came across the great mountain and Joe held his son and cried silently toward the sky.

The night grew cold. Joe shivered and the tears froze on his lashes and on his jacket. After a time the moon rose and cast the shadow of the man and his son across the stones, across the dry earth. The wind slowly died, now only a breeze, now an icy breath carrying the lonely call of an owl across the sleeping mountain.

Another shadow appeared beside those of Joe and his son, and with it came the sound of hooves on stone. A small girl leaped from her pony and stood beside Joe holding the reins in her fist.

"Father," she said hesitantly in Navajo.

Joe's eyes opened and were slow in focusing.

"Ya aat' eh, Little Daughter," he said in a thick voice.

"Old Man Walker sent me for you."

Joe looked down at his son.

"We can put him on my pony," the girl said.

Joe allowed the girl to help him to his feet. His movements were stiff and clumsy as he picked Lance up in his arms and laid him across the pony's blanket. The girl tied Lance's hands and feet beneath the belly of the animal so he would not fall off.

"Come," the girl said. Joe followed her down the mountain. He had no sense of time passing, nor distance covered, only movements repeated over and over, scuff of feet, whisper of his breath, jingle of the pony's bridle. The wind had gone and the moon and stars shined with an icy brilliance through the clear night air.

They came to an old hogan standing alone upon a wide plain. Its silvered log walls gleamed in the moonlight and the plume from its smoke hole stood straight up in the sky. A dog barked from among the gray, shapeless silhouettes of the sheep which stirred nervously until the girl spoke and the dog fell silent. She loosed her pony in the pole corral beside the hogan and led Joe inside.

The old man Joe had met on the mountain was sitting cross-legged on the floor beside the fire. Its light flickered on his face that was wrinkled and worn like the land. Its light filled the hogan with shifting shadows and cloaked the objects on the shelves in mystery. A basket suspended from a roof beam swayed as if something had brushed past it, then became still.

Old Man Walker's eyes stared beyond the log walls, outside the time of sunrise and sunset. His gnarled hands rested on his knees, and his yellow Chin Lee blanket was around his shoulders and he did not move as the girl guided Joe to a place beside the fire.

Joe sat where she put him and stared blankly into the flames. The girl looked from Joe to Old Man, then went to her bed against the wall and lay down. She pillowed her head on her hands. The fire reflected brightly in her emerald green eyes, eyes that contrasted strangely with her black hair and brown skin.

After a time Old Man stirred and reached for the pile of wood at his side, added a stick to the fire, and drew a deep breath and sighed.

"I knew your father," he said in Navajo. Joe stared at the fire and did not answer.

"He was a great warrior," Old Man said, nodding his head. "Brave and smart, generous to all the people. His feet always followed the Blessing Way, and so, even when he grew old he was beautiful.

"The body of a man grows old and weak with age, Grandson, but his spirit does not. If a man lives his life in the Light, his spirit grows strong like a towering tree, putting out new leaves each season. He grows stronger and richer in his spirit until, at the end, he puts aside his used up body and flies beautifully into the next world."

Old Man spread his hands like a bird and their shadow flew among the roof beams. Joe looked up and tears ran down his cheeks.

"My son—," he said, catching himself. For it was not appropriate that a Navajo should use the name of the dead, or even their relationship, in talking about them. "The young man who died . . . he was to be married," he said.

"Yes." Old Man dropped his hands. "That one was a warrior like his father and his father's father, and he followed the warrior's path into the next world, not knowing the name of that which he fought. And even had he known—." He shook his head.

"He was hunting for a man," Joe said, holding out his hand. "A crazy man, but only a man, Grandfather."

The blind, filmy eyes turned to Joe with a fierce, unblinking gaze, as if Old Man could see Joe clearly and did not like what he saw, and Joe was forced to look away uneasily.

"When you faced the Yellow Men of the East, you fought bravely and well, and the *bellicanos* rewarded you. What did they give you?"

Joe's face twisted. "They gave me medals."

"And what did you do with those medals?"

"I put them away," Joe whispered.

"Yes, and now it is time to put something else away," Old Man said calmly. "You must put away your attitude."

"I do not understand," Joe moaned.

"Your attitude." Old man cocked his head to the side. "Your *bellicano* attitude that nothing matters, nothing has purpose. You have been acting like the whole world is just one big coincidence."

"Grandfather, you are not making sense," Joe said.

"I am making perfect sense," Old Man said. "Your friends have been killed in the most terrible fashion. You have lost that beautiful young man, and yet you believe it is a man up there," he jerked his head, "on the mountain." He rapped his own head with his knuckles. "How much must you lose before you will listen?"

Joe rubbed his face with his hands. "What would you have me believe? That we have been hunting a *chindi?* That ghosts kill men and walk about in daylight?"

"A *chindi!*" Old Man snorted. "You think a simple *chindi* could cause so much death? Could drive the Ancient Ones from their canyons? Could call up the winds and the animal spirits?" He produced a growling sound in his throat. "It is no *chindi* out there, in the night. The Ancient Ones had a name for it, but that name has been forgotten. The one who taught me called it Eater-of-Souls."

Joe glanced uneasily over his shoulder as the girl whimpered in her sleep. The shadows seemed to thicken and swirl as the warmth of the fire faded. He held his hands out toward it, suddenly aware of how cold he was. His face was gaunt and his eyes were sunk deep beneath his lowered brow.

"You are right about me, Grandfather," he said in a voice barely more than a whisper. "I am empty. Perhaps I died on the mountain with that young man, and have not yet fallen. I have no beliefs. I no longer walk in beauty."

"So." Old Man shook his head and clucked with his tongue. "Now you feel sorry for yourself."

But Joe merely stared into the fire silently, too tired, too filled with grief to respond. Old Man pulled his blanket tighter around his shoulders and let his head fall forward on his chest. Joe's eyes closed and his face became slack. His breathing deepened.

"You must find your belief if you are to avenge the deaths of the others," Old Man muttered. "Even so, the outcome is doubtful. Tomorrow is time enough. Tomorrow I will give a Sing for you, a Sing that has not been heard in your generation."

The calls went out quickly when Sheriff Andrews arrived in Mexican Hat. Since one of their agents had been killed, the regional FBI office was alerted sooner than it might normally have been. Both the Utah and Arizona State Police agreed to increase patrol activity and assume surveillance responsibility for all roads in the area. The Navajo Tribal Police were called in, as there was absolutely no doubt now that a homicidal maniac was loose in the vicinity of Navajo Mountain, which was Navajo Indian Reservation.

The sheriff picked up the telephone for one more call, massaging his forehead with his other hand.

"Hello?" a woman's voice answered.

"Anna? This is Nathan Andrews."

There was the slightest pause before she said, "What's happened?"

"Nothing Anna, nothing at all. I'm just calling to tell you not to worry about Joe and Lance. We had a little trouble this—"

"Trouble? Were they hurt?" Her voice rose an octave, and he lowered his in response.

"They're both fine, Anna. Just let me finish."

"All right. Sorry."

"We had some trouble this afternoon. There was an accident and two FBI agents were injured, one of them fatally." He heard her gasp and hurried to say, "We had to evacuate them immediately, and the winds got so bad that we couldn't reach Joe and Lance. So they're spending the night on the mountain, or near it. I'm sure you agree they can take care of themselves until we get back for them in the morning."

"You left them on Navajo Mountain? For the night?"

"Now listen Anna, there's no reason to worry."

"Did you bring in the . . . did you find Norman Sanders?"

"No. But we're closing in on—"

"Joe and Lance are up there with it." Her voice suddenly sounded dead, and before he could reply she said, "Goodbye Sheriff."

The dial tone filled his ear. For a moment he stared at the receiver before dropping it in the cradle. He sighed wearily and stood, reached for the hat that wasn't there, swore softly and retrieved his coat from the hook beside his office door, and walked out past the front desk. He paused to speak to the deputy on duty.

"How many men have we got for tomorrow morning, and who are they?"

"Thirty-eight, Sheriff. Twelve from our department, nine FBI men, seven from the NTP, including a couple of their best trackers. And, ah," he glanced at his call record, "Kane and Garfield Counties are both loaning us five men."

"Okay." The sheriff's face was lined with weariness and his mouth opened as if he had something to say, but after a moment he shook his head and lifted his hand in a weary gesture. "Good night. Hope it's a quiet one."

"Yes sir, Sheriff. Good night."

As the sheriff drove toward his home, Anna paced the trailer and wrung her hands. There was nothing she could do now. She had tried and failed. The situation was inescapable and irreparable, so she did what the *Dine'* have ever done when confronted with the impossible; she sat and waited for circumstances to change.

She draped her best blanket around her shoulders and sat on the living room floor and her breathing gradually became deep and even. Her face became dull and her eyes closed to mere slits. Her head slumped forward on her chest. No Tibetan monk or Zen Buddhist was more adept at self-induced trance than the Navajo. She would wait.

She was still sitting in the same position when the sun emerged from its place in the east and began to warm the trailer, and one hundred miles to the southwest a loose circle of men converged on the slopes of Navajo Mountain. The light had touched the mountain's jagged summit ten minutes earlier, and now, as the long shadows formed, sharpened, and began to shrink toward the mesas and stone spires which cast them, the men began to climb, clutching their weapons. And Anna sat and waited.

It was a cold morning as Joe buried his son. The girl, whose name was Bene', and whose Navajo name was Cricket Singing, helped Joe dig, but she did not touch the body. Joe himself rolled his son in the blanket and lowered him into the earth.

He had put his son's shoes on the wrong feet, so his spirit could not find its way back once it had made the journey into the next world. He buried a sack of corn tortillas and dried peaches by his son's side, so he would have something to eat on the journey, and his canteen, filled with fresh water, so he would not go thirsty. The journey into the next world was long and hard, but Joe's son would not go unprepared. When it was done, Old Man chanted:

"Now you go on your way alone.
What you are now, we know not.
To what clan you now belong, we know not.
From now on, you are not of this earth."

It was a simple ceremony, and when it was finished Old Man and Joe went back to the hogan while the girl took the sheep down to the good, green grass where they could feed all day. Old Man lifted a cloth sack from its nail beside the door. He opened it and took out his headband and tied it around

229

his head. It was soft brown rabbit fur with a finger-width, blue-and-white-beaded band in its center.

He was wearing a brown velveteen shirt, bound at the waist with a belt of silver conchos. When he reached to the woodpile the sleeve slid up his thin wrist, exposing a heavy silver bracelet. It was an eagle bracelet, with the wings folded backward to form the wristband, and an exquisite oval turquoise gemstone set in its breast.

"I am the last one who knows the Eagleway Sing," Old Man said when they were seated again in the hogan. "Our ancestors performed this Sing before they went into battle. It is the Sing of Monster Slayer, and Child Of The Water, the Hero Twins. To them it was given before they returned to this world after visiting their father the sun. And then they returned and slew the monsters that had come into the world.

"The monsters came out of woman in the beginning, out of woman and out of man. The First People copulated with animals, and with plants, and the monsters were born. Terrible creatures that lived only to cause evil. The Hero Twins killed the monsters, but one escaped by its great cunning and evil.

"Eater-of-Souls killed a man and ate his flesh. He put on the man's skin so that when Monster Slayer came looking for him, he saw only a man. The false man told Monster Slayer that Eater-of-Souls had fallen into a hole from which he could not return.

"So the monster remained hidden among the sons and daughters of the First People, ancestors of the *Dine'*. In the beginning he did little evil, fearing Monster Slayer and Child Of The Water. But in time those two went into the west and did not return. Then did he begin to feed on the sons and daughters. And many did he kill, and he gathered their power, and the others fled their homes and never returned.

"So the First People summoned their greatest warriors, and their wisest shamans, and they pushed Eater-of-Souls back into the world of darkness through a hole they made in a sacred place. And they closed the hole with powerful spells, and there the monster remained until the place was opened again by the *bellicanos*." Old Man held out a hand, palm up, and slowly clenched his knobby fingers into a fist.

"He is filled with hatred and evil beyond measure. For what the First People did to him, he intends to destroy the sons and daughters of their sons and daughters, the *Dine'*, every one. In the body of a man he is roaming the world beyond these walls, gathering his power objects, his necklace of human teeth. I think perhaps he already has them. The killing will begin soon.

"Could such a thing happen?" Joe asked. Old Man snorted.

"Plague," he said. "Famine. Insanity. Those are words they will use when the *Dine'* start to die. Eater-of-Souls is old and shrewd, and knows death in all its forms. His patience is limitless, and he thinks the *Dine'* are not the warriors they once were. If he is right, the *Dine'* will die."

"And if there is a warrior to face him?" Joe asked. A muscle twitched in his jaw. "If he is the one who slew that young man, and the others, I will track him down, and I will kill him with my own hand. I swear it."

"How can you kill something you do not believe in?" Old Man asked.

"I will try to believe," Joe said, bowing his head. "At the least, I will pretend to believe."

"Very well." Old Man sighed. "If that is how it must be, nothing can change it. You did not ask for this task, and I can ask no more of you. But the enemy is strong. Know well the danger." He sat with his head lowered, his old face sagging. His hand trembled as he stroked his jaw. Then he shook himself and clapped his hands.

"Time is short, Grandson, so let us begin!" he barked. "Take off all your clothes except your undershorts."

Joe did as he was told and Old Man handed him a blanket which he wrapped around his shoulders. Old Man held a gourd cup to his lips and Joe drank the bitter liquid it held,

231

then followed him outside and along a path that descended into a shallow arroyo where clear water seeped from a crack in the rock. Old Man lifted the flap of a small sweat house, crudely constructed of vertical logs caulked with mud. Joe placed the blanket in Old Man's extended hand and crouched to enter.

The flap fell back and he was left in darkness and stifling heat. Sweat popped out all over his body, ran down his chest and legs, stung his eyes. An upended log was the only seat, and he sat on it and waited. Several hours later the flap opened and he emerged, squinting against the light. Old Man handed him a sweat stick and he scraped his body clean with its sharpened edge, then wrapped the blanket around his shoulders.

On the way back to the hogan he had to stop and vomit as a sudden, violent cramp wracked his belly. Old Man waited, nodding his head in approval, then led him inside and seated him beside the fire. From the shelves, Old Man selected the materials he would require for the first part of the Sing. When he had a variety of jars, cans, pouches, and bundles arranged beside the fire pit, he began the dry painting on the floor near the door, where the light was best.

He distributed his materials on paper plates so they would be easy to use. Blue from dried larkspur blossoms. White from corn meal. Corn pollen for yellow. Powdered coral bean for red and charcoal from a lightning-blasted tree for black. Joe could not help staring in astonishment as Old Man created the painting from memory, working without benefit of sight, never hesitating or making the slightest mistake.

First he put the four sacred mountains at the four cardinal points. *Sisnajini* in the east, a lightning bolt through its heart driven deep into the earth, fixing it for all time in its proper place, gleaming white in the dawn. *Tsodzil* in the south, a blade of pure blue flint pinning it to the earth. *Dokaoslid* in the west, transfixed with a sunbeam, shining with abalone. *Dibentsa*, the great black mountain of the north, bound forever in its place by a rainbow. Beside each mountain, outside

232

the boundary of the painting, he thrust a brightly feathered prayer stick in each of the four cardinal points. Thus the boundaries of *Dinetah* were established.

Old Man chanted as he worked, and he worked with swift, sure motions. The sound was rhythmic and repetitive, never ceasing as his hands moved, pouring the colors from the crook of his finger perfectly and exactly. Quickly the figures came to life on the floor, the hard-packed dirt floor which was the earth itself. The meaning of the words became lost in the sound, and the sound became the meaning, and the chant was the air that embraced the earth, the swirling winds that gave it life, and it was the sound of the ceremony, summoning the powers that had accompanied the *Dine'* since their emergence into the present world. The air thrummed with the power of Old Man's chant.

Now Old Man created the sacred forms of the Holy People. He painted the War God Twins, Monster Slayer and Child Of Water, clothed in their armor of flint, carrying their bows and knives, quivers of lightning on their backs. Between them stood Talking God, maternal grandfather of all the gods, dangerous and unpredictable, storm clouds gathered about his grim face and mists rising at his feet.

Joe kneeled where Old Man placed him, in the center of the painting. A pipe was thrust into his mouth and he puffed on it. The smoke filled his nose and mouth with a sharp icy chill. He puffed again and it expanded in his lungs, filled him with a chill that burned. The smoke was acrid and yet strangely creamy, and it was the taste of the ceremony, and the smell.

The elements of the chant mingled until it was difficult to tell where sight stopped and hearing began. A word became blue, and white was the hiss of a snake. Sunlight smelled like a leaf of mint crushed between the fingers. The chant bound the two men in a separate place where nothing of the outside world could intrude.

Amidst the sound and the taste and the smell, Joe saw the gods step from the floor of the hogan, one at a time, and

233

dance the dance that was unique to them, and they were the look and the shape of the ceremony.

Old Man painted designs on Joe's face and body. He shook his rattles over him and brushed him with a branch whose leaves had an acrid odor. In Joe's right hand he put a prayer stick and in his left a knife of flint. The prayer stick was made from desert willow, its shaft smoothly polished, eagle feathers suspended from its end and a quartz crystal embedded in its tip. The knife was razor keen and its handle was bound with unblemished doeskin, and these were the feel of the ceremony.

All day Joe remained inside the hogan, and his inward journey led him far beyond its poor walls of mud and logs. Just before the sun went to its place in the west, Old Man carefully moistened Joe's body and touched it to parts of the paintings, his arms to the Hero Twin's weapons, his legs to their legs, his head to Talking God's head, so that their powers would enter him.

He helped Joe to his feet, then swept up every trace of the painting and carried it outside and gave it to the winds. He returned for Joe and they stood in the light of the setting sun as Old Man chanted and swept Joe clean with an eagle feather brush. The shadow of the mesa touched them and they returned inside, where Cricket Singing had prepared a meal.

"You must eat only a little," Old Man said. He put a spoonful of cornmeal mush in a bowl and handed it to Joe, who took a bite and washed it down with a sip of water, found it was all he could do to eat three small mouthfuls, for his appetite had left him.

"Do not worry," Old Man said. "Cricket Singing will eat enough for both of you."

The chant continued into the night. Old Man bathed him with a white powder that made his skin tingle, and later gave him the pipe again. He washed Joe with a damp cloth that took away the powder and made him shiver. Old Man stoked the fire higher. Some time late in the night he prepared a tea

234

that filled Joe's belly with its warmth and his nose with its aroma.

On the other side of the fire Old Man began a new chant, and as the words rolled forth a bright, clear light grew within the hogan until Joe could see every detail with amazing clarity. The words of the chant leaped and ran, high and free and brave.

> "In beauty may I walk.
> All day long may I walk.
> Through the returning seasons may I walk.
> Beautifully will I possess again.
> Beautiful birds.
> Beautifully joyful birds.
> On the trail marked with pollen may I walk.
> With flowers about my feet may I walk.
> With dew about my feet may I walk.
> With beauty may I walk.
> With beauty all around me may I walk.
> In old age wandering on a trail of beauty,
>   lively may I walk.
> In old age wandering on a trail of beauty,
>   living again may I walk.
> It is finished in beauty.
> It is finished in beauty."

Tears ran down Joe's face. He wiped his eyes with the back of his hand and opened them to find a stranger standing before him.

It was a young man, his face handsome and proud, and when he smiled his teeth were white against his brown skin. A strip of red cloth bound his head and his black hair flowed over his shoulders. He wore a blue satin shirt and leggings of doeskin with silver buttons on the side. A coyote sat beside him. Its fur was pure white and gleamed like the moon, and its eyes were emerald green.

Everything faded in comparison to the man and coyote. The hogan, the fire, even Joe's own hand reaching out toward them as if by its own volition, looked gray and lifeless beside those two splendid figures. They glowed with an inner radiance. The very air around them shimmered in a faint aura that scintillated with every color of the rainbow. A curious sound filled the hogan, and the memory came to Joe of a time as a child when he lay in a creek beside a waterfall with his ears under water, and heard thousands and thousands of silvery bubbles breaking as they rose toward the surface. Yes.

The young man did not speak, and with a look of gentle compassion he extended his left hand holding a knife, a knife black as midnight and sparkling like diamond. He tossed it in the air and caught it by the blade, offered the leather-bound handle to Joe. Joe hesitated. The man shook it impatiently and the coyote stirred, blinking its luminous green eyes.

Joe reached for the knife and saw the heavy silver bracelet encircling the stranger's wrist; an eagle with an exquisite oval turquoise gemstone embedded in its breast. He took the knife in his hand, and his eyes sought those of the stranger. "You will have to get close to use it," the man said. The coyote grinned and its red tongue lolled from a corner of its mouth. Then the young man and the coyote turned to the door and were gone.

Joe stared at the glistening blade, turning it this way and that. It looked very sharp. The way the firelight reflected from its mirror surface was mesmerizing. He put his fist to his mouth and he yawned. Suddenly he felt unutterably weary. He lay on his side and pulled the blanket over him, placed the knife on the blanket beside his head, and fell asleep.

When he awoke in the morning the hogan was cold. He sat up and reached for the blanket, but it was not there. He was dressed as he had been when he first set out days earlier . . . how many days? Three? Four? He shook his head and stood, looking about in amazement.

The hogan was empty. There was no sign that it had been occupied for many years. Dust filled the fire pit. Webs fluttered in the corners. Atop one of the roof beams was a ragged bird nest, and the floor beneath it was spattered white with droppings. Joe rubbed his face with his hands and looked again, but his eyes had not been playing tricks; the hogan was abandoned. He hugged himself against the chill and stepped outside.

He blinked and sneezed from the brightness of the sunrise. There were no sheep, no dog, no girl. No Old Man Walker. He made a complete circuit of the hogan and its crumpled pole corral without finding any tracks except his own. A faint path, overgrown with sparse grass and weeds, led him to a shallow arroyo where water trickled from a fissure in the rocks.

Joe drank and splashed his face in the small pool beside the rock. As he stood he saw a tumble of mud and sticks that would at one time have been a sweat house. He shivered and buttoned his jacket tighter under his chin, shoving his hands in his pockets. He hurried back up the path and stood in the morning light, letting it warm him.

As he lifted the hem of his jacket to hitch up his belt his gaze fell upon the odd, leather-bound handle protruding from his knife sheath. He drew it, and looked with eyes of wonder on the elegant obsidian blade that had replaced his old military knife. It was symmetrical, shaped like a throwing blade but longer, tapering gracefully to a needle point. The edge was so sharp that when he lightly touched it to his thumb the skin parted with no feeling of pressure.

He watched the drop of blood form, run down, drop to the dry earth. For the first time in his memory, he wished for a sack of pollen so he could make an offering to Dawn Girl, sprinkling golden grains on the earth as he faced the east. Even so, having no pollen, he let the blood fall on the earth and opened his arms to the rising sun and sang in Navajo:

"Wind behind me, wind before me.
With it I walk.
Clouds behind me, clouds before me.
With it I walk.
Thunder behind me, thunder before me.
With it I walk.
Lightning striking behind me,
Lightning striking before me.
With it I walk.
Now I come walking.
Into the dark places walking.
Wind, clouds, thunder, lightning.
I come walking."

He put his bleeding thumb to his face and painted two horizontal stripes on each cheek, one on his forehead. Then he held the knife up, between his face and the rising sun, so its shadow fell upon him and the light streamed past it in a bright corona.

"Walk in beauty, Old Man," he said. Then he turned and started walking toward Navajo Mountain.

After two days, the search for Norman Sanders had moved on. There was general agreement among the various law enforcement agencies that he was no longer in the vicinity of Navajo Mountain, and that if by some wild chance he was, the increasingly cold weather would drive him down. The search was now concentrating on the roads and towns, where a computer programmer from Los Angeles would doubtless appear sooner or later.

And added to the mystery of Sanders's disappearance was that of Joe Redhill and Lance. Even the Navajo Police trackers had found only a few traces of their presence; everything else had been scoured clean by the wind. They had not found the backpack, or the cave.

Sheriff Andrews had been trying to reach Anna for two

nights and days. She wasn't answering her phone and none of her friends or relatives had seen her. Now, as the search for Sanders and the Redhills became a more or less routine procedure, he was considering driving out toward Winged Rock when his telephone rang.

"Yeah?" he growled, holding the phone with his shoulder as he shuffled reports on his desk.

"Harold Lowtah on the line for you, Sheriff."

"Put him through." The sheriff's expression changed from boredom to alertness as he pushed the reports aside.

"Sheriff Andrews?" Harold's voice sounded worried.

"Yeah, hello Harold. What can I do for you?"

"Sheriff, Anna's shown up. One of our employees called to tell me she just came down to the dock and took the Whaler out."

"Oh." His eyebrows lifted in surprise. "She say where she was going?"

"Didn't say a word to anyone. But the employee, Chris is her name, said she thought Anna had a rifle or a shotgun with her."

"Well hell, that's just great. Now I've got someone else to look for." He ran a hand through his hair and bowed his head in thought. "I better drive out there Harold. Can you arrange to be free when I arrive?"

"Certainly, Sheriff."

Sheriff Andrews called the desk and told the deputy his plans, made a few more phone calls to update himself on the search effort, then hurried across the parking lot to his patrol car. He was ten miles out on Highway 261, beneath a leaden sky, when the heater finally started taking the chill out of his bones, and by the time he turned left at 95 he was toasty. But the air was cold when he rolled down his window to spit after clearing his throat, and Bears Ears Mountain off to his right had a dusting of white on its peak.

He left his car in the almost-deserted parking lot and was instructed by the middle-aged Indian woman at the information desk to go right in. Harold arose from behind his desk at the sheriff's knock and opened the door.

"Hello, Sheriff," he said. He wore a squash blossom neck-lace big as a horse harness over a black turtleneck shirt, brown wool slacks, and elegant, gray leather shoes.

"Harold." The sheriff gripped the big hand in his own, shook it once, and released it. "How're you making out?"

"Not too well." He shook his head mournfully. "Marina operations are in chaos with Joe and Lance missing. Good thing winter's almost here and business is slack. And now this thing with Anna . . ." He let the thought trail off, motioned toward a chair, and went behind his desk. The sheriff remained standing.

"Any idea where she's gone?"

Harold glanced up at him from beneath drooping lids that failed to hide the intelligence in his dark eyes or the wariness that he extended to *Dine'* and *bellicanos* alike. "No more than you do, Sheriff."

"Meaning you think, like I do, that she's gone out to find Joe and Lance."

Harold closed his eyes, raised his eyebrows, and nodded. "Yes, I'm afraid so."

The sheriff took off his crisp new Stetson and swiped his forehead with the sleeve of his jacket, drew a deep breath. "Well," he said, "guess I'm gonna have to go after her. First, I want to have a little talk with this girl that saw her leave. Then I'm afraid I'll have to commandeer you and your boat."

"Me?" Harold's eyebrows shot up. "Why me? If it's official business why not use one of your—"

"Because every minute we stand here talking is another minute she's ahead of me," the sheriff said calmly. "By the time I got a patrol boat up here it'd be another hour lost. You don't mind helping to find one of your people, do you?"

Harold sighed. "No." He shook his head sadly. "Of course not."

"Good. I'd like to get down to the docks."

Harold moved lethargically toward his coat and hat and told the woman at the desk his plans, then hurried to keep up

240

as the sheriff strode down the footpath to the marina.

"Hello, Chris," the sheriff said as they entered the rental office. He shook her hand gently, and when she didn't appear to recognize him added, "Nathan Andrews. We met this summer."

"Oh." She waved a hand in front of her face. "Oh yes, I remember now. Sorry if I seem a little out of it." Her hair looked stringy and her face was dull and lifeless.

"That's all right Chris. I'd be surprised if you weren't." The sheriff had seen how Chris and Lance were together during the time he spent at the marina earlier in the summer, during the search for the third pot hunter, and his voice was sympathetic as he said, "I expect the past few days have been pretty hard on you."

"Yes." She blinked her eyes and lowered her head, swiped at her nose with the back of her hand. "I don't know what I can tell you," she said as she looked up. "Anna came down to the dock, got in the boat, and left. She looked . . . I don't know, fierce I guess. She was carrying two bags, one looked like a small pack and the other was something long and slender in a sort of cloth carrying case. That's all I can tell you, except she went out of here at full throttle."

"How much fuel was in the boat?" the sheriff asked.

"Let me see." She stepped behind the counter and checked the fuel log. "It was filled two days ago, the last time it was used. Yeah, she's got full tanks."

"How was she dressed?"

Chris closed her eyes in thought. "Long pants, shirt, jacket. A red jacket. No hat."

The sheriff turned to Harold. "Sounds like she was prepared for something," he said.

"Yes, unfortunately it does," Harold said with an unhappy sigh.

"Well, thank you Chris." The sheriff touched the brim of his hat. "I promise you I'll do everything I can to find Anna, to find all the Redhills. And don't you worry, those men can take care of themselves. Okay?"

"Okay, Sheriff. Thanks." Chris managed a tired smile.

"Harold, let's see how fast that old boat of yours is." He gestured toward the door and Harold nodded at Chris and stepped out onto the dock.

"My boat needs fuel," Harold said.

"Fine. If you can handle it by yourself, I'll get some equipment out of my car."

"I'll meet you at the fuel dock." Harold turned away without awaiting a reply. Twenty minutes later they headed out of the bay. They passed the big houseboat where it had been moored in isolation beyond the maintenance building since being salvaged from the rocks. Harold stared at it angrily.

"I should have sold it," he muttered. He was sitting at the salon steering station since it was too cold outside on the flying bridge.

"Hm?" The sheriff gave him a confused look.

Harold's soft eyes glanced at him from beneath lowered lids. "Nothing," he said. "Where are we going?"

"Dungeon Canyon." The sheriff stood beside him, gripping the handrail and gazing at the smooth lake, water the color of slate. "If she's not there, she'll be somewhere close by."

"I suppose." Harold hunched his shoulders and withdrew his head like a turtle. His normally lugubrious features settled into a doomed expression and the sheriff, after one or two halfhearted attempts at conversation, fell silent as the boat sped down the lake. Gray water hissed beneath the boat and gray sky swirled overhead. The day grew colder.

"There's a boat," Harold said as they passed the broad bay of Oak Canyon.

"Where?" the sheriff squinted and shook his head.

"There." He pointed and the sheriff sighted along his arm. A small white dot was visible several miles distant against the darker shoreline.

The sheriff shook his head. "You've got good eyes."

"Yes. Do you want to check it out?"

"Yeah, good idea. We'll only lose a few minutes if it isn't her." But it was. The Whaler was beached and the outboards

242

raised clear of the water. Two bow lines were secured to anchors that had been carefully set in deep sand. Anna's tracks led up the beach, straight toward Navajo Mountain.

"Guess I better go after her," the sheriff said as they stood on the shore.

"And what if she doesn't want to come back with you?" Harold arched an eyebrow.

"Hadn't really given it much thought, Harold."

"I don't see that you've got any real legal grounds to make her turn back."

"What about this boat?" The sheriff nodded at the Whaler. "That's NTC property, isn't it? She got any authorization to use it?"

Harold smiled faintly. "Not really. But given the circumstances, I don't think I'd get much sympathy from the board of directors if I tried to press it. They've already expressed some concern about lawsuits in regard to this mess."

"Yeah. Well," he stroked the stubble of beard on his jaw, "maybe I'll lie." He gave Harold a thin smile. "You coming with me?"

"Do you need me?"

"I guess not."

"Then no, I'm not coming."

"Okay. You have any problem with waiting until I return?"

"I'll wait."

"Right. See you soon."

The sheriff got his equipment from Harold's boat: a canteen, first aid kit, walkie-talkie, blanket, and a package of assorted dried foods he had carried in his patrol car for almost a year in case he was stranded in the wilds. He had never tasted it and hoped he wouldn't have to. Everything but the radio went into a daypack.

He walked fast, because even to his inexperienced eye it was obvious from her footprints that Anna was hurrying, running occasionally, paying no attention to covering her trail. He tried to jog but could only maintain it for a mile or so with the pack beating his back and the straps chafing his shoulders, equipment belt dragging at his waist, his breath coming hard after only a few minutes. He swore at himself for his poor conditioning, but shortness of breath caused him to fall silent. And after several hours he was beginning to despair of even spotting her, much less catching her, when he topped a low rise and saw a tiny figure far ahead across the plateau.

"Well, hell's bells," he muttered. He could see it would take him more than an hour to get to where she was now, and night was fast approaching. If only she would stop to rest he might have a chance. He started on.

The sun had set, and he was stumbling along in the deepening darkness, when he spotted the flicker of fire ahead. The fire was built against a natural windbreak of sandstone, and as he drew near he could see someone crouched beside it, holding hands out to the warmth.

"Anna!" he called. The figure sprang upright and he saw the gun come up.

"Anna it's me! Nathan Andrews!"

"You come forward into the light." He recognized Anna's voice, cold and tense, and smiled, holding out his hands so she could see them plainly; Joe had taught her to shoot.

"It's just me Anna. Harold called and told me you'd gone looking for Joe and Lance. He brought me down the lake to find you." By now he was close enough that she should have been able to recognize him, but still she held the rifle trained on his chest. "Come on, Anna, I'm not here to cause any trouble. What's wrong?"

She approached slowly, one step at a time, and the rifle never wavered. When it touched his chest she stood on her toes and peered closely into his eyes. Her own were wide with uncertainty, and his lips had gone white with tension.

"Okay," she said, lowering the rifle.

"Hey, Anna, what the hell is this all about?" The sheriff's voice was angry and confused. She shrugged and went back to the fire, squatted beside it, and laid the rifle across her thighs. She drew a blanket around her shoulders.

"I just wanted to be sure you were who you said you were. It's night, a time to be cautious."

"Well, who else would I be? I'm pretty easy to recognize, aren't I?"

"Yes, Sheriff." Her voice sounded tired. "But out here thing's aren't what they seem. Especially now."

"What do you mean?" He squatted on the opposite side of the fire and held out his hands, grateful for the warmth. She looked past him, her face thoughtful.

"You wouldn't believe me." She shook her head.

"Try me."

"Okay. It's like this Sheriff, my men are out there," she tossed her head, "on that mountain. And so is . . . something else. I won't say its name in the night; the danger is bad enough without that. It's an old evil from the dark days of my people, and it's out there tonight, and so are my men. You and your police didn't find a damn thing, and be thankful you didn't find that creature roaming the night." Her eyes glittered coldly across the fire and the sheriff glanced around, hunching his shoulders.

"So now it's my turn," she said.

"How do you know they're still out there?" His mouth felt dry and he took a sip of water from his canteen, offered it to her. She shook her head.

"Because I know, in here." She touched her breast with her hand. She gave a mirthless bark of laughter. "You know how us Indians are, Sheriff; full of visions and hunches. Superstitious and crazy, every one of us."

"No," he said quietly. "I've never had anything but respect for your people and you know it. If you feel in your heart they're up there, I believe you." He gave her a minute to digest what he said. When she didn't comment he continued.

"I believe you, and if you'll just agree to go back and let Harold take you home, I'll go on myself. I'll find them and bring them back."

She snorted. "Nathan Andrews, you couldn't track an earthmover to save your life."

245

"The NTP trackers have been up there and didn't find a thing," he said. "It's not by tracks that I'll find them, if they're out there."

"How, then?"

"I'm not much of a tracker, Anna, I'll admit. But I'm stubborn, and persistent, and you know my reputation for putting two and two together and coming up with an answer. I've got a good record."

"Yes," she said quietly, "that part is true."

"Please Anna, go home. Let me handle it, and I'll spend whatever time it takes to find your husband and your son. You've got my word on it."

She didn't look at him, but gazed into the night. It was quite dark now, clouds hiding the stars and moon.

"Okay," she whispered.

"Good. Thank you Anna." He shivered and shrugged off his pack, got out his blanket. "It's too dark to go back now, have you got enough wood for the fire?"

"Yes."

"All right then."

For another hour or so they talked, then rolled up in their blankets and slept. It was an uneasy sleep for the sheriff, who kept hearing stealthy noises and sitting up to gaze into the impenetrable blackness of the night.

Eleven

Joe was climbing. It was the morning of his awakening at the deserted hogan and the sky was overcast and gray and cold. He was climbing a rocky talus and the footing was poor. Twice already he had dislodged large stones that crashed and tumbled below him, picking up others until a minor rockslide had resulted. Now, as he neared the intersection of talus and cliff, he was being extremely careful because of the large boulders perched precariously at the base of the cliff, slabs of stone that had separated from the cliff itself and appeared to be awaiting only a gentle nudge to add their debris to the rubble below.

A crow circled silently overhead. It had been following him all morning, having appeared when he was about a mile from the hogan. He hooked his thumbs in his belt and watched the bird soaring. It dropped lower and tipped its head to inspect him, as if aware of his scrutiny. Black glittering eye, black ebony beak, icy black feathers, black legs, black claws. It circled him twice, still maintaining a safe distance, then fluttered to a landing somewhere above, out of sight.

His mouth turned downward at the corners and his eyes narrowed. He hitched up his belt and began to climb more quickly. Small rocks clicked and pattered down the slope at his back as he scrambled diagonally across it, making for a place beside the cliff where he could rest.

An ominous grating sound caused him to look up. A cube of stone taller than a man fell slowly forward and thudded onto one of its flat faces, tipped up and hesitated at the point of balance, then plunged over and began to roll.

Joe was already running, his uphill arm outstretched for balance, touching rocks as he threaded his way through the detritus. A boulder shifted beneath his weight and his next

247

step slammed his toes painfully into another and he almost fell, staggered, scrambled onward. He sprinted, only a few yards from the shelter of a great slab of rock.

The boulder came with a thunderous, grinding noise, accompanied by a shower of rock and dirt, striking sparks, blasting stone into smoke beneath it. A fragment the size of a melon struck Joe in the thigh and he fell. He covered his head with his arms as the rockslide roared around him. Something struck him painfully in the back and he cried out, and smaller blows pummeled him; then it was past. He remained where he was, breathing hard, waiting for the clatter of pebbles and hiss of sand to cease before slowly and painfully rolling over to sit up.

The path of the slide extended all the way to the bottom of the talus, twenty feet wide where he sat. He had fallen beside a deeply embedded stone projecting no more than eight inches above the slope. Luck had saved his life. He winced as he stood and dusted himself off. His leg throbbed, a dull, rhythmic pain that echoed his heartbeat, but nothing appeared to be broken. And when he tried to straighten up, his back responded with a feeling like a knife thrust between the ribs.

The crow screamed in the sky above him, flapping to gain altitude, the first time it had made a sound since joining him that morning. Joe, hands on his knees, turned his head to follow its flight. His right hand sought the handle of the flint knife as his eyes filled with anger.

He forced himself to stand, gritting his teeth, and when the worst of the spasm had passed, he drew the knife and held it out before him. The knife looked real. His thumb still bore the cut from when he had tested its sharpness. So the knife had to be real, and the beautiful young man and the coyote must have been real. If not, then he, too, was going insane.

And that was how the *bellicano* would explain it. Yes. They would say he had found the knife, wandering aimlessly, out of his head with grief. They would say he had experienced hallucinations brought on by exhaustion and fatigue, and that he had blanked out any memory of finding the knife. Because the mind is uncontrollable and deceptive, they would say, Joe could not recall what had really happened, but had created a

248

fantastic dream to explain it. That was how the *bellicano* would explain it.

But he was alone, as the *Dine'* had ever been in their vast solitude, and the knife was real and sharp and dangerous in his hand. And Old Man Walker had seemed real, more real than any *bellicano* he had ever met. He had promised Old Man he would pretend to believe, and so he would. He had once been a warrior, like his father and his father's father, and a warrior answered only to himself.

Joe slid the knife into its sheath and nodded his head, his face firm in resolve. If dreams could be real as this knife, then shamans could cast spells that would kill, ghosts could ride the wind, and he had better cover his ass or he would be one dead Indian.

He limped to the edge of the talus and found a sheltered spot beneath the branches of a juniper. There he gathered some twigs and made a small fire and sat and warmed himself. He rubbed his hands and thought of gloves, but he had none so he pushed the thought away. The crow glided past and cocked its head to look at him, then tipped its wings and disappeared over the ridge above him. Joe reached the box of licorice out of his jacket breast pocket and opened it, shook its contents into his hand. Three pieces. He ate one and saved the others for later.

The first snowflakes fell as he started along the ridge behind the cliff. The mountain's summit was lost in cloud that extended in a single, unbroken plane as far as the eye could see, and when he looked up, he had a momentary dizzying vision that the world had somehow reversed itself and he was climbing down into a strangely swirling sea the color of granite. His fingers clutched involuntarily at the straps of his pack. His leg had begun to stiffen and his limp was more obvious. Also his back hurt, and he winced when he turned a certain way, or when he bent forward at the waist.

He had never been this high on the mountain before. The snow was not clinging to the ground, but melting into the thirsty soil, beading the leaves of the plants with moisture. His moccasins were getting wet but there was nothing to be done about it. Later, perhaps. Later he would stop and build another fire and dry his moccasins, but not now.

Feet had passed here, booted feet. Two pairs had ascended the ridge, but nowhere was there sign of bare feet, of feet unusually broad and flat. It didn't matter to Joe. Booted feet, bare feet, no difference. The path led where it led, up the mountain, higher and deeper into the wild desolation. Where *Dine'* shamans had come to fast and seek visions, where no hogan had ever stood or ever would, where few men had walked.

The snow began to fall more heavily and Joe blinked his eyes against the thick flakes. Now when he stopped to rest he blew clouds, clouds of warm breath turned to ice crystal that the wind snatched greedily and sent swirling away with the snow. He took his hands out of his pockets and blew on them, thinking of fire again, and warmth. But he would not rest quite yet.

This exposed ridge was no place to stop and he kept walking. He smiled to think the crow could no longer see him, magical or not. The visibility was so poor that he kept his gaze on the ground immediately ahead of him, avoiding trees that loomed suddenly and darkly out of the hypnotic whiteness of falling snow, snow that was beginning to collect on the ground and branches. When he paused, he could see no more than a stone throw in any direction.

He unfolded the cloth encircling his brow and brushed the snow from his hair, tied the cloth over his head like a scarf, turned up his collar, and kept on. The trees grew thicker but more spectral as he ascended into the clouds. He was soon weaving his way among the great dark columns of their trunks, the branches invisible somewhere above. The snow decreased as the mist thickened, and after a time Joe slowed, stopped, looked about.

He was in a forest. The ground beneath his feet was soft with a deep blanket of pine needles. His face filled with confusion. The trees were white firs, not uncommon, but he didn't remember ever seeing them this big, or growing so thickly. Easily 150 feet tall and four feet in diameter, their lowest branches had to be more than fifteen or twenty feet above the ground because he could see that far in the mist, and all he saw were great shadowy columns that disappeared overhead.

Joe walked quietly beneath the trees, where the ground was mostly level and seemed to go on and on for miles. Except for the plaintive whistle of a nuthatch, the silence was profound. He couldn't remember anyone speaking of a great forest on Navajo Mountain. Trees yes, in dark bands threading the steep slopes, twisted from their struggle to survive in the poor soil and hostile environment. But not like this. These trees were monarchs, centuries old, towering straight and proud, and there were thousands upon thousands of them in a strange, misty silence.

He no longer knew which direction he walked or how far he traveled. It was not as cold in the forest, but the shadows were deep, the mists confusing. He kicked his feet in the needles now and then, so he would know if he was walking in a circle. But he didn't think he was. The path still drew him onward and he let his feet go where they would, heeding its call. He had worked some of the stiffness out of his leg and found walking easier on the soft, level ground.

A fallen tree barred his path and he angled his steps to detour around it, then saw as he got closer that its trunk had been shredded. Bark and rotten wood were strewn across the forest floor beside it.

He didn't need to see the tracks to know a bear was responsible, because only a bear or a chain saw could make a log look like Swiss cheese, and there were no chain saws up here. But he did find tracks, and big ones, too. When he stepped in one it was almost twice the length of his own foot. Though he had never seen a track like this before, he knew what it was.

"Grizzly bear," he muttered. "Bear-that-walks-like-a-man. There are no grizzlies on Navajo Mountain." He felt a prickling sensation in the small of his back and glanced quickly around, ears straining for the slightest sound. Nothing moved, all was silence. After a minute he bent to examine the log. Great chunks of rotted wood had been torn out, typical of a bear seeking grubs and other insects. The more solid wood had been assaulted also, leaving gouges an inch wide and three inches deep.

He straightened, massaging the small of his back and gaz-

251

ing thoughtfully about. He walked more cautiously now, watching and listening, for though he had been born to the Bear Clan, on his father's side, he had no desire to encounter that unpredictable animal here, armed with nothing but a pistol and a knife.

"There are no grizzlies on Navajo Mountain," he repeated quietly as he stopped again to stare about. "Where is this place?"

No answer came from the silent forest, and after a moment he started on. The game trail he now followed was littered with old deer droppings that turned to powder when he touched them; no animal had been this way in many seasons. The forest was thicker and he could no longer see the sky. Only scattered snowflakes penetrated the canopy above, but the mist increased, and so he knew he was still climbing into the clouds.

The mists thickened and swirled among the dark trees, soundless as dancing ghosts, forming into sinuous shapes that became almost recognizable, only to dissolve. In the complete absence of sound it was easy to imagine unseen scurryings, faint noises, watchers lurking behind the trees, something sneaking up behind . . .

Joe whirled about, hand on his pistol, but there was nothing. He forced the fear away and waited for his breathing to return to normal. He shivered with more than cold. The trees seemed to crowd in around him, the damp mist to search every crease and fold of his clothing, inserting icy fingers to leech the warmth from his flesh.

The thought of a fire came again, but now there was something he wanted even more; to be out of this place, to stand somewhere high and open where he could see for miles, where the wind would blast him with its fury instead of clinging like spider web. Better to be battered, to fall from a high place, than to suffer the insidious death of a thousand small wounds. The image of his son's face arose in his memory and he forced it away, rubbing his forehead with his hands.

As he stood undecided, gazing about, a faint odor of fungus and decay wafted past, somehow familiar though he could not recall where he had smelled it before. He hunched his shoulders uneasily and slid his thumbs beneath the straps of his pack, took a few steps and stopped with a lurch. Something was standing just ahead, watching him, and his hand drew the pistol in a practiced, unconscious movement.

For several long heartbeats Joe didn't move, nor did the shadowy figure standing between the dark boles of the trees. Indeed, it stood so perfectly still that he had almost convinced himself it was merely a bush when it stirred and took a step toward him.

It approached silently, hand extended as if in greeting, but the long, spindly fingers were bent like claws and the legs bent oddly outward at the knees, as might those of a lizard, or a spider. The curtain of mist parted before it and Joe saw the wreckage of what once had been Norman Sanders. Its mouth gaped wordlessly, spittle dribbling from its lips, running down its chin. The eyes were sunk deep in their pouches, black and glittering and greedy.

"Stay away!" Joe shouted. He cocked the hammer as he took a step back. He kept the pistol pointed at the center of its chest and it paused, cocked its head to the side, and extended its hand pleadingly.

Norman Sanders's hair had turned white and he looked lumpy and ill-formed. His chest and shoulders were grotesquely huge in relation to the rest of his body, and the skin there was stretched taut, unlike the arms, where the skin hung in folds. Then again, the hands were unnaturally large and the skin was split at the finger tips.

He was wearing a rabbit fur across his shoulders, some sort of necklace that hung down on his chest, and a pair of dirty jeans. The jeans had white spots on the legs from kneeling, but the spots hung several inches below where the legs now bent, and the cuffs had been cut off raggedly and trailed threads around the coarse, bare feet. The musty smell was strong now, and Joe's face wrinkled in loathing as he took another step back.

But the worst was when it spoke, and Joe saw that Norman Sanders's mouth was perpetually open, the lips dry and cracked, gums black, and another set of lips and teeth moved within them, like an actor behind a mask. He recalled Old

Man's words: "Eater-of-Souls killed a man, and put on his skin."

"You remember me Joe Redhill. It's Norm, Norman Sanders, Joe. Remember me Joe? Come closer Joe, come over here and sit down and I'll tell you everything you want to know. Hah hah hah." Its speech had no cadence, was accented in the wrong places, and it laughed mirthlessly, an awful noise that deteriorated into harsh grunts and clicks, wet, guttural sounds. The inner teeth were yellow and sharp.

"Stay back," Joe repeated. He waved the pistol for emphasis. The face changed, dry skin cracking, exposing those yellow teeth in a horrible caricature of a grin, and the black eyes glittered fiercely.

"You wouldn't shoot an old friend, would you Joe?" It took a strange little hop toward him, hands flopping at the end of the long, limp arms. "Come. Sit down, let's talk."

It opened its mouth wide, wide, impossibly wide, and the face that had once belonged to Norman Sanders tore at the corners of the mouth and it leaped at him with astounding speed and power, hands sweeping inward with hooked fingers to seize and clutch him to those evil teeth.

Joe squeezed the trigger and the sound was deafening as he threw himself to the side, skillfully following his target with the pistol even as he landed on his hip and shoulder, rolling, coming up on his feet gritting his teeth against the pain.

The creature also rolled across the ground and came up on its feet, and for a moment Joe thought he had missed as he stared at it with wide eyes. But no, there was a hole in its chest, a hole big enough to stick your finger in and no blood coming out of it. Just a black hole. It laughed, low and ugly, and came at him again. Already the hole was closing.

"Shoot! Shoot!" it taunted, and he realized it was now speaking in Navajo. "What are you waiting for, warrior? Shoot me dead!" It crouched, preparing to spring, and Joe raised the pistol. But before he could squeeze the trigger a bellow of anger filled the forest.

A bear had emerged from the trees. It arose on its hind legs, towering nine feet tall, its massive head swinging back and forth as its nose sniffed the air. It looked first at Joe, then at the

Sanders-thing, then back at Joe, and its eyes were blue as the sky.

The mist swirled about the great bear in spiral currents. When it snorted, spouts of steam erupted from its nostrils, and its fur was coated with frost so that a shining white aura surrounded its enormous, dark bulk. It growled low in its throat, a sound like stones shifting underground.

Joe backed away slowly until he fetched up against a tree, but the Sanders-thing didn't move, seemed in fact to be smiling, and odd guttural sounds came from its chest, grunts and clicks. The bear growled again and looked at Joe, who moved very slowly and cautiously to the side of the tree, slipping around to place the trunk between him and the giant bear.

He would have to smash its brain with his first shot if it attacked, a bullet any other place wouldn't even slow it down. How many shots left? He tried to count and couldn't. And no way could he climb out of reach before it got him. No way. Only a miracle shot would save him if it attacked, a chance in a million.

The blue-eyed bear looked at Joe and growled again, waved its paws in the air, paws twelve inches wide with claws longer than Joe's fingers. And the Sanders-thing with a bullet hole through its heart crouched and smiled at the bear. It chittered and smacked its lips, gesturing with its flapping hand at Joe, but the bear turned its attention to the creature instead.

For a moment the bear was intensely still, nose quivering as it inhaled the creature's musty scent, and then its lips curled back from fangs like sabers and it emitted a bellow of rage. Its speed was incredible as it bounded toward the creature, covering forty feet in a few seconds, spreading its forelegs in deadly embrace, just as the creature had attempted to grab Joe only a minute earlier.

But for all the bear's speed, the other was quicker and sprang aside. The bear blundered past, and as it whirled to renew its attack, the creature disappeared into the mist. The bear reared up and swiveled its head in confusion, blinking and sniffing. It made a few half-hearted lunges into the forest, then returned to where the creature had evaded it and gouged the earth angrily with its claws, urinated, sat up, and looked

255

defiantly around.

Apparently satisfied that the creature was gone, the blue-eyed bear turned toward Joe and dropped to all fours. A questioning sound came from its throat as it took a step toward him. It took another, and Joe came from behind the tree and holstered his pistol. He held out his hands.

"Ya aat' eh," he said. The bear snuffled and shook its body. Ice crystals formed a glittering cloud around it that settled slowly to the ground. It turned and took several steps in the direction from which Joe had come, looked back over its shoulder expectantly. Smoke blossomed from its nostrils.

The bear and Joe stood in the mist looking at each other, and the mist moved lazily about them and was cold, and the bear's eyes glittered like the blue ice of the ocean. Joe took a deep breath and his lungs and nose and throat filled with the cold gray cloud in which he and the bear stood in a forest atop a mountain which might or might not exist and Joe shook his head.

"I cannot go back. I will find the Eater-of-Souls again, and I will end its evil in this world. Thank you for sparing my life." He raised a hand in farewell. "Walk in beauty." He turned his back on the bear and walked away. The bear snorted its disgust, gazing after him, then vanished into the forest.

Joe walked on until the trees began to thin and the sky to appear and the sun shined weakly and far off and offered little warmth. But at least he was out of the forest. Where he was exactly, he could not say. The snow had mostly stopped and he judged from the position of the sun that it was past noon. He gathered dry twigs from beneath the trees and started a small fire to warm himself and dry his moccasins.

He opened the box and ate one of the remaining two pieces of licorice, chewing it thoroughly and well, and washed it down with a swallow of water. Though the snow had now stopped completely, the clouds persisted, and he could see no more of his surroundings than he could in the forest. But the feeling of closeness of the big trees had left him and he breathed easier.

He looked at his watch. 1:10. He stared at the little black numerals that seemed to make no sense here, in this place of

256

clouds. The watch was of the *bellicano* world, a world of measurement and calculation, and the watch reminded him of his son and of how they had spoken just before his death, a death that might have been prevented but for Joe's lack of belief. He thought of the grandchildren he would never have, and the tracks beside his son's body, and he removed the watch from his wrist and threw it as far as he could.

When he was warmed and his moccasins were dry, he searched his pack until he found the cartridges for the pistol. He opened the cylinder and extracted the four spent rounds, reloaded and holstered it.

"For what it is worth," he muttered as he snapped the strap across it. He started on across the rolling land. There were still trees, but they were scattered and smaller, and brown grasses interspersed with brush covered the ground. The grasses and weeds were soft from the snow, which was melting, and his footsteps made no sound. He could see where someone had gone before him, and when he found a clear track it was broad and flat.

He walked all through the afternoon and the clouds never lifted. The land arose on either side of him until he was walking in a broad valley where the plants and grasses were white with frost. The sides of the valley steepened until he was in a canyon. A stream of icy water flowed down its center, but there was room on either side to walk, and the tracks were clear and easy to follow. When he kneeled on a flat rock and drank, the water tasted good and clean.

Twilight came to the canyon while the sun still shone up top, casting on the east wall a bright ribbon that narrowed rapidly. Joe forced himself to walk faster despite the increasing pain in his leg and back. There were too many places where an ambusher could hide, and he already regretted following the tracks into the canyon instead of keeping to the high land. And he especially didn't want to be in so dangerous a position come night.

He was watching for the creature to attack, something the size of a man, and so he almost failed to see the snake. The symmetrical markings of its skin caught his attention an instant before it struck from where it lay beside the path, half-

257

concealed by a rock, and he lurched back as it buried its fangs in the cuff of his pants. He kicked it loose and the rattler vibrated its tail angrily. Others responded, from the walls on either side of him, ahead of him, behind him, slithering from beneath rocks, from cracks, dropping from ledges, and all coming toward him.

He jumped atop a rock in the creek and drew his pistol. The water was cold, too cold for reptiles, but then, so was the air. He watched a snake as big around as his arm enter the stream and cross to the rock. Its flat, triangular head appeared over the edge of the stone and he fired and saw it explode into red tatters, saw the thrashing body swept away by the current. Immediately another took its place, mouth open, fangs extended, and he shot it, too, and another, and another.

When the hammer clicked on an empty cartridge he hastily reloaded, spent those six rounds, reloaded again. And still they came. One managed to sneak up behind and it was only the thick bullhide moccasin that prevented its fangs from reaching his foot. He kicked the snake to the bank and blasted it into three separate pieces before cursing himself for wasting ammunition. And soon he was down to his final six rounds.

Two more heads appeared and he vaporized them both with slugs from the big magnum. And then they were all dead. He stared at the bloody carcasses, dozens of them, a few still limply writhing, and when he replaced the pistol in its holster his hand was shaking. Carefully avoiding the snakes, he stumbled ashore and hobbled up the canyon.

He stopped to listen at a turn of the stream and leaned against the wall of gray hermosa shale. He thought he heard something but the noise of the running water made it difficult to tell. Nothing moved, either in the canyon or up on the rim. What had become of the crow? If the bird was the creature's accomplice why had it not been following his progress?

He hurried on, massaging his thigh as he walked. The muscle was too sore to rub very hard, but it felt like it might cramp if he didn't. And it mustn't cramp until he was out of this canyon. He could climb out even now if he could trust his leg, but the walls were high and practically vertical, and a cramp or missed grip could easily be fatal.

A low buzzing sound made him stop again to listen, and this time when he looked up there was something. But not like anything he had seen before. It was spiraling down toward the canyon floor like a maple seed, and spinning on its axis like a bull-roarer. The rhythmic sound and movement were mesmerizing. He stared upward in fascination, wondering what it could be.

It was spinning so fast now that it hummed, a blur of dark shadow, dropping directly toward him. He was unable to take his eyes off it. The sound was more like an enormous bumblebee now than a bull-roarer. A tingle of alarm nagged somewhere in the back of his mind, but he was enthralled by its movements that made it seem almost alive, by the sound ebbing and flowing in the canyon walls. Almost close enough to grab now, to find out what it was . . .

He yelled and lurched aside as his thigh muscle suddenly knotted painfully. At the same instant the object darted toward him and he felt a burning sensation in the side of his face. He gripped his leg with both hands, working the muscle, but it would not let up. He tried hobbling back and forth beside the stream, stopping long enough to pick up the thing that had fallen after striking his face.

It was a feather, one of the long wing primaries from a black vulture. The worst of the pain passed and he began limping in the direction he had been traveling, studying the feather in the fading light. Small eyes were scribed in the quill, which had been sharpened to a needle fineness. He touched the side of his face and his fingers came away with blood on them.

With an angry gesture he crushed the feather in his fists and flung it into the stream, saw it swept away. He had almost succumbed to such a simple weapon. Simple but intricate. And relatively harmless unless it struck its target, puncturing an eye. Or was it so harmless? What if the tip were dipped in some kind of poison?

He threw himself to his stomach beside the stream and splashed water vigorously onto his face, cleansing the wound until blood flowed freely. Then he dragged himself to his feet and pressed on. For the first time in many years, the sour taste of fear was in his mouth and stomach. Darkness was coming, and something evil enough to eat the flesh of humans and powerful enough to turn a feather into a weapon was stalking him.

Night was the time of power for *chindi* and other dangerous beings. With night the power of the Eater-of-Souls would increase. Already it had attacked him during daylight, and he had escaped twice by fortuitous accidents, once by the rescue of the blue-eyed bear. And the snakes! How could something cold-blooded even move in this cold, much less attack him? He had proven himself incapable of harming the monster or of protecting himself against it. What a fool he had been to pursue something he knew nothing about.

He was almost running now, throwing his leg forward like a cripple, lurching along and breathing hard. He was suffocating in the canyon, he had to get out into the open right away. His face was pale, and he was sweating in spite of the cold. Fear sweat. What a fool he was! If only he had some knowledge of magic he might have a chance, but no, he had a gun, which was useless, and a stone knife. A stone knife! What a fool!

He slipped and his foot plunged into the icy water. The moccasin squished now with each step and he would have to stop and build a fire before his foot got too cold. He would have to stop and build one soon anyway with night almost here, a fire to keep the bad creatures away, a fire against the ghosts. As if it would do any good. What a fool!

His despair increased by the minute until it was all he could do to keep moving. He wanted to stop and sit and rest, forget about the fire, forget about the thing that stalked him. Just sit down and rest. The slit in his face burned and throbbed and his leg ached, he couldn't draw a deep breath without a spasm from his back. If only he hadn't been such a fool! And then he realized he was out of the canyon, and he stumbled to a halt and stared in wonder.

He stood at the entrance to a massive crater, on the shore of a wide lake, and the lake was the source of the stream, and its water lay perfectly still and smooth and reflected the stars, which were beginning to glimmer in the purple sky. The shore was grassy and broad, and rose gently to the base of a towering cliff that completely surrounded the lake except for the gap at his back, and high atop the cliff was a more gradual slope covered with grass and bushes that climbed a thousand feet or more into the sky.

The cliff curved inward, and appeared to be riddled with holes, but as he looked more closely he drew a deep breath of amazement; the entire wall surrounding the lake was a single, vast pueblo. Row upon row of buildings, one atop the other, thousands of doors and windows, dark and empty and staring. On either side of him, what he had taken to be random stone was the regulated repetition of human construction. A city of the dead.

Joe shuddered; he had never been in a more frighteningly lonely place in his life. The desolation of the abandoned pueblo was more awful than the emptiest stretch of desert. Not a single living thing moved. No bird sang, no insect called, no frog croaked among the weeds of the shore and no fish leaped from the water. An icy breath issued from the darkness of the canyon at his back and touched his neck, clung to his skin like fine spider webs, and carried the musty scent of decay to his nostrils.

He hopped about and saw it crouched atop a wall to his right, saw it by the greenish glow of its eyes before he made out the rest of its shadowy form. It laughed tonelessly, a sound of rocks striking together.

"Welcome to my home!" it said to him. "You have done well. Come, hail the conquering warrior, my people." It arose and spread its arms, and from the empty rooms and corridors, the hidden kivas, from the windows and doors came whispers, countless whispers, soft as the wings of moths beating in the darkness, sad and lost, cries of ghost children and moans of their mothers, hopeless agony of the fathers, gentle as the fall of a feather, a feather of death.

"My people," it said with a chuckle. "They are all dead, as you soon will be also. For eternity they serve me here. Each of them gave me a gift, yesss—." Its voice trailed off into a hiss of laughter. "Strength of arm or leg, cleverness of brain, sharpness of eye . . . I wonder what you will give me? Your heart? I would like to have eaten your son's heart. He was young and

261

strong, and his strength would have become mine. But no matter. I am already stronger than you can imagine. I am a God. Everyone here serves me!" It stood and laughed and the sound echoed around and around the dead city.

"Ah, how I lust for you!" it said, leaning toward him from atop the wall. "How I hate you! You and all your people. I will cut you down like grass before a sickle. I will feed on your flesh and your strength. You cannot imagine how hungry I became while I waited in darkness, I waited to be set free. Look upon me. Look upon your death!"

Joe was shivering, his back against a wall of adobe. The creature seemed to have grown larger with the night, and now was a dark bulk in which the green sparks of its eyes floated as it bobbed its head and hissed. He could only dimly see it raise its hand and point at him, hear the low chant begin. The slash in his face started to burn and ache and despair filled him.

"No!" he shouted. Even knowing it was useless, he drew the pistol and fired. He pulled the trigger over and over as flame flared brilliantly from the muzzle and the report left his ears ringing. When it clicked empty he lowered it and stood shaking, blinded and deafened, blinking his eyes as he peered at the wall where it had stood. It was gone. Silently he cursed himself for his stupidity, but then realized that the wound had ceased throbbing, and there was anger where there had been despair.

The cartridges spent, he threw the pistol aside. Fire, he must have fire, he was shaking so badly he could hardly stand. Where had the creature gone? Waiting in the shadows no doubt, waiting to leap on him with its clutching hands and yellow fangs. Or jab his eyes out with a magic feather, or send spiders swarming over him—.

He pushed all other thoughts aside and made for a bush he had noticed when he first arrived. It was green, but there were enough dry branches underneath for his purpose. He gathered all he could find by feel and carried them to the front wall of the adobe nearest the canyon entrance. Quickly he scooped a hollow in the dirt a yard from the wall, laid a platform of slender twigs across it, added larger twigs crosswise atop those, then small sticks.

He struck a match and carefully lowered it beneath the twigs, muttered a silent prayer, and watched the flames blossom and grow. With his back against the wall, he added sticks until he had a good crackling blaze, only a foot or so in diameter but burning well. The warmth felt wonderful, and despite the fear churning in his stomach he sighed as he held his hands out toward it.

By the fire's illumination he could see for some distance in all directions. That was good. But it would not come that way, no. He looked up. Yes, that was how it would come, dropping on him from above. What could he do? Move inside? He shuddered. No, better to meet it in the open, beneath the sky, make it come to him here. If he had to die, he would die beneath the stars. But he didn't want to die. He wanted to kill the monster. He wanted to kill it worse than he had ever wanted anything.

His hand sought the handle of the knife and gripped it. He added more sticks to the fire. His feet were warming up and he sat and extended his legs, rubbed the stiffness in his thigh. He had been lucky so far, that much he knew. But what was luck in a dream like this? Luck would be to kill the thing even if he died in the process. If it killed him, would his anguished spirit wander for eternity in this empty place, adding its whisper of misery to those of the children and the mothers and the fathers? How do you kill a ghost?

The night was fully dark now and the stars overhead were bright in the circle of blackness trapped by the bowl. Soon he would let the fire die down a little, after he was fully warmed, if he could ever be warm in this place. After he was warmer he would let the fire die down and then his eyes would adjust to the dark and he would be able to see all around him by the light of the stars, almost as well as he could by day. Was that true? No, but almost.

Eater-of-Souls should have brought the clouds, if truly it could, because Joe had no doubt it could see as well, no, better in the night than during the day. Maybe it had made a mistake. Did Gods make mistakes? Sometimes, in the stories the *Dine'* told, sure they did. In the myths that were told, the Holy People were mysterious and powerful, but they were also emotional and unpredictable, and they made mistakes!

Joe straightened his back against the wall and looked up. Nothing there, perched, waiting to leap on him with clutching fingers and yellow fangs and glowing green . . . no. He pushed the thought away. He was almost able to ignore the throb of his leg as hope filled him; the Gods made mistakes. Would that help him tonight? What he needed was calm, emptiness. He chanted quietly:

"It is lovely indeed, lovely indeed.
I, I am the spirit within the earth.
The feet of the earth are my feet.
The legs of the earth are my legs.
The strength of the earth is my strength.
All that surrounds the earth surrounds me.
I, I am the sacred words of the earth.
It is lovely indeed, lovely indeed."

He wasn't sure he had the words right, but the song of the Earth Spirit eased the hammering of his heart. He pulled his jacket tight and looked up. Nothing there. Where had it gone, when would it come? If only it would come soon, while he was ready. But probably it wouldn't. Probably it would wait until later, when he started to drowse. Then it would drop on him like some horrible spider and sink those fangs into him. He looked up. Nothing there.

The night grew colder and he couldn't get warm. He let the fire die down anyway, kept just enough flame so he wasn't shivering. He couldn't concentrate on listening if he was shivering. Images of his home and Anna came to mind, sitting on the couch, watching television, warm and comfortable. Lance slamming the door . . . he jerked upright, realized he was starting to doze. But he mustn't!

He mustn't sleep and he mustn't think of that other world, that *bellicano* world of logic and comfort. Instead he thought of the evil creature, envisioned it as he had seen it when it faced him; its features hidden behind the dead skin of Norman Sanders's husk. And the blue-eyed bear chasing it off. No normal bear, that was certain. Did it mean there was more than just him, Joe Redhill, to fight the monster? Better not count on it. Nobody saved him from the rock slide but himself. Only a sudden cramp made the feather weapon miss him.

He hugged himself and rocked and tried to remember the words to Rainbow God's song from the Windway. But the words were lost to him, and trying to remember them made him think of other things, and he needed to be empty, to put aside the voices in his head, to sit and wait and not sleep. Why did the creature leave when he shot it this time? He looked up. Nothing there.

He put another stick on the fire and folded his legs so his cold feet were beneath his knees. He had to use his hands to help bend his right leg, and then it started to cramp and he straightened it, massaged the muscles, and tried again. Better. He cupped his hands around the toes of his moccasins and tried to rub some warmth into them. The stick caught and sent its flames licking upward, dancing along its length. Joe yawned and his head sagged. He jerked awake and looked up.

The stars went out as something big and dark dropped toward him and he willed his legs to move but they were folded stiffly beneath him and he screamed as the creature landed on him and bowled him over with a tremendous blow. Its arms went around him and it lifted him up, holding him easily despite his violent kicking and bucking. It drew back its head and its mouth opened and for an instant he looked into the creature's eyes. It was only an instant, but the madness and evil in its inhuman eyes were more terrifying than anything he had ever experienced and he jerked wildly and screamed as it lunged at his throat. The foul yellow fangs missed and drove deep into his shoulder.

Its jaws closed with bone-crushing force and Joe heard a crack as a wave of incredible pain roared through him. He saw the sky spin dizzily as his left arm went numb, and only through a supreme effort of will did he retain consciousness. The fingers of his right hand strained to reach the knife, touched its handle, couldn't quite get a hold of it. The monster shook him like a dog with a rat and his head whipped back and forth, sparks swirling in the darkness behind his eyelids. He slumped in its grip, and the monster cackled and shifted its hold slightly, releasing his shoulder for a moment as it opened its mouth to crush his throat.

In the split second it relaxed its grip, Joe reached the knife and jerked it free of its sheath, drove it upward into the monsters side with all his strength. Its howl of pain and rage shook the night and Joe was hurled to the hard earth. By reflex he twisted to take the brunt of the fall on his right shoulder, but the agony when he hit brought bile rising in his throat. The creature blundered past him in a maddened dance of torment, and the tattoo of its feet on the earth was a thunder in the night, a thunder Joe heard only dimly through the clouds of oblivion rolling through his mind.

Dimly he saw the beast throwing itself about with frantic energy, pawing at the bleeding gash in its side, tumbling across the earth, through the fire, sparks ascending in a cascade. And when his eyes closed, and he could no longer see the creature, and his awareness fled heavenward like those sparks streaming toward the stars, he could still hear its enraged howls echoing along the empty rooms and corridors as it fled through the great dead city.

In the moments of lucidity remaining to him, Joe Redhill wondered if he was dying, decided he probably was. He could feel his life blood pumping from the wound in his shoulder, and knew that wasn't good. He groped blindly for the cloth around his head, dragged it free, and wadded it into the wound. The effort was too much. His body was in terrible pain, but the receptors had been shut down and his mind was engulfed by the clouds now, soft and gray and flickering with distant lightning.

"Close enough," he murmured deliriously. Then he passed out.

Sheriff Nathan Andrews was suffering the reality of his promise to Anna Redhill. He had been walking all day without finding a trace of her husband Joe. His feet were blistered, both of them, on the heels, and he was cold and hungry.

Evening was approaching and the clouds looked like snow. Navajo Mountain was no place to be in a winter storm, or a summer storm either, for that matter, but the promise had been made, and Joe and Lance were his friends, and then there was his duty as a sworn officer.

"Joe and the boy would never have been out here if it wasn't for me," he said to himself in a loud voice. He nodded and continued up the ridge. Below, on the slope he had just crossed, he saw evidence of a recent rockslide he had somehow failed to notice while standing in the middle of it.

"Just confirms what Anna said about my tracking ability," he muttered. Then the first flakes of snow started falling and he swore quietly. Snow would make things worse. Especially if it began to come down heavily, which it did directly. He shivered and kept on, shoulders hunched, head down, falling into a sort of mindless rhythm as he maintained a course that took him generally up and into the rugged terrain. He was well inside the forest when he emerged from his trancelike state and stared about him.

"Be damn," he muttered. "Sure don't remember this." It was good to be out of the snow, however, and he looked about and said, "Now what would old Joe Redhill do?" He pursed his lips, nodded, and found a sheltered spot between two trees. He gathered wood for a fire and cooked dehydrated chicken soup and chocolate pudding and coffee. The food was awful.

And afterward he huddled beside his little fire and the mists swirled about him and the dark trunks of the trees pressed close. He held out his hands to the warmth of the flames and wondered aloud what he was doing there, but no answer came from the forest. So he gathered some more wood and wrapped himself in his blanket and lay down, legs curled up against his chest. Despite the pine needles, the ground felt hard beneath him and he couldn't get comfortable.

"God damn," he muttered. "Damn it all anyway."

Twelve

Someone was beating an enormous drum in Joe's dream. Each time the taut-stretched skin was struck, the booming sound jolted him physically and made his ears ring. He wanted to get away from the sound but it seemed to come from everywhere. No matter that he gritted his teeth and willed it to stop, it kept on, achingly repetitive, shaking the ground where he lay.

The hard cold ground where he lay and awoke to a world of pain. His mutilated left shoulder sent a booming wave of agony directly to his brain with each beat of his heart and he had to close his eyes and lie very still until he gained a slight measure of control over the nausea and dizziness. He was so stiff from the cold that when he realized the knife was still clutched in his right hand and managed to sheath it his fingers would not straighten until he pressed them against the earth.

He stared up at the looming walls of the pueblo, washed by pale morning light, and after a time decided he should sit up. It took several tries, able to use only his right arm, and the pain and nausea of the process caused him to be sick. When the heaving of his empty stomach subsided he studied his situation. He was several yards from the wall against which he had been leaning when the creature attacked him. The ashes of the fire were scattered and cold, but there were sticks and twigs lying about from the pile he had gathered.

Scooting on his seat, pushing with his heels and his good hand, he was able to scrape some of the sticks together. He gouged a depression in the soil with his fingers and kindled a tiny blaze, straddling it with his legs and leaning over its warmth, eyes squeezed shut against the smoke. He was wracked by chills, but whether it was from his wounds or from the cold was impossible to tell.

His shivering subsided slowly as he gathered more sticks and warmed himself, and eventually the late morning sun dipped into the bowl to bathe his upturned face with light. He gathered some loose soil in his hand and dribbled it to the earth, apologizing in Navajo for having no pollen. What a marvelous thing the sun was. Tears squeezed from his closed eyelids as he sang Dawn Boy's Song, what he could remember of it. Ah, how wonderful was the sun. The warmth and the light . . .

The song, and the sunlight, dispelled some of the awful loneliness of the place, which even in the light was almost overpowering. And as he warmed up and his thinking cleared, Joe was able to stand and hobble down to the lake and splash his face. The icy water made him sputter and gasp, and revived him sufficiently to consider tending to the wound in his shoulder.

Now he looked at it for the first time since awakening and he shuddered. The cloth he had stuffed in the ragged wound to stop the bleeding was clotted with blood, and he thought he saw the white glint of bone. He didn't touch it, but considered how he could heat some water. He needed a container, and his gaze turned to the pueblo.

His reluctance to enter the pueblo was great, but his need was greater. He walked slowly up the shore, away from the lake toward the nearest entrance. But before he reached it he paused to look at the trail the monster had left. The extent of its fury was evidenced by the torn earth, the scattered grasses, and the blood. It appeared to have bled a great deal, leaving viscous black stains in a trail that led somewhere to his left, angling toward the pueblo. Joe's eyes narrowed and he marked well the monster's passage.

He entered cautiously, searching the shadows with his eyes, listening for the slightest sound. The first room he came to was empty except for dust and dirt, and he was thankful for the soiled floor that would record the slightest track, and seemed to confirm that the monster had not passed this way. The next room was also empty, but in the third he found what he was seeking; pottery. There were a bowl and two pitchers. He took the bowl.

The decoration on the bowl, a single black line shaped like

waves, was unfamiliar. He filled it with water and bedded it in the coals remaining from his fire. Soon it began to steam and the pottery did not crack and he was faced with the task of cleaning and binding his wound.

He stripped to his waist, a task that almost made him vomit again from the pain, and when he could focus his eyes he tore his shirt into strips he soaked in the water and laid across his shoulder. It took quite a while to work the blood-soaked cloth loose from the flesh, and when he at last had the wound reasonably clean, his jaw ached from gritting his teeth.

"Nothing major," he muttered as he prepared a bandage from the remains of the shirt. "Just a little flesh wound, soldier." The shoulder seemed to be separated from the clavicle and any movement of the arm caused him to moan and tremble. He thought the clavicle might be fractured, and the ligaments and muscles were torn, and the lacerations were ragged and ugly, but there was no major bleeding. Until infection developed, as he was sure it would soon, he would be all right. He would not be good, but he would be okay. Sure.

He was thoroughly chilled again by the time he finished bandaging the wound, and he dressed, and stoked the fire, and warmed himself. Then he fashioned a sling for his left arm from the belly strap off his backpack and ate the last piece of licorice. With considerable difficulty, he tied the red cloth around his head as his people had always done before going into battle. The sun stood almost directly overhead as he entered the dead city to find the monster.

The trail was clear and easy to read. Splashes of black blood stained the floors of the rooms and passageways where it had run and Joe was amazed and frightened by the vitality of the creature even when injured. The distance between its footprints, when it was running, took him four or five. And it appeared to have raced aimlessly through the city, sometimes doubling back on itself, up and down through the levels.

The adobe walls were thick and the inner chambers were utterly silent. They extended far back, three, four, sometimes five rooms deep. The rooms in the back were the worst. There, the shadows were almost palpable, stirring as if disturbed by his presence, and more than once he started violently when he

270

imagined something lurching out at him from a darkened doorway.

And the rooms were orderly, as if the inhabitants had just gone out for a few hours and would soon return. The pottery, baskets, and storage jars were neatly put away. But whatever grain or food there might have been had long since turned to dust, and the metates had lain unused for centuries, and the sound of children's voices was only the sigh of the wind.

After several hours of tracking, Joe stopped to rest. His head was pounding and he ached everywhere, but the shoulder was the worst. He needed medicine and nourishment, which he didn't have, and rest, which he couldn't afford. He couldn't risk letting the monster recover. He had to hope it was injured worse than he, and that he could take it by surprise. He sipped from his canteen, splashed the cool water on his face and the back of his neck, then pressed on.

The tracks became closer together, and the spots of blood less frequent, and it was obvious the creature was tiring at last. He was on the uppermost of seven levels, out on the flat roof, and could see the canyon across the lake, which meant he had worked his way more than halfway through the pueblo. It was late afternoon.

His headache continued to worsen and he was beginning to feel weak and nauseated. He slumped against a wall and massaged his forehead with his good hand. Soon; he would have to find it soon. An hour, two at the outside. How far could it have roamed last night? Surely he must be close. He pushed himself upright and went on.

Because of his exhaustion, Joe at first failed to notice the change in the tracks. But when the difference penetrated the fog in his brain, he stopped and rubbed his eyes with the back of his hand and looked more closely. The footprints no longer plunged headlong through the pueblo. Now they wandered, they stopped just inside a doorway. He could see where the creature had turned to watch, looking back along its trail.

Joe turned and retraced the tracks. Yes, here was the corner where it had lain on a bed of dry grass, grass stained with blood. He stooped and peered closely at the tracks. They were sharp and clear, and meant the creature must be up and about and aware he was following. His hand sought the knife as he shuddered.

He moved more carefully now, silently, knife held out before him. The tracks led him back into the nethermost regions of the pueblo where the shadows were thickest, where the only light came through many doorways, becoming fainter at each one. He was breathing shallowly, straining to hear as he walked, when his foot stepped on something that crackled like paper.

He stopped, listening, then slowly crouched to see what it was. Old blue jeans, chopped off at the cuff, and something else, something oddly familiar. Joe recoiled and almost fell over backward as he realized he had found poor Norman Sanders. Or what was left of him. Like a snake, the creature had shed Sanders's skin. It was brittle as parchment and torn, with small bits of dried flesh still clinging to it. Nothing left but a husk. Joe stood and drew a shaky breath.

He heard a faint sound and cocked his head. Gone now. Sound traveled oddly in this place of almost endless rooms and passages, but he thought it had come from the corridor to his right. He stepped around the grisly remains and walked on the balls of his feet along the deserted passage. He passed a rectangle of light, filtered through five doorways, and saw tracks. He stopped to peer at them, and felt a chill. These toes were clawed. The monster had shed its disguise.

The tracks led to a dark hole in the floor, and into that dark hole they vanished. Joe stopped and crouched, listening. The poles of a crude ladder projected from the circular opening, an opening that Joe knew led to a kiva, an underground chamber once used by the men of the community for their ceremonials. He heard a faint, stealthy sound.

With a feeling of despair Joe realized two things; that he had cornered the creature, since kivas only had one entrance, and that the creature was safe as long as it remained there. He could not imagine himself climbing down into the darkness with only one good arm, his back exposed, the monster crouched and waiting. And even with both arms it would be risky. No, he could not climb down. The monster would spring on him in the darkness, where it had every advantage. It would

272

leap on his back and clamp its horrible jaws on his neck and he would die then and there. He must find another way. He sat down beside the hole, sheathed his knife, and massaged his forehead.

There was little time left. Already the sun was past the rim of the crater. He could not go in after the creature, so he would have to drive it out while daylight yet remained. But how? It was difficult to think with the ache behind his eyes, in his shoulder, his empty stomach gurgling. Food.

Joe looked up with a thoughtful expression. The rabbit it had killed while they were tracking it meant the creature ate flesh, human and otherwise. And if it ate flesh, it must breath air to fuel the burning of the flesh. While it existed in this world, it must obey some of this world's laws. And if it breathed air . . .

He climbed unsteadily to his feet and backed out the way he had entered, being absolutely quiet, stepping in his earlier tracks. He paused at the doorway and watched the opening for several minutes, but the creature did not emerge. Quickly then he made his way from the pueblo and out onto the shore where he gathered dry wood and green grass until he had a good pile of each.

He scooped the piles into his jacket, gathered it by the sleeves, and carried it back inside. Again he paused at the doorway to the kiva room and listened, waiting for his eyes to adjust to the shadows, searching the floor for any new tracks. When he was certain the creature had not climbed out, he dumped the contents of his jacket quietly in the corridor and went out for another load. He made three trips, and on the last he gathered a few fist-size stones also.

When he had his materials ready, he carefully approached the hole and laid several long sticks over it. The sound of movement came from below, followed by an inquisitive grunt. Quickly he laid smaller sticks crosswise, then twigs across those. The process took less than half a minute until he had a blaze burning.

Now he added fuel until the flames were leaping toward the

ceiling, working fast before the lower sticks burned through. The oxygen rushing up from the kiva fueled the fire and it roared. He saw it beginning to sag into the hole, and heaped on the grass. White smoke billowed up toward the ceiling and he moved back against the wall beside the door to wait. He took the cloth from his head, moistened it with water from the canteen, and held it over his nose and mouth.

The fire burned through the supporting sticks and the entire mass of burning wood and smoldering grass cascaded down into the kiva. A bellow of anger came from below. Joe drew a deep breath and scooted over to the hole, draped his coat over it, anchoring it in place with the stones. The monster howled.

Joe drew his knife and waited, eyes watering, nose running. He could hear it coughing now. The smoke was thick and acrid even in the open room where he crouched, seeping from beneath his jacket in yellowish white tendrils and spiraling toward the ceiling. And even though he was expecting it, Joe was almost taken by surprise when the creature burst upward through the jacket with a roar.

It swung its arms blindly, howling and pawing at its eyes, coughing smoke from its lungs. Its movements were unnaturally swift and violent, but Joe could see it was hindered by a massive swelling in its side where the knife had struck, a puckered white wound that dribbled black fluid.

He dodged its aimless blows, trying to find an opening, the wicked black blade extending between his thumb and index finger as he had been taught when he fought the Yellow Men of the East. But his shoulder sent terrible pains shooting through his brain with each movement, and he began to pant from the agony and exertion.

The monster seemed to hear him and suddenly froze to locate him, blinking its evil green eyes. In that instant of hesitation Joe saw the one chance he was likely to have and lunged, arm extended like a fencer's. But he was not quick enough.

The creature was already hurtling toward him as he threw his arm out to protect himself. Only this instinctive movement saved him from its fangs as it dodged the knife and struck him with its full weight. The knife grazed its neck as he was hurled across the room into the wall. He collapsed to the floor as it rolled to its feet, howling and staring at him, rocking back and forth and rumbling deep in its chest and flexing its fingers. There was madness in its eyes, and blazing hatred; above the sound of his own ragged breathing, he heard its teeth grinding against each other like a blade against a whetstone.

For long heartbeats Joe held its stare, the knife shaking in his hand as he kept its point protectively between himself and the creature mere yards away. Man and monster measured each other, looking for an opening, and the monster began to pace back and forth, head swiveling to keep Joe fixed with its unblinking gaze. Joe could feel blood seeping from his wounded shoulder, and the knowledge that he might pass out again made him desperate.

He struggled slowly to his feet, keeping the knife as steady as he could, never for a second releasing that malevolent gaze from his own. It paused in its pacing and bunched its shoulders, swiped at the trickle of black blood on its neck. Then it tipped back its head and screamed its rage, a sound that brought dust from the ceiling and caused the smoke-filled air to swirl in great eddies. Joe blinked, and in that moment the creature was gone. He rubbed his knuckles across his eyes and looked wildly about, but there was no mistake; it had vanished completely.

A chill of utter hopelessness threatened to overwhelm him and he fought against the feeling, standing fully upright and scorning the support of the wall. He had missed his chance, his one chance, and now the creature was loose again and night was coming.

He lowered the knife and sheathed it. His eyelids sagged as his hand mindlessly sought the jacket pocket where his licorice should be. It wasn't, of course. There was no food or drink, and night was coming, and his son was dead, and the creature was loose again and the only thing left to do was to follow it and prepare for his own death. Yes, death was surely his lot, as well it should be for his ignorance and his pride.

And yet, even now, perhaps he could buy with his own life the destruction of the dread thing he had tracked to this place. Even now, that slender hope made him take a shuffling step forward, and another, made him look down and find the smear

275

in the dust upon the floor where the thing's feet had slipped as it made the tremendous leap that had carried it from the room.

It had not simply vanished, as he had imagined, but had fled before him once again. Its tracks, after several more great bounds, settled into a steady pattern that showed Joe plainly, through the fog of exhaustion clouding his thoughts, that the creature was weaker now than before. Onward the tracks led him, through more countless rooms, in and out of ever-darker doorways, past the thick walls of ancient stone, deeper into the silent ruins than before, coming at last to a place where he stopped and panted and stared down into darkness.

It was a stairwell cut into the very rock of the mountain, and he could not see beyond the first dozen steps. He closed his eyes and drew a deep breath, resting for a minute against the wall before starting his descent. With the knife clutched in his fist, his knuckles brushed the rough wall for guidance as he walked down and down, the steps shallow and endless, until the darkness was absolute and it made no difference whether his eyes were open or closed.

Blind, weak from hunger and loss of blood, he descended the steps like a man in a dream, a waking dream, waiting for death to drop on him, to seize him in its crushing embrace and bury its fangs in his throat, to drag him screaming, screaming out his life, drag him into the place of utter terror where all childhood nightmares come true.

And with his eyes closed, body trembling from the effort, he continued on, on, down into the bowels of the earth, past the place where even the deep-searching roots of great trees faded to threads and no beasts of the world of light had ever ventured, save the ancient ones who had carved this portal into the netherworld for some purpose lost in the dimness of time.

With his eyes closed, his knuckles bleeding from the abrasion of the stone, Joe continued down and down, and the thought came to him that he was retracing the route of the first people, those brave ones who had fled the world of darkness and emerged into the world of light. The thought came that this was the hole between the worlds, and with the thought came the growing despair that he was truly and finally lost if he continued to track the creature to the place of its origin.

He stopped and leaned against the wall, breathing heavily, and the image of his own death came into his mind like a great dark bird whose wings filled the sky and blocked all light. Never to see his wife again. Never to roam again across the beautiful desert, no more to laugh or cry or feel the sun warm upon his face.

He clutched the knife with all his strength until his arm shook. His jaw muscles clenched as he choked back the sob welling up in his chest. He was, after all, just a man like any other, his life worth no more or less than theirs. Those who had died must be avenged, and those who yet lived must be saved. He started on.

The air grew warmer as he went, whether from the depth or the proximity of the ever-seething molten rock deep in the earth's heart, he knew not nor cared.

He knew only that he must keep moving, and that the creature he pursued waited somewhere ahead. His exhaustion was slowing his steps and fogging his brain so that he barely felt the warmth of his chest at first. But as it grew and grew, he swiped at it with his knuckles, smearing blood across his shirt and wincing. The pain made him open his eyes to see a faint glow illuminating his path.

At first the source of the light puzzled him, until he lifted his sleeve to wipe the sheen of sweat from his forehead. A shadow seemed to rush at him and he slashed at it with the knife, encountering only air, and realized it was the shadow of his own arm he was striking at. With a look of wonder he transferred the knife to his useless left hand and lifted the Four Mountains bundle at the end of its thong. It was pulsing with a pale, clear light, a bright spark at its center, the quartz crystal from the foot of the mountain *Sisnajini* echoing the beat of his heart. When he clutched the bundle in his fist the light streamed redly through his fingers and he could feel it expanding and contracting as he breathed.

He released it to hang against his chest, took the knife into his right hand, and rested for a minute, accepting the mystery of the light without question. The sense of urgency was long past, for the coming of night meant nothing down here.

As he rested, he surveyed what he could see of his surroundings. The passage was crudely made and half-again as high as he was tall, and a velvety gray fungus coated everything, walls and steps, making the tracks of the creature easy to see. Joe looked back the way he had come and saw the passage dwindle into infinity. He gritted his teeth and adjusted his arm in the sling, then started on.

He traveled long, as long again as he had come already, and arrived at last at a place where his foot stumbled, searching automatically for the next step, a step that wasn't there as his descent ended in a great natural cavern. Its limits were lost beyond the reach of his light. Slowly, cautiously, he walked out into its expanse, turning to look about with the knife held ready.

Columns of glistening white stone hung suspended from the ceiling, and other columns sprouted from the floor to meet them. Moisture dripping from the ceiling splashed into streaming pools and echoed along dark galleries that radiated outward from where he stood. The warm, moist air smelled of decay. The light pulsed brighter from the bundle hanging at his chest, and he held his breath as he heard the sound of something moving away from him quickly, footsteps splashing and resounding in multiple echoes from walls and ceiling.

Joe's movements as he followed the sound caused giant shadows to leap across the cavern, patterns of light reflecting upward from the pools, from the slimed columns, tinklings as of myriad bells mingling with the stealthy fall of his own feet. Everywhere about him were fissures and cracks, tunnels, openings in the walls, the ceiling, the floor. Several times he skirted gaping holes whose depth his light could not plumb, where the distant sound of rushing wind or water came faintly to his ears. The sounds came too from the branching corridors he passed, corridors that gave onto other caverns, where the sigh of wind or water might have been the whispering of unseen watchers.

And now, also, the shadows and light began to play tricks on his eyes, and he saw movements unrelated to his own passage, movements furtive and stealthy that made him grip the knife more tightly and made his breathing become shallow and tense. His heart lurched in his chest as he saw a figure waiting, immobile, beside a column he was passing, and it took several seconds before he recognized it for what it was; a pictograph pecked in the stone.

It was the outline of a man, twice his height and decorated in diamonds and zigzags. Its eyes were large blind circles. He passed it with many sideways glances, and as he passed, saw another. And another. Beneath the soft patina of gray fungus, the walls were covered with hundreds of figures. Silent and eternal the figures surrounded him, some with the heads of animals or insects, some with the bodies of creatures and the heads of men or women. The *Na ye'*, the monsters of the underworld, all destroyed by the Hero Twins. All but one.

Joe paused uncertainly and screwed his eyes shut as he fought the ache in his head, in his shoulder, tried to ignore the gnawing in his belly. When he opened them again he saw Hector.

The little man was standing a short distance ahead, almost beyond range of the light, head tipped to one side as he smiled sadly. Joe's mouth opened but no words came, and when he blinked his eyes to see more clearly, the vision was gone, only a pillar of stone remaining.

Laughter. Voices. Joe turned completely around trying to locate their source. Nothing but endless dark corridors, trickling streams, mute pillars. His mind must be going. He was alone. Terribly, dreadfully alone. Except for the creature. Where was it? What was it doing?

Without his watch Joe had no way of knowing how much time had passed, but his utter weariness made it seem like days since he had driven the monster from its den in the kiva. He turned slowly around and around and the towering figures loomed over him, oppressive, perverse, stifling, embodiments of everything ugly and unnatural in man. The weight of their presence pressed inward upon him until the air seemed almost too thick to breathe and sweat poured down his face.

He felt his legs growing weak, and his heart pounding, and he raised the knife above his head and shook it as he screamed his anguish and rage.

"Chindi! Devourer, Destroyer, Eater-Of-Souls! Killer of children and old women! Come and face me! Face a man!" He

gestured with the knife, pointing it at himself. "One man. I am only one man. Come now, come and face me if you dare, or stay forever here in darkness where you belong!"

His words echoed into unseen distances, dwindled into silence. He waited, listening, and after a time heard the sound of muffled weeping. It came from somewhere at his back and he turned and started toward it. The bright warmth on his chest throbbed hotter and stronger and he saw a huddled figure at the base of a pillar, a familiar figure, head resting on its knees, which were drawn up against its chest. Not the creature he sought . . . or was it his mind playing tricks on him?

"So, monster, you too weep," he said wearily. And the figure looked up, and he saw the face of his son.

"Father," the boy sobbed. Joe swayed and took a step back, his face filled with bewilderment. He stepped forward and held out his hand.

"Lance —," he said, "Lance —"

"Father, why did you let me die?" The boy looked up at him, tears streaking his cheeks. "Wasn't I a good son?"

"Lance —." Joe swayed and lowered the knife. He struggled to find words that wouldn't come as his son's eyes implored him for an answer to his death, his face mottled from the bites of a hundred spiders.

"You could have saved me," Lance sobbed. "Why wouldn't you listen to mother? Why, father? Why?" He held out a hand, a hand puckered with small wounds.

"Oh, Lance —," Joe moaned, his vision swimming. "I did not know. Please, I did not know."

"You didn't believe," Lance said. "You were always too full of yourself." A hard note crept into his voice as he added, "You live and I am dead, father. I was only eighteen. Why father? Why?"

Joe blinked to clear his vision, his mind whirling with grief and confusion, trying to find an answer to his son's accusations. He almost failed to see the figure of his son uncoiling like a snake, the face dissolving as the weakened creature, unable to maintain the illusion any longer, revealed itself and sprang at him.

Wildly Joe swung the blade in a sweeping blow, a blow fueled with all his rage and shame at this final betrayal, this ultimate insult.

It flew at him and Joe swung the blade in a clumsy but powerful stroke that caught the creature's arm directly across the thick meat below the shoulder. The blow completely severed the limb and it fell at his feet, taloned fingers still clutching and clawing. With a terrible bellow the creature hurtled past and was bounding away, the severed stump spurting black fluid that steamed and boiled as Joe turned to follow its retreating figure.

It howled and screamed as it ran, blundering into pools and pillars, filling the air with its rage and agony. Joe hobbled after, gasping, tears on his cheeks and icy hatred in his eyes. Back it went, back the way they had come, into the stairway and up, up.

Joe followed, pausing time and again to catch his breath. The walls were smeared with gore where the creature had stopped to rest, and several times he almost caught up with it before it screeched and raced ahead. Up and up, until his vision faded and the light at his chest flickered into darkness and he stumbled and caught himself, falling to his knees only to stagger upward once again.

"Up, soldier," he muttered at one point. "Move it, move it." He chuckled, and sobbed, and went on. Up and up, his head spinning, smelling the foul stink of its blood and the stench of decay.

He lifted his foot for the next step and missed, fell forward, and realized the floor was level and flat; he had re-entered the city of the dead.

On one hand and his knees he gasped for breath, and stared across the room, and saw the creature crouched in the corner. For a long time he met the gaze of the glowering green eyes, and then he spoke, and his voice was flat and emotionless.

"We meet on even terms now," he said, gesturing with the knife. "One arm for you, one for me."

The creature opened its mouth and hissed. Its tongue flickered forth, black and forked like a snake's. He saw it gather its legs beneath it. The claws of its hand scraped the stone of the floor and it made a slight half-turn toward a doorway to his left, as if about to escape once more. But the instant he shifted in the same direction it was bounding toward him and he brought the blade up. The force of its attack drove the blade to the handle in its neck as it struck him and sent him flying across the room into the wall.

Joe collapsed to the floor and watched the monster as finally, incredibly, it perished. The racket it made was astonishing as it jerked and thrashed, hurling itself about, beating the floor with its legs and remaining arm until bits of adobe rained from the walls and ceiling. The room shook with the power of its dying and Joe waited to die with it, certain the building was going to collapse atop him. But suddenly the creature was seized by a final spasm and arched its back as it lay on the floor and the sound was like a huge tree pulling free of the earth, creaking and moaning. And then all was still.

Joe lay stunned by the blow he had sustained, and the spectacle of the monster's death, hardly daring to believe he was still alive. A long time passed before he was able to drag himself upright against the wall, then to stagger a few steps toward the monster's carcass.

Its black tongue protruded from its great frog mouth, past the wicked yellow fangs. Its skin was gray and wrinkled like something long dead and its absurdly short, crooked legs were locked rigidly, holding its body half off the floor.

He couldn't bring himself to touch it and he left the knife embedded in its neck and turned his back on it and walked away. He stood numbly outside the pueblo and felt a breeze streaming past him from the door. The water of the lake was rippling and throwing sparks of light. In wonder he turned to let the breeze blow directly in his face as it streamed from the emptiness, and he breathed it in and it was fresh and cold and carried the faintest echo of children's laughter, or perhaps the singing of unseen birds.

The lake sparkled and the green grass high on the rim of the crater waved with the breeze. The walls of the pueblo gleamed white as marble and the sky above was a turquoise gem set atop the verdant slopes. The dead had flown from the city; now it was only empty. Joe closed his eyes to fix the image in his memory. Then he gathered his remaining energy and turned his weary footsteps along the shore of the lake.

His mind was blank during the journey out, recording only the endless jarring of each footstep. He later couldn't recall the towering walls of the canyon, or the icy stream, only fatigue and pain in waves that had to be ignored, only repetitive movements that had to be made one at a time, only a thousand separate acts of will that shuffled his feet forward like an old man's. And a time came when it seemed he could go no farther, and Cricket Singing was suddenly at his side, looking up at him from emerald green eyes.

"Take my hand, Grandfather," she said. He smiled down at her and enfolded her warm, soft fingers in his. And together they walked from that dark canyon, and came out into the sunlight on a hillside where the wind blew and was not cold, and the wind made the grasses nod and sway. He drew a deep breath and let it out slowly saying, "It is good to be up high, to be able to see a long ways off."

"Yes," Cricket Singing said, "it is good." She smiled up at him. "Walk in beauty, Grandfather," she said. Then she released his hand and ran skipping and laughing down the grassy slope, becoming smaller and smaller until, just before she vanished from sight, she stopped and called, "Don't forget me! Remember your promise!"

His face grew puzzled, but he said softly. "Walk in beauty, Little Daughter."

He was tired, more tired than he had ever been in his life, and the grass was soft and green, and he lay down to rest. He would rest for just a little while, then he would get up and walk down to the lake. Yes, that is what he would do, but first he would rest.

Sheriff Nathan Andrews had been wandering in the murky forest all day, and it was approaching dusk when he finally saw two clear tracks in the soft soil of a seasonal streambed. They were the first tracks he had found since entering the forest, and his face registered dismay when he realized they were his own.

"Well shit!" he muttered. He squatted on his haunches and scratched his stubble of beard, his eyes flicking back and forth nervously. He pulled out his radio and tried unsuccessfully to raise someone, anyone, for the hundredth time, then jammed it angrily back in its holster. He eased the straps of his pack and stood, looking about uncertainly, and caught a glimpse of movement amongst the trees. It was a coyote.

The animal was sitting in the open, making no effort at concealment, and its mouth was open in a toothy coyote grin. "What the hell are you laughing at?" the sheriff growled, but his tone revealed the sense of relief he felt at seeing some other living thing in this strange forest, even if it was only an animal. When the coyote continued to sit and gaze at him from its unusual green eyes he said, "I don't suppose you've seen a tough old Navajo wandering around have you? About five-ten, couple hundred pounds?"

The coyote arose and trotted past him, stopped and looked back over its shoulder. When he didn't follow immediately, it pranced nervously in a circle and whined, making its intent unmistakable. The sheriff's eyes widened in surprise and he dragged the back of his hand across his gaping mouth.

"You've got to be kidding," he murmured. But when the animal moved out in a lazy trot, he hurried to keep up. The coyote was strictly business now that the sheriff was following, and it danced along with a curious tip-toe gait that carried it smoothly and silently straight through the forest, its sharply pointed muzzle never swerving to either side. In ten or fifteen minutes they came out of the woods, and crossed a grassy slope, and the sheriff found Joe where he had lain down to rest.

"Joe!" He raced across the slope and dropped to one knee beside the motionless figure.

"Oh Christ, buddy, you don't look good at all," he muttered as he sought a pulse. Joe's heartbeat was weak and rapid, as was his breathing. His eyelids fluttered open as the sheriff removed his coat and put it over him.

"Joe!" he said, "can you understand me?"

Joe mumbled something unintelligible. Then his eyes focused and he said, "Nathan."

"Yeah, Joe, how are you feeling?"

"Not too bad. But not too good." He smiled faintly, then winced.

"Okay Joe. Listen, just relax and take it easy. I'm going to get you out of here." His voice radiated a confidence that his eyes did not reflect, but when he stood and tried his radio again, he was amazed to receive a reply.

"Freeman here. Is that you, Sheriff?"

"Jesus! Yes! What are you doing? Where are you?"

"I got orders to come looking for you. Some woman named Anna has been raging at everybody that will listen between here and Washington, D.C. I am, . . . ahh," there was a pause during which the sheriff became aware of the distant thump of rotors, "about ten miles northeast of Navajo Mountain."

The sheriff told him where they were, and please to come get them, and an hour later Joe was in the hospital where the doctors were fascinated with his wounds and wanted to know what had happened to him. He lied to them, and others, for three days, and then he was rescued by Anna and Rebecca who came and took him home.

In early December, on a bright sunny day when Anna seemed especially depressed and withdrawn, Joe suggested they go for a boat ride. It would do them all good to get out, to breath some fresh air. Rebecca, who was still staying with them, greeted the idea enthusiastically, but with the mature reserve that had become her manner. They dressed warmly for the journey and Anna was persuaded to make a picnic lunch.

A few hours later Joe anchored the boat in Cathedral Canyon and they hiked inland. Joe carried the picnic basket, and Rebecca carried a blanket. Sometimes, when a storm was coming, or if he overtaxed it, his left arm still hurt him badly and he had to wear a sling. But not today. Anna walked behind and apart from them, head down, a dull expression on her face.

"Where are we going Uncle Joe?" Rebecca asked.

"It is a surprise." He helped her up a steep ledge, but Anna flinched away from him when he reached to help her and his face filled with sadness; she had spoken no more than a dozen words all morning. He had hoped having Rebecca around would ease some of the pain of Lance's death, and perhaps it had, and Martha was still in no shape to care for a child, though she appeared to be recovering slowly. The wounds were deep in all of them, and would be long in healing.

They arrived at the deserted hogan. Joe had made three trips looking for it during the past weeks, and he watched Anna's face as he led her to Lance's grave. Like most Navajo graves, it was marked only by the rocks piled atop it to prevent scavengers from unearthing the remains, but it was on a small butte that afforded a grand view of the desert, the land her son had known and loved.

For the first time since Joe's return, he saw her cry. She buried her face in her hands and walked a short distance away from him and sat down on the cold, smooth stone and the grief that had been trapped inside her all these weeks poured out. Rebecca heard the crying and abandoned her exploration of the hogan and corral to hurry toward Joe and throw herself into his arms, also crying now.

He squatted and wrapped his arms around her. She put her head on his shoulder and her tears wet the cloth of his shirt. "Why Uncle Joe?" she sobbed. "Oh why? Why?" It was not the first time she had asked him the question, and again he had no answer. He stroked her hair and held her, which was all he could do. Anna came and put her arms around the two of them. The woman and the child cried of their loss, while Joe held them and did not cry, for he had said his farewells on the mountain.

And after a time their sobs lessened and they wandered with Joe down to the spring and drank its cold, clear water and washed their faces. Then they climbed back atop the butte and spread out their lunch, but ate only a little.

"Have you ever heard of a Singer named Old Man Walker?" Joe asked Anna.

"Old Man Walker?" She gazed at him curiously and he was happy to see a sparkle of life in her dark eyes. "I remember something —," she waved a hand and her face furrowed in thought, "— something, I'm not sure. Maybe a story my father told me when I was a little girl. Why?"

"Tell me what you remember." Joe sipped his coffee, gazing at Rebecca over his cup. Her eyes seemed unusually large and green today. Perhaps it was the clear light of winter.

"You know how fascinated my father was with . . . mysticism and shamans," Anna said with a quick glance at Rebecca.

Rebecca took a bite of sandwich and returned her look from innocent eyes.

"Witches," she said around the sandwich. "Don't worry about me, Aunt Anna."

"Of course. Well, I seem to remember Old Man Walker was some kind of a hero to my father, but not the rest of the *Dine'*. It's all kind of vague, but I remember father telling me that Walker had performed some great feat of magic that destroyed a witch or a spirit that had been tormenting the people of his area. For a few years he was highly respected, but a disease swept through the sheep and he was blamed and someone killed him while he slept. This happened a hundred years or so ago."

Joe nodded solemnly, and Rebecca chewed her sandwich, and after a minute Anna added, "That's gratitude for you," with a hesitant smile. "Now tell me why you asked."

So Joe told them the entire story, leaving out the most grisly parts, and when he finished they both stared at him from wide eyes.

"I think the *Dine'* owe Old Man Walker a large debt," he said. "One that they will never know of."

Rebecca stared at him with her emerald green eyes and he said, "I am going to give you a Navajo name."

She clapped her hands in delight and laughed. "What is it?" she asked.

"Cricket Singing," he said in English, then repeated it in Navajo. "Do you like it?"

Her face paled and he saw the lump in her throat as she swallowed her bite of sandwich.

"What is wrong?" he asked. "You do not like it?"

She shook her head back and forth, opened her mouth to speak, but no sound came out.

"What's wrong dear?" Anna reached to touch her hand and Rebecca jumped, looked around in fright.

"I . . . I knew it but I forgot," she said.

"What?" Anna's face showed her concern and confusion, and Rebecca shook her head angrily.

"I can't remember!" she said with exasperation. "Not exactly anyway. But when I was in the hospital, and the cut in my head got infected I had a terrible headache and a fever and the *worst* nightmares ever! And you were there Uncle Joe." She sniffled and wiped her nose with her sleeve. "In my dream you called me that name. At least . . . I think you did. I don't know. Do you think it's crazy?"

"No, Little Daughter." Joe smiled at her. "I think we have dreamed a strange dream together, and now we are awake. And it is time for us to go home." He stood and began to gather up the plates and wrappers.

"Home," Rebecca said in a small, lost voice. She looked up at him as she handed him a cup. "Am I going to live with you and Aunt Anna now, Uncle Joe?"

Before he could reply, Anna reached for the girl and hugged her to her breast, tears running down her cheeks as she said, "Of course you are Rebecca! And when Martha gets well she can come live with us too, if she wants. You'll always have a home."

Joe smiled and nodded. It would be a long time until their wounds healed, if they ever did, but they would have each other and perhaps that would be enough.

"Come," he said, "it is time to go home."

They walked back the way they had come, across the unchanging landscape of the desert, and a bird circled high, high overhead, the merest speck against the pale blue sky. As they climbed aboard the boat, the bird tipped its wings and glided straight and unswerving into the west to vanish with the light of the setting sun.